# The Retribution

# Gallows Gold Series Book 2

*Written by James Scott Thomson*

Action and Adventure Novel

THE RETRIBUTION
Gallows Gold Series Book 2

Published by FutureWest Publishing 2023
Perth, W.A., Australia
www.futurewest.com.au/JamesThomson

This is a work of fiction. Any similarity between the characters
and situations within its pages and places or persons,
living or dead, is unintentional and co-incidental.

For permissions contact:
James Thomson at James@futurewest.com.au

Cover photography from Shutterstock.com

Book and cover design by Steven Schaffert

Australian map is courtesy of Bruce Jones Design
and FreeUSandWorldMaps.com

ISBN: 978-0-6454800-6-1

Dedicated to Don Pang and Glen Anderson

Taken too soon

# PROLOGUE

## WORLD WAR ONE

On June 28, 1914, Archduke Franz Ferdinand of Austria was assassinated by the Bosnian Serb nationalist Gavrilo Princip. The assassination led to a war across Europe. During the conflict - Germany, Austria-Hungary, Bulgaria, and the Ottoman Empire (the Central Powers) fought against Great Britain, France, Italy, Russia, Romania, Australia, Japan, and the United States (the Allied Powers). The war ended on November 11, 1918, leaving an estimated seventeen million people dead.

## WORLD WAR TWO

An unprecedented rise to power by Adolf Hitler led to Germany's invasion of Poland on September 1, 1939. Great Britain and France declared war on Germany. Germany, Italy, and Japan (Axis Powers) fought Great Britain, France, Australia, the United States, China, and the Soviet Union (Allies). The war ended on September the 2, 1945, leaving an estimated seventy million people dead. The bombing of Hiroshima and Nagasaki marked the first time atomic weapons were used in war.

## WORLD WAR THREE

Tensions in the South China Sea led to conflict between China and the Philippines on August 8, 2031. South Korea engaged in the conflict by assisting the Philippine Navy. The United States declared war on China on August 17, 2031. During the conflict, the United States, South Korea, Israel, India, Japan, the United Kingdom and Australia (Allies) fought China, Russia, North Korea, Pakistan, Iran, and Vietnam (Central Allies). The war ended on October 22, 2033, leaving an estimated 2.7 billion people dead. This time, both the Allies and Central Allies resorted to the use of nuclear weapons during the conflict. Hundreds of cities worldwide were destroyed by missile strikes or deserted due to radioactive fallout.

# Chapter One

I waved several pestering bush flies from my face and scanned the dry and desolate country. Red dirt, scrub, and a gnarled gum tree as far as the eye could see. It is hard to imagine that spring would transform the landscape into a nature garden of pink, yellow, purple, and white wildflowers.

Fiona and I rode Jasper and Roger, our trusty and much-loved mounts. We were close to Devils Creek, 369 kilometres north of Perth, the former capital city of Western Australia (WA). Devils Creek is a speck of a town with a population of fewer than fifteen souls. You would have to search long and hard to find a more remote location to hide out. The area is appropriately named after the Devil, as no matter what time of year a traveller visits, they would find the creek as dry as a bone. A cruel fate indeed for a weary traveller dreaming of quenching their thirst.

Perth is now as deserted as the mid-west farming region we travelled through. On February 22, 2033, the Perth Central Business District was destroyed by a nuclear strike. The initial blast and subsequent radioactive fallout resulted in the death of an estimated 1.5 million residents, over half of the state's population.

Ten months had passed since Fiona and my best mate Clarry joined me in launching a mission into Perth to rescue the grandson of a rich and influential landowner. We saved the boy, but his kidnapper, Noel Patterson, managed to escape. I still have nightmares about that mission. We saw the destruction caused by the nuclear strike and encountered the rotting bodies of murdered civilians. Patterson, a former scientist working for the military, had used innocent people as guinea pigs, experimenting on them to discover a cure for cancer. Not for some humanitarian cause, but to preserve his own life and create an army of radiation-proof super soldiers.

Fiona rode alongside me, "You reckon we're almost there, Boss?"

I lifted my Akubra hat, "We shouldn't be far from his camp. And stop calling me Boss. We've been partners for almost a year now. It makes me feel bloody old," I lamented.

Fiona laughed, "You *are* old."

When I first met Fiona Katsaros, she had just turned twenty-one and worked as a skimpy barmaid in Kalgoorlie, a gold mining town in the Eastern Goldfields. I intervened when a young buck was getting the upper hand in a quarrel they were having. I was attempting to calm the situation when Fiona launched a high-heeled foot up between the young man's legs. Shortly thereafter, I reluctantly agreed to take her on as my apprentice and teach her how to survive and earn a living as a bounty hunter. Straight off the bat, she proved to be a natural, learning the tricks of the trade faster than anyone I'd known. During her first operation, she saved my ass during a 'Dead or Alive' bounty operation that went sideways. It didn't take her long to earn the right to be my partner, receiving a fifty-fifty split on all contracts and rewards.

We had been residing in the north-western coastal town of Geraldton for almost three weeks, searching the nearby area for a fugitive we had been chasing since mid-November. Lesley Maka murdered her three kids and then just up and disappeared. She'd poisoned the children in their beds and left them to be found by her husband the following morning. We were frustrated that the several leads we had received concerning her possible whereabouts led us down the garden path.

One of our informants received information from a working girl that Maka had hooked up with some carnie and moved to Darwin. Probably just another useless piece of hearsay information. For a week or so, I'd tried to convince Fiona that Maka had moved on, but she'd made this bounty personal and wanted to continue the search. Fiona portrays a tough exterior but has a soft spot for kids and animals, although not necessarily in that order.

Fiona was finally giving up on the search for Maka, and we were on the verge of heading south to search for work when the local bondsman offered us an unexpected contract. My former colleague, Marco Gizzarelli, had been tried and found guilty in absentia for murdering two farmers during a bar fight. It's now common to conduct a trial without the presence of the accused, which usually results in the judge delivering a guilty verdict and issuing a bounty.

The 'Dead or Alive' reward was set at two ounces of gold. The end of the digital age has altered the world's monetary system. Commodities such as gold and silver are once again the preferred payment methods for goods and services. Gold and silver coins are still minted, but the Government carefully controls their supply to avoid hyperinflation. The average bounty contract fetches one ounce of gold. The bondsman explained that Gizzarelli's contract paid the high price of two ounces because of the increased danger involved in capturing the proficient killer.

I've had more than one run-in with Gizzarelli, but we had always managed to end our confrontations amicably, meaning that we hadn't tried to *kill* each other. Last year we had even worked together guarding the water train and were on the same team during the assault on a gang in Norseman.

The water train travels from Northam to Kalgoorlie, providing the prosperous mining town with its sole water source. Gizzarelli and I were hired to guard the train from criminal gangs and desperate opportunists. On the day in question, we successfully repelled a band of outlaws named the Norse Men Gang (NMG), who were intent on capturing the train and its valuable cargo. Regrettably, Gizzarelli and I had a difference of opinion concerning an NMG member he had captured. I wanted to bring the criminal in for questioning, whereas Gizzarelli was in the process of beating him to death. I held my ground on this occasion, but he was filthy with the decision and made sure I knew about it.

Just over a month after the attempted train heist, Gizzarelli was a member of a militia team I led to free Norseman from the NMG's reign of terror. The NMG had enslaved the town, forcing the residents to mine for gold and service their desires. As I led a team down a decline mine, Gizzarelli rescued residents near the mine site's administration building. Before I could rendezvous with him, he executed fourteen unarmed gang members who had surrendered. I had no sympathy for the men, but they should have been captured and tried before a judge.

Fiona recently spoke to Gizzarelli's ex-wife, who stated he was known to frequent an old prospector's camp a couple of clicks east of Devils Creek. No love was lost between the volatile bastard and his former misses. We would have to be on our toes for this mission, as the bondsman's judgement was spot-on; the grizzled veteran would be a difficult and dangerous fugitive to capture.

As a bounty hunter, I abide by a personal code founded on four rules. Rule one is always go home at the end of the operation. No reward is worth giving our lives away, so we plan our operations to mitigate the foreseeable risks. Rule two is self-explanatory; never intentionally cause physical harm to an innocent. Rule three is a cardinal rule for most hunters; never steal another hunter's bounty. This rule can cause conflict when two or more hunters chase the same fugitive. The final rule is one that most hunters don't follow. We always attempt to capture and transport the perpetrator alive. I'm not an executioner and don't plan to take up the vocation. A few years back, I explained my code to my mate Clarry over a beer or two. He pointed out in his tongue-in-cheek manner that the final rule contradicted the first rule. So I repeated the rule and emphasised the word 'attempt.' If a fugitive tries to kill one of us to escape or out of hate, I'll always defend myself, which can mean using lethal force. I sleep well at night, knowing I do my best to follow this code.

We entered Gizzarelli's hideout just after 4 a.m., two hours before sunrise. I aimed to catch him unaware and subdue him with minimal force.

I retrieved the infrared binoculars from my pack and scanned the horizon. It didn't take long for me to spot a campsite consisting of an old tin shed beneath the foliage of a gum tree. My attention was drawn to a recently used fire pit. Its glowing embers were slowly dying in the cool morning. An old mine shaft with a rusted steel headframe sat twenty metres east of the ramshackle dwelling.

"So, what's the plan, Boss?" Fiona asked eagerly.

"We'll tie the horses up and approach from the west. With any luck, he'll be sleeping like a baby. And then Bob's your uncle, we'll get the drop on him."

Fiona raised an eyebrow, "We're after Gizzarelli, not some daft bank robber. Can't we just prop 250 metres out and take him down with the sniper rifle?"

"You know the code. That's not how we work."

"He wouldn't pause for a second before putting a bullet between our eyes," she rebutted.

"I'm not so certain about that. Anyway, when we return to Geraldton, I think it's best I tell you about the glass jar philosophy. It's been my moral compass since my former professor gave me a lesson about it."

Fiona chuckled, "Philosophy 101? As long as you're buying the drinks, I'll listen to whatever lecture you're giving Boss."

We tied Roger and Jasper's reigns to the trunk of a large eucalypt tree and hiked through the scrub from the west. I saw the tin roof through the foliage and signalled for Fiona to stop by holding my open hand up at shoulder height. We both knelt behind a weeping bottlebrush. I signalled for Fiona to enter his camp from the north and approach the rear of the shed. I planned to continue walking from the west and snake around the shrubs and mining machinery to the front door of the shed. If all goes to plan, we'll meet at the door and tactically enter hard and fast, catching him unawares.

The full moon provided enough light to avoid tripping over rusted junk and large rocks. As I approached the shed door, I was startled by the sound of bells ringing, followed by a high-pitched scream and a thud!

It was a matter of seconds before I found the cause of the commotion. Fiona was lying face down in the dirt, about four metres from the rear of the shed. Her legs were tangled in wire with small brass bells attached. Gizzarelli was standing above her, holding an empty champagne bottle by its neck.

As Gizzarelli grinned and stepped towards me, I glanced at Fiona's motionless crumpled form. "You thought you could bring me in. Shit mate, you've got dibs on yourself," he sneered.

"What did you do to Fiona?"

"She's trespassing on my property, so I gave her a bit of a whack with the old Dom Pérignon. But I think you should be more concerned about your own welfare."

I tried to keep the conversation light. There was still a chance I could reason with the man. "Dom Pérignon? I wasn't aware you had such expensive taste."

"I don't. The fella that's been squatting in my shed left it with all his other shit. If I find him, he's going to look a lot worse than the sheila over there," he said, pointing at Fiona.

"Why don't I check on her, and then you and I can have a chat about where we go from here."

He spat on the ground, "You can rest your silver tongue, O'Connor. Nothing you say will save you." He lowered his stance and lifted the bottle above his head. "This has been a long-time coming," he growled.

I shrugged my shoulders. "I guess it is what it is," I grunted.

I stepped backwards while Gizzarelli rolled his shoulders and followed me to the open space beyond the fire pit. I wasn't sure if Fiona was breathing, let alone conscious, but I wanted to create some distance between her and Gizzarelli, as I had no idea what was running through his mind.

I would be wasting valuable time attempting to negotiate with the man. He was stubborn, desperate, and pissed. And he was confident he would give me a flogging. At about five foot eight, he had a wrestler's frame, with thick forearms and broad shoulders. I had six inches of height on him, but he outweighed me by at least fifteen kilos.

I reached for the grip of my revolver as he sprinted towards me, dust spiralling into the air as the tread of his boots gripped the red dirt. Just after my revolver left the holster, he struck my gun hand with the bottle. I spun to the side, and the revolver flew out of my grip into scrub. I couldn't risk turning my back to search for it, and it was too dark to locate it at a glance.

Gizzarelli held the bottle like it was a sword. Forget what you have seen in old movies; ninety-nine bottles out of a hundred don't smash when you strike someone. He watched me like a hawk as I circled and tested my right hand for injuries by forming a fist. He stretched his neck to the left and right, touching his ears to his shoulders, causing his vertebrae to crack and pop in response.

As I raised my fists to my jaw, he hurled the bottle at my head, narrowly missing when I flinched like I was slipping a punch. He charged forward like a raging bull and threw a right hook toward my jaw. Reacting with muscle memory, I bobbed and weaved under his punch. With surprising speed and grace, he instantly regained his balance and rotated on the balls of his feet to face me.

I smirked, "Jeezus! You move fast for an old boy. But I notice that you're puffing pretty hard. Do you need a bit of a lie-down, grandad?"

I intended to enrage him and provoke a mistake. I just needed an opening to win the fight so I could check on Fiona. *Come on, Gizzarelli, throw a haymaker.* But unfortunately, he had other plans.

When I threw a quick cross, he slipped to the outside and launched an uppercut into my liver. I instantly doubled over, clutching my stomach in excruciating pain. He didn't hesitate to take advantage of the opening. He drove his right knee into my jaw.

My vision blurred, and I fell to my backside in a heap. Gizzarelli wasted no time taking advantage of my vulnerability, attacking me with the ferocity of a Tasmanian devil claiming its kill - raining down punches and elbow strikes without respite. Reflex and instinct took over. I managed to block most of his blows with my forearms.

When he realised most of his strikes were missing the target, he altered his attack by pressing one of his hammy fists across my throat, forcing his weight down with grim determination. Then, breathing heavily, he growled, "Say goodnight to *grandad*, you cheeky fuck!"

I struggled to breathe as I desperately reached for my knife. Thud!

# Chapter Two

Blood from Gizzarelli's temple was smeared over the pommel of my FS-Fighting knife. I kissed the blade that had once again saved my backside. A knife passed down from grandad to dad and finally to me. Before I served in the Australian Defence Force (ADF) during World War Three, both men had carried the knife in different wars – one in the jungles of Vietnam and the other in the mountains of Iraq and Afghanistan.

Gizzarelli moaned in a semi-conscious stupor as I hogtied him with cable ties, securing the back of his ankles to his wrists.

Wasting no time, I ran over to Fiona and rolled her onto her side. She was breathing shallowly and had an enormous haematoma on her forehead. I was shocked by the size of the lump and her uncanny resemblance to the alien in the classic movie *Close Encounters of the Third Kind*. To keep the negative thoughts at bay, I reminded myself that these types of injuries often look worse than they are. Upon careful examination, there were no apparent indications of a fracture or clear fluid leaking from her ears, indicating a brain haemorrhage. At least not yet! After unravelling the wire around her ankles, I carried her into Gizzarelli's shed and gently lowered her onto a foam mattress. I placed her in the lateral recovery position in case she vomited from the concussion.

I stuck my head outside the shed door and saw Gizzarelli struggling to break free of his restraints by flexing his muscular arms and rolling in the dirt towards a boulder. He could try with all his might to break his bonds, but with experience, I knew the plastic cables would hold. If he planned to use the boulder to snap the ties, the weathered surface of the rock would not do him any favours. If it weren't for my concern for Fiona, I might have found the situation comical.

I found Gizzarelli's pack in the corner of the shed and discovered his wallet in the side pocket. I was surprised to find a photo of him standing between an attractive middle-aged woman and a pretty young lady. After locating his water bottle and a clean shirt, I soaked the material and placed it on Fiona's forehead.

Gizzarelli had given up on his attempt to perform a Houdini and was lying on his side with his back against the boulder. I knelt beside him in the dirt and showed him the photo. "Who are these ladies with you?" I asked curiously.

When I saw his expression, I thought, *I'd be a dead man if looks could kill.*

"None of your fucking business," he replied bitterly.

After I watered the horses, I inspected Fiona's injury, noting the swelling in her forehead had worsened. To say that I was worried is an understatement. I knew it wouldn't do much good, but I had to do something, so I drenched Gizzarelli's shirt and placed it back on her forehead. The sun started to rise over the horizon to welcome a new day, and I prayed it would be a day to remember for all the right reasons.

When I returned to deal with Gizzarelli, he must have noticed my concern. "Is the girl alright?" he mumbled.

"No, she's not, thanks to you," I replied with a grimace due to my aching jaw where he'd punched and kneed me.

I ignored the pain and changed the subject. "So, will you tell me who the ladies are in the photo?"

Gizzarelli sighed. "You're a nosey fuck, O'Connor. If you must know, Katie's a new bird I've been seeing. The young lady is her daughter, Rebecca."

"I'd say good for you, but you'll probably be swinging by your neck within the next 48 hours."

He smirked before replying, "The only thing I like about you,

O'Connor, is that you're an honest man."

"I find it's best to tell it like it is. Don't you?"

He nodded before he let out a long sigh. "I can't help but find it ironic that you're asking me about them, as they're the ones who got me into this mess in the first place. It's the story of my life. Women are constantly getting me in the shit."

Men like Gizzarelli always had a list of people to blame, yet he still piqued my curiosity. "How's that?"

"For the last year or so, I've been living with Katie in Geraldton. Everything was hunky dory until the night Rebecca came home crying. It was plain to see that she'd been roughed up. Katie finally got it out of her that she'd been raped in the carpark near the hotel dumpster. My blood was up, so I went down to the bar and had words with the boys. The rest is history, which I can do fuck all about now."

His words led to violence and the subsequent death of two young men. "You could have dealt with it differently. But I guess you're not one to hold your temper."

"Yeah, right, O'Connor. And what would you've done?" Before I could reply, he continued, "Anyway, as you like to say, it is what it is." He licked his lips and looked towards the shed. "I tell you what, I have three ounces in my pack. Take it and cut me free. I'll pick up Katie and Rebecca and leave WA for good. I swear you'll never see me again."

I looked him dead in the eye. "You're jumping the gun, mate. You should know that your offer is mute if Fiona doesn't make it. I'll be bringing you in, that's for sure," I stated in a grave tone.

He opened his mouth as if to respond but must have thought better of it as he closed it without saying a word and rested his head in the dirt. I was surprised that he didn't argue, knowing that if Fiona died, it wouldn't be long before he joined her.

Fiona is like the little sister I never had. She entered my life at a time when a visit by the 'black dog' was a daily occurrence. I was wallowing in my misfortune and dealing with my despair by self-medicating between high-risk bounty operations. My focus quickly moved from dwelling on the past to preparing and training an apprentice I was responsible for. Over the last twelve months, we've been through some heavy times together, and her optimism and willingness to confront her demons have rubbed off on me.

After eating a can of baked beans for lunch, I left Fiona's side to make the short journey to collect Roger and Jasper. Roger's an Australian Stock Horse with large eyes, a long arched neck, a deep chest, and a solid, broad back. Australian Stock Horses are bred for their courage, intelligence, and stamina. Fiona's mount, Jasper, was a stockier and more compact dark brown Brumby with a thick neck and a large, elongated head. He has a calm temperament, which I hoped would positively influence Roger, for he could be a grumpy bastard. Come to think of it, Roger's disposition was not dissimilar to Gizzarelli's.

Upon my return, Gizzarelli was staring off into the distance. I noticed that he looked utterly parched. In his situation, most men either begged for their lives or yelled deadly threats. I had to respect the man's stoicism.

"I'm going to cut your ankle ties so I can move you out of this sun. Don't even think about doing something stupid," I warned.

"What am I going to do, run off into the bush with my wrists tied and no water?" he grunted.

I retrieved a rope from my pack and searched his pockets and body for weapons. I then cut the cable tie linking his wrists to his ankles and led him to the shade of a nearby eucalypt tree. I helped him sit down and secured him to the tree by tying his torso to the trunk. I was mindful that he may appear compliant, but if I gave him as much as an inch, he'd use extreme violence to escape. I secured his ankles with cable ties before cutting the links to his wrists with my combat knife, so I could tie them to his front. He was grateful when I placed the water bottle in his hands, which he greedily guzzled.

Fiona was still out cold, but I was relieved her pulse and breathing were strong and steady. I kept busy by watering and feeding Roger, Jasper, and Gizzarelli's mount, named One-eye. A few years back, Gizzarelli was holding court during a drinking session, recounting how One-eye took a bullet for him during a gun fight with a fugitive. He was adamant that the horse walked into the line of fire to save him.

That night while riding home from the pub, I imparted the story to Roger. He snorted as if to say, *'I'm not losing an eye for your sorry-ass.'*

Just before sunset, Fiona roused from her unconscious state. She moaned and grabbed her forehead as she attempted to rise, using her elbow as support.

"Just relax mate, and lay back down," I said soothingly. I was relieved she was conscious but knew she wasn't out of the woods yet.

She groaned, "Fuck, what happened? I've got a splitting fucking migraine." She rolled onto her side and vomited onto the red dirt floor.

After throwing her guts up, I supported her neck as she swallowed two ibuprofen tablets and drained a bottle of water. When we go bush, we carry enough water for ten days, even if we plan on trekking for two, which equates to a total of 45 litres.

Gizzarelli had a pile of firewood and kindling leaning up against the shed. I re-started the fire using my flint and heated a can of potato and leek soup.

Gizzarelli sniffed the air. "Am I getting some of that?"

"What do you reckon?" I replied sarcastically.

Fiona sat up, rested her back against the shed wall, and sipped the soup from her dented aluminium mug. The bump on her head still looked horrible. I silently prayed that she didn't ask for a mirror.

"How are you feeling?" I asked.

"Thankfully, my migraine has turned into a dull headache. I just feel bloody exhausted," she replied wearily.

As Fiona closed her eyes, I settled into my sleeping bag and watched the fire flicker and dance on the logs. The occasional spark popped and launched into the air, then took off in the wind like a firefly fluttering through the night. Gizzarelli was snoring like a bear as he slept against the eucalypt trunk. I was looking for a shooting star or a falling satellite as my eyelids became heavier and heavier.

~

The bright morning sun beamed over the campsite. With a big yawn, I unzipped my sleeping bag and stood up to stretch my stiff shoulders and back. Although my jaw and ribs were aching from the previous day's fight with Gizzarelli, I decided to leave the ibuprofen for Fiona. She needed it more than me, and if I was being honest, I wanted to stay clear of painkillers, given my previous dependency issues.

"Get on with it then," Gizzarelli growled.

I rubbed the sleep out of my eyes and turned toward Gizzarelli to find Fiona standing above him, pressing the muzzle of her Glock pistol into his forehead as he sat huddled against the tree trunk.

Her gun hand shook as she spoke, "You could've killed me, you fucker! Look at my bloody forehead. I look like the elephant man."

I noticed that she was holding her compact mirror in her left hand.

"You still look beautiful to me, lass," he joked.

Good one, Gizzarelli, I thought. It wasn't the brightest idea to piss her off more than she already was, especially when she's had a chance to inspect the severity of her injury.

I attempted to calm the situation. "I'm not saying he doesn't deserve it, but I reckon you'll regret pulling the trigger."

"Why? He's a fucking murderer anyway," she replied without taking her eyes off him.

I handed Fiona the photo of Gizzarelli with Katie and Rebecca. "He killed the men when confronting them about raping the young lady in this photo. He's shacking up with her mother."

Fiona glared at the photo and then paused, her inner turmoil evident to me, before shaking her head and re-holstering her pistol. "Fuuuuck! He's going to hang anyway."

I motioned for her to stand with me by the old mine, out of Gizzarelli's earshot. "Yeah, about that. He's offered us three ounces to let him go. He wants to pick up his misses and her daughter and leave the State for good."

Fiona rolled her eyes, "Jeezus, Boss. You're a bloody pushover. You do know that, right?"

"Well, I took you on as an apprentice, didn't I?" I said jokingly, regretting the words as soon as they left my mouth.

Fiona gave me the evil eye, but before she could say a word, I said, "Sorry, my bad. It was a terrible piss-take. Look, what can I say?

I've got history with the man, and even if you don't believe his story about the rape, he doesn't deserve to die over a bar fight. I've never taken a man in for a fair fight that's gone wrong."

Fiona kicked the dirt and stormed off towards the shed. She tipped the contents of Gizzarelli's pack onto the dirt near his feet and picked up a leather satchel. Inside she found 6 one-ounce gold coins and several silver coins. She held four gold coins under Gizzarelli's nose. He squinted from the sun's glare as he counted the coins in her palm.

"Four ounces, and we let you go. I know you won't give a fuck, but I want to make it crystal clear. I'll *kill* you if we ever cross paths again," she warned.

To Gizzarelli's credit, he didn't smirk or counter with a facetious remark. "I understand completely. If I can help it, you'll never see my ugly mug again."

"You better hope so," she spat.

I unloaded Gizzarelli's firearms and gathered all of his ammunition from his belt pouch and saddle bag. I filled his pack with the ammo and saddled up Roger.

I turned to Fiona, "If you're up to it, you can pack our gear while I'm gone. I'll only be twenty to thirty minutes. And I know I don't need to mention it, but I will anyway because you've had a knock on the head. Under no circumstances untie his bonds, even if he needs to go to the dunny. He can shit in his pants," I instructed while pointing at Gizzarelli.

"Oh ye of little faith," Gizzarelli snorted.

Roger enjoyed stretching his powerful legs as we cantered five kilometres north of Gizzarelli's camp. A flock of crows pecking at the carcass of a camel was a reminder of the harsh environment in which we were venturing. I dismounted Roger near the wreck of an old, rusted truck and emptied the ammo into the tray. Under no circumstances did I want Gizzarelli anywhere near his ammo when I set him loose.

Upon returning to Gizzarelli's shed, Fiona stood near our packs and took a sip of whisky from my flask.

Gizzarelli squinted up at me as I approached. "Your ammo is in the tray of a truck about five kilometres almost directly north of here. I'm going to cut you loose. Don't be a daft bugger and head back to Geraldton. There's other hunters' looking for you, and if the coppers put two and two together and think we let you do a runner, then we're in the shit. And that's a dog act considering I'm letting you go. You can send Katie a letter to meet you wherever you end up. Do you have a problem with that?"

Gizzarelli shook his head. "You've done me a solid that I won't forget."

After I unsheathed my knife to cut his ties, I heard the *crack* of a rifle and saw a puff of red dust erupt from the ground near Gizzarelli's leg.

"Seek cover," I yelled.

Fiona sprinted to the horses, untied them, and swiftly led them to the back of the shed as my blade cut through Gizzarelli's cable ties like a hot knife through butter. I then started to run towards the rear of the shed. Gizzarelli must have felt the effects of being tied up for twelve hours as he hobbled after me like an old man with a knee injury. I heard him holler in agony before he fell head first into the dirt. Without stopping to think, I hurried back to him, grabbed him under his armpits and hauled his ass behind the shed.

"Some fucker shot me," growled Gizzarelli.

"No shit, Sherlock. You win the 'state the bloody obvious' award," Fiona joked breathlessly.

Gizzarelli gritted his teeth as he grabbed his upper thigh, where a dark red stain was rapidly rising through his jeans. He took off his shirt and singlet and used them as a makeshift gauze and bandage to stem the blood flow.

"What's the plan, Boss?" Fiona asked.

"Given that he took his second shot about two seconds after the first, I reckon he's firing a bolt action rifle." When I glanced at Gizzarelli, his expression switched from a painful grimace to a stubborn scowl. His attempt to put on a brave face didn't fool me for a second. We needed to act and act quickly. I turned to Fiona, "We could wait until dark to make our move, but the grumpy bastard will most likely bleed out. Considering the position of the wound, the shooter will be lying doggo south of us."

"Well, he's not after us. So let's mount up and get the hell out of this shithole."

I shook my head. "I'm not willing to take that chance. And if he's a bounty hunter, then he's a disrespectful bastard who I'd like to speak to."

"The shooter could be a family member of the men he killed," Fiona retorted while jabbing her trigger finger toward Gizzarelli's chest.

"It's not the time for a debate, but I'll add that the shooter could be a thief, a serial killer, someone we've wronged or just some crazy bushmen. We won't know until we have a meet and greet."

Fiona had the good sense to grab my pack when she fetched the horses. I retrieved my fold-up shovel and dug into the compact red dirt. Sweat soaked my shirt, sticking the cotton to my skin like honey on a spoon. It took me about five minutes to dig a hole big enough to allow me to crawl under the rear wall of the shed.

I took a quick swig of water and told the other two to stay put before sliding under the shed wall.

"Pass me my rifle," I whispered once I was inside. Fiona was careful not to knock the scope as she slid the weapon to me. Standing two metres from the shed door, I fired a couple of rounds through the tin wall. I quickly detached the scope and peered through the bullet holes to spot any movement from our would-be assassin.

From inside the shed, I overheard Gizzarelli grumble, "Fuck this," and immediately noted the rifle fire echoing through the scrub. I peered through the scope, adjusted the focus dial, and spotted a middle-aged bloke wearing a baseball cap resting his rifle barrel on the trunk of a fallen tree. He had no bipod, and the weapon looked like a beat-up farmer's rifle used to shoot vermin.

I crawled back outside and asked them both, "What happened?"

Fiona sighed, "Hero over here decided to try and make a run for it. It was quite pathetic. He hobbled into the open to be used as target practice."

Blood was now freely seeping through his makeshift bandage. I took out gauze and bandages from our first aid kit, and with Fiona's assistance, we placed pressure on the wound to reduce his blood loss.

"Okay, new plan. The shooter is propped against a fallen tree about 200 metres south of us. Fiona, I want you to fire a round into the ground every twenty to thirty seconds. I'm going north, and then I'm backing around to get behind him. And Gizzarelli, do me a favour and stay put."

They looked displeased but reluctantly nodded their heads in agreement. It was now or never. I picked up my rifle and jogged north.

# Chapter Three

As soon as Archie was out of earshot, I gave Gizzarelli a piece of my mind. "Archie is risking his life for you. I don't give a flying fuck if you do a runner, but the least you can do is help us help you."

Gizzarelli was tight-lipped as I regained my composure. I pointed to a rocky outcrop fifteen metres to our west, "I'm going to run to those rocks so I can get a bead on the shooter. If I can't take him down, I'll at least keep him busy while Archie approaches." I drew my Glock from my holster. "I'm giving you my pistol so you can fire some distraction shots."

Handing the violent sod my pistol may seem irrational, but given the circumstances, I thought it was worth the risk. Archie's my mentor, partner, and big brother. He wasn't going to risk his life while I just sat on my ass behind the safety of the shed.

The Glock's grip disappeared in his meaty hands. He glared at it momentarily before giving me a sly grin. For a split second, I thought he was going to turn the muzzle on me. But instead, he pointed at a nearby tree and fired one round into the trunk. Before he pulled the trigger to fire a second round, I dashed to the rocky outcrop with my .223 Ruger rifle in my grasp.

I skidded to a halt behind a head-high boulder that had weathered the elements for over half a billion years. I peered down my scope, scanning the landscape for a fallen tree and the shooter. After no success, I moved to another section of the rocky outcrop and looked through the scope again. I ducked my head behind the rocks when I suddenly heard gunshots - *pop, pop, pop* - staying hidden until I finally realised it was just Gizzarelli taking potshots at the tree. *I almost shat myself.* I had been so focused on finding the shooter that I momentarily forgot about giving the ingrate my pistol.

"Hey princess, are you still awake?" Gizzarelli snickered.

*Christ, he's a fuckwit,* I thought. "Shut up and try not to bleed on my pistol," I replied tersely.

I changed position for the third time and peered through the scope. I wish Archie hadn't taken the sniper rifle. Not that he wanted me to go all G.I. Jane in the first place, but the Blaser R93 Tactical would have been handy right now. It was a beautiful and deadly weapon used by Australian snipers during the War. The rifle had an effective range of 1500 metres and was a straight-pull bolt-action rather than a turn-bolt, allowing faster follow-up shots.

"Got you," I whispered. The shooter's baseball cap and firearm were visible behind a fallen paperbark tree. It was time to blow this fucker's head off. I placed my index finger inside the trigger guard, took a deep breath, and exhaled as I acquired my sight picture. *What the fuck?* I was about to pull the trigger when I saw Archie creeping up behind the shooter with his revolver pointed at his back. I removed my finger from the trigger and sighed in frustration. If the bloke turned around to take a shot, I wasn't confident enough to fire and risk hitting Archie.

Through my scope, I could see Archie pointing his muzzle at the back of the shooter's head. He then stood up slowly with his hands raised, leaving his rifle leaning against the white tree trunk. When Archie grabbed the bloke's arm to secure his wrists, a kookaburra flew overhead into the branches of a gum tree and started to laugh his feathered head off. I wish I had his sense of humour. I left the rocky outcrop and trekked through the bush, humming the nursery rhyme, 'Kookaburra sits in the old gum tree.'

By the time I arrived at Archie's location, he was standing above a middle-aged bloke sitting on the fallen trunk he had used as a shooting platform. He was fit-looking and of average height with badly sunburnt forearms, face, and neck. He was wearing denim shorts and a white t-shirt with a giant rooster sitting on a soccer ball printed on the chest. Not the most ideal clothes for the bush,

I pondered.

"Fiona, meet Jon. Jon's a prospector who's been down on his luck and decided to start working as a bounty hunter. But you're not licensed, are you, Jon?" asked Archie rhetorically.

"Look, this was a misunderstanding. I apologise for cutting in on your bounty, but I didn't know you were hunters," Jon explained in a London accent.

Before I could respond, Jon gazed up at me and inquired, "Hey, what's wrong with your head?"

"None of your fucking business. And how could you know if we were hunters if you didn't bother to ask?" He just shrugged his shoulders in reply and looked down at his dirty sneakers. "You know what, Jon, you're a fucking wanker! You could have killed us," I sneered venomously.

Archie stepped in close to me. "Are you okay?" he whispered in my ear.

"I am now, but when I saw you sneaking up behind Jon here, I thought you were suffering from heat stroke. That was a bloody risky move, Boss."

As is his habit, he deflected my comment, "I'm guessing Gizzarelli's done a runner?"

I was about to slap my forehead to acknowledge my stupidity when I remembered the state of my bruised and swollen head. Fuck, I forgot all about Gizzarelli. *What's going on with me today?* Oh, that's right, I'm recovering from a concussion.

We escorted Jon back to the shed, and as expected, Gizzarelli hadn't missed his opportunity to take off. At least he left our gear and horses, taking only his belongings and mount. The operation wasn't a total waste of time, I contemplated. Gizzarelli's four ounces of gold still sat in my pocket, and hopefully, he would be true to his word and leave WA for good.

"So, what are we going to do with the 'bounty hunter of the year'?" I asked, looking at Jon.

Archie paused and looked around as if the answer was painted on a sign in the bush. "I guess we cut him loose."

That's my boss, a man of many words. "Okay then. Should we beat him up first to teach him a lesson?" I asked Archie, knowing what his answer would be.

Jon gulped, "No need for that, Luv."

Archie smirked, "She's just pulling your leg, mate."

"Am I?" I grumbled as I strode toward Jasper to prepare him for the four-day ride back to Geraldton.

There is no doubt that Archie is one tough bastard. I've seen him fight through physical and mental adversity whilst taking significant risks to help others. A small number of hunters would call him brave, while the rest would consider him stupid. Those who don't know him well would be surprised to hear that he's also a bit of a softy with a conscience - rare traits for a bounty hunter. Most hunters would have shot Gizzarelli from afar, cut his head off and claimed the bounty. Even when we're chasing sadistic and dangerous fucks with a 'Dead or Alive' bounty on their heads, he still refuses to kill them on sight unless they're shooting at us or trying to slit our throats. About three months back, we were chasing Cameron Lewis, a convicted serial killer who we snuck up on while he was taking a leak in a back alley. We could have legally shot him in the back of the head, but no, that was not an option, according to Archie. He had to choke him unconscious while the dirty fucker pissed all over my jeans.

Archie searched Jon's belongings and removed all of his .223 rifle and .45 calibre pistol ammunition. He slowly drew his knife from the leather sheath and approached the nervous-looking prospector. Archie cut the cable ties securing Jon's wrists and returned his unloaded pistol and rifle. It's not for me to advise Jon, but it would be in his best interest to give up trying to play bounty hunter.

"You can't leave me without any ammo. How am I supposed to protect myself from scavengers?" Jon whined.

When Jon spoke of scavengers, he was referring to gangs, thieves, and your everyday psychos, who would take advantage of a lone unarmed traveller at the drop of a hat.

"Mate, you're lucky you came across us. Ninety-nine percent of the hunters out there would have gutted you for interfering with their contract," Archie replied earnestly.

Archie wasn't lying. Most hunters would have shot Jon for attempting to steal their contract, especially after shooting at them. It's just another example of Archie being too soft.

We left Jon to collect his belongings as we rode east. The journey on horseback was not helping my thumping headache. I sipped sparingly from my water bottle to conserve what little we had left. A mob of kangaroos were chewing on bush grass as we rode by, their ears twitching as a prominent buck stuck out his muscular chest with his head held high. His body language made his intent crystal clear – *'If you try to mess with my mob, then you'll have to deal with me!'*

A little more than an hour into our journey, we located Gizzarelli's one-eyed horse munching on grass without a care in the world. He was standing only ten metres away from Gizzarelli, lying face first in the scrub alongside his pack. Archie dismounted and rolled him onto his back. His bandage and jeans were soaked with blood. I did my best to stop the bleeding by placing pressure on the wound and applying a fresh gauze and bandage. This was nothing but a short-term fix. If we didn't get him to a doctor soon, he would cark it for sure.

Archie knelt beside Gizzarelli and slapped his face to rouse him. The only response he elicited was from the flies that buzzed on and around the fugitive's face. Archie looked at the man with sadness and pity.

I stood and placed my hands over my face as I raised my head to the sky. "Oh, for fucks sake!" I exclaimed.

Archie looked up at me with eyebrows raised, "Are you upset? I didn't think you cared for the big lug."

"I'm not upset about that wanker. It's just that I'm going to suggest something that's going to really piss me off."

Archie looked on impatiently, "Okay, what is it?"

"My former girlfriend lives on a farm just outside of Mullewa. It's not more than fifteen kilometres away. We can take him there, I guess."

Archie looked exasperated. "Why didn't you say something before now? We could have headed straight there so we could resupply and give you a chance to recuperate."

Archie could be as thick as a brick sometimes. Sure, he's unaware of the circumstances that led to my break-up with Sally, but why would he think I'd want to rock up to my ex-partner's doorstep looking like the elephant man? I reckon Archie would be lucky to score two out of ten on an emotional intelligence test.

We struggled to lift the unconscious fool onto One-eye's well-worn leather saddle. First, we used rope to secure his upper body to the back of One-eye's neck to ensure he didn't fall out of the saddle. Then, we examined our map before setting off at a trot toward Fitzpatrick's Farm, where Sally worked as a cook.

Sally and I first met at her family's farm, not far from Fitzpatrick's property. In the WA bush, 'not far' means any distance from one to one hundred kilometres. At the time, I had no coin, no employment opportunities and nowhere to stay. I was fortunate to land a job on her family farm as a general hand. Not only did the job pay well, but I was also provided free board and food. Being one of a handful of women meant that Sally and I were destined to hang out at the end of the working day. So when I observed the massive task of cooking the meals to feed her family and workers, I felt obligated to help.

One night after dinner, we were washing the pots and pans and laughing about some funny incident that I've now forgotten, and then within a blink of an eye, we were gazing at each other as we held hands under the hot soapy water. I was about to lean forward and kiss her when I caught her glancing at the Christian cross hanging from the kitchen wall. I soon learned that the Fitzpatricks were devout. They never failed to miss their nightly prayers and Sunday Mass and certainly didn't accept same-sex relationships.

I don't have much time for God – it's not as if he stopped my parents and half the planet from being obliterated. Later that night, I snuck into Sally's bedroom. It was not the most romantic beginning to a relationship, but there was a definite spark, and she became my first true love. My only true love.

Sally's dad, Mr Watson, was a hard taskmaster who didn't suffer fools, but I was determined to earn his respect. So for nine months, I worked hard, learned new skills, and volunteered to help with the unpopular jobs - shovelling shit, cleaning grain bins, and killing rats. He must have seen I was keen as he taught me how to shear, mend fences and operate the tractor. He even paid a local vet to teach me medical skills, which came in handy as workers were constantly getting injured around the farm. I treated everything from abrasions to broken bones. It wasn't long before the men came to my door after hours. Brawls, motorcycle accidents, falls from horses, and injuries from everyday shenanigans kept me busy. I realigned broken noses, stitched facial wounds, and reset dislocated fingers and shoulders.

Three years before I arrived on the farm, Sally's older brother died in a horrific tractor accident. Mr Watson had high hopes that Sally would meet a capable local man, have three kids or more, and take over the farm when he could no longer work the land.

Late one stormy night, Sally and I were preparing the horse feed in the stables. One thing led to another, and we started making out. Her father barged into the stables and witnessed me passionately pressing his daughter against the stable wall. He immediately did an about-turn and marched out, shaking his head and swearing under his breath. I should have known that this was the beginning of the end for Sally and me.

The following morning Mr Watson ordered me to vacate the property by sundown. In response to my eviction, Sally had a massive dustup with her father and stormed off the property holding my hand. We both found work at Fitzpatrick's Wheat and Sheep Farm, just thirty kilometres from her family's farm. Fitzpatrick didn't care who was fucking who, just as long as you worked hard and didn't cause any trouble.

Sally didn't come out and say it, but I felt her resentment for causing her family bust-up. It was clear by Sally's demeanour that she missed her parents and the farm and blamed me for her estrangement. She sulked at night and criticised me for trivial issues, such as failing to do the laundry, wearing boots inside our room, and being tired at the end of the working day. One night she even accused me of flirting with one of the farm hands. This caused a huge row that had tongues wagging all over the farm.

Instead of doing the right thing and ending our relationship, she sabotaged my trust by making out with a shearer behind the shed. Upon learning of her betrayal, I immediately handed in my notice to Mr Fitzpatrick, packed all my belongings and left the farm for good. That was the last time I had set eyes on Sally. Numerous times I've attempted to write her a letter, but after reading the second or third line, I felt the words were either clumsy or inadequate, so I would crumple the paper into a ball and throw it into the nearest bin or fire.

# Chapter Four

*Sunday, February 9, 2042 from 10:30 a.m. – Fiona*

Sitting on Jasper's saddle on the summit of a steep hill, I looked out over the brown pastures and could just make out the profile of the Fitzpatrick homestead. As we rode toward the farm's main gate, I was horrified that my trepidation at seeing Sally was accompanied by a tinge of excitement. Nevertheless, I buried my emotions and scanned the grounds. It wasn't surprising that the property looked the same as when I left it. The limestone homestead was a colonial-styled one-storey, with an extensive wraparound verandah built to keep the occupants cool in the summer heat.

Looking over my shoulder, I noted Gizzarelli was still unconscious on One-eye's back. "Is he still alive?" I asked.

Archie dismounted Roger and checked Gizzarelli's pulse. "Yep, he's still with us."

"I shouldn't be surprised. He's one hell of a stubborn bastard." I let out a long sigh, "I guess I'll go knock on the front door and say hello."

Archie nodded. "No problem, we'll wait here. Don't take too long. He may be a stubborn bastard, but he looks as pale as a ghost. You don't have to be a surgeon to realise he's not long for this world."

As I expected, there were no guards positioned at the gate. In fact, I couldn't see anyone on the grounds. I wondered if Archie was shocked by the lack of security. Most southern farms deter gangs and thieves by positioning armed guards at strategic locations around the property. Small family farms may have a worker with a shotgun or rifle, whereas wealthy farms have a team of armed security patrolling the property.

The Fitzpatrick farm was a relatively small northern property in the middle of nowhere. When I lived here, I only saw workers carry firearms to put down animals or head out bush to hunt.

Archie dismounted and opened the gate so I could trot up the red dirt track to the homestead. I secured Jasper to the hitching post at the main entrance and tapped my knuckles on the fly-screen door.

"Hello, it's Fiona. Is anyone home?" I bellowed.

"Give me two secs. I'm just getting dressed," Mrs Fitzpatrick hollered back.

In a jiffy, Mrs Fitzpatrick came bustling down the entry hallway. She was a large-bosomed lady in her early fifties, with short curly brown hair beginning to grey. There were constant rumours around the farm that she'd sleep with the young male shearers whenever she got the chance. But, of course, I didn't pay any attention to the farm gossip. And anyhow, she was always kind to me, and if she had some young buck on the side, it was none of my bloody business.

In a heartbeat, Mrs Fitzpatrick's expression transformed from uncertainty to recognition. She opened the screen door and looked me up and down before embracing me. "Oh my god, Fiona! What happened, Love? Are you okay?"

Given how I had abruptly left the property, I was so focused on gauging her reaction to my sudden appearance at her doorstep that I'd forgotten about my head injury and how I must look.

"I'm fine, Mrs Fitzpatrick, just a little banged up. Sorry to impose, but I'm here because I have a friend, well, sort of an acquaintance, who's been shot. He's in a bad way, and If he doesn't get medical attention soon, he's a goner for sure. So I was hoping you could help."

"Well, you'd better bring him into the house. While you do that, I'll organise the sewing room and tell Daniel to fetch old Harris. And please call me Jennifer, Love. I feel old being called by my married name."

Daniel is Mrs Fitzpatrick's husband, and Harris is one of their neighbours who provides veterinarian services and assists in medical emergencies. Harris was the vet who taught me most of what I know about patching people up. He plays a vital role in the community, as the nearest hospital is in Geraldton, almost one hundred kilometres away. By the colour of his skin, Gizzarelli desperately needed a blood transfusion. If Harris didn't get here quick, the grisly oaf would surely meet his maker before nightfall, or in his case, chat with the red fellow with horns and a pointy tail.

"The injured bloke is with Archie. He's my partner. They're waiting outside the main gate for me to return. I'll bring them both to the house if that's okay with you?"

Mrs Fitzpatrick raised her eyebrows. "Your partner?"

Not that it was any of her business, but I clarified our relationship to avoid confusion. "Archie's my business partner. I'm now a licensed bounty hunter. Please ask Mr Fitzpatrick to tell Harris that our friend has lost a lot of blood and needs a blood transfusion."

Archie tied the horses to the hitching post, and with my help, we managed to drag Gizzarelli from One-eye's back without dropping him. Archie carried the dying man under his armpits while I lifted his feet. Like experienced removalists, we manoeuvred him through the front door and down the hallway to Mrs Fitzpatrick's sewing room. She cleared her jarrah sewing table, which she mentioned was used as a dining table shortly after they married. And now it was about to be used as an operating table. If only furniture could talk. I'm sure it would say something like, 'What the fuck?'

Mrs Fitzpatrick busily placed clean sheets on the table, along with four towels, two jugs of water and a medical kit. We carefully lifted Gizzarelli onto the table and placed him so his head faced the door and his boots hung off the edge. After checking he was still alive, on a wing and a prayer, I searched the medical kit for any type of painkillers or anaesthetic. Unfortunately, except for some bandages and a scalpel, the kit was next to useless.

Archie retrieved our medical kit from his pack while I untied and removed Gizzarelli's blood-soaked bandages. He handed me the scissors, which I used to remove the unconscious man's jeans so I could examine his wound. Fortunately, the bleeding was reduced to just a trickle, which is probably the reason he was still alive. But, if I were honest, I didn't have much hope that he'd survive the surgery.

His face was as pale as a Scotsman's ass, and his breathing was as shallow as a pauper's grave. Of course, it didn't help his cause that I was an amateur surgeon who had only seen a bullet removed on one occasion. And I was the patient at the time.

Archie pressed a towel over the wound. "Are you going to go fishing for the projy?"

Archie was referring to the lead projectile jacketed by a thin layer of copper, which was embedded in Gizzarelli's thigh. Jon shot him with an old .223 rifle, the weapon of choice to kill dogs, pigs, and goats. I wouldn't want to be Jon if Gizzarelli survives. *Dead man walking comes to mind.*

I gave Archie a grave look. "I can cut the bullet out, no problem. But I'm guessing it'll probably kill him. He needs a blood transfusion which I don't have the knowledge or equipment to perform." I turned to Mrs Fitzpatrick, who was standing by the door. "Can you boil a litre of water, please? Ah, can I also have some disinfectant or soap and some more towels? Oh, and can I use some of your sewing thread?" Mrs Fitzpatrick held an address book and wrote what I assumed was the list of items I had requested. "Sorry, I know I'm asking a lot of you, but can you also please ask one of the boys to look after our horses?"

"No problem, Love. I'll put the kettle on and get you some disinfectant and towels. I have plenty of thread. You'll find it in my green sewing box under the mannequins. I'll get one of the boys to take the horses to the barn and give them water and feed." Before she left the room, she smiled and added, "See, old Jennifer hasn't missed a beat."

I must have been stressed, as it felt like Mrs Fitzpatrick had only just left the room when she came bustling in holding a boiling kettle, soap, and a bag of ice. She clarified that the ice was for my forehead.

I was about to place the ice on my bump when Harris briskly entered the room holding a black leather medical bag. He was slightly more stooped than I remembered. He stood by the table, lifted Gizzarelli's eyelids, and then raised his thick grey eyebrows as he examined the wound. The old fella was all business. He didn't even take the time to say hello.

"Fitzy mentioned that your friend's been shot. I've never had to remove a bullet, but I can assist you in monitoring his vitals. First, I'll need to give him some blood. Do you know his blood type?"

Before I could clarify that he was not my friend, Archie opened Gizzarelli's notebook and read the inside cover. "He's O positive."

Most bounty hunters record their next of kin's contact details, blood type and allergies on the inside cover of their notebook. It's a form of insurance, more than anything. They know they have a greater chance of meeting an angel than receiving adequate medical care. But they still hope a Good Samaritan will contact their next of kin and inform them where to find their body.

"I'm O positive. But if I'm going to take this bullet out, I need to have my wits about me," I explained.

"Not to worry. I can take it from anyone with O negative as it's compatible with any blood type."

Mrs Fitzpatrick raised her hand like she was about to ask a question in class. "Daniel is O negative. I'll tell him that the jobs around the farm can wait so he can roll up his sleeve."

While Harris took blood from Mr Fitzpatrick in the loungeroom, I cleaned and disinfected a scalpel, forceps, clamp, and needle. Thank God Harris had a decent medical kit. I then wrote notes from my recollection of when a nurse removed shotgun pellets from my shoulder and breast. *A fucking bitch shot me when I was guarding the water train.* I listed the procedure from beginning to end - from cleaning the entry point to stitching him up.

After reading my notes over and over, I felt more confident. Just like Archie says – proper planning and preparation prevents piss poor performance - the seven P's.

Harris returned with 500 millilitres of blood in a plastic bag. He held Gizzarelli's arm and placed a small needle into a vein. I could see the blood flow from the bag through a rubber tube into Gizzarelli's vein through the needle.

"I'd give him some anaesthetic if I hadn't run out," Harris said apologetically.

"I'm just grateful that you're here to help me through this."

I cleaned the wound with a warm cloth soaked in soapy water and then made an elliptical incision around the entry wound with a scalpel. I grasped the elliptical area of the skin with the Allis forceps and then incised downwards from the edges on both sides towards the centre. After taking a deep breath, I used the forceps to enter the wound and attempted to grasp the projectile. I couldn't help but wince when blood flowed freely from the wound. Just as I could feel the forceps apply pressure around the lead projy, Gizzarelli suddenly woke and screamed in agony.

"Bloody hell, hold him down, Boss, or I'll never get this damn thing out," I pleaded in frustration.

Archie pushed down on Gizzarelli's shoulders, "Settle down, big man. Fiona's trying to take the bullet out, and you're not helping things."

He attempted to push Archie away and screamed, "Get off me, you fucker!" and then suddenly went limp and blacked out.

The bullet was so deep inside his thigh muscle that I was beginning to worry that I wouldn't be able to pull it out. With steely resolve, I dug the forceps deeper until I could finally feel the bullet between the teeth. While careful not to release the pressure, I pulled the bloodied projy from his leg and held it triumphantly between the tips of the forceps, like a prospector discovering a gold nugget.

After I breathed a sigh of relief, I closely examined the bullet. The lead and metal were conjoined to look like a mini mushroom cloud. I smiled as I pondered if Gizzarelli would like to keep it as a memento to remember the time I saved his miserable life.

My daydream was interrupted by Harris' offer. "Good job, Lass. I'll stitch him up for you while you put some ice on that lump of yours and get some fresh air."

"Cheers. I'll take your advice," I replied while picking up the bag of ice.

As I strode toward the front door, Mrs Fitzpatrick was busy cleaning dishes over the kitchen sink. "Here, Love, have a brew," she said before passing me a mug.

I strolled out to the verandah with the mug and bag of ice. Upon my first sip, I was pleasantly surprised to taste milk. The cost of distributing and refrigerating milk makes flat whites an expensive habit, so I'm accustomed to guzzling long blacks. My caffeine addiction intensified during my career as a bounty hunter. When searching for fugitives, we often worked late into the night and rose early in the morning. The magic bean helped keep me alert. Archie would be the first to admit that he's a bit of a 'coffee connoisseur.' His words, not mine. He would often whinge about the quality of the beans or the shortage of trained baristas that could make a decent cup. The beans are imported from New South Wales (NSW) and Queensland, with the truckies avoiding the gangs in South Australia (SA) by travelling through the Northern Territory (NT).

As I was only a kid when the War ended, Archie educated me about the world events that made this country so fucked up! *Those are my words, not his.* Archie said it took just three months after the end of the War for the Australian States and Territories to separate from the Federal Commonwealth. The crash of the global economy and the destruction of communication systems caused the Government to crumble. He reckons law and order was one of the first government systems to fail. The SA government lost complete control of the State and is now ruled by outlaw gangs who terrorise the local people. Archie and I joined a militia and rescued the residents of a WA town that had been enslaved by an SA gang that crossed the border to rape and pillage. They chained the Norseman residents in neck irons and forced them to work in the town's gold mine and service the gang's whims and desires. It was a bloody affair that left me with more than a few ghastly memories. But it was worth it. We rescued most of the residents, including a bright twelve-year-old girl named Helen, who I've grown quite fond of. Helen was adopted by our close friends, Elizabeth Ross and her husband, known to most as the Captain.

The tree branches danced in the breeze as a flock of sheep chewed grass in the paddock. Hearing footsteps approaching from behind, I instinctively reached for the grip of my holstered pistol.

A familiar voice asked, "Fiona, is that you? Are you alright?"

As I turned to face her, Sally raised her hand to her mouth to conceal her shock. Unconsciously I returned the ice to my forehead to cover the lump before doing an about-turn and marching back into the house. On my way to the bathroom, I banged my cup down on the dining table and swore under my breath.

The twenty-two-year-old staring back at me in the bathroom mirror was a blonde, athletic young woman with a massive purple and black haematoma bulging from her forehead. For a split second, I regretted saving Gizzarelli's life. *That stupid, aggro fucker!* Letting him die would have been a just punishment for giving me this ugly injury and putting me in this shitty situation.

I placed the bag of icy slush back onto my forehead and groaned as I recalled Sally's shocked expression. What frustrated me the most was that I cared about what she thought of me. *Fuck you, Sally!*

Someone knocked on the bathroom door. "What is it? I'm busy," I said sharply. I was acting like a cranky bitch, but in my defence, I was sore, exhausted, and hungry.

"I'm just checking that you're okay," Archie stated in a worried tone with enough volume to resonate through the timber door.

"I'm all good," I lied. "Is Gizzarelli still alive?" I asked more out of curiosity than concern for the man's welfare.

"For now, he is. Mr Fitzpatrick is cooking lamb chops on the barbie. Are you hungry?"

"Give me two minutes, and I'll meet you out there. It's all good, don't worry about me," I said, trying to convince myself as much as I was Archie.

There was a short pause, "No problem. We're out in the backyard."

We were often in dangerous situations that required us to trust and rely on each other. There's a bond that grows, and sticking your nose into your partner's business is a consequence of that bond. I pondered what Archie was thinking. Was he worried about my injury, or did he have an inkling I was shitting bricks about seeing my former lover?

I returned my gaze to my reflection in the mirror and whispered, "Toughen up, princess. You've been through hell and back. Surely you can face an ex without falling to pieces."

With fresh resolve, I abandoned my temporary haven and followed the scent of cooking meat to the backyard. Mr and Mrs Fitzpatrick, Harris and Archie were seated in camp chairs on a patch of rich green manicured grass. The English picnic scene looked out of place in contrast to the brown paddocks and the bush scrub in the distance.

I sat next to Archie, and before I could get comfortable, Mrs Fitzpatrick handed me a bowl filled to the brim with cabbage, fried crickets, mashed potato, and a lamb chop. Mrs Fitzpatrick must have noticed my unease as I considered whether I could consume such a huge portion, as she couldn't help but comment, "Eat up, Love, you're far too skinny." It wasn't the first time I had wondered why fat people were so concerned about my weight. I don't tell them to lose weight. So why should they ask me to put on weight?

To my annoyance, Archie joined the chorus of concerned spectators. "You need your strength. Dig in."

"Yes, Dad," I replied churlishly.

I grasped the chop by the bone and chewed on the succulent meat, burping appreciatively before spluttering, "Wow, this is really good!"

Archie raised a bottle of home brew to Mr Fitzpatrick, "Cheers to the cook." We all responded by raising our glasses to the man. I noticed that Mr Fitzpatrick had lost a lot of weight, and his usual brown weathered skin was ashen. After he coughed violently into his fist, I pondered whether he was ill.

Chronic diseases in this day and age were more often than not a death sentence. It's not as if Mr Fitzpatrick had the option of booking an appointment with a medical specialist. Most of them were killed in the nuclear strikes or during the evacuation. Even if they could locate a doctor that could help, what could they do without medical equipment? MRIs, CT scans and any technology with a chip were destroyed by either the nukes or electromagnetic pulse weapons (EMPs). I have no idea what these abbreviations stand for, but during my training, Harris told me that these machines made images of a patient's organs to assist doctors in diagnosing diseases. I'm sure a photo of Mr Fitzpatrick's organs would point to some type of cancer. A disease that Harris reckons was treated with radiation. I found that pretty ironic, given that radiation from the nukes caused so much death and misery. *Fucking Wankers!*

I spooned grilled crickets and mash into my gob and commented, "Fuck me! I tell you, Mr Fitzpatrick, this is bloody good!" Then, remembering that the Fitzpatricks were sticklers for swearing, I swiftly added, "Excuse my language."

Mr Fitzpatrick chose to ignore my use of foul language and beamed at the compliment. "The secret is in the marinade. I marinate the crickets in garlic, spices, and olive oil before grilling them."

The extortionate price of red meat meant that insects were now the primary source of protein for all but the wealthiest of civilians. As a result, I grew up eating all sorts of creepy crawlies while Archie's palate had yet to diversify. He would rather eat a sausage roll left in a bain-marie for two days and risk food poisoning than eat a delicious cricket sandwich.

After lunch, Mrs Fitzpatrick handed me a fresh bag of ice and suggested I use the spare room to take a nap. I didn't need much convincing. I was so exhausted that I could hardly keep my eyes open. However, I was curious whether the operation had been a success, so I decided to check in on Gizzarelli before heading to bed. Several pillows propped him up as he slurped lamb soup dripped over potato mash.

He gazed up from his bowl. "There's my saviour," he chirped, seemingly unaware that he had mash hanging from his chin.

I noticed that Harris had bandaged his thigh. "How are you feeling?" I inquired.

"I'll live," he replied, grinning.

I left him finishing his meal and collapsed onto the bed in the guest room. For at least an hour, I couldn't settle, with visions of Sally invading my thoughts and preventing me from falling asleep. I attempted to block her from my mind until weariness finally won the battle, and I drifted off into a deep slumber.

I woke to complete darkness and peered out the bedroom window. The farm was eerily quiet in the glow of a half-moon. I checked my watch: 11:15 p.m. I had slept for almost ten hours.

It was so warm that my shirt and tracksuit pants were sticking to my wet skin. Not wanting to wake anyone, I crept over the ancient jarrah floorboards to the bathroom and had a quick cold shower. After putting on a clean pair of jeans and a shirt, I decided to get some fresh air. I winced as the hallway's floorboards creaked with my every step. Gizzarelli was still asleep in Mrs Fitzpatrick's sewing room, snoring like an old steam locomotive. I walked out the front door and gazed at the starry night sky, appreciating the spectacular sight that never grows old.

With no particular destination in mind, I strolled down a pathway toward my old living quarters. The workers were quartered in a large farm shed that had been converted into private rooms using old shipping containers. A shearer who probably named his dog 'Dog,' christened the living quarters 'The Shed.' A brown kelpie pup ran up to me before skidding to an abrupt halt and barking his little head off.

I couldn't believe my bad luck when I noticed Sally exiting the Shed. "Shut the hell up, Brandy. Some of us are trying to get some sleep," Sally barked, louder than the dog.

Brandy was as obstinate as the man snoring his head off in Mrs Fitzpatrick's sewing room. He kept barking, so Sally retaliated by taking off one of her thongs and throwing it at Brandy's backside. She was dressed in white satin pyjama shorts and a black muscle top with a Jim Beam logo printed on the front. That was Sally to a T, soft in some areas and tough in others. She was a beautiful woman with long red hair, sexy hourglass curves, and ample breasts. She was the opposite of my athletic runner's frame, with no hips and no tits. Her looks had fooled many a dim-witted male. She may appear girly, but she can be hard to handle in equal measures, possessing a right hook that could knock most men out.

Sally noticed me standing on the path and paused before asking, "Fiona, is that you? Are you okay?"

"Yep, that's the second time you've asked me that today. I'm just getting some fresh air."

"Well, if you've had enough of that, do you want to come in for a drink?" she inquired.

I was about to decline but then thought, what do I have to lose? I followed Sally inside the Shed and down the hallway. I glanced at the name tags on each donga door, recognising some old names and noting some new ones. She placed her key in the lock and opened the door to our old room. Just as I was about to cross the threshold, I heard a door creak open and peered down the hallway. Mrs Fitzpatrick exited a room and fixed her hair. Sally stood on her tippy toes and craned her neck around my shoulder. Mrs Fitzpatrick noticed us and waved before strolling outside. "Mrs Fitzpatrick must be doing Robbo," Sally deduced.

Sally was not the most organised person in the world. She had underwear, shoes, jewellery, and clothes scattered throughout the room, on the floor, dresser, bed and bathroom. When we were living together, it used to bug the absolute shit out of me. Every second morning I'd pick up the clothes and dump them in the cupboard. Annoyingly the clothes were like boomerangs, as by the following afternoon, they would once again be scattered everywhere.

Sally opened the cupboard door and found a bottle of whisky and two glasses under a pair of overalls. She poured us two fingers as I plonked on the desk chair. We clinked glasses, said cheers and took a sip before she relaxed on the bed with her back leaning against the steel wall.

"So, where do we start?" she asked after taking another sip.

I was at pains to avoid the whole conversation about how I left, why I left, and the predictable accusations that would follow. I had played out the argument in my head a million times – '*You cheated on me. You were ignoring me. We no longer loved each other. You ran off!*' I knew the conversation would end ugly, and I didn't want to deal with it. Some may accuse me of cowardice for avoiding the confrontation, but I had a new life, and I'd moved on. As they say, let bygones be bygones.

"I've been working as a bounty hunter. I'm earning good coin, travelling around the state, seeing new things, and meeting new people. It's pretty exciting at times. What can I say? Life's been good."

At best, I was putting a positive spin on the last two years. At worst, I was bragging about my new life and rubbing her nose in it. I unashamedly chose not to mention my job as a skimpy, the number of people I've killed, and the horrific events I've witnessed. *I didn't owe Sally a damn thing!*

She gave me a warm smile. "Good for you. Sooo, are you shacking up with that islander hunk I saw you with earlier today?"

I had forgotten how she could get under my skin like an aggressive tick. She got one thing right, though. At six-foot-two with a six-pack and exotic movie star looks, most women turned their heads and went weak at the knees when Archie walked into a room. He looked islander, but his mum was Korean, and his father's ancestry was a mix of Irish and Jamaican.

I not only set her straight, but I couldn't help but throw a verbal jab. "I still just go for women. Not like yourself, that is," I replied.

I learned the hard way that Sally plays for both teams. Good for her, whatever floats her boat, but you would think she'd have the decency to tell me.

Sally raised her glass, "Touché and cheers."

After I downed my whisky, she scooted off the bed and poured me another. When she sat back down, she separated her long smooth legs just enough to let my imagination run wild as I glanced at the point where her inner thighs met her loose-fitting satin shorts. *Fuck me! I still found her so hot!* Unconsciously my glance turned into a gaze, which I swiftly averted when she cleared her throat. I was deeply mortified when I noticed the glint in her eyes and a knowing smile. I told myself, '*Get a grip. I know you haven't had sex for over a year, but that's no excuse to embarrass yourself.*'

"So, do you want an explanation?" she asked earnestly.

"No, actually, I don't. It's a surprise to hear myself say it, but I really don't. I don't know how to say this without sounding like a bitch, but I've moved on," I explained in a deadpan manner.

I sculled the remnants of my second glass and was about to get up and leave the room when she stood from her bed, brought the whisky bottle to her lips, and took a quick swig. I noticed that she didn't swallow. Instead, she straddled my lap and kissed me passionately. I opened my lips, and her tongue darted into my mouth as the whisky spiralled down my throat. I turned my head and coughed. She laughed while she slipped off her muscle top to reveal her beautiful breasts. I was about to push her away when she slid her hand down the front of my jeans and kissed my neck. Before I knew it, we were in bed, acting as if we had never broken up.

~

I couldn't help but feel like a creepy voyeur as I gazed at her angelic face whilst she slept. It frustrated me that I still had feelings for her. Over the previous two years, I'd used my anger to convince myself otherwise. I peered at the luminous hands of my watch: 4:45 a.m. I crept out of bed and silently slipped on my jeans. Before I tiptoed from the room, I took one last look at Sally.

It didn't take me long to locate Archie. He was standing outside Mrs Fitzpatrick's sewing room with a frustrated expression. "Gizzarelli's gone. Again!" he remarked bitterly.

It didn't surprise me one little bit. Archie walked over to the table and picked up a knife resting on a note. He passed me the message and the blade.

U saved mi life. This is for u. Giz

I gripped the polymer handle and examined the knife that wouldn't have weighed more than 200 grams. The Glock brand was inscribed on the grip and near the guard. With a fifteen-centimetre long blade that has a sawtooth spine, it looked savage. It could be considered a nasty cousin of the Ka-bar knife Archie gave me the year before.

Archie whistled. "The blade is phosphate coated to prevent corrosion. It will last you a lifetime. By giving you his knife, he's not just saying thank you. He's saying he respects you."

I wasn't quite sure how I should feel about receiving approval from a stone-cold psycho like Gizzarelli.

"Come on, we need to leave," I told him.

"What's the rush?" he asked with a quizzical expression.

There is no way in hell I was going to explain that I was avoiding an awkward goodbye with my ex-partner, whom I'd just slept with. So instead, I asked rhetorically, "Aren't you the one that's always saying that we have to keep moving?"

# Chapter Five

*Wednesday, February 12, 2042 from 10 a.m. – Archie*

Fiona barely spoke as we journeyed towards the coastal town of Geraldton. We rode thirty-odd kilometres during daylight for three days and hunted for dinner in the afternoon. I shot a roo and made a stew, and Fiona bagged a goat, which she roasted over the campfire. We were comfortable in each other's company, and she accepted that I'm not much of a talker unless I was partaking in an alcoholic beverage or two. It was evident that something had occurred at the Fitzpatrick's farm that she didn't want to discuss. And that's fair enough. I've told her I'm willing to listen if she ever needs to talk.

I'm somewhat of an introvert who tends to bury issues deep down. I'd be the first to admit that this coping mechanism has not worked well for me in the past, so I had been trying to open up a bit. Fiona's also an introvert, but unlike me, she bottles her feelings up until she explodes. It's like shaking a fizzy drink and taking the top off; it can get messy, but at least the problem is out in the open.

When I lost my wife in the War, I retreated from the world and self-medicated with oxycodone. The 'black dog' chased me from one town to the next, nipping at my heels. I made terrible decisions. This almost got me killed when a bounty operation went sideways. Fiona was my apprentice at the time. I was responsible for another human being for the first time in years. So how did I handle this new responsibility? I placed her in a deadly situation with insufficient training and preparation. The consequences were dire. My mentor, Sal, died. My back and chest were sliced open, and I was about to eat a machete blade before Fiona stepped in and saved my ass. After the dust had settled, I apologised to Fiona for my actions and made her a full partner, with the rewards split fifty-fifty between us.

I had hit rock bottom and decided to clean up my act after my best mate, Clarry, called me out on my addiction. He then helped me get off the pills. Clarry Ugle is a proud Whadjuk man from the Noongar nation, who I treat like a brother from another mother. He's also the most brilliant bloke I've ever had the pleasure to know. We wouldn't have had a hope in hell of venturing into contaminated Perth and rescuing ten-year-old Raj Singh without his scientific expertise and know-how.

Fiona and I rode to Bushy's stables, located within walking distance from Geraldton's town centre. Bushy's a wiry chap in his late thirties who dressed like a hippy from the sixties. He sported a jet-black beard and shoulder-length hair. He had a side hustle as the local mull dealer, so I had always wondered if his dress was a type of uniform. Bushy was busy shoeing a horse when we entered the stables.

"Hey, Bushy. We're here to drop off Roger and Jasper. Although I'm not sure for how long."

Bushy released his grip from the horse's rear leg. "No problem, man. Let me take them off your hands, and I'll get 'em settled in. Pay two weeks up front, and then we'll settle up when you return. I know you're good for it."

We had been residing at the Geraldton Ocean Hotel in the town centre. We had interconnecting rooms on the third floor overlooking the deep blue Indian Ocean. Fiona and I agreed to meet at 1 p.m. for lunch. I dumped my pack on the bed, retrieved my silver flask from the side pocket, and strolled onto the balcony. I took a swig of whisky before leaning over the railing to gaze at the picture-perfect coastline. The white sand, the gentle breeze and the waves lapping onto the shoreline helped clear my mind. Of course, the whisky didn't hurt either.

Over the previous nine months, the opportunities for bounties and private contracts had been meagre. Frequenting flashy hotels like

'The Ocean' would not be an option unless we pulled our fingers out and had some success. I retrieved my journal from my pack, sat on the edge of the bed and reviewed the previous year's takings. I kept an accurate log of completed bounties, security guard jobs, private contracts, and our expenses. My meticulous records are a hang-up from my days as a contract lawyer.

| Issued | Fugitive | Capture | Reward |
|---|---|---|---|
| 29/1/41 | Lewis Hutchins | 1/2/41 | 2 ounces |
| 15/3/41 | Curtis Gates | 17/3/41 | 1/4 ounce |
| 16/3/41 | Water Train | 16/3/41 | 1 ounce |
| 17/3/41 | Raj Singh | 12/4/41 | 25 ounces |
| 12/4/41 | Noel Patterson | | |
| 14/5/41 | Water Train | 14/5/41 | 1/2 ounce |
| 17/5/41 | Holly Hunter | 13/8/41 | 1/2 ounce |
| 19/5/41 | Caleb Tran | | |
| 14/7/41 | Arnold Cussler | 15/10/41 | 1 ounce |
| 15/8/41 | Water Train | 15/8/21 | 1/2 ounce |
| 14/10/41 | Cameron Lewis | 9/11/41 | 2 ounce |
| 14/11/41 | Lesley Maka | | |
| 16/11/41 | Esperance Police | 16/11/41 | 1/2 ounce |
| 5/2/42 | Marco Gizzarelli | | |

Technically we didn't commit an offence by failing to honour the bounty on Gizzarelli, but it wouldn't do our reputation any favours if it was widely known that we let him go. So I thought it was best to omit recording the four ounces that we appropriated from him.

As was often the case, my eyes focused on the Singh contract, by far the biggest reward I'd collected in nine years of hunting. We rescued Raj and were paid handsomely by his grandfather, a wealthy landowner named Kadesh Singh. Fifty ounces of gold split two ways was nothing to sneeze at. You could purchase a lovely four-bedroom home in a major town with fifty ounces of the yellow metal. But like a financially illiterate lotto winner, we'd been burning through the reward. We are not yet paupers by any stretch of the imagination, but we've been living it up, staying at five-star hotels, eating steaks, and buying quality booze.

We weren't entirely self-indulgent with our newfound wealth. We decided to give funds to Clarry to set up a functional science lab in Esperance. He used to work for the Commonwealth Scientific and Industrial Research Organisation (CSIRO) as a supervisor in the Health and Biosecurity unit, and he yearned for the opportunity to continue his research. Given that he was pivotal in rescuing Raj, it was only fair that we helped him out.

Even though of late we've had no luck in capturing fugitives, we're not yet destitute, as we still have a total of eight ounces of gold secured in bank vaults in Esperance, Kalgoorlie, and Geraldton. In case of emergency, I also have four ounces buried in the outback fifty kilometres north of the town of Norseman.

I unfolded the contract that would solve all of our financial worries. Kadesh Singh issued us a fifty-ounce private contract to capture Patterson and escort him to his Northam farm to settle a debt. I knew the debt was a farce, and Singh's true motive for capturing Patterson was to exact retribution for kidnapping his grandson. Nevertheless, I had no moral issues in accepting the contract, as Patterson was a sick bastard who murdered more than a hundred innocents. He had it coming in spades.

If we could locate Patterson, we would be financially secure for the foreseeable future. Our biggest problem was the absence of leads to his whereabouts. This wasn't due to a lack of effort. We had been travelling from one town to the next, pounding the pavement, interviewing residents, offering financial inducements for information, and searching for signs of unusual activity. So naturally, we were becoming frustrated and disheartened by our lack of success.

I Kadesh Singh, owner of the
Singh Farm in Northam,
contract Archie O'Connor and
Fiona Katsaros to escort Noel
Patterson to the Singh Farm
in Northam for the purpose of
settling a civil debt.
Upon Noel Patterson's
delivery Archie O'Connor and
Fiona Katsaros will be
rewarded with a total of 50
ounces of gold.

Archie O'Connor   Kadesh Singh
12th of April,    12th of
2041              April, 2041

My old man was a hard taskmaster. His military experience
indoctrinated a genuine belief that it was imperative for young men
to be capable, both physically and mentally. He took an interest in
my school studies and enrolled me in extracurricular activities such
as martial arts and Scouts. I didn't mind attending the Cub Scouts
or the martial arts. It was my dad's criticisms that bugged the hell
out of me. He found fault in everything I did, whether I received an
A-minus in a school exam instead of an A, lost a tournament bout,
or failed to erect a tent to his standards. I could hear him now - *'Why
didn't you check your answers during the exam? Why didn't you beat
that boy to the punch? You're better than him! For fuck's sake, that's not
how you put up a bloody tent.'*

One of the key impetuses for volunteering in the Army Reserves
whilst working sixty-hour weeks as a solicitor was to prove my old

man wrong. I kicked myself for it, but I was also seeking his approval.

The principle of being prepared was instilled in me by the army and the legal profession. Every week, without fail, I checked the serviceability of my tools and audited the items in my pack. My survival items and necessities include-: dehydrated meals, Leatherman multitool, map book, flint, lock pick set, water purification tablets, compass, night vision goggles, duct tape, rope, torch, batteries, folding spade, first aid kit and two pairs of merino wool socks. I needed to visit the local pharmacy and convenience store to purchase bandages, gauze and dehydrated meals.

I had an hour before meeting Fiona for lunch, so I stripped, cleaned, and conducted a serviceability check of my rifle and revolver. At every available opportunity, we clean and ensure our firearms are functional. Our lives depended on our firearms going *Boom* rather than *Click*.

I was reassembling my rifle when I heard a knock on the door. I picked up my revolver and tactically approached the door.

"Don't shoot me, you suspicious bastard," Fiona bellowed.

I lowered my revolver and invited her inside. "Everything all good?"

"I wish you'd stop asking me if I'm good. Why wouldn't I be?" she remarked snidely.

"Okay, what's up with you?" I asked as I returned to the task of reassembling my rifle.

Fiona stepped inside the room. "Nothing, just joking around. A bit sensitive today, are we?"

She was deflecting my question by trying to piss me off, and I'm an easy-going bloke, so it takes quite an effort to get under my skin.

Fiona's shoulder slumped, and she pouted, "Look, I'm sorry if I've been acting like a bitch, but I'm going through some personal stuff. No offence, but it's not something I want to talk about. And you can't help me anyway. You'll just need to trust me on that. But I'd appreciate it if you joined me for a workout." She held out her hand, tilted her head and smiled, "Friends?"

I couldn't tell if she was being genuine or facetious, so I shook her hand and examined her eyes and posture for signs of deception.

With the collapse of higher education, Fiona didn't have the opportunity to become book-smart. But she's a problem solver who can manipulate people like an ingenious fraudster. Fortunately, I'm used to playing cards with sharks, so I've got a pretty good idea when someone's trying to swindle me.

~

It's crucial in our line of work to keep physically fit. We may need to run or fight for our lives at a moment's notice. We run, lift weights and spar whenever we get the opportunity. I returned the items to my pack and secured the thirty-five-kilogram load to my back, tightening the waist and chest strap before exiting the room. We jogged down the Geraldton coast on a gravel track for about five kilometres before turning around to run back. The south-westerly blew the salt air into our faces as we picked up the pace. Fiona's pack is about twenty kilograms lighter than mine. We don't need two of everything, and I'm thirty kilograms heavier than she is, so it's only fair that I carry more. Fiona is highly competitive by nature, so it wasn't much of a surprise when she challenged me to a race over the final 150 metres. She raised her hands and shouted triumphantly as we sprinted across the invisible finishing line. I laughed breathlessly with my hands on my hips as she performed a victory dance.

After we recovered our breath, we completed a circuit of push-ups, lunges, and body squats until we fell to the grass in exhaustion. While I rested on my back and took deep breaths, filling my lungs with oxygen, I spotted shapes in the clouds, recognising Aladdin's lamp, a giant mushroom, and a fat rabbit.

I thought our workout was over. Fiona must have thought otherwise. Without warning, she lunged toward me like a jackal attacking its prey. She mounted my torso and began her assault. At a glance, bystanders may have thought we were engaged in a lover's tryst, but if they looked closer, they would see it was a simulated game of life and death. First, she attempted to perform an Ezekiel choke, placing downward pressure on my windpipe with her left forearm while wrapping the other behind my neck and then gripping her opposite forearm. She aimed to either make me submit or choke me unconscious.

I must give credit where credit is due; Fiona's technique had improved by leaps and bounds. But my size and experience gave me a distinct advantage. I escaped the choke by gripping and pulling her top forearm while bridging and rolling her off my chest.

We rolled for forty-five minutes, transitioning from various chokes to limb extensions and joint rotations. Even though I tested her abilities, making her work hard for submissions and escapes, I was careful not to smash her with pressure. An instructor should never dominate their student, and I still had concerns about her head injury.

After the gruelling workout, we lay on our backs and gazed at the blue sky.

She turned toward me. "I feel a bit better now," she said breathlessly.

"Glad to hear it. Now let's get back to the hotel. I'm bloody starving."

~

After a quick shower, I met Fiona in the hotel dining area for a bite to eat. The dining room was swanky, with clean white tablecloths, expensive-looking cutlery, tasteful art hanging from the walls and well-dressed wait staff. I sighed inwardly and pondered whether this decadence was the cause of our sharply declining funds. I ordered a roo burger, and Fiona ordered a fried cricket sandwich. I still can't comprehend how her generation eats bugs, even when they have a choice not to. Don't get me wrong, if I have to eat creepy crawlies, I will, but I'll swallow it down with a swig of whisky. I asked the waiter to bring us a jug of beer.

My eyes were drawn to a cricket leg sticking out from the corner of Fiona's mouth. "So, Boss, tell me about your philosophy."

I went blank for a second until my brain clicked into gear.

I recalled telling her I would explain my university professor's philosophy on mental well-being.

"We've dealt with some horrific stuff over the last twelve months, and I just thought you should be aware that exercise and acting stoic might not be enough to keep you sane over the long run."

"Stoic?" she asked.

"You know, detached and unemotional," I explained.

"And you think I'm stoic?"

"It's not a bad thing. It's just not something to rely on. You know I don't have a good record of dealing with stress. And I don't intend to lecture you. I just thought it would be a good time to discuss mental well-being." Fiona furrowed her brows, crossed her arms, and sat straighter. "I'm not asking you to talk about specific issues. It's just a philosophical chat."

Fiona took a sip of her beer. "As I said, Boss, I'm willing to listen as long as you keep buying the piss."

It was tradition in the law firm where I was employed for the boss to pay for the drinks at the end of the work day. Fiona had caught onto this cultural hang-up that I had unwittingly perpetuated. It also hadn't escaped my attention that she tends to call me *Boss* when she wants something.

"I had this professor at uni who was pretty switched on. He used a glass jar and a bag of marbles as a metaphor to explain his theory of mental well-being. But I think I can make do without the marbles."

Fiona laughed. "Marbles? I hope you're not telling me that I'm losing my marbles. Because that's not a good start to your lecture."

I asked the waiter to bring over a jug of water and an empty glass. By the time I took another bite out of my burger, the nimble waiter had placed the jug and glass in the middle of the table.

I held the empty glass. "This glass represents an individual's conscience and state of well-being, and the jug of water represents loss, regret and guilt. We're all born with an empty glass, as we are innocent and free of negative emotions. Do you agree?"

"If you're asking me if I think we're born innocent, yeah, I don't think you can look at a baby and think it's evil."

Fiona sculled the rest of her beer and immediately poured another one. She was drinking like a sailor who had just started their shore leave. This may be a perfect time for this little talk, I thought. I ordered another jug of beer from the attentive waiter.

I continued what Fiona referred to as 'the lecture.' "Life can hit us with challenging circumstances. Like when we found the bodies in the hotel and lost our mates on the train." I poured water into the empty glass. "The water filling up the glass represents the loss, regret and guilt we feel due to the horrible situations we experience." I poured more water into the glass so it was three-quarters full. "If we don't acknowledge, process and manage the fallout from these emotions, it can all start to build up." As I poured more water into the glass, causing it to overflow onto the tablecloth, I explained, "If it overflows, we can react in an unhealthy manner and harm ourselves or even hurt the ones we care for."

Fiona's eyes narrowed. "Dealing with relationship issues is a bit more complicated than an empty glass and a jug of water, Archie!"

Fiona grabbed the fresh jug of beer from the table and stomped toward the hotel stairs that led to her room. I was left somewhat dumbfounded. Who the hell mentioned anything about relationships? We were discussing the consequences of experiencing death and destruction. I feared her head injury may have rattled her brain more than I'd anticipated. Or perhaps this was a conversation best had sober.

# Chapter Six

*Monday, March 3, 2042 – Fiona*

After returning from a morning run, I was standing before the bathroom mirror, examining the injury to my forehead. It had been a day over three weeks since Gizzarelli struck my noggin with a bottle. The swelling had disappeared entirely, and the bruising was a light shade of yellow. Excuse the pun, but I don't think anyone would have accused me of having a swollen head if I said the young woman staring back at me looked healthy and fit. Archie and I had been exercising every day, and when we weren't running or sparring, we were either at the gun range practising marksmanship and movement drills or riding Jasper and Roger along the beach and bush tracks.

Archie had been concerned by our lack of funds. He had been visiting the bondman's office first thing in the morning for two weeks to inquire about new bounty contracts. We had been shit out of luck. He mentioned that if we didn't find a job soon, we would need to apply for work on the water train. It was not exactly my favourite gig, but it paid alright. I had guarded the train travelling from Northam to Kalgoorlie on three occasions. During my first run, we repelled a gang that attempted to capture the train. It was messed up! *Bullets were flying everywhere - Cars were ramming the train - And we were fighting hand to hand on the carriages.* It was thrilling and terrifying. The following two runs were as boring as bat shit.

During dinner, I mentioned to Archie that I'd join him on his daily pilgrimage to the bondsman's office. I was hoping our luck would change. I purchased a couple of toasted cheese sandwiches and two long blacks from the hotel diner and met Archie at a park bench across from the hotel. Archie was facing the beach and performing his breathing exercise. He conducts this weird-looking exercise where he sucks in his lower abdomen during deep inhalation and then holds his breath for ten seconds before exhaling for fifteen to twenty seconds. He repeats this cycle for up to twenty minutes. I don't have the patience to sit and focus on my breathing for twenty minutes. I would rather do push-ups, chin-ups or lunges. Plus, as I've already mentioned, it looks *weird*.

Archie must have had a whiff of the melted cheese toasty because he opened his eyes and greeted me before I could say a word. We ate breakfast whilst watching the waves crash onto the foreshore. The gulls brazenly glided nearby, fixated on the toast in our grasp.

After brekky, we moseyed to the stables to collect Roger and Jasper before riding to the bondsman's office. The business of bounty hunting sounds quite simple. A licensed bounty hunter is issued a contract from the bondsman. Once the fugitive is captured or killed, they deliver them to the local police station to receive a handover document as proof of capture, which they then take to the bondsman to collect the reward. It's a shame that claiming a bounty is more challenging than it sounds. But then again, if it were easy, everyone would do it. And it would be for *shit pay*.

We tied the horses to the hitching post, removed our rifles from the scabbard and strolled through the front door of the bondsman's office. Brad Hill had his back turned as he stood in front of a five-foot-high metal cabinet. He was reading a giant book titled 'White Pages 2018'. I was introduced to Brad last year when he acted as the Esperance bondsman while Charlotte was on holiday. Brad turned around as we approached the counter. He was a tall thin man with a thick black lumberjack beard.

"What are you reading, Brad?" I inquired.

"That's a good question, Fiona, and I mean no disrespect by saying this, but given your age, you've probably never seen one of these. This is a book they used before the Internet to assist in contacting people. It had people's names with their addresses and phone numbers alongside." He placed the book on the counter and encouraged me to open it. The print was so tiny that you needed to look really close to read it. "I'm thinking of asking the local mayor to consider creating a similar book. It would make my job a lot easier."

"You're a real thinker, Brad. Now, tell me that you have some new bounties for us," said Archie.

"The one thing I can say about you, Archie, is that you're persistent."

Archie smirked. "Not to mention desperate, mate. Have you got anything for us? I've brought my lucky charm this time." When Archie pointed at me, I crossed my fingers.

"I hate to be the bearer of bad news, mate, but I don't have a contract for you. However, I've heard the coppers need some guns for hire to execute an arrest warrant," he replied apologetically.

I'm not dead against assisting the police with their operations, but they don't pay well, and I am yet to work with the Geraldton coppers. Last November, the Esperance Police hired us to shut down an illegal southwestern gambling ring running bare-knuckle no-holds-barred cage fights, along with dog and cock fighting. Most of the fights, including the human contests, ended in the death of a combatant. We had worked with the Esperance Sergeant in the past, and he'd done us a favour or two, so we felt obliged to assist. Even if that wasn't the case, I would have helped out. I hate cruel assholes that use and abuse animals. And I'm referring to the feathered and furry kind. We made the arrests without incident moments before the start of the entertainment. The three ring leaders are serving twenty years of hard labour at the Eastern Goldfields Regional Prison. *Suck shit!*

"Do you know how much they're paying?" I asked.

Brad looked apologetic. "Only a quarter of an ounce per gun."

One quarter is certainly not worth risking your life for. Especially when it's not our operation. Any job where you don't have control and ultimate say on how it goes down is considered high risk.

Archie leaned on the edge of the counter. "What did the fugitives do?" he inquired.

"They weren't particularly original. They robbed the town bank."

Archie's expression suddenly went dark. "Christ!" he muttered under his breath.

We said our farewells to Brad and walked out the front door. "What's up?" I asked with concern.

Archie replied with his hands resting on his hips, "I'm just praying they didn't get into the vault. We have four ounces in that bank. Most likely, those four ounces are now in some robber's greedy mitts."

So much for being a lucky charm, I pondered. When we entered Brad's office, we were hoping to collect a two-ounce bounty contract. But, instead, we left thinking we were four ounces in the hole.

Before we walked into the Geraldton Police Station, Archie confided, "I've never met the coppers here. Clip your hunter's license to your shirt pocket. I don't want them to get the wrong idea about us rocking up with rifles. They're bound to be jumpy due to the robbery."

Our rifles were slung over our shoulders, and our sidearms were holstered. It's normal for civilians to wear a sidearm, but it's a strict rule to hand over your longarms upon entry to any establishment, especially a police station.

We entered the station and approached the light blue laminate counter. A young constable with thick black sideburns and a square chin was searching through a green canvas duffle bag. He looked up and asked, "How can I help?" He rudely continued his search, making me think he wasn't interested in our answer. He removed clothing, a torch, and cable ties, placing them on the counter in front of us.

Archie cleared his throat and took the lead. "My name's Archie O'Connor, and this here is Fiona Katsaros. Brad next door advised us that you're looking for assistance to arrest some fugitives who robbed the bank."

The constable gave us a blank look. "We're both licensed bounty hunters," I explained, pointing to our license.

The constable immediately placed the bag on the counter and gave us his full attention, glancing at our license for the first time. He leaned forward, placed both palms on the counter, and lowered his voice in a conspiratory manner, "That's great news. Senior Constable Yeu is on annual leave, so we're a bit light on. We've put the word out to our volunteers, but only Mark and Nicky have offered to help out."

I thought, are we supposed to know who these people are? The constable failed to introduce himself, but his name tag read Constable JONES. He must have noticed our blank faces as he finally explained that Mark and Nicky were regular volunteers who assisted the station when they were short on numbers. This usually involved manning the counter and logging evidence and stolen property. Mark manages the post office and is an upstanding citizen in the community, but he's also an elderly gentleman with arthritic hips. Nicky's a seventeen-year-old lad who desperately wants to join the police force and has applied for the cadet school. I pondered, who would want to be a copper? They are paid peanuts to put their life on the line and are rarely thanked for their service.

Archie impatiently tapped his fingers on the counter as the constable ranted and raved about how short-staffed they were, their lack of equipment, the minimal opportunities for training and the miserable budget they were given. Archie glanced at his watch and then cut him off mid-sentence, "Did they get into the vault?"

"Yep, they made off with 750 ounces after killing the teller and bank manager. There was no damage to the safe, so they must have opened it up before they were offed. So, are you signing up to assist in their capture?"

"Before I answer that question, I need to have a chat with your sergeant," Archie replied cautiously.

By the look on the constable's face, he had taken offence to Archie's request. As if on cue, a bald man in his early fifties stuck his head out from the hallway, and with a gravelly smoker's voice, he bellowed, "Jonesy, we're starting the briefing. Finish up at the counter and lock the front door, would you."

"Sarge, we have two hunters here that are thinking of volunteering. They want to have a quick word with ya."

The sergeant considered us for a brief moment before approaching the counter. "Is that right? I'm paying a quarter of an ounce. Do you want to join me in my office, and we'll complete the paperwork?"

Archie and I walked around the front counter and followed the sergeant down the hallway to his office. On his desk sat a framed photo of the sergeant at the beach with a lady and two teenage boys, who I assumed were his wife and kids. It wasn't one of those fake family photos where you had to threaten the kids to smile. They actually looked genuinely happy. Hanging from the wall above his desk were a couple of plaques and a picture of him in a blue suit shaking a senior officer's hand. The sergeant asked us to place our rifles near his jacket stand in the corner of the office and gestured for us to take a seat.

The sergeant sat behind an expansive jarrah desk. Archie didn't hesitate to get down to business. "My name's Archie, and this is my partner, Fiona. Look, Sarge, I know you're a busy man, so I'll cut to the chase. We're happy to help with the op as long as two conditions are met. First, we had four ounces in that bank vault, so I want that back, and second, we want an additional one ounce each. Paying a quarter of an ounce for a job like this would result in the commission of a second robbery, and we'd be the victims."

The sergeant stroked his chin with his thumb and index finger. "So you're Archie O'Connor, the man who led the Esperance militia to victory in Norseman."

Archie stalled as his cheeks turned bright red, so I took the opportunity to butt in. "He also saved those nurses in Darwin during the War. I'm pretty sure having a fucking war hero on your team is worth an extra one and a half ounces." Archie hates it when anyone mentions his exploits during the War, but we desperately needed the gold. Watching him squirm with embarrassment was a bonus.

The sergeant smiled and raised his palms. "That sounds fair. I'll have to clear it with the mayor, but it should be fine. And young lady, I'd prefer it if you didn't use profanities in my presence. As a bounty hunter, you're a representative of the law, and it's not befitting for you to swear like a trucker."

*What the fuck? Did we just enter a time machine and return to the nineties?* As I was thinking of a rebuttal, I noticed an ornamental jade cross sitting on his cupboard shelf beside a leather-bound Bible. *Pious bastard!*

"Noted, Sarge. When and where's the briefing?" Archie asked before I could respond.

The sergeant pointed to the ancient Epoch typewriter sitting on the corner of his desk. "I just need to update the operational order. Ask Constable Jones to make you a coffee, and we'll start the briefing in about thirty minutes. It's great to have you on the team, Archie."

*And what am I, bloody window dressing? Fucking dinosaur!*

Archie thanked the sergeant, and we left his office with our rifles slung over our shoulders. Archie whispered to me as we walked down the hallway, "You don't need to convince me. I know the sergeant is a bit of an uppity prick, but let's just play nice, so we can get our gold and leave town."

I gave him the evil eye and was about to give my two cents' worth when I bumped into Constable Jones, who was barrelling down the hallway holding two Kevlar vests. "Fair bump, play on," the constable chuckled before leading us to the crib room.

I once asked Archie why coppers referred to their meal break as crib. It was a mistake thinking I would receive a straightforward answer because he went on to give me a bloody history lesson. *I vividly remember feigning interest during his explanation.* In his defence, he was a lawyer before the War. He explained that his grandad told him the term initially derived from Cornwall in England and meant a container for animal fodder. His grandad argued that it made perfect sense because most coppers behaved like pigs. Archie warned that I should take his grandad's opinion with a grain of salt. His grandad also swore that their family was related to C.Y. O'Connor, the engineer who developed the pipe in the early 1900s to pump water 590 kilometres from Perth to Kalgoorlie. It was used for over 130 years until the nukes contaminated the water source. Archie explained that an Aussie miner would argue that it's called crib because in underground mining, 'cribbage' was used to support the area where the miners had their meal breaks. He then added that if you asked a copper, they'd explain that in the late 1800s, the officers would play the card game 'cribbage' during their meal breaks.

An older gentleman and a young chap who didn't look a day over eighteen were seated at a cheap plastic rectangular table that dominated the centre of the crib room. Wanted posters and advertisements for local diners were pinned to a corkboard on the far wall. Archie walked up to the board and closely examined the posters. He took one of the posters down and folded it before placing it in his back pocket. That was a bit weird, I thought. The constable switched on an old stainless-steel kettle and put a heaped tablespoon of instant coffee into two ceramic mugs with 'visitor' scrawled on the side in black marker. Even with my caffeine dependence, I struggled to swallow the muddy liquid that was, at best, a distant cousin to coffee.

The older gentleman introduced himself as Mark Mosley. He wore glasses with thick coke bottle lenses and had a kind face. He came across as an elderly man who wouldn't hurt a fly. Mark explained that he manages the local post office and volunteers as an auxiliary officer in his spare time.

The young fella sitting across from Mark was named Nicky. He was bright-eyed and bushy-tailed. He made no effort to hide his infatuation with joining the police force. He explained that since he turned sixteen, he'd assisted by manning the counter, attending vehicle accidents, and taking reports of low-level crimes such as thefts and property damage.

The uptight sergeant entered the crib room, stood in front of the fridge, and read the operational order. He explained the situation and repeated the mission statement before detailing how we would execute the entry to the premises. We gathered our notebooks and recorded the critical parts of the plan. I was relieved to learn that Archie and I would be entering the rear of the house side by side. After hundreds of hours of training and numerous operations, we had developed into a well-oiled team. When we reached the pointy end of a mission, we could almost read each other's minds. With minimal words required, we tactically responded to the other's movements and hand signals, often in life-and-death situations.

#### **** OPERATION DESPERADOS ***

**SITUATION**: AT 0745HRS ON MONDAY, MARCH 3, 2042, TWO MEN AND ONE WOMAN, NOW KNOWN TO POLICE AS LILLIAN QUINN, BRUCE QUINN, AND SEBASTIAN HUSSAIN, ARE SUSPECTED OF ROBBING THE GERALDTON TOWN BANK. THEY ARE ACCUSED OF FATALLY SHOOTING MONICA HAWKINS (TELLER) AND GABE PORTER (BANK MANAGER). THEY STOLE 750 OUNCES OF GOLD FROM THE BANK VAULT. A WITNESS SLEEPING IN A NEARBY PARK WAS ALERTED TO THE ROBBERY WHEN HE HEARD SHOTS BEING FIRED. HE RECOGNISED THE THREE SUSPECTS WHEN THEY DECAMPED FROM THE PREMISES IN A WHITE FORD CORTINA SEDAN. THE WITNESS STATED TO POLICE THAT HE ATTENDED HIGH SCHOOL WITH THE THREE SUSPECTS AND DID NOT BELIEVE THEY SAW HIM WHEN THEY DECAMPED. LILLIAN AND BRUCE ARE SIBLINGS WHO ARE KNOWN TO POLICE FOR SELLING DRUGS AND ENGAGING IN UNDESIRABLE BEHAVIOURS AT LOCAL LICENSED ESTABLISHMENTS. SEBASTIAN IS A KNOWN ACQUAINTANCE OF THE QUINNS AND HAS BEEN CONVICTED OF STEALING A MOTOR VEHICLE.

**MISSION**: TO EXECUTE A WARRANT AND ARREST THE THREE SUSPECTS (LILLIAN QUINN, BRUCE QUINN, AND SEBASTIAN HUSSAIN) ON MONDAY, MARCH 3, 2042, AT THEIR LAST KNOWN PLACE OF ABODE - 32 JENARK ROAD, GERALDTON.

**EXECUTION**:

**PHASE 1**: AT 1145HRS, THE TEAM WILL TRAVEL IN VICTOR 1 AND VICTOR 2 TO THE CORNER OF PLACE ROAD AND JENARK ROAD, GERALDTON, PARKING APPROX. 100 METRES FROM THE CORNER.

**PHASE 2**: UPON ARRIVAL ROMEO ONE AND ROMEO TWO WILL CONDUCT FORCED ENTRIES AND ARREST THE THREE SUSPECTS.

**ROMEO ONE**: SERGEANT ROACH, CONSTABLE JONES AND AUXILIARY OFFICER NICKY ALLEN WILL BREACH AND ENTER THROUGH THE FRONT DOOR OF THE PREMISES.

**ROMEO TWO**: BOUNTY HUNTER ARCHIE O'CONNOR, BOUNTY HUNTER FIONA KATSAROS AND AUXILIARY OFFICER MARK MOSLEY WILL ENTER THROUGH THE REAR DOOR OF THE PREMISES.

**ADMINISTRATION & LOGISTICS:**

A POLICE RADIO WILL BE ISSUED TO EACH MEMBER OF THE TEAM.

EACH TEAM IS TO CARRY DOOR BREACHING TOOLS (RAM, JIMMY BAR, HINGE PULLER, BOLT CUTTER).

EACH MEMBER IS TO BE ARMED WITH SIDEARMS AND LONGARMS.

**VEHICLES:**

VICTOR ONE: CONSTABLE JONES, BH O'CONNOR, BH KATSAROS

VICTOR TWO: SERGEANT ROACH, AO ALLEN, AO MOSLEY

**COMMAND & SIGNALS:**

POLICE CHANNEL 5

\*\*\*

"Are there any questions?" asked the sergeant.

Archie raised his finger. "Yep. Do you have any intel on what weapons they have access to?"

"No idea, other than the victims appeared to have been shot with small calibre rounds," he confessed.

"How many occupants are staying at the house?"

The sergeant rubbed the back of his neck. "Not sure, but we'll find out soon."

"Do you know if the place is fortified?" Archie fired back.

The sergeant looked flustered. "Look, these are small-fry thugs. Shall we stop playing twenty questions and do the job?"

Archie looked concerned as the sergeant placed a Kevlar vest over his head. It was a poor fit, as it failed to cover the girth of his potbelly. *I was getting a bad feeling about this job.* Jonesy handed out mug shots. The wanted crims held a piece of A4 paper to their chest, stating their name, height, weight, and the date the photo was taken.

Constable Jones drove Archie and me in Victor One, a battered chestnut brown 1971 Holden Kingswood station wagon. Before I even had a chance to attain my learner's permit, most of the nation's modern vehicles were rendered useless when major powers launched nukes and EMP weapons during the first two weeks of the War. All those electronic parts and computer chips in cars manufactured after 1975 just stopped working. I couldn't help but grimace when I thought of how the twelve-year-old me had a meltdown when my H-phone stopped working. I was more concerned with gossiping with my friends' holographic composites than contemplating the horrific consequences of the War. The hard truth is that I was a spoilt brat with my head up my ass. And I feel bloody guilty about it.

I was riding shotgun with the portable police light between my feet. The seventy-year-old suspension failed to do its job, with every bump, rock and pothole vibrating through the springs of the old seat, shaking my spine like a rattlesnake's tail. I was thankful we weren't transporting old rifles or shotguns. A combination of severe knocks and faulty safety mechanisms would probably cause the longarms to go *Boom!*

Archie was carrying his .38 Smith and Wesson six-shot revolver, and I had my nine-millimetre Glock 19 semi-automatic pistol with a spare fifteen-round magazine holstered to my belt. We also had our knives sheaved by our sides. I decided to bring the wicked Glock blade Gizzarelli had gifted me two weeks earlier. I wouldn't divulge it to Archie, but I fancied wearing the matching items – *Why can't I still be a tough bitch and look good?*

Before we left the station, Archie and I decided to task Mark with securing the backyard while we cleared the house. Archie wasn't confident that Mark would abide by the four firearm safety rules. One of the first tasks Archie gave me was memorising the four rules: treating all firearms as loaded, pointing the weapon in a safe direction, identifying your target and surroundings and keeping your finger off the trigger until you're ready to shoot. We were concerned that he would either step into the line of fire as we cleared the house or unintentionally shoot us. The old fella didn't appear happy when Archie asked him to remain in the backyard to secure our six. He folded his arms over his chest and snorted '*fine by me*' in a churlish tone. Not such a kind elderly gentleman, after all.

Constable Jones parked behind Victor Two on the corner of Jenark and Place Road. We exited the vehicles and walked down Jenark Road towards a cream brick single-storey home with an arched carport. The sergeant, constable, and Nicky quickly marched to the premises' front door. Archie and I jogged down the side driveway towards the rear of the house, with Mark hobbling behind us. Archie carried a ram to smash the rear door down; if that didn't work, I grasped a hinge puller.

"Remember, we do this slow and steady," Archie said as we approached the backyard.

Shortly after the sergeant's briefing, Archie took me aside and warned me about a secondary threat. He wasn't keen on the sergeant's plan of conducting a simultaneous entry at opposite ends of the premises. He was concerned that if we weren't careful, there was a risk of being hit by friendly fire. The belligerent bastard of a sergeant wasn't interested in anything we had to say and didn't answer any of our questions.

I flinched as gunshots erupted from inside the house. My heart pounded, and my senses were heightened as we stepped towards the rear door. *Here we go again.*

I pointed my muzzle at the door as Archie rested the door ram against the rear wall. He nodded to me as he turned the handle. But, of course, it was locked. What robber wouldn't want to protect their belongings from pilfering shitheads like themselves? He picked up the ram, swung it rearwards and struck the wooden door beneath the lock. The door splintered and cracked open. Archie drew his revolver as the ram left his fingertips. I took a deep breath as we tactically entered the premises.

*Bang, bang, boom, boom, bang.* Multiple shots from different calibres rang out. Before advancing into the main living area, we cleared the laundry and bathroom. We both yelled, "Clear." Archie marched through a small hallway to the left while I pivoted to the right. We entered a sunken loungeroom that led up two steps to the kitchen. A male fitting the description of Hussein was using the far kitchen wall as cover as he fired down the entry hallway towards the front door. He was so occupied with shooting at the officers that he had no idea we were standing behind him. I fired two rounds into his upper back and one round into the side of his skull. He dropped onto the kitchen tiles with a sickening thud!

A round buzzed past. Archie yelled, "On me", and we peeled into the kitchen. I stood above Hussein's carcass as Archie leaned his shoulder against an old fridge. Multiple rounds were being fired down the hallway. Archie yelled like a drill sergeant on parade, "Sarge, Jones. Hussein is down."

Bullet holes in the loungeroom wall to our rear were multiplying. *Bang, bang, bang.* Archie's initial fear of being shot by the coppers was duly warranted. We were stuck behind the safety of the kitchen wall, without any means of advancing down the hallway to provide Romeo One support. Archie went down on one knee and took a risk by sticking his head out to peek down the hallway.

Archie looked troubled and frustrated. Then, finally, he let out a deep breath and yelled over the gunfire, "The sergeant has been shot in the gut and - *Bang, bang, bang* - he's lying near the front door. A barrel of a longarm is sticking out from the nearest doorway on your side."

*Bang, bang.* I was trying to think of a plan of action I could suggest to Archie when I heard a bloodcurdling scream. As Archie turned his muzzle toward our six, Mark hobbled down the middle of the loungeroom with his Colt .45 revolver pointed at the ceiling. He was screaming an indecipherable challenge. Archie held out his arm, attempting to stop his momentum, but Mark brushed past him with his awkward gait and lowered his muzzle, repeatedly firing down the hallway. *Bang, bang, bang, bang.* He appeared to be on some bizarre suicide mission.

Archie's brows furrowed. "On me," he shouted. We darted down the hallway behind Mark. I'm not ashamed to admit that we intentionally used him as cover. It was seconds of utter chaos. Time slowed down. My amygdala, the tiny part of my brain that controls the fight and fright response, was surging cortisol through my bloodstream. My training took over.

Focusing on my area of responsibility, my attention was drawn to the doorway to my left. Archie was on my right, matching my pace as we advanced down the hallway. He fired multiple rounds. Slender arms grasping a sawn-off shotgun launched from the doorway. SHIT! I squeezed my Glock's trigger as I stepped forward. The shotgun fired. I witnessed Mark fall to the ground in my periphery. He crawled on all fours as I discharged four rounds through the doorway into a woman's chest and neck. I couldn't help but flinch when she fired the shotgun into the wall as she fell to the carpet. I entered the room, kicked the shotgun from her grasp, and roared, "Clear!" Blood sprayed from her mouth as she gasped for one last breath.

I was forced to step over Mark's corpse to exit the room. I held my pistol close to my chest while surveying the scene around me. The sergeant had been shot in his beer gut, right where it hung below his vest. Archie knelt beside the man, who moaned in agony as he sat against the security screen door, pressing his hands over his wound. Blood flowed freely between the gaps in his chubby fingers.

A man who I assumed was Bruce Quinn lay on his back in the sunken loungeroom with multiple wounds to his face, chest, and legs. His lifeless eyes were the spitting image of his sisters, the woman I had just dispatched.

Within reach of Quinn, Constable Jones was lying facedown, pistol still in his grip. I re-holstered my Glock and rolled him onto his back. He was a gruesome sight, with gunshot wounds to his right eye, nose, and forehead.

"I'm going to take the sergeant to Victor One. You find Nicky and meet me out the front," Archie ordered.

Archie marched over to the constable's body and retrieved the car keys from his pants pocket. He then grasped the sergeant under his armpits and dragged him out the front door. The sergeant stifled a scream before repeatedly swearing under his breath. I didn't think it was in good taste to remind him that swearing was *not befitting* for a representative of the law. I chuckled at my own joke.

While I searched the premises, I called out for Nicky. I was terrified that I would find his bullet-riddled corpse. "Nicky, where are you? We need to get the sergeant to the hospital."

I walked into the loungeroom and was relieved to find Nicky kneeling in a ball behind a well-worn two-seater couch. He gripped his ancient revolver between his legs with his eyes shut tight. When I saw the bullet holes scattered all over the backrest, I thought, *you lucky little bastard!*

"It's all right, Nicky. It's all over. You're safe now," I said in a soothing tone. I placed one hand on Nicky's back while I firmly gripped the revolver's cylinder with my thumb behind the hammer. "I'm just going to unload your revolver, Nicky. We don't want any accidents," I explained as I removed the firearm from his grasp.

I unloaded his firearm, dumping the rounds from the cylinder into my palm before returning it to him. The last thing I needed was for him to accidentally pull the trigger and shoot himself, or worse yet, shoot me. I held Nicky by the shoulders as I led him to Victor One. The poor kid was shaking like a leaf in a cyclone.

The neighbours across the road were having a sticky beak from the edge of their driveway. They would have had to be deaf not to hear all the commotion.

I leaned against the car door and whispered, "I'm going to search the house and find what we came for."

Archie gave me a wink. "Be careful. If you get lucky, I'll meet you back at the station. If not, I'll return and help you search." Archie handed me the keys to Victor Two. "Happy hunting," he offered before driving off.

I waved and smiled at the neighbours. "Nothing to see here, just a domestic argument that got a bit out of hand," I lied.

Even though the coppers had jemmied open the security screen, I still managed to close it after a firm kick and a solid shoulder bump. I retraced my steps and searched each room from the front of the house to the rear. 750 ounces is about 21 kilograms, so they could have hidden the gold bars in numerous spots. I searched the cupboards, draws, couches, kitchen cabinets, the fridge, oven, and the most obvious place, under the beds. This wasn't the first time I had searched a house. We've been in situations where fugitives had scampered from their premises. So we'd search for clues that could lead us to their whereabouts. Archie taught me to search systematically, focusing on ground level, mid-level, and probing high. I glanced at the ceiling in the hallway and noticed finger marks on the manhole cover.

I strode out the rear door in the hope of finding a ladder. As I walked to the shed, my eyes were drawn to the turf near a large olive tree. The lawn looked like it had been recently disturbed. A thirty-by-thirty centimetre clump of grass was distinctly yellow and slightly raised.

The first thing I noticed when I opened the shed door and peered inside was a giant spider's web hanging from the pitched roof. A redback climbed the web, desperate to escape the clutches of a daddy-long-legs. I'm not exactly an arachnophobe, but I still go out of my way to keep my distance from the creepy bugs. While being careful not to touch the web, I noted an extendable ladder, an ancient lawnmower and various garden tools scattered throughout the shed.

I bent down and picked up a well-used shovel before exiting the shed and leaving the spiders to continue their deadly dance. The breeze was blowing the branches of the olive tree as I pierced the clump of dead grass. I dug into the dirt until I struck a solid object wrapped in a brown blanket. I felt a tingling sensation running up my neck to the top of my head as I unwrapped the blanket to discover 20 one-kilogram gold bars and numerous ten-ounce and one-ounce bars. I gazed in awe at the riches. *They were bloody beautiful!* It was hard to believe that I had gold worth more than three million pre-War dollars in my possession. If it wasn't for Archie, I would have placed a couple of the ten-ounce bars in my pocket.

Carrying the gold bars in plain sight would likely provoke a shoot-out, so I covered the hole with dirt before jogging down the road to retrieve Victor Two. I reversed the vehicle down the side driveway and loaded the gold onto the back seat, concealing it under the blanket from prying eyes.

# Chapter Seven

*Monday, March 3, 2042 – Archie*

The sergeant was as pale as a ghost when I carried him into the emergency waiting area at the Geraldton Hospital. As the nurses wheeled him into the operating theatre, I wondered if the old boy would make it. When I walked back to the car, I noticed that the sergeant's blood had soaked the front of my shirt and pants. It was a pity there was no time to get changed. I looked like I had just finished work at the abattoir.

I shoved the Kingswood's column shift into drive and headed back to the police station to ascertain if Fiona had returned. Nicky was shaking in the passenger seat as he gazed out the side window. I would lay a hefty wager that he was considering other career options. Policing is not for everyone.

Victor Two was parked in the station's staff carpark. Fiona was sitting on the bonnet picking dirt out of her fingernails, acting like nothing out of the ordinary had occurred.

"How'd you go?" I asked in anticipation.

She gave me a cheeky smile. "I thought about doing a runner and heading east. But I changed my mind after considering how you couldn't cope without me."

I raised an eyebrow. "I take it that you found the booty."

"Back seat," she replied while gesturing with her thumb.

I opened the vehicle's back door and whistled in admiration. I had never seen so much gold in my life and most likely never will again. I smirked as I, too, contemplated 'doing a runner.' I pondered what that would look like. I would start by journeying up to the Northern

Territory and lying low for a couple of months before spending up big and buying a boat and a luxury house. The bubble burst when I envisaged looking over my shoulder for the rest of my life, waiting for a bounty hunter to track me down and target me in their rifle scope.

I shook my head, quickly dismissing my pipe dream and placed my hand on Nicky's shoulder. "Mate, do us a favour and fetch the mayor. Be a good fella and let him know it's urgent."

I found the station's door key on Victors One's key chain and unlocked the station's rear door. Fiona and I carried the gold bars into the crib room and placed them in the centre of the dining table. After taking another moment to gaze at the gold, pondering what could have been, I picked up a couple of mugs and found the jar of instant coffee in a cupboard above the sink. Even though my morning cuppa was awful, my caffeine craving would not be denied. Without thinking, I made the coffee and was about to take a sip when I noticed the names *Roachy* and *Jonesy* inscribed on the mugs. *Poor buggers*. I tipped the coffee down the drain and made fresh cups in the visitor mugs.

Fiona screwed up her face. "This shit is terrible", she griped.

A man I presumed was the mayor strolled into the crib room and stood before the gold. Nicky shuffled into the room behind him. The kid refused to look me in the eye when I greeted him. Instead, he moved to the far corner of the room and leaned against the wall with his head bowed.

The mayor was a bear of a man, standing six-foot-four with a massive barrel chest. He gestured for me to follow him out to the hallway. Before leaving the crib room, I snapped my fingers to get Nicky's attention. "Is he the mayor?" I asked. Nicky nodded his head solemnly by way of reply. Fiona began to make Nicky a coffee as I sauntered down the hallway. The mayor was waiting for me outside the sergeant's office with an air of impatience.

Given the sergeant was either dead or fighting for his life, I thought his behaviour was callous when he plopped his fat ass into his chair. "Grab a seat, Archie. Nicky hasn't told me much about what occurred, but I managed to get the gist of things. I believe you killed the bad guys, and old Roachy and his young sidekick bit the bullet."

I instantly disliked the bloke. "The sergeant was still alive when I dropped him off at the hospital. Sorry Mayor, I didn't get your name?"

He fixed a wan smile. "That's because I hadn't offered it. You can call me Jim. Jim Falster."

The mayor reached across the sergeant's desk to shake my hand, which I left hanging in front of me as I retrieved my notebook from my pocket. I swiftly scribbled my insurance policy.

*On 3/3/42, Mayor Falster of Geraldton received 20 x one-kilogram gold bars, 14 x ten-ounce gold bars and 32 x one-ounce gold bars from Archie O'Connor. As agreed, Archie O'Connor and Fiona Katsaros have been paid a total of 2 ounces in gold for assisting with Operation Desperados. They have also retrieved four ounces that had been secured in the Geraldton Bank in the name of Archie O'Connor before it was robbed.*

I passed the mayor my notebook and asked him to sign and date directly under the statement. After the big man read my notebook, he sneered, "You obviously don't trust me, Archie."

"Don't take it personally, Mayor. I trust only a handful of people in this world."

The mayor glared at me in uncomfortable silence before asking, "And what happens if I don't sign it?"

You could cut the tension in the air with a knife. My mind was bursting with questions – Is he trying to screw us? Is he planning to steal the gold? Or is he just an egotistical asshole?

I took my right hand off the desk, leant back in the chair and rested it on the grip of my revolver.

I paid close attention to his hands. "If you do, we'll get out of your hair. However, I'll take the gold to the bank if you choose not to scribble your moniker."

The mayor's right hand moved under the desk. I returned the four legs of my chair to the carpet and discreetly lifted my revolver from my holster. And then holstered the revolver just as discreetly when a man of Asian descent wearing board shorts and a billabong t-shirt marched into the office.

"What the fuck happened?" the surfer asked.

The mayor sighed and acknowledged the man with a look of disappointment. "Good afternoon, Senior Constable Yeu. Where the hell have you been?"

Senior Constable Yeu looked flustered. "I'm on leave. I've been camping down south. I'll ask again, what happened? Where's the sarge?" he fumed.

Before the mayor could answer, I promptly stood, shook the senior constable's (S/C) hand, and introduced myself. I put the poor bloke out of his misery by summarising the situation in a nutshell. I informed him that Sergeant Roach was still alive and kicking when I dropped him off at the hospital and then gave him my condolences for the loss of Constable Jones. We left the dodgy mayor in the sergeant's office with his mouth agape and returned to the crib room.

Fiona and Nicky sat at the kitchen table, sipping their hot mud. Nicky looked somewhat calmer, explaining how to wax a surfboard. Young men were attracted to Fiona like bees to nectar. She was easy on the eyes, great at spearfishing, could shoot a roo at 200 metres and knew more about cars and cage fighting than most blokes. So when a young fella asked the inevitable question, he would feel crushed when she made it clear that she batted for the other team.

S/C Yeu looked like a stunned mullet. Who could blame him? After returning from a camping trip, he learned his colleague had been slaughtered, and his sergeant was fighting for his life. Not to mention the 750 ounces of gold sitting on the crib room dining table.

It pained me to disturb his reverie, but we had places to go and people to see. "Senior Constable Yeu, can you please sign my notebook? Nicky can verify that everything I've stated is true and correct."

S/C Yeu suddenly returned to the land of the living when he realised we were all staring at him in anticipation. He cleared his throat and said, "No problem. And please call me Yewie." He then turned toward Nicky. "Nicky, do me a favour and grab the property receipt book from the front counter." Before Nicky exited the room, he added, "Oh, by the way, I'll need your services for at least the next fortnight."

Before Operation Desperados, I would have sworn that Nicky would have been over the moon upon receiving S/C Yeu's request. But his numb and disinterested expression said it all - what should have been called 'Operation *Debacle*' had caused him to think twice about a career in the police force.

S/C Yeu crossed out the mayor's name in my notebook and replaced it with his own before signing the page. He also wrote me a property receipt for the gold and handed me the four ounces we recovered and two ounces in earnings. He stated that as soon as he put his uniform on, he and Nicky would meet the acting bank manager and return the gold to the vault. Upon leaving, he thanked us for our assistance and said he owed us one. That was good to know, as having the constabulary onside could be particularly useful in our vocation.

Nicky was still blushing when Fiona released him from a warm embrace. I shook his hand firmly and said, "Hold your chin up, mate, and keep moving forward."

As the words left my mouth, I could have kicked myself for offering advice that my old man imparted – '*Get back on that horse*' - '*Keep a stiff upper lip*' - '*Meet adversity head-on*' - '*Pain is weakness leaving the body*' – '*Never give up, Archie*' - blah, blah, blah. I muffled an audible groan as I mused over the prospect of turning into my old man. Nicky didn't need to hear that crap.

Before we left, I decided to make amends and guided Nicky to the far corner of the office, out of Fiona and S/C Yeu's earshot. I placed my hand on his shoulder and said in a low voice, "Forget that BS I just told you. Go home and have a good cry on your mother's shoulder. Yewie seems like a good bloke, go and have a beer with him and have a good chat. You can bet your bottom dollar that he's had similar experiences. You'll get through this, mate."

After my conversation with Nicky, I felt better about myself. However, I realised another oversight as I unlocked and opened the station's front door. There was one further task to perform. Fiona and I had a quick word with S/C Yeu and returned to 32 Jenark Road in Victor One to transport Constable Jones and Mark to the morgue. It was the very least we could do.

# Chapter Eight

*Tuesday, March 4, 2042 – Archie*

Whilst strolling back to our hotel from Bushy's stables, I examined the wanted poster I had removed from the police station crib room. The fugitive's expression portrayed intelligence and smugness, with wide eyes, thin lips, a square jaw, and a smile that failed to reach his eyes. As I stared at the poster, I chastised myself for the hundredth time for letting the bastard escape.

Fiona sat on our favourite park bench, enjoying the sunshine, and chewing on a fried egg and cricket toasted sandwich. A group of kids were kicking a football back and forth and leaping onto each other's backs to take a specky. Their exuberance took me back to the days when I'd meet mates after school to kick the footy. I probably would have joined them for a kick if I didn't have my revolver on my hip. Who am I kidding? At thirty-six years of age, I'd struggle to leap into the air as I did in the past.

I sat down beside Fiona. "How are Roger and Jasper?" she asked with her mouth half-full.

As Fiona spoke, I couldn't help but notice a concoction of chewed cricket, cheese, and egg in her mouth. We were a successful team because we balanced each other's strengths and weaknesses. Don't get me wrong, I enjoyed working with her, but from time to time, her idiosyncrasies irritated the hell out of me! Not only did she chew with her gob open, but she also took my gun cleaning kit without asking, hardly ever offered to clean the dishes, snored like a trooper, and I'd even caught her using my toothbrush.

I diverted my eyes from her mouth and watched a young fella dive for the ball with outstretched arms. "As expected, Bushy is treating them well. Jasper seems happy, and Roger is his usual grumpy self. I also have some intriguing news to share."

Fiona snatched the poster from my hands with her greasy paw. She spat out a cricket or two as she exclaimed, "Fucking Patterson. Yes! Finally, we have a lead. So, he was last seen in Darwin. Wow! They've put ten ounces on his head. When are we leaving?"

Fiona was overeager, but for good reason - we had a private contract worth fifty ounces to escort Patterson to Mr Singh's farm. Patterson was an evil murderer who needed to be brought to justice. About a month after he escaped from our grasp in Perth, Sergeant Lee from Esperance Police Station took our witness statements, along with the testimony from three victims we rescued from Patterson's torture laboratory. We had taken it upon ourselves to seek payback on behalf of his victims - the hundreds of innocents he had killed during his experiments. This was personal!

Until I read the wanted poster, I was unaware that the judiciary had tried and convicted Patterson in absentia for multiple murders. A 'Dead or Alive' bounty had been issued. It didn't shock me that we weren't summonsed to give evidence at the trial, as we were always on the road and difficult to track down. The judge must have convicted him after hearing the victims' testimonies. I'm sure Mr Singh would have been an influential witness. A ten-ounce reward is an enormous and unheard-of bounty. Hunters would be searching for Patterson far and wide. If we managed to nab him, our reward would total sixty ounces of gold. A bloody fortune!

"We'll head out tomorrow morning as we have a few things to take care of first." I pointed to my notebook as I rattled off the list of things to do. "We have to buy supplies and ammo. Then, I need to settle the cost of servicing the Beast with Bill. And, of course, we need to pick up the bounty contract. Ah, and don't let me forget that I have to send Clarry a letter to let him know of our plans."

Fiona finished the last bite of her toasty. "What about Roger and Jasper?" she asked.

"I've sorted that out with Bushy. The cost of agistment is not cheap. It was fortunate we recovered our four ounces."

"I'll miss them both, but I'm not riding up to Darwin. Sooo, what's the plan for the rest of the day, Boss? What do you need me to do?" she asked.

"You grab the supplies and ammo and replenish our packs while I visit the bondsman. Then I'll pick up the Beast and drop by the post office to send Clarry a letter. After that, we'll meet up for dinner and have a debrief about Operation Desperados." Fiona's expression turned from exuberance to wariness. "There's nothing you or I did wrong. But, as usual, I want to discuss some learnings," I clarified.

Fiona gestured with a nod. "Too right it wasn't our fault. The op was a real clusterfuck because of piss poor planning," she snorted.

Fiona headed off to catch a taxi while I sauntered down the road to Bill's Motors. After the War, the local council's responsibilities were greatly diminished. Litter scattered the footpaths, thick tree roots cracked the pavement, and potholes filled the streets. Homeless people sat outside every second shop front, begging for food. I handed a box of sultanas to a ten-year-old child sitting outside the motor shop, knowing it would likely be his only meal for the day.

My baby was sitting in the garage with her bonnet up, flaunting her powerful V8 5.6-litre engine. I nicknamed her the Beast shortly after purchasing her. I took a moment to admire the beautiful 1971 Chrysler VH Valiant Charger. The midnight black hardtop coupe had an aggressive wedge-like stance and sharp lines that personified devilish speed. It's fair to say that I fell in love the day we met.

Bill was a diminutive man who wore grease-stained overalls like a second skin. Whether I spotted him at the pub or down at the shops, he was in his overalls. I've pondered whether he wore them to bed.

Bill noticed me standing in his garage. "She's purring like a lioness," he bragged.

I thanked and paid the man before reversing out of the garage and driving to the bondsman's office. I strolled through the front door to discover that Brad was nowhere to be seen. Standing behind the counter, I bellowed a greeting. Brad shuffled out from the back office, holding a coffee and rubbing sleep from his eyes.

He gave me a mock salute. "Good morning, Archie. How can I

help?"

"Morning. Quick question, mate. Have you been holding out on me?"

"What do you mean?" Brad replied innocently.

I placed Patterson's wanted poster on the office counter. "You didn't give me the heads-up about this contract, which happens to be worth a whopping ten ounces."

I intentionally omitted information concerning our private contract with Singh. Brad's a good bloke, but he gossips like an old woman. The competition would already be fierce. If it were widely known that we had a fifty-ounce contract for Patterson's capture, we'd have hunters from Timbuktu trying to steal our reward.

Brad picked up the poster and considered it with a quizzical expression. He then searched through a tray of envelopes at the back of the office. Finally, he pulled out a contract. "I must have missed it when the mail came in." Brad handed me a copy and remarked, "Far out! You're dead right. It's worth ten bloody ounces. That's a first for me. It makes me consider becoming a hunter."

Brad might have a different perspective if he could see my physical scars and hear my mental ones. The grass is always greener on the other side, I pondered.

After leaving Brad's office, I dropped by the post office and purchased an envelope, stamp and writing paper. The destruction of the Internet has resulted in a letter and postcard renaissance. The State Postal Service may travel at a snail's pace, but it's considered pretty reliable if you're sending mail intrastate. I have absolute respect for the courageous postmen and women who risk their lives to deliver the mail. They work by themselves for an average wage and are often forced to flee from gangs and fight off bandits.

I returned to the Beast, locked the doors and rested my revolver on the dash to persuade any would-be car thief to move along and rob someone else. Then, I leaned against a clipboard and penned a letter to Clarry.

*Dear Clarry,*

*I hope you are well and haven't blown up your lab :). We're all good. I just wanted to let you know that we're heading up to Darwin as we have a lead on Patterson. Please say Hi to Xena, Zeus and the Ross family for us. We'll come down and visit you as soon as we get back, I promise!*

*Yours Sincerely,*
*Archie*

As I placed the envelope in the post box, the sun began to fade over the horizon. I tipped my hat to the brave postie tasked with delivering the letter. My reverie was broken when I heard my stomach rumble. It was time to meet Fiona for dinner.

Fiona selected a table in the corner with a clear view of the restaurant's ingress and egress. I've taught her to remain vigilant and prepare for threats, whether visiting a bar, ordering a coffee in a café, or going to the loo. Due to the sheer nature of the job, bounty hunters inadvertently make a load of enemies, from felons sentenced to hard time to family and friends of those sentenced to hang. There are also crazies and fame-seeking individuals that crave the notoriety of killing a hunter. After I sat down, she poured herself a glass of lager and offered me the same. I refused and ordered a scotch with dinner.

"How'd you go today?" I asked.

"I bought the ammo for a pretty good price. We've got 300 rounds of 9mm, 200 rounds of .38, 100 rounds of 12-gauge slugs and 50 AAAs. I also picked up plenty of water and food. But we're running pretty low on funds, Boss."

I could feel the tension in my shoulders and let out a deep sigh. As soon as my scotch arrived, I took a much-needed swig. "We still have our emergency stash, but I get your point." I passed the copy of Patterson's bounty across the table. "We'll head up to Darwin and focus on Patterson. If we get lucky and catch the bastard, we're all sorted for years to come."

Fiona looked over the contract. "Fuck yeah," she exclaimed.

I salivated when I saw the waiter approach the table with my hamburger and chips. Fiona's fish 'n' chips arrived shortly after, and we wasted no time digging in. On the other side of the restaurant, a man wearing dapper clothes was cutting into a large steak as he scanned the front page of a newspaper while his wife was shovelling pasta into her gob and guzzling a bottle of wine. I can't help but feel a tad guilty when I eat so well, knowing there are those like the young lad I passed on the street, starving without a roof over their head.

"A penny for your thoughts," Fiona said with a smile.

Oh, I don't know, I thought - guilt, poverty, hopelessness. I decided to focus on what we could control. "So, if you were in charge of Operation Desperados, how would you have executed the Op? And before you start, don't focus on the personnel. We had who we had."

For a pleasant change, she finished her mouthful of chips before answering. "Ok, the first thing I would have done is performed a recce. We had no idea whether they were even home. It would have been helpful to have someone walk by the house to see how many cars were out the front, if there were lights on or music blaring, the type of door or security screen they had, and whether there were dogs in the yard. We were walking in as blind as a bat."

"Good thinking, I agree. What are your thoughts on the execution of the door entry?" I asked.

Fiona contemplated her answer while she ate a chip. "Making a simultaneous entry through the front and back door was bullshit. We were lucky we didn't get shot. I know you don't want me to focus on the entry team. But fuck, I have to point out the obvious. Our team consisted of an untrained teenager and an old dude that went berserker."

I raised my palm. "Yep, I understand. But how would you have executed the op if you were in charge?"

Holding a chip, Fiona turned her head slightly to the side and replied, "I would have had Constable Jones with the ram and Sergeant Roach assisting with the forced entry. You and I would have made entry, with the connie and sergeant tailing us, advancing down the hall as we cleared the front rooms. I would have had Nicky and Mark prop near the back shed with instructions to take down the shitheads if they attempted to escape out the back."

I was impressed with her strategy. "I like the way you think Ninety-Nine. There are only a couple of things I would add. First, the house was likely built in the eighties. It would have been handy to source the house plans from the council, so we had an idea of the layout prior to entry. Secondly, most stations have stun grenades stored in their armoury. Throwing one through the window would have been useful to create some noise and sparks to distract the occupants as we made entry."

"Cool, noted. And, who's Ninety-Nine?" she asked with an upbeat tone.

I finished my scotch. Without TV and the Internet, I sometimes forget that Fiona's pop culture references were few and far between.

"It's a reference from an old TV show I watched with my grandad. Maxwell Smart is a bumbling secret service agent, while his partner, Ninety-Nine, is the competent one. It used to really crack me up."

"Oh, I get it. So then it's a mirror image of us?" she snickered.

"Smartass," I replied with a smile.

# Chapter Nine

*Wednesday, March 5, 2042 – Archie*

We planned to journey north on the coastal highway to Carnarvon and head up to Broome after a brief stop. We would then travel east to Kununurra before crossing the Northern Territory (NT) border and travelling to Katherine. Then it was just a hop, skip and a jump to Darwin, the former capital city of the NT, where Patterson was last sighted.

We expected the 3700-kilometre journey to be fraught with danger. Due to the prevalence of organised gangs, criminals, and desperate individuals using the highways as hunting grounds, the risks were significant. But so were the rewards. With regular stops and a pinch of luck, the journey shouldn't take us more than three days. I felt like we were in a race against time, even though, for all we knew, Patterson had already departed Darwin.

We had enough fuel stored in the boot to reach the small thriving community of Carnarvon. The town of four thousand souls is located 475 kilometres north of Geraldton. The local farmers focus their efforts on cattle, goats, sheep, and fruit, and being a coastal town, fishing is also a significant part of their economy. In addition, the town is fortunate to have a salt mine located on Lake MacLeod. As the community has limited access to electricity and refrigeration, salt is heavily relied upon for food preservation.

It's a pity Clarry was not with us, as during the 1960s, NASA set up a tracking station in the town to support the Gemini and Apollo space programs. Clarry was fixated on everything to do with space and would have loved to visit the site and examine the enormous dish.

As I drove the Beast down the highway, I continually scanned the horizon for threats and suspicious activity. It's easy to fall prey to predators if you allow the never-ending flat and dry pastures and empty plains to lull you into a false sense of security. Complacency can kill even the most dedicated professionals. Fiona peered out the passenger side window and then glanced in the side mirror.

Fiona was right to feel anxious. We've been attacked twice on the road in the last twelve months. One of these occasions involved bandits in a Holden ute shooting at us while their buddies chased us on dirt bikes. Instead of taking evasive action, I slammed on the brakes, causing our pursuers to smash into our rear end. The bandit in the ute's tray flew over the Beast's bonnet while the driver ate his steering wheel. I was distraught over the damage to my baby until the day Clarry brought her home looking brand spanking new. Clarry had secretly organised for his panel beater mate to work his magic. That's why he's my best mate.

Fiona rode shotgun in every sense of the phrase - sitting in the front passenger seat with quick access to her twelve-gauge. To provide support, I could draw my trusty Smith and Wesson .38 calibre revolver at a moment's notice. It's no secret that I favour revolvers over semi-automatic pistols. Compared to most semi-autos, the .38 special can't compete in stopping power or speed of fire. And she can only hold six rounds in the cylinder, whereas Fiona's Glock has a fifteen-round mag with one in the chamber. This is why most people prefer a semi-auto. But on the flip side, people rarely consider the revolvers' reliability. She has fewer parts to maintain and is almost indestructible. An important feature when travelling in the middle of nowhere, with limited access to gun stores and parts.

We were only thirty kilometres south of Carnarvon when I saw a distant white box shimmering off the bitumen. I feathered the brakes. "Heads up!" I warned.

The opportunity to go bush bashing and avoid the possible threat up ahead was an attractive one. However, I quickly dismissed the idea when I envisioned the Beast bogged right up to her axles in the red dirt. I love my girl to bits, but there were times when I recognised that a big four-wheeler would offer a more practical ride.

I pulled over to the side of the road, about eight hundred metres away from the single-axle white caravan sitting in the middle of the highway. The Beast's engine rumbled while I drew my revolver from its holster and considered our options.

"How do you want to play this, Boss?" Fiona asked nonchalantly.

I considered her poise and reflected on how much she'd matured over the last twelve months. "I need a better look." I reached into my pack and retrieved the binoculars. The weathered pop-up caravan was hooked up to an old Land Cruiser that looked like it was on its last legs. My suspicions were raised when I failed to observe any movement on the road or in the nearby bush. I scanned our six and was comforted when I couldn't see anyone sneaking up on us.

"Have you got your whistle?" I asked. Fiona nodded and took out a silver whistle from her buttoned shirt pocket. Even though your voice can carry in the bush, whistles are more effective in alerting your partner. One blast of the whistle communicates, '*I'm all good.*' Two blasts mean, '*it's not urgent but come to me.*' Three blasts signal that '*the poo has hit the fan, and I need urgent assistance.*'

"I want you to take the rifle and head out bush to get a bead on any threats. Don't approach the caravan but be ready to engage. I'll give you ten minutes to get into position before I slowly drive down the road with the shottie at the ready. Any questions?"

"Okie dokie, Boss, let's have some fun." Fiona holstered her Glock and reached for the sniper rifle in the back seat.

"I'm too old to call this fun. Let's just stay safe and clear the mess ahead so we can continue on our journey. Now hang on."

I accelerated forward off the shoulder of the highway, so the driver's side was parallel to the caravan, and the front end was parked up against a clump of four-foot-high bush. I was careful not to get the girl bogged. After I wound up the tinted window, Fiona slowly and quietly opened the passenger door and exited the vehicle. She crept into the bush, crouching like a leopard stalking its prey. You won't survive long as a bounty hunter unless you understand that Homo sapiens are predators. Like all other predators, our eyes are positioned forward, allowing excellent depth perception to locate our prey. We are also attracted to fast-moving objects, be they prey or predators. I've taught Fiona how to move slowly and quietly to avoid attention. I hope she can sneak up on any threat so we can both avoid being the prey today.

With the shottie ready and waiting in my lap, I peered through the binos, searching 360 degrees for threats. After hundreds of ten-minute grappling rounds on the mats, I instinctively knew when the time limit was approaching, but I glanced at my watch out of habit. Fiona had been stalking for just over nine minutes. Close enough is good enough. My boot gently pressed the pedal, and the V8 engine rumbled to life. I accelerated down the road at ten kilometres an hour as I engaged my diaphragm and performed a deep breathing exercise, clearing my head and preparing to react - *'slow is smooth, smooth is fast.'*

Before arriving at the caravan, I heard the double tap of handgun fire echo through the bush. My heart rate jumped from 60 beats a minute to 120. *Action time!*

# Chapter Ten

*Wednesday, March 5, 2042 – Fiona*

Archie taught me how to stalk like a cat. I was careful where I placed my size seven boots, avoiding dry leaves and sticks so I didn't alert anyone to my presence. When my peripheral vision detected fast movement to my left, I turned to see a giant monitor lizard skirting over the red dirt, its feet moving so fast it appeared to be sprinting in mid-air.

I stalked 400 metres west before turning north and snaking around the bush toward the caravan. When I was approximately fifty metres from my destination, I was alerted to the sound of the Beast's powerful engine.

I knelt on my right knee and peered through the rifle scope. I should have been shocked, but I wasn't. A middle-aged dark-skinned man was lying face down on the highway near a Harley-Davidson motorcycle. A pool of blood surrounded his upper body, his head barely hanging from his neck by a fold of wrinkled skin. An unravelled purple turban danced in the hot breeze as hundreds of blowflies buzzed around the carcass. If Clarry were here, he'd make some quip that sounded like a quote from a Sherlock Holmes novel - '*There appears to have been some foul play afoot, young lady.*'

My inspection of the dreadful scene was interrupted by a high-pitched scream from inside the caravan. Archie specifically told me *not* to approach the caravan, but my blood was up after hearing the ear-piercing shriek. I firmly believe that some rules are written in sand. When conditions change, the rules disappear with the wind or the rain and are no longer relevant.

After placing my rifle over my shoulder, I drew my Glock and cleared the immediate area. I cautiously approached the caravan door and preceded to step up into the enclosed space with my pistol at the ready. A samurai sword with blood smeared all over the blade rested on a tiny laminate dining table near the entry.

Shabby venetian blinds covering the windows swayed in the breeze. There was enough light to see a man thrusting back and forth on a bed at the far end of the van. A woman's screams were muffled as flies buzzed around the man's hairy ass.

I pointed my Glock at the back of the man's head.

"HEY, CUNT!" I yelled.

A thirty-something-year-old pot-bellied bloke wearing a wife-beater singlet swiftly rose from the bed and turned around to face me. His expression was not 'oops, I've been caught doing something wrong'. Instead, it was more like, 'Bloody hell, where did she come from?'

"Come over here and stand behind me," I instructed the young lady on the bed.

The sobbing naked woman of Indian descent dashed past me and out the van door. I instantly noted two details that were unrelated to each other. First, she had blood running down her inner thighs, and second, she reminded me of a girl I went to school with. We would often swap lunches; my Vegemite and cheese sandwiches, for her butter chicken. It is strange what details come to mind during stressful situations.

Meanwhile, Mr Wife-beater raised his hands high in the air. "We have a misunderstanding here. They tried to rob me, and after I defended myself, the young lady wanted to make it up to me," he explained with a smirk.

"Oh, why didn't you say so in the first place? I'm so sorry," I said sarcastically.

His confused look almost made me crack up. "So, I'm alright to leave then?" he asked.

"You move a muscle, asshole, and I'll put sixteen holes in you," I warned.

While keeping my muzzle pointed at his chest, my eyes drifted towards an old green photo album and a Polaroid instant camera sitting alongside the samurai sword. Just like driving past a traffic accident, I couldn't help but take a quick peek, even though I might see something disturbing that could stick with me for the rest of my life. I opened the album cover and read aloud a sentence scrawled in black marker –

*It's a righteous path to conquer men and own their women*

I winced in disgust as I quickly flicked through plastic sheets that contained numerous photos of bound naked women and mutilated men.

I glared at the repulsive killer. "What do you do with a wild and dangerous dog?"

He started to open his mouth when I fired two 9mm rounds into his groin. The projectiles obliterated most of his cock and scrotum. He released a shrill scream peculiarly similar to the lady he'd been raping. As he squirmed on the bed with his hands gripping his ruined crotch, I struck his temple with the butt of my rifle, knocking him out cold. I then wreathed his arms back to secure his wrists with cable ties.

"You neuter them."

I grabbed a blanket from the bed and stepped outside into the warm breeze. The woman was crying on Archie's shoulder. Not only is Archie a good-looker, but he also has one of those kind and trustworthy faces. Archie held out his right hand, and I passed him the blanket, which he wrapped around the woman's shoulders before leading her to the back seat of the Beast.

Archie returned to the scene and stepped inside the caravan while I checked out the black and chrome Harley with its image of a silver skull crudely painted on the petrol tank. Minutes later, he stood beside me with the samurai sword sheathed in its scabbard. He looked toward the caravan and raised his eyebrows as he rubbed the back of his neck. This was Archie expressing that something was troubling him.

"What's wrong, Archie?" I asked, anticipating a lecture.

"That's a real mess in there," he stated as he turned to face the van.

I reckon Archie suspected I could have avoided putting two rounds into Mr Wife-beater's groin. And he'd be right. He just didn't want to come out and accuse me of it. The thing is, I just didn't give a shit because the sicko deserved what he got.

"He's got an album in the van with photos of all his victims. He's a psycho that doesn't deserve your pity, Archie," I retorted defensively.

Archie shook his head, looked down at his feet and sighed. "The girl you rescued is named Vanessa. She's shaking like a leaf in the back of the Beast. I've put a bandage on the bloke you shot, but it's a pretty rough job." He pointed to the corpse and vehicles as he said, "I'll move this poor chap and the vehicles off the road while you check on the crim in the van."

I bit my tongue as I thought, *fuck that*! I'm not giving that piece of shit medical care. Archie placed his hands on his hips and gazed down the highway. He looked like he had the weight of the world resting on his shoulders. Clarry once explained over a beer that Archie was a man of contradictions. At the time, I didn't know what he meant. But, on reflection, it made perfect sense. Over the last twelve months, I've never heard Archie utter a single curse word, but I've seen him torture a man. He risks our lives by attempting to capture fugitives on 'Dead or Alive' bounties instead of shooting them but then escorts them to the executioner to be hanged. He's a bounty hunter trying to employ the morals of a saint. I just couldn't understand where he was coming from.

Archie jumped into the Land Cruiser and moved the caravan to the side of the highway. He then grabbed the old Indian man's ankles and dragged him off the road and into the scrub.

"Do me a solid and grab the shovel from my pack." He pointed to where he dragged the body. "I'm guessing that poor fella is Vanessa's father."

Just after Archie righted the Harley, Mr Wife-beater, still stark-naked, sprinted from the caravan and looked at us bug-eyed before legging it down the road with his wrists still secured behind his back.

I should have hogtied him. My bad. But the sight of him bobbing his head like a chicken being chased by a fox was still funny as fuck. When I muffled a chuckle, Archie gave me a look of disapproval.

Archie expelled another audible sigh. "We'll pick him up down the road."

"It's my mess. I'll clean it up," I offered.

I extended the sniper rifle's carbon bipod and was about to move to a prone position on the side of the road when Archie repeated, "I said we'll pick him up down the road. We'll drop him off at the coppers, and then he'll hang."

"Fuck that, Archie. It's a waste of time and effort," I whined.

Archie's right hand sprung as quick as a threatened tiger snake, snatching the rifle clean out of my hands. In a moment of insanity, I clenched my right hand and considered striking him. After looking down at my fist, he glared at me in frustration before shaking his head.

My outrage quickly subsided, leaving me feeling frustrated and ashamed. It had nothing to do with shooting Mr Wife-beater. It's just that Archie didn't deserve my anger and disrespect.

Archie turned his back. "We'll talk about this later," he said quietly. He then grumbled something under his breath as he pushed the Harley into the bush to hide it from scavengers.

I frowned and was about to ask him, 'Don't you think the old man and Vanessa deserve vengeance?' But instead, I searched the caravan for a towel and clothes to give to Vanessa, who was sobbing and shaking in the back seat of the Beast. A woman of similar age who had much greater grievances than mine.

# Chapter Eleven

*Wednesday, March 5, 2042 – Archie*

I understand there is a lot of evil in this world, probably more so after the War than before, and sometimes it's necessary to take out the trash. Still, I worry that Fiona is enjoying handing out retribution. As we thundered down the road to Carnarvon, I pondered what my old professor would make of Fiona. He may have gone so far as to say she has a crack in her glass.

Before continuing our journey, we locked Vanessa's Land Cruiser and caravan, let down the tyres, and removed the vehicle's spark plug leads and battery to make it harder to steal. I hid the scumbag's Harley behind bushes about two hundred metres from the highway. To get the best price, I suggested selling the bike in town to Vanessa. I gave her a ballpark figure of its value so she wouldn't be taken for a ride. *Excuse the pun.* I might have made her an offer on the hog if I had the funds and a secure place to store it. With a bit of luck, the vehicles would still be there when she returned with a towie.

I peered into the rear vision mirror while Vanessa explained what had happened. Vanessa and her father had been travelling to Carnarvon to visit her Auntie and Uncle. Her old man stopped to help a man lying in the middle of the road alongside his motorcycle. Unfortunately, they were tricked into believing he had fallen from his bike. Her father had paid the price for being a good Samaritan when the scumbag almost cut his head clean off his shoulders with a samurai sword.

Fiona passed Vanessa a water bottle. I was a bit parched myself after digging a six-foot-long grave in the red dirt. I wrapped Vanessa's father in a blanket and placed him in the shallow grave to provide some protection from dingoes, foxes, and birds. That way, Vanessa would have the option of retrieving the body and burying him in the Town's cemetery.

I shoved my foot on the brake when I saw the scumbag lying motionless in a foetal position in the middle of the road. With his crotch looking like it had been shoved into a meat grinder, the coppers wouldn't require the services of a forensic pathologist to determine the cause of death. It's not often that I drag two corpses from the highway before lunch. After I stretched my back and shoulders, I grabbed the instant camera from the Beast's back seat and took a photo of the killer's face. The picture took ninety seconds to develop. I placed it in my pocket with the intention of giving it to the coppers. I decided the scumbag didn't deserve the dignity of burial, so I left him in the bush for the local fauna to feed on.

We planned to drop by the Carnarvon Police Station to give the local constabulary our statements. They'll likely tick the boxes and close the investigation before their crib break. Police investigations are not what they used to be. And who would blame them given their lack of resources and three thousand percent increase in violent crime? I, for one, should be grateful that the boys and girls in blue are running around chasing their tails. That's why they require the services of bounty hunters like us to capture their quarry.

Vanessa grasped a silver cross that hung from her neck as she whispered a prayer. By the early 2030s, religion was waning from the public conscience, with only half the population identifying as religious in the national census. It came as no surprise to me that religion was experiencing a renaissance. Desperate people were seeking solace for the atrocities and hardship that plagued them. And what have people turned to throughout history when confronted with misery and helplessness? - *The promise of hope through faith.*

My mother was a Christian who took me to church every Sunday. To my mother's disappointment, Dad lost his faith during his tour in Iraq. Upon his return from the War, he wouldn't allow any talk of the Father, Son and Holy Ghost in our home and would rant and rave at my mother if she ever spoke of her beliefs. My mother was not one to back down and gave as good as she got, threatening to leave him and take me with her. Christmas was anything but a merry time in my family home. It was more like a battleground.

I'm sure my agnosticism could be explained after several visits with a shrink. But I didn't have the time or inclination to explore my upbringing and beliefs. So during one of our piss-taking sessions, I was amused when Clarry accused me of sitting on the fence, as this was coming from a man who hops from one side to the other. I retorted by asking him, "You're a Whadjuk man of the Noongar nation, a scientist, and a believer in Christ. How can you wear so many hats?" He shrugged his shoulders and replied, "There's plenty of room for us all under the stars."

An elderly lady carrying a pug dog exited the front door of the Carnarvon Police Station as I parked the Beast out front. I had never stepped foot inside the station and had no idea who was posted there. However, when I walked through the door, I noticed a familiar face sitting at the counter, munching on a Vegemite sandwich.

Constable Atkins looked like a surfer, with an athletic stature, shaggy blonde hair, and blue eyes. We have had our differences in the past, and I'm equally to blame for our frosty relationship. The problem with Atkins was his level of sensitivity. He took himself far too seriously. It was like he was holding up a sign that said, 'Make fun of me!' The last time I saw him, I couldn't help but give him a ribbing about getting shot in the bum. We were members of the militia that defeated the NMG in Norsemen. Sergeant Lee from Esperance Police Station told me over a beer that Atkins broke every tactical rule in the book while they cleared one of the gang's strongholds. He started to clear a room by himself, and then BANG, he ran outside, screaming and clutching his backside.

"Hey, Atkins, it's been a while." I peered over the counter, "It's good to see you no longer need to sit on a doughnut cushion."

Atkins scowled and deflected my comment, "It's Sergeant Atkins to you."

I glanced over at Fiona and raised an eyebrow in bewilderment.

"Congratulations," we both said almost simultaneously.

The powers that be must have decided to do away with merit-based promotion and return to the time-served arrangement, whereby as soon as an officer achieves his time at rank, he is automatically promoted. From what I've witnessed, he definitely wouldn't have been promoted through merit. I felt sorry for the constables reporting to the miserable sod.

"I'm a busy man, Archie. I've got a station to run, so stop wasting my time and tell me what you want."

More like busy chewing on your sandwich and wasting taxpayers' dollars, I thought. Atkins was the sort of man that worked harder to get out of work than just getting on with the job itself. So, for Vanessa's sake, more than anything else, I forced myself to be the better man by zipping my lips and extending an olive branch.

I placed the album, camera and samurai sword on the counter and gestured toward Vanessa. "Vanessa has had a traumatic experience on the highway. Some scumbag killed her father with this sword. Fiona was forced to defend herself when she came across the murderer who was assaulting Vanessa at the time. The album is his trophy collection which may help you solve several missing person cases."

Atkins flicked through the album. "Fuck me!" he exclaimed as the colour drained from his face.

"You'll find the murderer's body on the side of the highway twenty-five clicks south of town. Vanessa will need a tow truck to recover her car, caravan, and motorcycle, which we parked about five clicks down the road from the body."

Atkins frowned. "Thanks, guys, you've caused me a lot of bloody paperwork," he grumbled.

Fiona sneered, "Don't mention it, Atkins. Fuck you very much!"

I smiled in agreement with her potty mouth.

# Chapter Twelve

*Wednesday, March 5, 2042 – Fiona*

After we gave Atkins our statements and wished Vanessa good luck, we returned to the road and continued our journey. We used the four hours of remaining daylight to cover as much distance as possible. Even for a man that doesn't talk much, Archie was uncharacteristically quiet. I assumed he was giving me the *dreaded silent treatment.*

~

Late in the afternoon, Archie turned into a side gravel track. We were in the middle of nowhere. He mumbled, "We'll camp for the night and get back on the road at first light."

The rough track rattled and jolted the Beast to the extent that my legs vibrated and I had to place my palm against the roof to stop my ass from leaving the seat. It was rare for Archie to drive his car so carelessly. He finally parked about four kilometres from the main highway.

The day's heat began to cool as the sun fell below the horizon. While Archie prepared the fire, I shone my torch on the map I had placed over the bonnet. We were camping a couple of clicks north of the Yannarie River. It was a pity the river was dry this time of year, as I could have really used a wash. I lifted my arm and placed my nose near my armpit, "Poowee!" I hollered.

It was too late to hunt for our meal, so I grabbed a billy pot and two dehydrated meals from my pack. Archie sat by the fire as I stirred the mushroom, cricket, and garlic soup. I noticed he had his gun cleaning kit in his grasp. I had watched him clean his revolver more than a hundred times. On each occasion, he performed the task in the same systematic manner. First, he places his gun cleaning kit on a blanket, opens the cylinder and unloads the Smith & Wesson, letting the rounds fall into his palm. Next, he dips the bore brush into cleaning solvent and then slides the brush into the barrel to remove any gunpowder residue. When satisfied with his work, he removes the brush, attaches a clean piece of fabric to the rod, and inserts it back into the barrel to remove any remaining grit. He then replaces the cloth and cleans the cylinders. He's bloody fastidious. He then pours a small amount of gun oil onto a rag and wipes the outside surface of the firearm, careful to avoid the hand grip and the interior of the barrel and cylinders. Finally, before reloading, he wipes the excess oil with a clean rag. When he was finished, his .38 special shone impressively in the light of the fire.

"Pass me your Glock, and I'll clean it for you," he offered.

Was this an olive branch? We needed to get this conversation over and done with, even if I was scared of the outcome. "Are we going to talk about whatever's bugging you?" I asked.

He re-holstered his revolver and looked at me intently above the top of the flames. "I've got a couple of issues that we need to discuss," he said in a calm and measured tone.

I nodded, "I'd rather get whatever's going on between us out in the open."

Archie cleared his throat and placed his hands on his knees. "I'm not saying that the scumbag in the caravan didn't deserve it, but you know my code. *Our code!* We should have brought him back to town so he could be tried and then hung." Archie sighed and paused for a long moment before confessing, "I'm also worried you're beginning to enjoy the killing."

Rather than biting back, I stood up and scooped our meal into two bowls. Archie looked up at me with a frown. "I'm listening. I just don't want to burn this," I explained. He waited patiently and thanked me when I passed him his bowl. He curled the corner of his upper lip as he stirred the soup. He hates bugs, but them's the breaks when you don't do the shopping.

Archie spooned a mouthful into his gob before continuing. "Look, I'm not one for ultimatums, but I work the way I do because it's important to me. So we'll take this Patterson lead as far as we can, and then you can let me know if you'll respect the code moving forward. But, in the meantime, try to stick to it. Agreed?"

I let his question hang in the air for a second or two before getting up from my perch and shaking his hand. "Agreed, Boss. And I'll think about what you said."

After finishing my meal, I laid out my sleeping bag and gazed at the stars. Archie was snoring like a bear as I contemplated his comments. The new world favours the bully. Plenty of mean fuckers with the 'survival of the fittest' attitude take advantage of the weak. Before Archie took me on as an apprentice, men used and abused me, taking advantage of my weakness. Thank Christ, the tables have turned. I now have the training, guns, and expertise to make evil men pay for their vile acts. Getting a bit of vengeance also made me feel good. Archie made it clear on day one of my apprenticeship that I could leave our partnership whenever I wanted. I snuggled deeper into my bag and pondered whether it was time to go it alone.

# Chapter Thirteen

*Thursday, March 6, 2042 – Archie*

As daylight broke, I boiled some water in the billy and had a quick coffee before hitting the road. Besides a fuel stop, our next planned rest break was in Port Hedland, a coastal town about 570 clicks north of the Yannarie River. I recall Clarry telling me over a beer that the area is known as Marapikurrinya by the Aboriginal people, meaning a 'place of good water'. According to the Aboriginal Dreaming beliefs, a huge blind snake lived in the landlocked water area known as Jalkawarrinya. This landlocked area was now used as the turning basin for the massive ships that entered the port to trade their goods.

As the name suggests, the town's business revolves around the port, with the residents either supporting or directly involved in coordinating the shipping in and out of the natural deep harbour. Before the War, the port was the primary fuel and container receival point for the region, exporting 520 million tonnes of iron ore, with most of the ore heading to China and India. When I practised law, I brokered hundreds of contracts for mining and shipping companies in the region. As iron ore is no longer a commodity in demand, trade now consists of grain and rice from Southeast Asia and fuel from the middle-east. The port receives eighty-five percent of the state's fuel through its harbour, ensuring the survival of thousands of WA and NT families.

For most of the trip, neither of us felt like chatting, so we listened to mixtapes of my heavy metal favourites. The barren highway was surrounded by low-lying bushes and red dirt. We wound down the windows to seek relief from the oppressive heat. It felt north of forty-five degrees. The balmy air blew the beads of sweat from my temples. Of all the modern conveniences – computers, televisions, microwaves, smartphones - I miss air-conditioning the most. I read that before the War, 2.8 billion air conditioners were installed worldwide, accounting on average for twenty percent of energy usage within a building.

Arriving at Port Hedland, the Beast rolled into the town's one and only service station. A bullet-riddled sign advertising 'Jake's Garage' was bolted to a Shell petrol sign. I had no idea who Jake was, but I knew that a consortium of companies owned the station, one of the largest being the Pilbara Port Association. During drinking sessions and poker games, I'd overheard that the town possessed an impressive, well-armed militia similar to the Goldfields. Just as Esperance and Kalgoorlie militias were prepared to protect the towns from Gangs targeting the potable water and gold, Port Hedland was trained to protect the fuel and grain from Southeast Asian pirates.

Before the War, piracy was a concern in the Straits of Malacca near Indonesia, the Indian Ocean adjacent to Somalia, and the Gulf of Guinea within reach of West Africa. The Pirates' modus operandi (MO) typically involved boarding oil and cargo ships and kidnapping, torturing, and killing the crew. By 2030 the central powers' navies were working together to mitigate the pirate threat and had enormous success in destroying the criminal enterprise. Sadly for seafarers and the people that needed the fuel and food they were transporting, the end to piracy was short-lived, as the destruction of the world's navies brought lawlessness on the oceans to a new extreme.

Typical, I thought, the fuel pump was not working. I repeatedly pressed and depressed the nozzle to no avail. I felt irritated as I stomped towards the store's entry. The argument with Fiona was still on my mind, and I was keen to refuel and continue our journey to Broome. The more time we spent on the road, the greater the chance Patterson would once again slip from our grasp.

The station door had a 'closed' sign hanging from a hook. As I looked around for a worker, I noticed Fiona walk towards a crowd of kids mucking around on skateboards. I marched into the garage feeling frustrated with the lack of service. A mechanic in blue overalls was working under an old brown Kingswood station wagon hoisted at head height.

"Hey mate, the fuel pump is on the fritz," I said, attempting to grab his attention.

While he inspected the vehicle's underside, he hollered, "No, it's not."

He didn't even have the courtesy to look at me. My blood started to boil as I walked within arm's reach of the mechanic. "Look, mate, I've just tried to pump some gas, and I can tell you now that it's not working."

The bloke just ignored me and continued to work on the wagon. I felt like grabbing him by the collar and shaking him, but instead, I ranted through gritted teeth, "Are you trying to piss me off? Because if you are, it's bloody well working."

He finally turned around with a frustrated expression and explained, "It's working. There's just no gas. Look, you missed the run, mate. There's nothing I can do about it. Blow-ins have been lining up since opening. They, too, want to fuel up and get out of town."

"Why? What's going on?" I asked, dumbfounded.

"Pirates have taken over the harbour. I've got to fix this old girl to get my family out of town. So if you'll excuse me, I've got work to do," he huffed.

"The militia must be fighting back. Why aren't you with them?" I asked in an accusatory tone.

The mechanic sneered at my comment and bent down at the waist to lift his pants' legs, displaying his prosthetics. "I'm not much use to them. Now fuck off!"

I felt like a real asshole as I trudged back to the Beast. Whilst digesting what I had just heard, I was drawn to a commotion in the carpark. Fiona was surrounded by a group of teenagers screaming abuse at her as she held a hoodlum in a headlock. A ten-year-old kid was on his backside at her feet, crying and bleeding from his nose. We don't have time for this, I thought. Fortunately, the teenagers were so focused on Fiona restraining their mate that they didn't notice me sneak up behind them.

Just as one of the delinquents lifted his skateboard to crack Fiona over the back of her head, I ripped the board from his grasp and swept his feet. After he landed hard on his backside, his mates ceased hollering and considered the new threat.

Before they had an opportunity to egg each other on, I snapped the board in two over my knee and threw it over my shoulder. "Get a move on before I decide to snap something else," I warned.

As soon as Fiona released her grip, the hoodlum ran off with his mates down the road, leaving the ten-year-old boy to gaze up at me with curiosity.

Fiona was just about to speak when I cut her off, "I don't want to hear it. We have bigger bullies to deal with. Pirates have taken over the harbour, so the town's out of fuel. We need fuel. The State needs fuel. We're heading to the police station to see if we can help."

We jumped into the Beast, and I turned the ignition key. "Pirates? You've never mentioned anything about pirates. So what the fuck?" she exclaimed wide-eyed.

I couldn't help but smirk at her bewilderment. "I guess it's just never come up. Living south, you don't have to worry about Pirates, but our Northern brothers and sisters are constantly on the lookout for them. Without a navy, the nation's northern waters are unprotected, and the pirates take advantage of this by robbing cargo and transport ships."

"Who are they? Where do they come from?" she asked.

I shrugged my shoulders, "A mixture of peoples, but mostly Indonesians, Malaysians, Filipinos and Papua New Guineans. I've heard that Aussies and Kiwis also join up to reap the rewards."

I was forced to park down the road from the South Hedland Police Station due to their public carpark being full to the brim. We entered the station's front doors and were met with a chaotic reception. Men and women of all ages were darting all over the place, carrying firearms, radios, and ammo, shouting instructions, getting into arguments, and generally looking panicked.

An enormous man that stood close to seven feet tall, wearing a police uniform with sergeant stripes on his shoulders, boomed instructions over a megaphone, "Unless I've personally given you a task, please attend the port office on the Esplanade. There's a staging area in the carpark. Please sign in and await instructions. I repeat, please sign in at the port office carpark."

I tapped Fiona on the shoulder, and we weaved through the packed crowd to reach the exit. On the way to the Port Association, Fiona asked excitedly, "So, Boss, are we going to help the coppers out? Take down some fucking pirates?"

I didn't have time to be concerned about her enthusiasm to get into the thick of the action. She had no idea of the dangers involved in battling pirates.

"I've never met the sergeant, so I'm unsure if he'll want our assistance. We'll just have to wait and see. Our big problem is we're going nowhere without fuel. We still have another 2400 klicks to Darwin."

The staging area at the Port Association carpark was just as chaotic as the police station. But at least they had a marquee erected to record the names of volunteers. While we waited our turn at the end of a lengthy line in the bitumen carpark, I was beginning to wilt in the extreme heat and humidity. It felt north of fifty degrees Celsius. Even though I've got dark brown skin, I was thankful to be wearing my Akubra wide-brimmed hat and a long-sleeve shirt. I glanced at my watch; it was just past 1 p.m. My stomach grumbled in response to the waft of sizzling sausages. A couple of elderly volunteers at a nearby marquee served hot dogs and cups of water.

"Do us a favour, mate. Can you grab us both a hot dog and water? I'm bloody starving."

Fiona must have also been hungry as she nodded without complaint and swiftly headed off to line up.

A young bloke in front of me turned around and looked down

at my holster. He squinted with suspicion. "Are you with the militia, mate? It's just that I haven't seen you around these parts."

He was smartly dressed in a red check shirt neatly tucked into his clean blue denim jeans. I noticed he wore a Berretta pistol with a customised mahogany grip holstered at his left hip. I picked him as a mollydooker poser with an air of arrogance.

"I was just passing through and thought I'd volunteer," I explained.

He stood on his toes and looked around the crowd like a meerkat on guard duty. I took my bounty hunter ID from my back pocket and showed it to him. "My name's Archie O'Connor. I'm not a spy, mate. Just relax. Like I said, I'm just here to offer my assistance."

The young bloke inspected my ID. "Sorry, mate, I'm just a bit on edge," he explained. He held out his hand, and we shook as he introduced himself. "Scott Bridle. I'm the mayor's nephew. You can ask me if you need to know how things work around here."

My assumption was close to the mark. Scott was undoubtedly born with a silver spoon in his mouth. His smooth hands, unblemished clothes, and eagerness to drop his auntie's name said it all. It was lucky for the sake of the operation that I wasn't a spy, as he sprouted information about the state of their armoury, patrol boats, and militia.

"I heard from my auntie that the pirates have a gunboat in the harbour and have taken a tanker captive. They're not leaving without a chest of gold," he explained.

We continued to move forward in the line, although at a snail's pace. I speculated how the pirates got past the port's patrol boats. Someone dropped the ball, that's for sure. My morale received a shot in the arm when Fiona returned with hot dogs and water. The arrogant young bloke in the line turned around and gaped at Fiona with puppy dog eyes. I munched on my dog as I again pondered whether she had any idea of her alluring effect on men.

"What are you looking at? This is my hotdog. Go get your own," she told him in a matter-of-fact tone with her mouth full of sausage.

The lad was saved from any further embarrassment when a no-nonsense lady with turkey wing arms sitting behind the marquee desk hollered at him to step forward.

After the lad had provided his details, I took a giant step toward the desk before the fastidious lady could holler at me. She asked for our names and occupations in a clipped tone. After we advised her that we were bounty hunters, she raised an eyebrow and inquired, "Have you been members of a militia?"

"Fiona and I have been involved with operations with the Esperance Militia," I replied.

This must have sparked her interest as she leaned forward, resting her substantial arms on the desk and asked, "Do you have any military experience?"

My military experience was not a topic I liked to discuss, but neither did I want to deal with the wrath of this stern-looking lady. "I served as a corporal with the First Battalion during the War."

Her demeanour changed instantly. She smiled warmly and asked in a friendlier tone, "Did you serve in Darwin, Luv?"

After I nodded, she took two cards from a tin container and placed them in my hand. "Thank you for your service. Present this to the guard at the front door of the port office and go upstairs to the Incident Control Centre. The harbourmaster will want to speak with you."

The cards had a number in the top right corner and the words 'Security Pass VIP' typed in the centre. We marched around the corner and presented the cards to the armed guards standing outside the Port Association's front doors. Wasting no time, the senior guard told us to clip the cards to our chests and make our way up the stairs, where a guard would be waiting for us outside the Incident Control Centre (ICC). The guard spoke on the radio as his colleague unlocked the doors.

We both marched upstairs and identified ourselves to the guard at the ICC. He seized our firearms and knives and then conducted a pat search before unlocking the door and disappearing inside the room.

"It's a pity the harbour wasn't as secure as this building," I whispered facetiously.

The guard returned and ordered us to follow him inside. We

were confronted with a hive of activity as we crossed the threshold. Thirty-odd people were busily examining maps, answering phone calls, and typing documents. The colossal sergeant we saw earlier in the day was standing near the ICC's far window, staring out over the harbour. We walked over to introduce ourselves. At six-foot-two, I'm not a short man, but I felt like a midget compared to the towering sergeant. His height wasn't his only striking feature. Without the megaphone hiding his face, I could see his impressive bushy ginger moustache. My father was the last man to intimidate me, but if there was ever a fellow to make me sit up and take notice, I was standing before him. I glanced at Fiona, who was displaying her usual self-assured demeanour.

My right hand almost disappeared in his massive paw as we shook hands. The sergeant was polite but direct, asking poignant questions about my military experience – 'Where did you serve? Who did you serve with? What operations were you involved in?'

"Do you have any experience with amphibious operations?" he asked.

"I've had some," I replied.

The sergeant's expression and tone softened. "Look, I appreciate your service, and I know you blokes don't like to talk about the War, but I'm not asking you to list your medals. I just need to know about your experience. We're in a bind here and on the clock."

I sighed. "Understood, Sergeant. I led an operation near the end of the War, whereby we rescued a group of civilians who were being held captive on an enemy frigate."

The sergeant looked like I had just told him he'd won the lotto. "You two are coming with me. Follow me this way," he ordered.

We followed the human skyscraper down a corridor to a corner office with a view of the harbour. A man and a woman in their early sixties were busily examining a large map spread on top of a square mahogany meeting table. The gentleman with a working-class air had short-cropped grey hair and labourer's hands. He wore a short-sleeved khaki shirt and a vintage diver's watch. The lady sitting alongside him appeared to be a well-heeled professional who wore a sharp black business suit and several diamond rings on her manicured fingers. The odd couple looked up from the map as we entered the office. The sergeant swiftly introduced us to the harbourmaster and the mayor before requesting we take a seat.

To my immediate right sat the harbourmaster, and across from me was the mayor, the aunt of the arrogant lad I met in the carpark. The sergeant sat next to Fiona; his massive frame made it appear that he was seated in a primary school chair. They had been examining a map of the harbour and its surrounds, which had three toy boats situated just inside the mouth of the harbour, one green and two blue.

The sergeant cleared his throat. "Mayor, Sir, Mr O'Connor here led an operation during the War which involved rescuing captives on an enemy ship. I remember reading about it. It was a group of nurses, I believe. Is that correct, Mr O'Connor?"

I feel embarrassed when anyone mentions the rescue op, as my team and I just did what was expected, nothing more, nothing less. We were taking a beating towards the end of the War, and any good news story was used as propaganda, and this was one of them. I lost three of my eight-man team that night. It still haunts me, which is why I put the op to the back of my mind and try to discourage people from discussing it.

"Yep, that's correct, Sarge. And please call me Archie."

An uncomfortable silence ensued. Fiona nudged me with her elbow, "I think they want you to elaborate, Boss."

I stared at the map as I reluctantly told them the summarised version. "Near the end of the War, I led an eight-man team on a mission to rescue eleven nurses who were held captive on a Chinese frigate. It was messy and bloody, but we got the job done. Not all of us made it back. Three good men gave their lives. Brothers."

The mayor and harbourmaster must have been remarkably familiar with how one another thinks. They turned to face each other and appeared to communicate without needing to say a word. Then, with a slightly raised eyebrow, a gentle nod and a wan smile, a decision was made in the time it took for Fiona to pick the dirt from under the nail of her trigger finger.

"You may be able to help us, Mr O'Connor. As you are probably aware, we're in a crisis of the highest magnitude. Pirates have captured the harbour and a Saudi fuel tanker. They're holding us to ransom," the mayor explained with a deep frown.

"What are their demands?" I asked.

"500 ounces of gold. They've promised to leave upon payment and permit the tanker to berth. But of course, we cannot comply with their demand," the mayor replied.

I had a fair idea why they'd be loathed to contemplate the pirates' demand, but I had to ask, "And why not?"

The mayor placed her elbows on the map and said, "Mr O'Connor, are you aware of what occurred in England during the late tenth century when the Vikings came ashore?"

"Sadly, my bachelor of law lectures weren't that interesting, but if the TV shows I watched were even partially factual, I'm guessing they were doing a lot of raping and pillaging."

The mayor clasped her hand. "You're not wrong, but do you know what the English did about it?" I was pretty sure she wanted to tell me the story, so I just shrugged my shoulders and gestured for her to continue. "The King decided to pay the Vikings a vast fortune to leave their shores and never return. But regrettably for the English, the Vikings repeatedly returned and demanded more gold and treasure until the Crown's coffers were empty. They were then humiliated when a Danish King named Cnut not only defeated their army but inserted himself on the throne."

I glanced at the other occupants in the room to judge their mood. The sergeant and the harbourmaster wore grave expressions while Fiona appeared genuinely excited.

"I get your point. I'm guessing you want to go to war."

The mayor placed her lithe hand over the harbourmaster's burly forearm and gestured for him to answer my question. "We will not be intimidated by thugs, Mr O'Connor, which is why it's our intent to take the fight right to their door. And I believe *you* are the man to lead us," he declared.

Fiona and I made eye contact, and she nodded in agreement.

"Okay. Can you take us to your tower so I can get a bird's-eye view of what we're up against?"

The forty-five-metre-high shipping control tower was attached to the port offices. The concrete tower provided a 270-degree view over the inner harbour and shipping channel. I walked over to a pair of powerful binoculars fitted to a tripod on the observation deck and focused my attention on the pirates' patrol boat. The boat was anchored about eighty metres from the wharf within the inner harbour. Her previous name had been painted over and haphazardly replaced with her new name – 'KUSA'. There were eight men of Asian appearance on the main deck, and I could just make out two men on the first deck. All but two of the men were holding Avtomat Kalashnikova assault rifles (AK-47s). Unfortunately, I couldn't see inside the bridge due to the tinted glass.

An 'old salt' who reminded me of my good friend Captain Ross, coughed into his fist and pointed towards the boat. "She's an Armidale Class Patrol Boat. I know this because I served with the navy up until the early noughties. After I retired, I picked up a job at Austal in Freo. Austal built the boats up until 2008."

During my days as a lawyer, I had a mate who worked at Austal. They were a global shipbuilder operating out of Fremantle in WA, building commercial and defence ships for the Royal Australian Navy (RAN) and the United States Navy (USN).

When I offered the bloke my hand, he didn't hesitate to shake it with a firm grip. "I'm Archie, and this is Fiona."

"You can call me Simmo. I'm retired now, but I help out in the tower when I can. I've been watching the pirate's movements since they arrived. I've counted sixteen individuals on the boat and four on the trawler. Are you going to help us get rid of these miserable sods?"

Spoken like a true sailor. "We're going to try Simmo. What do you know about the boat's capabilities?"

Simmo rubbed his chin, "The old girl's a 300-toner and about fifty metres long. She has a Bushmaster 25mm cannon at her bow and two Browning 50 cal machine guns at her stern. The scum fired warning shots with the cannon within minutes of their arrival, so we know she's functional."

"How did they get hold of a navy ship, and how can they even sail it without the electronic systems?" Fiona asked.

"She's a boat, Miss, not a ship, but good question. I'm not sure how these bastards stole her, but by the end of the twenties, the RAN replaced the Armidale with the Arafura class. A bigger boat with more firepower. I believe they gave the Armidales' to Indonesia and the Philippines under the proviso that they'd help us patrol for people and drug smugglers. You can operate most navy boats manually. It's a bitch to operate, but you can do it. We do the same with the Arafuras."

I gestured for Fiona to return the binoculars. The Kusa had two Zodiac Rigid-Hulled Inflatable Boats (RHIB) secured at her stern on the starboard and port sides. "Have they launched the Zodiacs, Simmo?"

The old boy let out a long sigh. "Up until a couple of hours ago, they were doing runs up and down the channel. Bastards were firing their AKs in the air like they were almighty conquerors. They scared the shit out of the port workers and the public," Simmo answered.

"When did they last make contact?" I asked the mayor.

"They came to shore on a rubber boat at about 8:30 this morning and demanded 500 ounces by 5 p.m. They threatened to sink the tanker and kill the crew if we didn't comply."

The mayor appeared visibly shaken by the prospect. I pondered whether she was more concerned about the welfare of the foreign crew or the fuel loss. The harbourmaster squeezed the mayor's shoulder in a sign of either solidarity or affection. They made an odd couple, but people always say that opposites attract.

"The month's supply for the entire Pilbara region is stored in that tanker. Livelihoods will be lost without that fuel. We're talking about 400,000 barrels," the mayor stated emphatically, making her priorities crystal clear.

I empathised with her as it's not easy being in charge, with your constituents' livelihoods and concerns resting on your shoulders.

They were looking to her to manoeuvre them out of this crisis.

"They won't sink the tanker, Mayor. They're probably planning to take her to a Southeast Asian port to sell." I turned to face the harbourmaster, "Where do they currently have the tanker?"

"The pirates have boarded her and are positioned in the outer anchorage about fourteen kilometres out. They have a fishing trawler guarding her right now. We have eyes on her constantly. I'll show you through the binos."

We stood on the observation deck and looked out over the harbour. I was considering a plan that most would consider insane - crazy enough that it might just work. But, first, I needed reliable intel and breathing space to convince my benefactors and partner that we could pull it off.

I noticed the big sergeant and harbourmaster conversing quietly near an obsolete computer screen. They awkwardly ceased their conversation when I approached. I suspected they were deliberating whether they could trust me. Putting myself in their shoes, I couldn't blame them in the slightest - *A couple of bounty hunters walk in off the street and offer to take over their operation.* For all they knew, I could be working with the pirates.

I directed my question to the harbourmaster, "How'd they get past your defences? I thought you had two Arafura patrol boats protecting the harbour."

I have never boarded an Armidale, but I was given a lift on an Arafura during the War. They're an eighty metre long, 1600-ton formidable boat, with a 40 mm Oto Marlin autocannon and two fifty cal machine guns.

The sergeant looked embarrassed. "By the whisky bottles lying near our blokes, we surmised they were having a drinking session instead of doing their job and guarding the boats. Regrettably, for all concerned, it cost them their lives. After the pirates cut their throats, they firebombed the Arafuras' engine rooms. They won't be serviceable for at least three months. Our only saving grace is we managed to catch one of the bastards."

"I need to speak to the prisoner as soon as possible. Regarding resources, I need a tugboat and five fit soldiers that can dive. I need them to be kitted out with assault rifles and scuba gear. You might call me greedy, but if possible, I'd like M4s. I also need someone that knows their way around explosives. A shot-firer will do if you don't have ex-military." The sergeant took his notebook from his front pocket and started taking notes. The mayor's stern expression turned to one of hope, which quickly faded after I hit her with the big ask. "Oh, before I forget. Mayor, I need 155 ounces of gold."

"What heavens for?" she spluttered in a high-pitched tone.

"Look, I know this request requires a leap of faith, but I don't have time to prepare an operational plan to convince you that I know what I'm doing. So the best I can do is to suggest that you call the Esperance Mayor and Sergeant. They will vouch for me. But I can tell you now that I intend to return all 155 ounces to you in the next twenty-four hours."

The mayor crossed her arms and then looked at the harbourmaster and sergeant in search of guidance. The sergeant averted his gaze by looking out over the inner harbour, and the harbourmaster just shrugged his shoulders.

"I'll consider your proposal, Mr O'Connor. And I will be making a call to the Esperance Mayor. But help put my mind at ease. Why are you assisting us? You haven't even asked for a reward."

I told her the simple truth. "We need fuel."

The mayor and harbourmaster looked perplexed while the sergeant's booming laughter was so loud that port workers would have heard his glee from the wharf. He then slapped me on the back with such exuberance that I almost faceplanted onto the carpet.

"Ha-ha, that was a good one," the sergeant said, wiping the tears from his eyes. "There's no issue in taking you to the prisoner. But I'll need two hours to locate every item on your list. Every item but the gold, that is." Then, he turned to face the mayor, "I'll respectfully let you handle that request, Mayor."

We left the mayor and harbourmaster to discuss my proposal. I imagine they needed to make the necessary calls and talk to the port owners and the bank. We followed the sergeant downstairs to his vehicle, a yellow XB Ford Falcon coupe. I respected his taste in automobiles. The muscle car looked like it could have been used in a Mad Max movie. He drove us to the station and wasted no time escorting us straight to the cells, which was a shame because I would have killed for a coffee.

A man of Chinese ancestry in his late twenties was lying on a concrete bench in the farthest cell. He had dreadlocks, several nose rings, and an impressive tattoo of a fire-breathing dragon on his bare chest. Most Anglo-Saxons are incapable of distinguishing one Asian ethnicity from another. Being half Korean, I have a pretty good record of determining someone's ancestry from their skin colour and the shape of their cheeks, nose, and eyes. I glared at him between the iron bars for several minutes, appraising his physical attributes, body language, and demeanour. The prisoner vehemently glared back at me until he yelled with a New York accent, "What the fuck are you looking at?"

His skin was clear of blemishes, and he had smooth hands and straight clean teeth. Clearly, this bloke was a poser, someone pretending to be a 'hard man.' I took my knife and firearm from my belt and handed the weapons to the sergeant.

"Unlock the door, Sarge. Give me a couple of hours alone with him," I instructed, ensuring I was loud enough for the prisoner to hear. I wanted him to think this would be a long-drawn-out process, but I estimated it would take ten minutes at the most.

The sergeant unlocked the cell doors and left me to my work. Fiona leaned against the far wall nonchalantly while I stood at the cell entry and continued to glare at the man. The army trained me to interrogate prisoners to extract intelligence. Admittedly, I had mixed results until a colonel taught me skills conveniently missing from the curriculum. I didn't enjoy the process. In fact, I hated it! But by the end of the War, we were all doing things we weren't proud of. *Inhumane things*.

For five minutes or so, I stared at the man while he yelled profanities in my direction. Finally, when he stopped posing, I stepped into the cell and slapped him hard across his cheeks four times. In retaliation, he attempted to stand. I instantly struck him to his solar plexus with my palm causing the back of his head to slam into the concrete wall. After he crumbled in agony, I gripped him by his throat with one hand and pushed him hard against the wall. He sobbed relentlessly. Then, I ripped out his nose rings. As blood flew over his cheeks, he screamed like a pig being torn to pieces by wild dogs. I intentionally didn't say a word during the entire ordeal.

After watching him sob for a while, I asked Fiona to pass me her combat knife in a loud, clear voice. She slid her Glock blade from the sheath and handed me the knife in clear view of the pirate.

I turned to Fiona, "Have you ever seen someone being scalped? I have. During the War, I scalped traitors for sport." I pointed my index finger at the pirate. "This scum is a traitor working for the enemy." I cackled like a lunatic and stepped forward with wide eyes. When I stood within an inch of his face, I held the blade near his hairline.

"Take his balls instead, Boss. I saw a stray dog outside that looked bloody starving."

I wasn't exactly sure whether Fiona was acting in the pantomime or being serious. Which I found a little disturbing.

"Good idea. And to think I was going to ask the mayor to let him go after he told us everything. Aren't I an idiot for being an optimist?"

Obviously, I've never scalped anyone or messed with anyone's testicles. I've pulled teeth and fingernails, but nothing more. The Colonel explained that interrogation is centred on psychology – the loss of control - the fear and expectation of violence.

I moved the point of the blade toward his groin.

The terrified man placed his palms in the air, "Okay, okay. I'm sorry! What do you want? I'll tell you anything. I'll help you. Just please don't!"

Henry Bai spilled his guts, telling us all about his pirate life, including titbits that were of little interest to me – his desire to move to Australia – find an honest job – marry a buxom blonde. It seemed that the pirate life and all it entailed was incompatible with his constitution. He confessed that he was living in constant fear of dying at the hands of his older cousin, the captain of the pirates. I would hazard a guess that a clinical psychologist would diagnose Henry with post-traumatic stress disorder (PTSD). As he spoke, I could see Fiona rubbing her index and thumb together in my periphery, pretending to play the world's smallest violin. At first, I did my best to ignore her, but when she continued with her antics, I asked her to fetch Henry a cup of water so I could continue the interrogation without interruption.

Henry's temperament towards piracy was the antithesis of his older cousin, Captain Julian Jun Feng. He explained that before the War, they were spoilt rich kids living the high life in Singapore. Their wealthy parents lavished them with the five big C's – Cash, Car, Credit card, Condominium and Country club. Even though they had it better than most, Henry wasn't surprised that his cousin desired something more. After graduating from university, Julian coveted power and respect. But most of all, he wanted to be feared. So what better way to achieve his lofty goal than seek out and ingratiate himself with the local triads? He sold drugs to teenagers at his family's country club for a powerful gang, the Jiangshis. It wasn't long before he was invited to be a member of the gang, and within twelve months, he was running his own club in the heart of the city on Orchard Road. Henry exploited his cousin's notoriety by partying with the attractive women frequenting the club and snorting all the coke he could get his hands on. While Julian was in the thick of gang life, squeamish young Henry cautiously avoided becoming entangled in the gang's criminal enterprise.

When the missiles struck Singapore, the cousins were fortunate to be partying in the Malaysian city of Kuala Lumpur, one of the few cities that escaped the devastation. Being a criminal entrepreneur who never missed an opportunity, Julian recruited a bunch of local cutthroats and stole the Armidale patrol boat from a rival Malaysian gang. Over the past nine years, they had raped and plundered throughout Southeast Asia. That was until Julian decided to harass Aussie Ports. They were familiar with sailing the flat waters of the South China Sea, so the journey from Malaysia through the

Timor Sea to Australia was destined to be a rude awakening. The treacherous and unforgiving waters caused discontent amongst the crew, with some begging the captain to turn back and return to calmer waters. In Julian's paranoid-riddled mind, he feared a mutiny, so he retaliated by setting an example and murdering three of his crew.

Henry informed me that just two of the sixteen pirates had military experience. But I confirmed they were all killers armed with AKs, with several capable of operating the Kusa's heavy machine guns. However, on the upside, he also confided they were low on ammo for the canon.

After extracting the intel from Henry, we entered the crib room to find the sergeant making a coffee with a plunger. The nutty, spicy aroma of the beans was so enticing that the top of my mouth could almost taste the coffee.

"You've been holding out on us, Sarge. Where did you come by those beans?"

"Ah, you're a man that likes your coffee, hey. The sailors on the middle east oil tankers trade their Arabica coffee for Kununurra mangoes. Smells good, doesn't it? Do you both want a cup?"

"Does a Koala eat gum leaves?" I asked rhetorically.

As I enjoyed one of the best coffees I've had in the last decade, the sergeant explained that he'd sent his constables out to beg, borrow and steal the equipment I required. He had also asked the commander of the Pilbara militia to round up the personnel I requested. The man was efficient, drove a sweet ride and made a marvellous coffee. I must confess that I was beginning to develop a bit of a man crush.

The sergeant drove us back to the port office to meet with the mayor. Even though I had requested the gold, I was still surprised to find the 155 ounces waiting for me on the mahogany table. It's not every day someone you have just met gives you a fortune in gold. Only three days ago, I was gazing at the gold stolen from the Geraldton bank. If only I was a dishonest man - I'd be filthy rich!

"I appreciate your trust in me, Mayor," I stated earnestly.

"Don't worry. I've performed my due diligence. And I don't think we have any choice but to trust the saviour of Norseman," she replied with a thin-lipped smile.

"I hope I can live up to the hype, but to be brutally honest, I'd be happy to get out of this alive," I said with a grave expression.

The mayor gestured for us to take a seat. "I still want to hear your plan, Mr O'Connor."

I glanced at my watch – 3.05 p.m., just under two hours before the pirates delivered on their promise and executed the tanker crew.

As I outlined the mission and how I intended to execute it, the three community leaders sat in stoic silence. After my presentation, I was pleased to hear that the sergeant was impressed with my plan. I was less concerned with the look of terror plastered on the mayor's face and the expression of doubt from the harbourmaster. What did they expect? I only had two hours to develop a plan.

# Chapter Fourteen

*Thursday, March 6, 2042 from 4:45 p.m. – Archie*

Fiona was displeased when I informed her that she wasn't accompanying me on my meet and greet with the pirates. We didn't have time to prepare for an assault, so I had to literally *buy* us some time. I tasked her with positioning herself on the second storey of a neglected storage building just ten metres from the wharf. Her job was to watch the pirates through her scope as I played *my part*. I told her, "If the poo hits the fan, kill as many pirates as you can so I can escape." If it came to that, I knew my chance of fleeing was slim, but I couldn't let her know my thoughts, as she wouldn't have let me leave the wharf without her. Besides, she was an outstanding shot, and I wanted her to take out as many of the bastards as she could, especially Captain Julian.

Fiona astutely asked how she could identify Captain Julian. She thought I was taking the piss out of her when I said, "Look for the bloke with an eye patch."

"Does he also have a peg leg and a parrot on his shoulder?" she asked sarcastically.

At times Fiona could be a real smart-ass, but I found her reply quite humorous. Henry had explained that his cousin lost sight in his right eye when his AK-47 blew up in his face. The most probable cause was either a poorly maintained weapon or faulty ammo. Servicing your firearm regularly is essential, but it's especially crucial when the gun is constantly exposed to salt air.

Simmo, the old navy vet I met in the observation tower, bravely volunteered to ferry me to the Kusa. He explained with a lop-sided grin that he had nothing to lose but his life. I wondered if he was related to my good friend Captain Ross, as they were cut from the same cloth.

I requested the oldest tugboat in the port's fleet. And they didn't disappoint, as the sixty-plus-year-old boat was clearly on her last sea legs. Even though it wouldn't have surprised me to learn that gaffer tape was holding the faded orange and blue tug together, she did have her endearing qualities: blue eyes and prominent dark eyelashes painted on the front of the wheelhouse, with a toothy smile on the bow. She was affectionately referred to as Mrs Fugsly by the port workers. I was informed by Simmo that a mischievous employee had even decided to paint over her old name to make her new name official. Even though Simmo swore Mrs Fuglsy was reliable, I was grateful that we didn't have far to travel, with the Kusa anchored in the middle of the 170-metre-wide inner harbour.

At my request, we flew a white flag from the mainmast to advertise our intentions. I was about to play the role of a Port Association administrator. If I had known in high school that my acting skills could one day save my life, I would have switched on during drama class and spent less time chatting up the girls. The harbourmaster loaned me a well-worn Port Association uniform which I wore with my shirt tucked in. The 155 ounces of gold were in a duffle bag at my feet. It may have weighed slightly more than four litres of milk, but it was valued at half a million pre-war Aussie dollars.

After Simmo steered Mrs Fugsly to the stern of the Kusa, I exited the wheelhouse to greet six pirates pointing AK-47s at me. We were both unarmed and at the mercy of the pirates. Covertly wearing a firearm or knife was guaranteed to get me killed, as I had no doubt they would search me. Before we left Tug Haven, I advised Simmo that if I got into serious strife, retreat full throttle back to the wharf or dive overboard and make a swim for it. But, of course, we both knew his chance of evading the two Browning 50 calibre heavy machine guns was a long shot at best.

With my hands raised in the air, I hollered, "Permission to come aboard, Captain." I then slowly pirouetted to show the pirates I was unarmed.

A rotund Asian man wearing a brown and yellow stained Bintang tank top gestured with his hands while yelling, "Come close. Throw me a rope."

The tug's engines rumbled as we pulled alongside the Kusa. I threw the tug's two bow lines to Bintang, then ambled to the stern, and threw the remaining lines to his shipmates. I didn't know whether to laugh or duck for cover as they caught the lines while pointing their AK muzzle in every which way while resting their finger on the trigger. Bloody Amateurs! The first thing you teach someone learning to shoot is the four safety rules: always point the firearm in a safe direction, treat all firearms as loaded, identify your target and surroundings, and keep your finger off the trigger until you're ready to fire. The pirates broke every rule in the book.

Before becoming a hunter, I worked with a bloke in the fight game who had a dark sense of humour and loved to tell stories. Over a beer, he divulged an embarrassing incident involving his pistol and his mother-in-law, who he notoriously loathed. After shooting targets in his backyard, he turned the door handle to enter his home while grasping his pistol in his opposite hand. Unfortunately, his finger was on the trigger as his mother-in-law approached the door from inside the house. And then BANG! His mother-in-law screamed in agony and fury. He shot the tip of her left big toe clean off. I almost pissed myself laughing as he described the story in great detail, mimicking his mother-in-law's reaction and recounting his wife's outrage. I jokingly asked whether he had shot the poor woman out of spite or if it was an accident caused by interlimb interaction – a simultaneous movement of his opposite fingers. He deflected my question by confiding he was no longer invited to the in-laws for dinner.

Even though I immediately identified Captain Julian by his eye patch, I was careful not to acknowledge him and risk fuelling his suspicions. Putting myself in his boots, he was floating in an enemy port, and his cousin was missing. But, of course, Henry's capture was only one possibility. He could have just as likely been killed or hightailed it out of town to find a buxom beauty to woo. After all, he didn't need to be Nostradamus to recognise that Henry wasn't happy in the pirate business.

"I'm bringing two bags aboard your ship. One has gold in it, and the other has whisky. I'm unarmed and wish you no harm," I shouted nervously to Bintang.

With all these amateurs waving AKs around, the last thing I needed was to be suspected of bringing a bomb or firearm aboard. I stepped onto the Kusa's main deck at the stern with the duffle bag hung over my shoulder and my right hand grasping the carry bag. To play the part of an employee who feared for his life, I stood with hunched shoulders and wore a nervous expression. Given my current predicament, performing the role of an anxious man wasn't a difficult task. Five surly pirates closely surrounded me on the deck. They were a mixed group of Filipino and Indonesian cutthroats.

I noticed a shaggy dark-haired bloke standing behind a fifty-calibre machine gun on the starboard side. By the manner in which he gripped the weapon, with his bunched shoulders and a sly grin, I could tell he was itching to let her rip.

The pirates stepped aside so Captain Julian could point the muzzle of his chrome Desert Eagle pistol at my forehead. The ostentatious pistol matched his dress sense. He wore a white silk shirt and black leather pants tucked into elaborately embroidered Stetson boots.

"Daliman, search him," Julian ordered Bintang in an American accent.

As Bintang pat searched me, I was forced to turn my head to avoid his garlic and onion breath. He avoided searching my groin. An error that could prove fatal. My morale was lifted when I noted that Captain Julian had failed to correct his henchman's blunder. The amateur hour was on display.

"Place the bags on the deck and slowly open them. Start with the green bag," instructed Julian.

I slowly placed the bags at my feet and pulled the zipper of the duffle bag to reveal the 155 ounces of various gold bar denominations. The captain gave a hint of a smile while his crew whistled and cheered. With the same level of care as the first, I opened the carry bag to reveal the twelve Johnnie Walker black label whisky bottles. It came as no surprise when the pirates' reaction to the whisky was just as raucous as it was to the gold. The whisky's value skyrocketed in 2032 after the Scottish distillery was destroyed by artillery fire. Authentic bottles are as rare as hen's teeth. I thought I saw a tear beginning to form in the corners of the harbourmaster's eyes when I detailed my plan of gifting the bottles to the pirates.

Julian removed the gold bars from the duffle bag and placed them in an orderly line on the deck. He individually inspected each bar, picking them up and running his fingertips over the surface. The pirate captain was searching for any irregularities in the colour. Gold is naturally non-magnetic, so he placed a magnet against each of the bars to test for a reaction. I was confident that he wouldn't find any, as I personally checked each bar before we left the wharf – trust nobody. If he had trioxo nitrate acid in his possession, he could have added a small drop to a scratch on the bars' surface. If the gold failed to react with the acid, it's legit, but if a green or milky colouration were observed, this would indicate the gold was fake.

After he'd inspected each of the bars, he stepped toward me. "What the fuck is this? Where's the rest of it?" he whispered vehemently in my ear in his New York twang.

Maintaining my act, "I'm sss...sorry SS...Sir. They told me to gg... give you a message," I stammered.

Julian slapped me hard across my cheek. I noticed his right shoulder twitch a fraction of a second before he struck me. My instinct was to duck and launch a left uppercut to his chin. But instead, I flung my head to the side and held my palm to my cheek while I whimpered another apology. It was a shame that my thespian skills did not extend to producing tears at a moment's notice, but a man needs to know his limitations.

Julian's spittle struck my face as he screamed, "Daliman, Loong, bring this snivelling piece of shit to my cabin."

Julian bent down and grabbed a bottle of whisky before dramatically turning on the heels of his Stetsons and leading the way past the Zodiac to the boarding party access door. Bintang and his mate gripped me by my arms and manhandled me in Julian's wake. They both stood at the door with awkward expressions when they discovered they could not enter the door while standing side by side.

"Hurry up, I don't have all day!" Julian yelled from inside the boat.

I swiftly ducked my head when Bintang single-handedly shoved me through the door. The pirates escorted me down a hallway past the galley. It was an absolute pigsty, with noodle packets, opened cans of food and bottles of beer strewn all over the galley's counter. Discipline and cleanliness did not appear to be the order of the day.

Bintang opened a door with the title 'CO's Cabin' inscribed at eye level and pushed me through the doorway. I stood in a cramped four-by-three-metre office with white aluminium walls. Julian surprised me by ordering his henchman to wait in the hallway and close the door behind them. Either he's a cocky little bastard, or my act was more convincing than I had hoped.

Julian sat at a small desk and gestured for me to sit opposite. I noticed a half-peeled sticker of a Philippine flag on one side of a cupboard door and an old navy crew roster on the other. A torn 'Pirates of the Caribbean' movie poster of Captain Jack Sparrow took centre place on the rear wall. It appears the captain may have a sense of humour after all. I remember watching the movie as a kid, as it was one of a handful of times my old man took me to the cinema. He said something about the actor drawing inspiration from a member of the Rolling Stones, one of his favourite bands. The name of the actor and musician was on the tip of my tongue.

"What's your name?" Julian asked as he scratched his chin.

"Johnny, Sir," I replied meekly.

"Don't call me Sir. Call me Captain. What do you do at the port, Johnny?" he asked inquisitively.

"I work in supplies, Sir. I mean, Captain."

Julian leaned back in his chair, placing his hands behind his head. "You have any kids, Johnny?"

"No, Captain, I've never had much luck in that area." I did my best to appear frightened and nervous, lowering my head and avoiding eye contact, speaking quietly, and licking my lips.

The pirate inspected the seal of the Johnnie Walker bottle before pouring two fingers into a couple of glasses resting on the table. He brought the glass to his lips but changed his mind before taking a sip. "Bottoms up," he said, gesturing for me to drink first. When I considered drugging the crew, I thought of several things that could go wrong, this being one of them. As a whisky man, I appreciated and savoured the smooth, smoky texture. Julian poured me another before finally taking a sip from his glass. As I downed the second glass, I felt a mixture of regret and remorse at giving the bastard the fine whisky.

The pirate captain suddenly changed his persona, just like an actor after the director had yelled cut. He lowered his voice and said, "Look, man, what's going on? You brought me less than a third of what I asked for. I don't want to be a hard ass and come down on you like an asshole, but I must keep the boys happy. You know how it is. Now, I'll ask politely. Where are the 500 ounces?"

"I understand, Captain. I......"

Before I could finish my answer, he flung his glass against the cabinet and screamed, "We need to get paid, or I'm going to have to let my boys loose, and you don't want that, believe me! So where's the fucking rest of it?"

*I thought, bloody hell, this bloke is a schizophrenic.* "The mayor told me to advise you that they're in the process of collecting the rest of the gold, and I'll bring it to you by 12 noon tomorrow. They wanted to give you the gold they have available and the whisky as an act of good faith," I explained in a soft, whiny voice.

"Not good enough. You tell your boss that I want the gold by 6 a.m. tomorrow morning, or I'll execute the tanker's entire crew and then blow a hole in her at the mouth of the harbour. And I'm charging interest. I want another 400 ounces. Do you understand?"

"Yes, Captain, I understand. 400 ounces by 6 a.m., or you'll kill the crew and sink the tanker. I'll tell the mayor as soon as I return."

He was bluffing, he'd never sink the tanker as she was worth a fortune, and he needed the crew to set sail to the next port to sell the ship and fuel. If the mayor complied and supplied the pirates with the gold, he'd still sail away with the tanker. And the mayor was correct. Julian and his cutthroats would be back for more.

"Daliman," Julian yelled.

Bintang opened the door, "Yes, Boss."

"Take him on deck and give him a pair of binoculars. Make sure he's watching the tanker's bow. Right above her name."

As Bintang grabbed me by my arm, I pleaded, "Please, Captain. I'll do my best to get your gold. Please don't do anything rash."

Julian held a two-way radio to his mouth as Bintang dragged me from the cabin. I asked Bintang if I could go to the toilet to stall whatever Julian planned. I received a swift punch to my liver in reply. He pushed and shoved me back outside to the stern of the boat. He thrust a pair of binoculars against my chest and pointed toward the tanker anchored in the outer harbour. "Look near White Pearl," he sneered.

The ship's name, 'The White Pearl,' was painted in large white letters at the top of the black hull. I stopped looking through the eyepiece and scanned the deck for Julian. He was nowhere to be seen. Bintang swore and shoved the back of my shoulder, gesturing for me to use the binos. I observed two men on the tanker's deck gripping the arms of a young man of middle-eastern appearance. One of the pirates pointed a handgun at his temple. Even though I was aware of the distance, the artificial magnification of the scene tricked me into anticipating the sound of gunfire. Blood sprayed from the man's skull as his head fell forwards. The guards laughed as they pushed the young man from the tanker's side into the ocean below. *Bastards!*

I turned to Bintan. "I need to speak to your captain urgently," I pleaded.

Bintang coward punched me in the back of my head. I took a deep breath and slowly exhaled, willing myself to not react. He again gestured for me to look at The White Pearl. The pirates shoved a middle-aged lady to the tanker's edge and cut her throat before callously throwing her overboard. I could feel the tension in my jaw muscles as I clenched my teeth together. This was my fault. I caused their deaths. This was on me!

Bintang ripped the binoculars from my grasp and gestured for me to return to the tug. "You go now. Bring back our gold, Gweilo," he said with a toothy grin.

He referred to me as a 'gweilo,' meaning 'foreign devil.' It was a spiteful rebuke for someone of Asian descent. However, if he thought of me as a 'foreign devil' as I stood on the deck pretending to be 'Johnny the weakling', I couldn't wait to hear what he thought of me when we next met.

# Chapter Fifteen

*Thursday, March 6, 2042 from 4:45 p.m. – Fiona*

A squawking seagull flew overhead as I opened the rear door of the storage building. After trudging up the rickety stairs to the second floor, I searched for the ideal spot. I laid a brown rug on the ancient timber floorboards near a smashed window that looked over the inner harbour.

Over the past 12 months, I've improved my shooting accuracy, or as Archie would say, 'my marksmanship'. I've practised on targets at the range, but the real sign of improvement is evident when I'm hunting. Archie reckons there used to be a national code for shooting roos, which mandated the requirement for a single headshot. For a muscular animal that can weigh up to ninety kilograms and grow to two metres tall, they have tiny skulls about the size of a man's fist. So the most humane method of hunting them is shooting them to the forehead, temple or just below their ears in the back of their head. I hate letting an animal suffer, so I've become very accurate.

I adjusted the bi-pod of the Blaser R93 Tactical 3 Sniper rifle before moving into a prone position. The .338 calibre rifle had an effective range of 1500 metres and was used by Australian snipers during the War. Archie inherited the rifle when a fellow guard working with us on the Kalgoorlie water train was killed in an attack. I was absolutely chuffed when he gave me the Blaser at Christmas. I reciprocated by giving him a carton of beer brewed at the Duke of York Hotel in Narrogin. He constantly raved about their pale ale. We greedily drank the entire carton over a messy three-day weekend.

As I lay on the rug, I scanned the patrol boat's rear deck, anchored just 250 metres from my position. I held my breath when I sighted a mob of pirates armed with AKs surrounding Archie.

"Hello, Captain," I whispered as I aimed the crosshair at his chest. He was dressed like he was attending a Halloween party. I placed my finger on the trigger as he waved a massive silver pistol at Archie's head. Archie instructed me not to shoot unless his life was in 'imminent jeopardy'. If it came to that, I aimed to execute fancy pants first before doing my darndest to kill as many of his crew as possible.

Two thugs suddenly grabbed Archie by his arms and dragged him below deck. *Fuck!* My mind was racing as I thought of worst-case scenarios. Every scenario was uglier than the previous.

I glanced at my watch. Archie had been out of sight for almost fifteen minutes, but it felt more like an hour. I was sweating like a pig being led to the slaughter. When the pirates finally shoved him back on deck, I could feel the tension in my shoulders release. As soon as the tug arrived at the jetty, I breathed a sigh of relief before packing up my rifle and returning to the shipping tower. *Thank fuck I didn't have to shoot.*

When I entered the shipping tower, I initially noted that Archie had yet to arrive from the jetty. Then I quickly realised there wasn't a man or woman that didn't look shocked or upset. I felt like I was attending a wake. The harbourmaster swore under his breath while the mayor stood motionless with her hand over her mouth. Totally bewildered, I gazed out over the harbour, wondering what I had missed, as it all seemed to go to plan. I felt like the odd person out until the sergeant noticed my confused expression and explained what the merciless pirates did to the tanker crew. *Poor bastards!*

Undoubtedly, Archie took a considerable risk by venturing out to the pirate's boat. I know we need the fuel to capture Patterson, but what's the point in dying to acquire it? If Captain Ross and Clarry were here, they would have told him that boarding the boat was foolhardy. I could see it play out - Archie would raise his palms like he was defending himself in court and explain he was taking a calculated risk. He has a habit of placing himself in harm's way, which I don't begrudge as long as he doesn't try to wrap me up in cotton wool. I won't stand for the attitude of – 'Do as I say, not as I do.' I'm a grown ass woman, and I'm no longer an apprentice.

We waited for Archie in the harbourmaster's office. The mayor, harbourmaster and sergeant sat at the timber desk, making small talk to relieve the tension. I leaned against an office wall, too on edge to sit down and talk shit. Archie looked stressed when he entered the office. Knowing Archie, he'd be taking the deaths of the tanker crew personally and would likely brood over it for days to come. Don't get me wrong, it pisses me off that the fuckers killed the crew members to prove a point, but I wouldn't consider it a personal failure. It's not our bloody fault!

The sergeant stood from his chair and shook Archie's hand. The big man's body language and facial expression said it all – *Sorry, mate. I know what it feels like. I've been there.*

Archie sat down and cleared his throat, "My focus is now to prepare for phase two of the operation. Have you got my team and the necessary equipment ready to go?"

"We have four ex-military personnel that can dive waiting at the station. Two served in the RAN. I can vouch for them, as they're all members of the Pilbara militia. I've also located the kit you requested. It's all at the station. It took a bit of wrangling, but I've rounded up a shot-firer who knows his business," advised the sergeant.

"What happened on the boat?" the mayor asked Archie in a concerned tone.

"Their leader has agreed to give us more time, but only until 6 a.m." Archie looked at his watch before he continued, "We have just over eleven hours before it's go time, so I have to get prepped. I also need a power nap to clear my head. I'd love to take the time to debrief you all about what happened on the boat, but we don't have the time."

When the mayor opened her mouth to speak, she was interrupted by the sergeant, "Sounds like a plan. Let's return to the station and get it sorted so you can put your head down. We need you in tip-top shape if this mission is to be successful." The sergeant looked at the mayor with piercing eyes as he stood from his seat, "We all appreciate your assistance Archie," he stated emphatically.

The mayor looked miffed. She glared at the sergeant with her arms folded as we stood to leave the office. She reminded me of Sister Anne, the woman in charge of the Catholic orphanage I attended. She was a strict disciplinarian who always got her own way until a *certain* child was fed up with her draconian rules and decided to rebel and run amok. Just after my fifteenth birthday, I had the bright idea of sneaking into her bedroom and placing a bright green grass snake in her pillowcase. Later that night, the entire orphanage could hear her screaming like a banshee. When I wouldn't own up to the prank, even after a severe beating, she had the same frustrated expression as the mayor – a powerful matriarch unaccustomed to being defied.

As the sergeant drove us back to the station, I thought about making him an offer to buy his cool yellow coupe. But, of course, we'd have to capture Patterson first. The sergeant was switched on enough to know that Archie was in his own world and avoided making unnecessary chit-chat. However, he would be wrong if he thought Archie was thinking about the death of the tanker crew. I know him well enough to tell he's focused on tomorrow's operation. He was like one of those supercomputers I learned about at school, analysing every tiny detail and contingency – when, where, who, how, what, and why?

We were about to enter the station's rear door when an unshaven skinny white dude approached Archie. "Archie O'Connor, I'm a reporter with the Pilbara Times. Can you tell me how you're involved with the pirate negotiation?"

Archie ignored the reporter's question and turned the door handle. Unperturbed, the man took a photo of Archie with a camera hanging by a strap around his neck and then asked, "Has the mayor.....?"

With surprising speed for a big man, the sergeant stepped toward the reporter, grabbed him by his chicken neck, and shoved him firmly against the wall. "If you say one more word or speak of this to anyone, so help me, God, I will cut your tongue out, Andrew. Don't test me!" he boomed.

We stepped inside the station as the sergeant released the shaken reporter. The sergeant led us down a hallway to the crib room, where four hard-looking men were playing cards. The sergeant introduced us to each man as they stood and shook our hands. It's tough to describe exactly why, but they each had an 'air of confidence' that was unmistakable and not too dissimilar to Archie's. It was how they held themselves, with assured body language and a relaxed demeanour. Not one looked me up and down or asked stupid questions like most men I met. On the contrary, they were polite and professional. They asked me about my rifle and what I knew about the pirates and their weapons.

Archie spoke to the sergeant in the hallway just outside the crib room. My ears pricked up when I heard the sergeant mention scuba, M4s, grapple hooks, and nylon ladders.

Archie returned and addressed the group, "Thank you for your patience. Give me twenty minutes to inspect the equipment for the op, and then I'll speak to you individually before getting this show on the road."

While Archie and the sergeant gave the equipment a once-over, the men invited me to play poker. We used matchsticks as an alternative to chips and played for bragging rights rather than gold or silver. They asked me how long I'd known Archie and what it was like being a bounty hunter. They were interested to hear about the Norseman mission from someone who was in the thick of it. And surprisingly, I actually enjoyed telling the story.

They then each took turns telling me their story. Jamal, a retired US Navy Seal in his mid-forties, was working on an oil rig in Australian waters when the War broke out. Unable to find a passage home, he volunteered with the RAN. At the end of his tour, the harbourmaster offered him a job guarding the port on the Arafura boats. The muscular African American described in detail what he wanted to do to 'Henry the pirate' for blowing up *his* beloved Arafuras' engines.

Jayden was a handsome thirty-something-year-old Queenslander who served with the Australian Army as a Commando. He grew up on a farm, so after he was discharged, he returned to his roots to work on a cattle station thirty kilometres out of town. He was also a lousy poker player. I unashamedly won at least half of his matchsticks.

Thomas was a Tasmanian in his early forties who served as a helicopter pilot in the Army. He worked with Jayden on the cattle station and had a weekend side gig performing security duties at the port. Thomas and Jayden were keen recreational divers and hunters. I guessed they were lovers by the way they kept glancing at each other.

Yasar was a combat systems operator who served with the RAN and spent two years on HMAS Broome, an Armidale class boat almost identical to the pirate boat sitting in the harbour. Until a couple of days ago, he was stationed with Jamal guarding the port on the Arafura boats. His motivation to be involved in the op was similar to Jamal's. He wanted payback for what they did to *his* boats. In his late fifties, he was the oldest team member but looked just as fit and eager as the younger men.

As I considered my rotten cards, I wondered what was holding up Archie. My curiosity and impatience got the better of me, so I excused myself after folding my hand and ambled toward the sergeant's baritone voice. I found them both at the lock-up counter discussing the four men in the crib room. I walked to the nearest cell and peered inside to see five machine guns, three boxes of ammo, and scuba equipment - including tanks, wetsuits, fins, and goggles. Two wicked-looking steel hooks attached to nylon ropes were leaning up against the cell doors. They were about thirty centimetres long, with four saw-tooth claws. I pondered their purpose and couldn't think of anything other than for catching killer whales.

I heard 'Henry the pirate' call out in a meek tone from the farthest cell, "Can I please speak to someone?"

I was about to walk to Henry's cell when a man's sudden and loud exclamation made me flinch. "HEY, FUCKERS! Can someone please make this whiny little shit shut his mouth? He's been grizzling for two hours. It's Goddamn torture sticking me in a cell next to this fella. You're breaking the Geneva convention or some bloody convention. I'd rather have my toenails ripped out."

"What's this bloke's story?" Archie asked the sergeant.

The sergeant scratched his jaw and leaned against the lock-up counter. "Look, I didn't have much time to find someone with the expertise you requested. Deuce is a shot-firer who's worked in the mining industry for forty years. But unfortunately, he's also an alcoholic wanted for blowing up a man's cow."

"I can hear you," bellowed Deuce from his cell.

"He did what?" Archie asked in disbelief.

"Tell whoever you're talking to the truth of the matter, Theodore," Deuce bellowed.

Archie smiled and raised an eyebrow, "Theodore?"

The sergeant glared, "Deuce has known me since I was a little tacker. He was my daddy's drinking buddy when they worked in the mines. And by the way, it's Theo."

I followed Archie as he moseyed down to Deuce's cell. "What's your story, mate? Maybe we can cut a deal if it's a good one."

If anyone needed a hearty meal, it was Deuce. I could see his ribs sticking out under his ripped Hawaiian shirt as he sat on the toilet. He appeared none too concerned about doing a shit in front of visitors. That was until he noticed me standing behind Archie and the sergeant.

"Can I have some bloody privacy," he uttered testily.

In dismay, the sergeant put his hand on his forehead. "Then pull your bloody pants up, Deuce."

"Tell the sheila to turn around, so I can finish up."

I didn't need to be asked twice. The last thing I wanted to see was the old man's shrivelled cock, or *any* cock for that matter.

After hearing the toilet flush, I turned back around to see Deuce gripping the bars of his cell door. "Old man Jackson owed me money for blasting some stumps on his property. He didn't pay up because he said I damaged his ute when a part of the stump hit his windscreen. It's not my fault he parked too close to the stump. So later that night, I got hammered and blew up his prized bull. It was a stupid thing to do, but being sentenced to five years of hard labour is bullshit. It's a fucking death sentence at my age."

"Just how good are you with explosives?" Archie asked.

"Boy, I can blow anything up with the right ingredients."

"If I can reduce your sentence, will you help us?"

"I'll tell you what, if you wangle me a written pardon, I'll help you steal the crown jewels."

I'm known to be nosey, so I had to ask, "Why do they call you Deuce?"

He grinned as he stuck his right arm between the bars and wiggled the two remaining fingers on his right hand.

After we left the lock-up, Archie turned to the sergeant, "Can you speak to the mayor and organise his pardon? This man is pivotal to the plan. We need him if she wants her harbour and fuel."

"It won't be a problem, Archie. I'll handle it," he promised.

Archie borrowed the sergeant's office to meet with the men individually before returning to the crib room to find us debating whether Prince was a better singer than Bruno Mars. Jayden and I voted for Bruno, while Jamal was adamant Prince beat him hands down. Archie wrote 'Operation Poseidon' at the top of the whiteboard with a black marker. Underneath, he penned the headings – Situation, Mission, Execution, Admin / Logistics, and Command / Signals. He included dot points under each of the headings. The men and I couldn't help but keep one eye on the whiteboard as we continued our conversation. He drew an outline of a boat on the top left-hand side of the board, labelling the front of the boat as the bow, the rear as the stern, the right as starboard, the left side as port, and the middle as midship. It was clear to all in the room that he labelled the boat for my benefit, but I appreciated that no one felt the need to mention it. On the right-hand side of the board, he illustrated a map of the port, including the current location of the pirate's boat.

Archie stopped scribbling on the board and cleared his throat. When this failed to have the desired effect, the sergeant ordered everyone to "Listen up!"

Archie stood beside the whiteboard and addressed the men.

"Again, thank you for your patience and willingness to accept this mission. Operation Poseidon is named after the Greek God of the sea and the protector of seafarers. Our mission is to breach the pirate boat Kusa at 5:40 a.m. on Friday, March 7, 2042, and take control of the vessel. I repeat, our mission is to breach the pirate boat Kusa at 5:40 a.m. on Friday, March 7, 2042, and take control of the vessel. The situation is...."

While Archie explained the situation, his two-way radio erupted, first with static and then a clearly identifiable transmission from the harbourmaster. He excused himself and swiftly left the room to converse with the harbourmaster. When he returned, he used his thumb to erase the pirate boat from the board and drew it facing the opposite direction, with the bow facing toward the town. By his deep frown and the sweat on his brow, it didn't take a psychologist to recognise he was feeling the pressure.

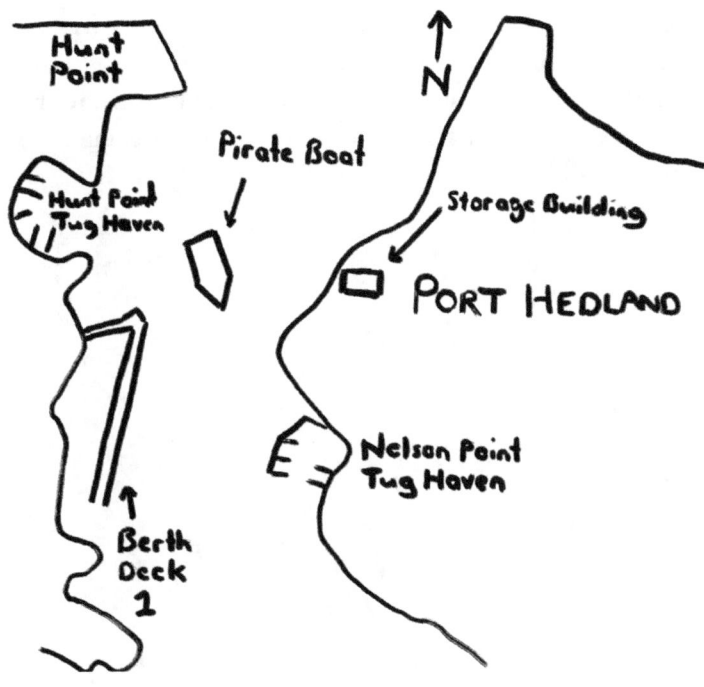

As Archie delivered the order, the four men and I paid close attention, jotting down notes and asking questions. When Archie tasked me with the sniper role, Jayden turned in his seat and gave me a wink. The men would be relying on me to clear a path for them and protect their backs as they cleared the deck. Butterflies fluttered in my stomach as I thought of everything that could go wrong. What happens if I miss a pirate and shoot one of our own?

While I cleaned my rifle and privately fretted, Archie and the team used the remaining four hours to inspect the equipment and finalise the finer details of the operation. The sergeant was true to his word and issued Deuce a signed pardon. After Archie completed the briefing, Deuce looked how I felt, absolutely shattered. At 1:15 a.m., we said goodnight to the team, knowing we'd meet in less than three hours for the big show.

The sergeant booked rooms at the nearest hotel for the four ex-servicemen. He led Archie and me to his quarters, a clean two-by-one annex attached to the station. Blissfully we each had a bed. Before we hit the sack, Archie set the alarm for 4 a.m. I laid out the clothes I'd be wearing for the op alongside my rifle, ready for when the alarm sounded. I had no doubt that it was going to be an eventful morning.

# Chapter Sixteen

*Friday, March 7, 2042 from 4:00 a.m. – Archie*

The twin bell analog alarm clock did its job and blasted my eardrums from the bedside table. Fortunately, there wasn't a snooze button to tempt me, as it was time to get up. Fiona was groaning in the bed on the opposite side of the room. She was not a morning person, but admittedly, at 4 a.m., neither was I.

Just after I slid on my cargo pants, I heard a rat-a-tat-tat on the bedroom door. "Are you decent?" the sergeant asked in a muffled tone. Still half asleep, Fiona gingerly pulled up her jeans, "Yep, all good," she replied. The towering man ducked his head under the door frame and handed us a mug of his marvellous Arabica coffee. "God bless you, Sarge," I proclaimed.

The sergeant was fully kitted and raring to go. I could see from the confusion on Fiona's face that I had forgotten to give her an update. Thankfully, she continued to sip on her coffee and kept any mischievous thoughts swirling around in her head to herself. After last night's briefing, Sarge informed me that he intended to join the team for the pointy end of the operation. He disagreed with my suggestion that he should coordinate the contingency strategies from the shipping tower. He looked down at me and grumbled with his moustache bristling, "I'm a competent diver. I can use a firearm. And I'm not sending men into danger without being by their side." I wasn't in a position to argue with the man, nor did I want to.

After we exited the station's front doors, Fiona and I bumped fists and wished each other good luck. She picked up her gear and walked towards the old storage building. I was kind of surprised she hadn't complained about her role. I had anticipated a debate that would kick off with her asking, "Why can't I go with you and the team? I'm not confident I can do this." I had rehearsed a carefully worded counter-argument, "You're as accurate with the rifle over two hundred metres than any civilian I've ever met. Sure, you haven't been formally trained as a sniper, and this job is undoubtedly a big challenge, but I've seen you hunt, and you're up to it. Just last month, I witnessed you shoot two roos in the head at a distance of no less than 250 meters in under three seconds. You're ready!" It was almost a shame I didn't have an opportunity to give the speech a whirl.

The assault team was due to rendezvous at the Port Association's shipping tower at 4:20 a.m. I glanced at my watch – 4:15 a.m. The mayor and harbourmaster greeted us with nervous smiles. The tired-looking mayor started to play twenty questions, which is something I didn't need right before an op. The harbourmaster must have read the sergeant's expression as he distracted the mayor and led her to the opposite side of the tower. When I peered through the tower's powerful binoculars, I was relieved to see that the boat had not altered position. If all goes to plan, the action will commence at 5:40 a.m. Deuce had spent the night clandestinely preparing Mrs Fugsly for what would hopefully be her final adventure.

I recognised the tightening of my stomach as just the normal jitters before a big op. My old mentor, Sal Willis, believed that nerves were a good thing – 'It's your body and mind reminding you to switch on,' he would attest. Sal was a former commando who taught me everything there was to know about bounty hunting. On February the 1st of last year, a sadistic fugitive he was hunting tortured him to death. It occurred during Fiona's first operation. Her baptism of fire, so to speak. I was fortunate Fiona ignored my instructions to flee, as she saved my backside after I engaged Sal's killers and came off second best. It comforts me to envisage Sal looking down on me. When under pressure, I often contemplate, 'What would Sal do?'

The big sergeant must have sensed my apprehension. "Don't you worry. The men will arrive on time."

On cue, Thomas and Jayden marched into the tower, with Jamal and Yasar not far behind. They may not have been clearance divers or frogmen, but they were ex-military with years of recreational diving experience in these waters. I felt blessed to be surrounded by competent operators as I prepared to enter the fray.

Each man had a Colt M4 Carbine assault rifle strapped to their back. Jamal could not hide his delight when he discovered we were using the M4s. The big American maintained that the Aussie military's F92 Austeyr was a decent rifle, but the M4 was known to be reliable for amphibious work and had smoother mag changes. He also asserted that the F92's sights were next to useless in low light.

It took me ten minutes to brief the men, reinforcing the critical elements of the operation. We then loaded the scuba gear, grapple hooks and rifles into the rear of a ute. The sergeant drove us to the Nelson Point Tug Haven carpark. We found Deuce smoking in the dark, leaning up against an old jeep. One of the men muttered something about Deuce giving away our position. I wasn't too concerned as it was customary for port employees to work all hours of the night with a cigarette hanging from the corner of their mouths.

"You all set, Deuce?" I whispered.

Deuce flicked the butt into the water and raised his thumb, "Does a bear shit in the woods?" he giggled. Deuce must have read my apprehension. "You kept your word with the pardon, and I'll keep mine," he said with a sly grin.

We huddled together and synchronised our watches. "Deuce, set the wheels in motion at 5.35 a.m. as planned. That will give us time to get into position."

All the men looked at Deuce and waited for his response. He quietly chuckled, "Don't worry, boys. Have some trust in old Deuce. This is my wheelhouse."

The sun wasn't due to rise for another twenty minutes. We checked the equipment one last time and then donned our wetsuits and webbing. My stomach was churning as I slipped on the dive boots. We each had four 30-round spare mags for the M4 secured to our webbing, our preferred pistol holstered, and a combat knife sheathed to our belt.

Jamal couldn't help but give me a gentle ribbing when he noticed my 6-shot revolver. "Are you planning on challenging a pirate to a duel, partner?" he joked.

"Nope. A friend of mine told me to shoot first and ask questions later. I was going to ask him why, but I had to shoot him," I replied in my best John Wayne impersonation.

"Why are you using an American accent?" asked Jayden.

"I agree he shouldn't give up his day job, but it's clear he's doing John Wayne," said Jamal.

"Who's John Wayne?" asked Jayden.

"How old are you, twelve?" laughed Jamal.

The friendly banter helped my stomach relax a notch.

I was disappointed to learn the harbourmaster couldn't locate the port's rebreathers, and we didn't have the time to look elsewhere for replacements.

Rebreathers provide a stealth advantage over conventional tanks as they don't exhaust bubbles. The sergeant acquired some steel scuba tanks from the station's seized-property room. I was consoled by the thought that if Deuce did what he promised, the pirates would have greater concerns than searching for our bubbles. Even though the tanks looked well and truly past their used-by date, the sergeant was adamant they would do the job. I hoped for all of our sakes, he was right.

We slipped on our masks, fins, and tanks before checking our buddy's tanks and webbing to ensure all was secure. I gave the thumbs up to my buddy and placed the regulator in my mouth before taking a giant stride from the jetty edge into the warm water. I've been told the temperature in these waters averages 30 degrees Celsius. It was like taking a bath compared to the southern waters I was familiar with. Our destination was about 150 metres the way the crow flies, but we planned to swim 200 metres west before turning north for a further 100 metres towards the starboard side of the Kusa.

Jamal and Jayden were on point with grapple hooks strapped to their backs, followed by Yasar and me, with the sergeant and Thomas at the end of the line. We were swimming at a shallow depth of eight metres, heading for the northern tip of berth deck one. The berth deck was a massive steel structure where the ships moor to load and unload goods, minerals, and fuel. It felt good to be moving towards our target. In my experience, waiting for the operation to commence was always the most challenging part of the mission. The self-doubt and negative thoughts spinning in my mind were energy-sapping. Whereas, once the op began, worries and nerves disappeared, replaced with determination and focus. The mission was everything.

Jamal and Jayden were treading water, patiently waiting for our arrival at the most northern concrete pylon. I removed the regulator from my mouth and checked my watch - 5:35 a.m. The swim had been more taxing than I had anticipated. Clearly, the sergeant also required a moment to recover his breath. I noted with jealousy that the other men were breathing like they had partaken in a relaxing swim.

The pirate's boat looked eerily quiet, the only movement being a lone figure on the bridge, possibly tasked with keeping watch. I was hoping that the pirates' evening was spent drinking the twelve bottles of Johnnie Walker, getting absolutely blotto.

The sergeant whispered breathlessly, "Heads up". We turned towards Nelson Point and witnessed Mrs Fugsly's masthead light flashing on and off five times. It signalled she would be leaving the tug haven in five minutes. And our warning to make our next move.

Jamal spat water out of his mouth and whispered, "Good luck, gentlemen," before reinserting his regulator and descending to a 5-metre depth.

So far, so good - time to execute phase 2 - breaching the Kusa. We followed Jamal towards the stern of the Kusa. We swam the 100-metre leg 'nice and slow' to ensure we weren't gassed for the upcoming fight.

My initial recce failed to give me much insight into the boat's layout. We were fortunate that Yasar had served on an Armidale class boat. His knowledge was invaluable in sketching the vessel's schematics and formulating the plan's breaching phase. I asked Yasar during our one-on-one, "How would you breach this boat?" He smiled and replied, "I've already considered a couple of options."

Yasar's familiarity with the boat's engine room made him the perfect choice to command Bravo Team. His task was to lead the sergeant and Jayden to the starboard side and wait for the signal. Their primary objective was to climb aboard and secure the engine room by any means necessary.

I selected Jamal to lead Alpha Team as he was the most experienced operator in the group. Our objective was to secure the bridge. We swam under the hull and popped up on the port side, close to the stern. As I breached the surface, Jamal was already slipping off his steel tank, letting it sink to the harbour floor. I did the same and then looked up to see the underbelly of the Zodiac. The former chopper pilot, Thomas, gave me the thumbs up after dropping his tank. He followed my lead by pointing his M4 muzzle towards the main deck as we trod water in our fins.

I turned towards Port Hedland and saw Mrs Fugsly approaching the bow of the Kusa with her wheelhouse lights shining and a large white flag flapping in the breeze from her mainmast. The pirate on watch would be expecting the tug to deliver the gold. Just as she was within spitting distance - BOOM! There was a one-second delay. And then another BOOM! Deuce had placed enough ANFO and fuel in Mrs Fugsly to blow the wheelhouse sky-high. He had rigged the steering and set the timer to perfection.

The first explosion was Jamal's cue. He threw the grappling hook over the boat's railing and then tested the tautness of the nylon rope before climbing the ladder. Thomas and I did our best to cover him. If a pirate popped his head over the railing, he was a sitting duck. Then, BOOM! The unexpected third blast startled me, causing me to momentarily lose focus.

"Go up, Archie," Thomas hissed. I swiftly slipped off my fins and swung the M4 over my shoulder. I grabbed the first rung and climbed up the 2.7-metre nylon ladder. When I reached the top, Jamal gripped my webbing and heaved me over the side with the ease of a powerlifter.

As soon as the soles of my dive boots hit the main deck, I reached for my M4, first scanning for threats at the stern and then focusing my attention on the bridge. I couldn't see any pirates, but I could hear men yelling in panic. We were positioned at the stern of the Zodiac, which was hooked up to a crane and hanging a metre off the deck. Jamal, who was on point, commanded, "On me!" Thomas squeezed my shoulder, and we were on the move, advancing to the port midship main access door.

One moment all was quiet, and then all of a sudden, all hell broke loose. The boat's flood lights weren't the only things that lit up. Automatic gunfire erupted. And we were the targets. Rounds pinged and ricocheted off the steel deck. Thomas and Jamal fired in multiple directions while I engaged a pirate shooting at us from the bridge. He fell in a heap as my M4's 5.56 calibre rounds raked his torso and chest.

We used the Zodiac and crane as cover as we returned fire. Meanwhile, three pirates exited the door we planned on entering, firing their AK47s in our direction. We were pinned down. While Thomas and Jamal returned fire, I glanced up to see pirates firing their machine guns from the rear of the bridge.

We were up against superior numbers and firepower. My plan had gone FUBAR! I yelled, "Reloading," and dropped to one knee. I felt Thomas' knee in my back while ear-piercing rounds zipped overhead. As I inserted a new mag, our luck suddenly changed. The three pirates' midship were dispatched when three high-calibre rounds tore into them in quick succession. *You little beauty, Fiona!*

# Chapter Seventeen

*Friday, March 7, 2042 from 4:25 a.m. – Fiona*

I had mixed feelings when Archie took me aside to explain my role as a sniper. I have never had to shoot at multiple targets surrounded by friendlies. When Archie noticed my concern, he said the magic words, "We need you, Fiona." *Expert negotiator, my ass! He's more of an expert manipulator!* I'm not ashamed to admit that I was nervous. I hadn't been trained for this, but I steeled myself for the task ahead and gave myself a much-needed pep talk, *'Toughen the fuck-up princess. Archie and the team are relying on YOU!'*

There is no way I would reveal it to Archie, but I was relieved to learn I wouldn't be diving with the team. I'm petrified of swimming in dark waters with no visibility. And you don't get much murkier than the harbour before sunup.

When I worked as a deckhand on Captain Ross' fishing boat, he told me countless horror stories about shark attacks, including when he received 163 stitches after being chomped by a great white. In my experience, most blokes love telling furphies, but when a fisherman with a hideous scar running from his shoulder to his lower back tells you a shark story, you listen and take notice.

Growing up in Perth and frequenting my local beach in the summer, I was frightfully aware that at least one person a year was attacked and killed by a great white or tiger shark. Sometimes authorities would fail to locate a body, and a day or so later, a piece of the victim's bathers, goggles or surfboard would wash up on the shore. So even knowing I had a greater chance of dying in a car or bike crash during the journey to the beach did nothing to deter my jitters when I took a dip in the ocean.

From my observation position in the storage building, I noticed the pirate boat hadn't moved since Archie's briefing. I had a clear view of the boat's port side but little else. I considered searching for a new spot but then quickly disregarded the idea. There wasn't time. And there was no guarantee I would find a better vantage point anyway.

I lay prone, looking through the rifle scope with the butt resting against my shoulder. The bridge lights were on, but the remainder of the boat was in complete darkness.

I searched for Archie and the team but couldn't sight them. Which was a good thing because if I couldn't see them, neither should the pirates. Patience has never been one of my strong suits. What felt like an hour was barely a fifteen-minute wait. BOOM! BOOM! Bloody Hell! The tug was blown to smithereens. Even though I was anticipating the explosions, it still came as a shock. The windows rattled while I felt a vibration through the timber floor.

Suddenly every fucking light on the boat was switched on. BOOM! Another explosion. Muzzle flashes at the stern caught my eye as a barrage of automatic gunfire reported its intentions to anyone within earshot. 'The killing had commenced.'

Frustratingly I couldn't sight anyone. It was like a bloody war being fought by invisible people. Then, finally, Jamal's head popped up in a flash near the rubber boat and disappeared just as quickly. "Fuck me," I whispered. Where is the rest of the team?

Finally, I had something to aim at. Three pirates exited a midship door and started firing their AKs at the stern, right where I sighted Jamal performing his impression of a jack-in-the-box toy.

I peered down the scope, took a deep breath and then let it out before squeezing the trigger. The .338 round impacted the side of the pirate's head at 940 metres per second, causing his skull to crack like an egg, but instead of yolk, blood and brain matter erupted from the bullet hole as he fell lifelessly to the deck. I immediately pulled the rifle bolt and retook aim. Crack! Another pirate bites the deck.

The rifle felt like an extension of my arm. I actioned the bolt. Aimed. Crack! Strike three. "I'M ON FUCKING FIRE!" I cheered.

The excitement and thrill of the engagement felt like a drug coursing through my veins.

Jamal, Archie, and Thomas disappeared inside the boat through the door the *unfortunate* pirates had just moments before exited. "Ha-ha. Unfortunate to be in my sight picture," I giggled. A pirate sprinted down the deck from the stern towards that very door. *No, you don't.* As he reached for the door handle, he turned toward Port Hedland and paused. Eerily, it was as if he was looking directly at me. I could have sworn time slowed as I squeezed the trigger and shot him right between his eyes, watching with pleasure as his skull exploded. *Now you can join your mates in hell, mutherfucker!*

I scanned the boat's length and glimpsed a fat man with an AK in his grasp climbing a ladder at the stern. I had a side view of his massive gut. I took aim and squeezed the trigger. Fuck a duck! *Missed.* He kept climbing. He gave me a clear shot as he walked to the bridge on the top deck. How stupid is this bloke? He was tapping on the bridge window with his muzzle. I exhaled with my finger on the trigger and whispered, "See ya later, alligator." Crack!

# Chapter Eighteen

*Friday, March 7, 2042 from 5:50 a.m. – Archie*

Thanks to Fiona, the path to our ingress point was clear. Take-Two. Jamal again yelled, "On me," and advanced toward the port midship main access door. Thomas and I fired at pirates positioned outside the bridge as we tailed Jamal. Just within reach of the door, a lanky pirate abruptly stepped out from the doorway with his AK muzzle pointed to the sky. He closed the door behind him and looked towards the bow before turning his head and noticing our approach from the stern. Like the laughing clowns in the sideshow alley game, his mouth formed a huge O. I may have considered his expression comical in another time, place, and circumstance. Instead of feeding a ball into his mouth, Jamal fed him a hail of lead.

Goddamn it! I felt a sudden, painful sting in my backside. Either I had just pulled my gluteus maximus, or I had been shot. There was no time to take a pit stop and check.

Jamal covered the door while Thomas protected our six. Meanwhile, I stepped over the lanky pirate's corpse and pulled the door lever up, opening the heavy steel door. I placed my hand on the back of Jamal's shoulder, and he swiftly entered the boat. I advanced closely behind the big man. We marched down a grey corridor I hadn't had the pleasure of visiting during my recent tour. The corridor width made it tight, with Jamal and I barely able to stand side by side. Without any available cover, we were at the mercy of opposition fire, but on the flip side, only a small number of combatants could engage us simultaneously.

Just as I heard Thomas shut the door behind us, two pirates

armed with AKs ran down the stairs three metres to our right. They had no idea what they were running into. The sound of gunfire was deafening in the enclosed space. I will never forget their expressions of terror as we mowed them down with our M4s.

With Thomas covering our rear, Jamal swiftly cleared the stairs to our left. Even though tactically unwise, I couldn't help but glance at the bullet-riddled pirates who blocked the stairwell. The broad American bellowed, "Clear," and strode past me. "This is the way to the bridge. On me," he instructed. He climbed the stairs and covered the door at the top of the landing while I squeezed past him. I took a deep breath and turned the handle. As soon as I opened the door, Jamal stepped into the corridor without hesitation. I followed him up yet another set of stairs before striding down a four-metre dog leg passageway.

While focusing on the path ahead, Jamal jested, "We've arrived. I hope you enjoyed the tour." Then, he swiftly stepped onto the bridge and engaged pirates to his right while I cleared the left. Meanwhile, Thomas marched straight up the centre.

Multiple gunshots rang through the air to my right as I pointed my muzzle at the pirate captain's head. Julian stood within striking range as he held his Desert Eagle pistol by his leg and his two-way radio near his mouth.

"Put them both on the ground nice and slow, or you're a dead man," I warned.

Once Julian had followed my instructions, I shoved him against a panel of defunct electronic screens and secured his wrists with cable ties. I scanned the room and inspected the carnage. I noted the corpses of the three pirates Jamal had dispatched. Jamal was injury free, while Thomas was not so lucky. He was lying on his back, pressing his hands over his throat in a futile attempt to stop the blood gushing from his wounds. Grief-stricken, Jamal knelt by his side as he passed. Poor bastard, I thought as I shook my head in dismay.

I pushed Julian into the comms chair and pressed the muzzle of my revolver to his forehead. I let out an audible sigh when I noticed an empty bottle of Johnnie Walker sitting near the ship radio. I could really do with a drink, I lamented.

Jamal was back to business, piling the pirates' corpses against the bridge door, creating a morbid but effective defensive position. He was preparing to engage any of Julian's men stupid enough to try and recapture the bridge and rescue their captain.

Julian expressed a knowing smile when he finally recognised me as Johnny, the weakling who boarded his vessel to deliver the whisky and gold. I wasn't in the mood to negotiate, so I didn't allow him the opportunity to spurt any bullshit. Instead, I shoved my Smith and Wesson's muzzle under his jawline with such force that I could feel the cold hard steel pressing against his teeth.

"Get on the radio and order your men to stand down. If you go off-script, I'll splatter your brain all over the bridge," I ordered through gritted teeth.

Julian laughed with false bravado. "Why should I? You're just going to kill me anyway."

Time was of the essence; I didn't want anyone else to lose their life unnecessarily because I failed to seal the deal. So I drew my knife with clear intentions, holding the point of the blade an inch from his one good eye. "My partner and I had a bet on how long it would take to make your cousin talk. She timed me as I severed Henry's ears. It took just fifteen seconds." I had extinguished Julian's bravado. "I'm confident I can break the new record." I glanced at my watch. "I'll start with your nose and then your balls. I'll leave your eye until last so you can witness my handiwork before I blind you."

If Fiona was here, she would say something like, 'Shit just got real for Julian'.

Julian looked like he was about to puke all over the bridge. "You're, You're, fucking crazy," he stammered.

I held the boat's comms transmitter to Julian's mouth as he ordered, "This is your captain. Drop your weapons and stand down. I repeat, stand down." He then repeated the order in Malay.

I removed the radio from my webbing and tore open the plastic bag. "Bravo team, this is Alpha team. Can you read me? Seeking a sitrep."

"Crshhh, Roger. Alpha team receiving. We have secured the engine room. Crshhh. Five enemy combatants KIA. One captive."

"Roger. Stay in position. Wait for further instructions," I transmitted.

"Roger."

I located a radio on the captain's chair and confirmed the correct channel before pressing the button to transmit. "Good. Now radio your men on the tanker and tell them you have the gold. Then, order them to leave the crew alive and disembark the tanker."

"That wasn't the original plan. They're going to think something's up. They would've seen the explosion and heard the gunfire," Julian whined.

I recalled peering through the binos at the tanker and witnessing a pirate shoot a poor hostage. I couldn't hear a thing. Not even a distant pop. But surely they heard the explosions. I manoeuvred the knife closer to his eye, "Make it believable, Julian. Tell them you blew up the tug. Draw on your thespian abilities. Your life depends on it."

Julian squirmed in his seat. "Ajimin, can you hear me? Ajimin, are you there?"

"Yes, boss man. I'm here," his henchman transmitted from the tanker.

"Change of plans. We have the gold. I've done a deal with the gweilos. Leave the ship and do not harm the captives. Meet us twenty-five kilometres north. And Ajimin, we will be back to plunder, so do as I say, or it will be very bad for you."

I was about to ask Julian if he had squirrelled away a bottle of Johnnie Walker when I saw an obese man tapping on a port window with his AK. He rested his palm on the pane and peered through the tinted glass with a stupid look on his face. Knowing that the windows were bulletproof, I felt more baffled than concerned. Ah, I recognise you, Bintang! The pirate that had slapped me around the ears was standing dumbstruck in front of the window. His jaw dropped before gaping holes suddenly appeared on both sides of his neck. I had seen this before. He had been shot with a large calibre round, almost severing his fat head from his body. It was obviously

Fiona's handiwork.

I felt all the built-up tension release as I took a deep breath and slowly exhaled, feeling my stomach loosen a couple of notches and the weight lift from my shoulders. As expected, the adrenaline was dissipating, and fatigue was setting in. While watching the sunrise through the tinted windows, I radioed the shipping tower and provided a sitrep, confirming that we had successfully secured the bridge and engine room. The harbourmaster executed phase three of the plan by instructing four tugs of armed men ready and waiting to approach and board the Kusa.

# Chapter Nineteen

*Friday, March 7, 2042 from 7 a.m. – Archie*

On arrival at the wharf, we received a hero's welcome, with a hundred or more civilians cheering and hollering out their congratulations and gratitude. It was both unexpected and quite embarrassing. A young lady planted a kiss on my cheek, and an elderly man shook my hand as kids ran around my feet and members of the crowd patted my back and shoulders. Jamal and Yasar received similar treatment, with the American's infectious booming laugh placing a smile on the faces around him.

The sergeant skirted around the crowd with the recovered duffle bag of gold hanging from his broad shoulders. He expertly avoided attention as he escorted Jayden, with his head lowered and his wrists secured behind his back with cable ties. When Jayden learned that Thomas was dead, he threatened a murderous rampage, demanding Julian and the two surviving pirates be immediately executed on the deck of the patrol boat. The sergeant argued that a trial was necessary as he didn't have the legislative power to conduct an execution, and the public wouldn't stand for it. When his attempt to reason with Jayden fell on deaf ears, he was forced to disarm and restrain him. I empathised with Jayden, but the sergeant had made the right decision.

The sergeant later explained that Jayden and Thomas were partners with a long history. Poor bastard! I know what it's like to spiral into the abyss when losing a loved one.

The constables escorted the captured pirates to the police station lock-up. Meanwhile, a harbour pilot was sent to the tanker to guide and secure the vessel to the berth deck. Much to the relief of the authorities and civilians, the fuel was safe and secure.

A core group of port employees volunteered to go after the pirates who had disembarked the tanker and escaped in a fishing trawler. However, the harbourmaster dismissed the idea as folly. He explained that without radar, it would be like finding a needle in a haystack.

As I weaved through the crowd to speak with Fiona, a young man hollered, "Extra! Extra! Read all about it! Pirates defeated!" and shoved a copy of the Pilbara Times in front of my face. Fiona placed a silver coin in the boy's hand and held up the newspaper's front page. I was horrified to see my face covering a quarter of the page. "Bloody reporter," I fumed.

"You're famous," Fiona teased.

"I'll tell you this. I wouldn't want to be that reporter after the sergeant reads this."

"He's just doing his job. And besides, at least he got your good side," she giggled at my expense.

I threw the newspaper in the nearest bin as we moseyed over to a vendor selling coffee. I bought us a much-needed long black. As we walked to the station and sipped our coffees, I asked, "I'm guessing you dispatched the three pirates on the port side. And Bintang must have been one of yours."

"Bintang?" Fiona asked, perplexed.

"Obese bloke tapping on the window outside the bridge," I clarified.

"Oh, yeah. I took out five in total. I got one sneaking up on you just before you entered the boat."

"Bloody good shooting, mate."

I was genuinely impressed and thankful she was there to cover our backsides. Which reminded me of my injury. There was a small hole in my wetsuit right in the middle of my right bum cheek. While waiting for the tugs on the Kuza, I applied a bandage over the wound to stop the bleeding. It didn't hurt that much. It was just painful to the touch.

Fiona turned around and noticed me inspecting my rear. "Have you been shot?"

"Yeah, I reckon I have."

"I'll take a look at it when we get back to the station. My pack is still at the sergeant's place."

I wasn't too keen on Fiona inspecting my rear end. "It's okay. I'll stop by the hospital after we've fuelled up."

"Don't be silly. It'll only take five minutes. It might just be a flesh wound. We don't want to waste the doctor's time, do we?" she said with a cheeky smile. Great, just great, I thought to myself.

We stepped through the station door and were met by the sergeant at the front counter. He shook our hands in gratitude. "It's been hectic. That's my excuse for not yet thanking you both. You did a bloody fantastic job, and it's appreciated by all of us, even if certain officials aren't here to thank you in person. Anyway, we need to talk, so let's head to the crib room."

We sat at the crib room table. "Would you both like a coffee?" the sergeant offered.

Fiona shook her head, "No thanks, Sarge, I'm keen on getting some shut-eye."

Even though I had just finished a cup, I struggled to keep my eyes from shutting. "If you're serving up that middle-east blend, I'd love one."

I sat on the edge of the chair with my right ass cheek hanging over the side, carefully avoiding placing pressure on the awkwardly positioned wound. Upon reflection, I could *almost* sympathise with the pain and indignity the recently promoted Sergeant Atkins felt after being shot in his posterior. But not quite. After all, I wasn't shot in the process of running away from a fight.

The sergeant sat at the table and was about to speak when yelling emanated from the cells.

"CONSTABLE, IF THE PRISONERS' WON'T SHUT THE HELL UP, HOSE 'EM DOWN," the sergeant bellowed, his moustache bristling with anger.

I winced in pain as I almost jumped out of my seat. It was the first time I had heard the big man yell, and I was glad I wasn't on the receiving end.

"Sorry about that. Prisoners that are due to hang either sit in quiet contemplation or panic and go stir-crazy," the sergeant explained.

"Sarge, I don't want to appear pushy, but I'm keen on collecting our fuel and getting a move on. As the saying goes, we have places to be and people to see."

The sergeant deflected my request, "I asked Jamal to escort Jayden to the cattle station and stay with him until the trial is concluded."

"The trial's in session today?" I asked, genuinely surprised.

"Yep, we run a tight ship here. With Jayden and Jamal obviously unavailable and Yasar preparing the captured patrol boat in case the pirates return, you'll need to *hang around* and give testimony. Pardon the pun."

Neither of us smiled at his unsuccessful attempt at levity. "It's time we should be going," I said apologetically.

"I understand. And I know we are testing your patience, but I promise, as soon as the hearing is over, I'll give you enough fuel to travel around the entire country," he said reassuringly.

In my experience, it's rare for bounty hunters to be summonsed to attend court. In fact, since the end of my law career, I've only set foot in a courtroom on two occasions.

One of those said occasions involved a violent confrontation between two landowners. The defendant hired me to negotiate a settlement with his neighbour. He accused his neighbour of stealing a portion of his land when he erected new fencing. Initial negotiations were promising, but when they stalled over the cost of restitution, my client decided to take matters into his own hands. After a night of heavy drinking at his local, he knocked on his neighbour's front door and shot him in the foot when he answered, causing his foe to lose three toes. I was summonsed to appear in court to testify for the defence. I obviously tilted my testimony in favour of my client, assisting his lawyer in arguing a defence of provocation and temporary insanity. Although, I thought he had 'Buckley's chance' of convincing the Judge.

During one of my university legal lectures, I was interested to learn the origins of the 'Buckley's chance' saying. After being convicted of receiving a bolt of stolen cloth, Englishmen, William Buckley, was sentenced to transportation to the British penal colony (Australia) in 1802. Less than two months after arriving, the six-foot-five, long-haired convict escaped under gunfire into the bush. Despite dire predictions he had perished in the outback, he survived by living with the Aboriginal Wathaurong people for thirty-two years. Then, in 1835, he strolled into a settler's camp wearing kangaroo skins and carrying Aboriginal weapons. He received a pardon shortly after his reappearance and then worked as an interpreter before settling in Tasmania. He was a fortunate man indeed.

After hearing the verdict, I was positive my client didn't leave his fate to chance like old Buckley. He was treated with kid gloves, receiving a mere two weeks in the lock-up and ordered to pay two ounces of gold in reparations to the complainant. Shortly after the trial, I heard on the grapevine the Judge had purchased a forty-foot yacht. *I wonder where he found the funds for his new toy.*

The only other occasion I was required to front the court was because of an incident at the York Hotel in Kalgoorlie. While enjoying a pint and minding my own business, I witnessed a well-known hustler named Frank Gillard accuse a young shearer of cheating during a poker game. The young man cleaned Frank out after being dealt a royal flush.

Gillard abruptly stood from the table, placed his hand on the grip of his pistol and called the young shearer out. The kid refused and remained seated, declaring he won fair and square and didn't want to fight. My excuse for getting involved in the dispute was threefold; Gillard was a known bully whom I detested, I felt sorry for the kid, and as I later confessed to the court, I was somewhat inebriated at the time. In front of the voyeurs, I hollered, "Stop being a sore loser, Gillard. Leave the kid alone." Gillard's cheeks reddened with anger, and he raised the stakes by demanding that I act as the kid's proxy. It's an unwritten rule that the person being 'called out' can select the form of combat – gunfight, knife-fight, or fist-fight. I stupidly agreed and caused laughter in the crowd after I loudly belched, excused myself, and bombastically announced, "I choose fishes. I mean fists." Gillard rushed forward and punched me in the eye before I countered with a hook to his jaw, causing him to fall backwards and strike his head against the corner of the oak bar.

Unfortunately for all involved, he carked it two hours later. I was accused of murder and ended up in court before the local Judge. Six patrons, including the young shearer at the centre of the affair, stated under oath that I had partaken in a fair fight. Even though I knew I was on the right side of the law, I was immensely relieved when the Judge's gavel hit the jarrah sound block and grumbled, 'Not guilty.'

My reverie was interrupted when Fiona asked, "Sarge, can we use your house? Archie has an injury that I need to attend to."

"Of course," he replied to Fiona before turning to me and asking, "Why didn't you say so, man?"

"It's just a scratch," I lied, waving him off. I was making every effort to avoid telling him the location of the wound.

"Thanks, Sarge. He's been shot in the ass," Fiona clarified before chuckling. While I glared at her, the sergeant did his best to hide a smirk.

As I cleaned my cup in the sink, the sergeant handed Fiona a key to his annex. "Once you're done, meet me back at the station. If he needs to go to the hospital, speak to a nurse named Aria and tell her the station is taking care of the bill."

We moseyed next door and unlocked the front door of the sergeant's home. "You get ready in the loungeroom while I grab my first aid kit," she ordered.

She was back in a jiffy, carrying her first aid kit, a bowl of hot water, a clean sheet, and a towel hanging over her shoulder.

"Why aren't you ready? Get your gear off," she instructed.

She laid a sheet on the carpet and pointed to it like a drill instructor commanding me to drop and give her twenty. I expelled a loud sigh, dropped my pants and was about to lay down on the sheet when she raised an eyebrow, "And your boxers."

"Well, turn around then," I pleaded.

She laughed, "You're like a bloody kid."

After she turned toward the opposite wall, I quickly stripped and lay face down on the sheet.

"Jesus Christ!" she exclaimed.

"What? What's wrong?" I asked, genuinely concerned.

"Your ass. It's like a bloody round peach. How do I get an ass like that? Are you doing extra squats or lunges? Tell me your secret."

"Ah, I don't know whether you're taking the piss or not, but can you please get this over with," I urged.

I felt her fingers probing the wound. "Good news. It must have just been a bit of shrapnel whizzing past. All you'll need is five or six stitches. And you'll have another scar to show off to the laaadies!"

I could feel the needle piercing my skin as Fiona joked, "Hey, now you and Atkins have something in common."

"Be careful. Next time we wrestle, I'll choke you out," I warned.

"Promises, promises," she snickered.

"Arrghh," I groaned when she poked the needle through my skin.

I couldn't help but turn my grimace into a smile. I was happy that we had moved on after the messy situation on the highway.

# Chapter Twenty

*Friday, March 7, 2042 from 10 a.m. – Fiona*

We both cleaned up and had brekky before ambling to the station. The sergeant's fridge was something to behold – eggs, bacon, cheese, milk, steak, and a wide selection of vegetables and fruit. Meat and dairy products are luxury food groups for the average person. The port must subsidise his living expenses, as there is no way in hell he could afford to eat this well on a police officer's wage.

As we strolled past the lock-up to the crib room, we noticed the prisoners had been removed from the cells. We bumped into the sergeant in the hallway. He was smartly dressed in his police uniform, a navy-blue jacket with silver buttons and a white peaked hat. He was carrying a large black leather briefcase. During the drive to court, he informed us that the prisoners had been transported to the court cells.

The court was situated in South Hedland opposite an old run-down motel. It was a single-story red brick building with Aboriginal artwork painted along the facade. A boisterous crowd of at least 200 people were milling around in front of the court. Food and coffee vendors were plying their trade while a bunch of kids played backyard cricket on the roadway, with a bin substituted as wickets.

Workers were busily finalising the erection of the jarrah gallows in the motel's parking lot. Most WA towns use portable gallows constructed from wood or galvanised steel that can be assembled on short notice. I pondered the reaction of patrons who had booked a motel room for a romantic evening, only to awake and peer outside their windows to discover a raucous crowd awaiting an execution. It would certainly spoil my morning.

As we entered the court, the sergeant acknowledged the two constables standing guard. The gallery was packed, with people from all walks of life awaiting the start of the trial. The sergeant approached the court clerk, a lady in her late thirties wearing black-rimmed glasses, with her hair pulled so tight in a bun that her skin was stretched from hairline to brow. She was standing behind a jarrah desk positioned below the Judge's bench, busily flicking through files of paperwork.

The no-nonsense clerk craned her head back to gain eye contact with the towering sergeant, "Good Morning, Theodore. Are you ready to prosecute your case?"

"Indeed I am. I instructed Constable Shepherdson to deliver the prosecution brief."

The clerk frowned while she flicked through her files. "Yes, I have it here. But I haven't had a chance to review it as I was only advised about the case forty-five minutes ago. The Judge is still getting dressed in his chambers, and the defence counsel is meeting with the defendants," she snapped in frustration.

The sergeant rubbed the back of his neck with his enormous palm, "I apologise, Margaret, but it was out of my control. The mayor wants this dealt with as soon as possible."

The clerk tutted in reply and continued to compile the court documents in preparation for the hearing. Seeing the sergeant intimidated by someone half his size was odd but quite amusing at the same time. Finally, a greasy-looking gentleman sporting slicked-back ginger hair strolled over to the clerk's desk. His crisp cream suit failed to hide his ample pot belly.

He nodded in the clerk's direction before shaking the sergeant's hand. "Is this your first witness, Theo?" he asked while pointing his thumb at Archie.

"This is Archie O'Connor. He's the only witness I plan on calling. I doubt I'll need anyone else. But if required, I've entered several people on the witness list. Have you had a chance to speak to the defendants?"

Archie raised his eyebrows, adjusted his collar, and looked

towards the gallery. He appeared uncharacteristically nervous. He hates being the centre of attention.

The ginger lawyer adjusted his collar. "I've had the displeasure of listening to their pleading, whining and crying attempts to bribe the Judge. The sooner we get this over and done with, the sooner I can visit a new client of mine. She's a widow who's in dire need of legal assistance in the settlement of a will. It should be an eventful afternoon, if you know what I mean," he exuberantly chortled, causing his chin to wag and his belly to bounce.

*What a fucking grotesque jerk! He made me want to vomit!*

The clerk stood and faced the gallery. "All stand for the Honourable Judge Bodey," she hollered in a surprisingly loud voice.

With the support of a cane, an elderly gentleman wearing a red robe and a white wig limped into the courtroom. While he settled behind the bench, placing on his glasses and thumbing through a pile of paperwork, I noticed his wig was fitted at an odd angle, and he had a three-day growth of white whiskers.

"You may be seated," the clerk advised the citizens in the gallery.

The sergeant directed Archie and me to sit in the front row of the gallery in seats I presumed had been reserved for witnesses. He then opened his briefcase on the smooth jarrah surface of a long thin table that faced the Judge's bench. To the left of him, at the other end of the table, sat the defence lawyer slumped over an old brown satchel.

"Good morning, Your Honour. I'll be prosecuting the case before you today," the sergeant boomed.

"Thank you, Sergeant. And make sure you speak up. You know I'm hard of hearing," instructed the Judge gruffly.

I wondered if hearing aids were on the list of electronic devices disabled by the EMPs during the War.

The sleazy lawyer grudgingly stood from his seat. "Good morning, Your Honour. I'll be representing the accused," he shouted.

"Very well, Mr Smith. Bring in the defendants, Constable. And this is a poignant time to remind the citizens in the gallery that if there is any untoward behaviour, I will have the constables remove you from the court."

One of the constables left the courtroom for a brief moment before returning with three defendants shuffling behind him in chains secured to their wrists and ankles. Captain Julian, his cousin Henry, and his one remaining crew member were seated in the dock.

"When you're ready, Sergeant, call your first witness, if you will."

The sergeant turned around and gestured to Archie. Archie marched to the witness box and remained standing while the clerk approached him with a Bible. Archie placed his palm on the cover. "I swear by Almighty God that the evidence I shall give in this case shall be the truth, the whole truth and nothing but the truth."

After Archie sat down, the sergeant rose from his seat. "Please tell the court your full name and address."

"Archie Dae O'Connor. I currently have no fixed place of abode."

"Mr O'Connor, what do you currently do for a living?"

"I'm a registered bounty hunter."

"Did the Mayor of Port Hedland engage your services to assist her in removing pirates threatening the port?"

"Yes, that is correct."

"Did you meet with Captain Julian Jun Feng on the afternoon of the sixth of March?"

"Yes, I did."

"Is the defendant present in this court, and if so, please point to him."

Archie pointed at Julian, who was sitting nervously in the dock.

The sergeant turned to the Judge, "Please let the court record show that the witness is pointing to Julian Jun Feng, one of the defendants present in court."

The Judge slowly lifted his head. "Yes, thank you, Sergeant."

The sergeant approached the witness box. "Mr O'Connor, please explain to the court what occurred during your interaction with the defendant, Mr Julian Jun Feng and his crew on the afternoon of the sixth of March up until this morning."

You could hear a pin drop in the gallery for the first twenty minutes of Archie's testimony. He detailed what occurred during their first meeting on the main deck to the moment he breached the boat's bridge and arrested Julian. Near the end of his evidence, when he described Thomas' death, there were sudden gasps and sobs from the gallery crowd. The three defendants sat in the dock with anxious expressions.

Once Archie had answered the sergeant's questions, the defence lawyer placed his meaty hands on the sturdy table, awkwardly rose from his chair, and trudged toward the witness box.

The lawyer theatrically turned his gaze from Archie to the crowd and then back to Archie. "Mr O'Connor, are you a killer?"

"Excuse me?" Archie asked, clearly taken aback by the question.

"You heard me, Mr O'Connor. Are....you....a....killer?"

The big sergeant stood from his seat as quick as a whip. "I object, Your Honour. What is the relevance of my learned friend's question?"

When the Judge failed to reply, the crowd reacted with giggles and muffled speech. To put it kindly, the old fella appeared to be resting his eyes.

"Judge, I OBJECT!" the sergeant thundered in a blatant attempt to wake him.

The Judge moved his shoulders from side to side and lifted his head like an old bird ruffling his feathers. "What was that, Sergeant? Speak up."

The lawyer butted in, "Disregard, Your Honour. I withdraw the question."

"Mr O'Connor, did you witness any defendants kill anyone?"

"No, Sir, but as I stated during my evidence-in-chief, just after my initial conversation with Julian Feng, I was forced to watch the execution of two crew members on board the tanker through a pair of binoculars."

"Judge, I have no further questions for this witness," the lawyer stated as he returned to his seat.

"Sergeant, would you like to re-examine your witness?" the old Judge asked.

"No, Your Honour."

"Mr Smith, do you have any witnesses?"

"Your honour, I would like to call Julian Feng," the lawyer replied in a confident tone.

"Very well, Constable, please unchain the defendant and escort him to the witness box."

The constable gripped Julian's arm as he led him to the witness box and stood beside him as he took a seat.

The lawyer cleared his throat, "Mr Feng, have you ever killed a man, woman or child?"

"Never have, Sir, and never will."

I whispered to Archie, "He'll never have a chance to kill anyone, as he'll be hanging from a noose before the end of the day."

Archie whispered back, "Don't get your hopes up. Anything can happen with this old Judge. I think he may be a tad senile. I feel sorry for the coppers if he gives a 'not guilty' verdict. There'll be a bloody riot."

The defence lawyer paraded in front of the court like an overweight peacock. "Have you ever ordered a crew member to kill anyone?"

"Never, Sir," he responded like butter wouldn't melt in his mouth.

The lawyer's questions provided Julian with an opportunity to deny all wrongdoing. At one stage, I thought he would recommend the pirate captain for the 'citizen of the year' award. They were two peas in a pod. Slithering serpents, both of them.

The sergeant stood from his table and approached the witness box to begin his cross-examination.

"Mr Feng, prior to your arrest, were you the Captain of the Kusa?"

Julian looked at his lawyer with uncertainty. The sergeant continued, "Mr Feng, I have statements from your fellow accused. Please answer the question."

"Ah, yes," he replied nervously.

The sergeant turned to the Judge. "Your Honour, I have no further questions for the defendant."

Pre-empting the Judge's question, the lawyer stated that he had no further questions for the defendant and would not be calling other witnesses.

I was shocked that the sergeant didn't ask Julian any further questions. "Why didn't the sergeant drill him with questions?" I whispered to Archie.

"He doesn't need to. Under international maritime law, the captain is ultimately responsible for protecting the crew and passengers from injury."

There was a murmur through the crowd, with most people sitting on the edge of their seats while the sergeant and lawyer provided their final submissions. The defence lawyer argued that the prosecution could not prove beyond a reasonable doubt that the defendants' had killed anyone. He spoke for less than five minutes and appeared to be just going through the motions.

The sergeant simply stated that as Captain of the Kusa, Julian was responsible for his crew, and it was apparent to all present in court that all three defendants had committed the offence of terrorism.

The Judge coughed loudly into his fist and banged his gavel. "After hearing all of the evidence brought before me today, I find the defendant Julian Jun Feng, guilty of murder and terrorism. I find the defendant Wiranata Park guilty of murder and terrorism. Finally, I find the defendant, Henry Bao Feng, guilty of terrorism."

The gallery erupted with jubilation, with members of the crowd standing and clapping while Julian stared into the distance with a terrified expression. Henry was sobbing into his palms. The crew member, Wiranata Park, was hit with a baton over the back of his head when he attempted to desperately escape his chains.

The Judge shouted with all his might as he grabbed his chest, "BE QUIET!" He took a deep breath before continuing. "Sergeant, are there any submissions relating to punishment?"

"The Town of Port Hedland would like to see the death penalty for Mr Julian Feng and Mr Park. I have spoken with my learned friend. It has been agreed that the state would recommend to the court that Mr Henry Feng receives twenty-five years hard labour due to the assistance he provided the authorities in apprehending his fellow convicted felons."

Julian stared daggers at his cousin before he suddenly leapt forwards with his fingers extended toward his neck, only to be prevented from carrying out his attack by the restraints securing his wrists to his ankles.

The Judge yelled, "Control Mr Feng this instant, Constable."

The constable swiftly knocked Julian into submission with his steel baton.

"Thank you, Constable. Now, where were we?" the Judge asked with a confused expression.

"Sentencing, Your Honour," the sergeant reminded him.

"Ah, yes. Very well. The court hereby sentences Mr Julian Feng and Mr Wiranata Park to be hanged by their neck until they are dead. Mr Henry Feng is to serve twenty-five years of hard labour, with no opportunity for parole. Thank you, Clerk. That is all for the day."

The officious clerk stood and bellowed to the gallery, "All rise."

Archie and I stood with the crowd as the Judge shuffled out the rear door, most likely to go for a nap. The constables then led the three defendants to the court cells while we waited for the sergeant to pack his briefcase.

The defence lawyer patted the sergeant on the back of his shoulder. "I'll see you later, Theodore." He then turned to face Archie and said, "Sorry about the line of questioning. I must at least make it look like I'm trying to get them off. After all, I do have a reputation to uphold."

I almost scoffed at the absurdity of his suggestion. *Reputation? What, for being a sleazy, slippery liar?*

We followed the sergeant and the remaining crowd from the courthouse, where we were confronted with a carnival-like atmosphere. Several barbeques were erected on the front lawn, deck chairs and picnic rugs were occupied by people drinking beer, and kids played cricket in the street. The executioner, wearing his black hood, was standing beside the gallows with his chest out and hands on his hips. He was waiting for the convicted men to be brought before him so he could commence the show.

"Are you two planning on watching the hanging?" the sergeant asked as he surveyed the crowd with an eagle eye.

"Nah. You've seen one, you've seen them all," I replied, knowing that Archie would be in agreeance.

When a felon has been convicted of killing a friend or someone I've worked with, I'd usually be at the front of the crowd to watch them hang. Archie preferred to be anywhere else, which was generally waiting for me at the pub. He believes I've seen too many people hang. He reckons that witnessing violence and death can cause you mental harm. I don't believe in any of that, as I've never had trouble sleeping after an execution. My thoughts returned to the present when I reflexively snapped out my arm and plucked a tennis ball out of the air that had been slogged for six by a skinny kid swinging an age-old cricket bat. I immediately threw it back to the twelve-year-old bowler. I might disagree with Archie's opinion on watching a hanging, but that doesn't mean I think you should bring your kids.

Every hanging pretty much follows the same format. The executioner places a noose around the felon's neck before pushing them off the gallows platform. If luck is on their side, the jolt at the end of the six-foot drop breaks their neck and severs their spinal cord, ensuring a merciful death. If they're not so fortunate, they'll experience painful strangulation that may last up to twenty minutes. I've witnessed hangings where family members have rushed forward to mercifully pull down on their loved one's feet to release them from their suffering. Then, just before death, their bodies twitch, and their bowels release before the jeering crowd. As I mentioned, the gallows is definitely not a place for children.

The sergeant threw Archie the keys to his vehicle. "Take my car and head back to my place. I'll sort you out with the fuel as soon I return. This will take about two hours by the time we pack up and complete the paperwork. If I were you, I'd get some sleep before you leave. You can stay at my joint as long as you want."

The aroma of sausages on a street vendor's grill was a temptation we couldn't ignore, so before we left the festivities, we bought a couple of hotdogs and a beer to wash it down.

I had just finished my dog when the tenacious reporter appeared to pop out of thin air. "Can I get a photo of you for the local rag, Mr

O'Connor?"

The irritated expression on Archie's face was priceless. "Go on, Archie. Don't be a spoilsport," I said, rubbing it in.

"Sure, why not," Archie said, taking me by surprise. He then smiled and wrapped his arm around my shoulders. "This is Fiona Katsaros. She was a pivotal part of the operation."

*Damn, I thought. I stepped into that one.*

Before the reporter took the picture, I said, "Hang on," and used the tip of my sleeve to wipe sauce from Archie's chin. "You're like a bloody child," I joked.

*SNAP*. "Thanks for your time. The article will be in tomorrow's edition," explained the reporter.

"Just make sure you spell her name correctly. Fiona Katsaros. K...A...T...S...A...R...O...S," Archie clarified.

As Archie drove slowly down the street in the sergeant's wheels, we saw the constables escorting Julian and his mate through the crowd to the awaiting executioner. The cheerful mayor strolled arm-in-arm with the harbourmaster to the gallows to watch the show. *What a romantic evening! Not!*

# Chapter Twenty-One

*Saturday, March 8, 2042 from 4:45 a.m. – Archie*

I woke at the sparrow's fart and peered at my watch: 4:45 a.m. The sergeant's annex was blissfully quiet. Fiona was snoring like a trooper and constantly tossing and turning on the springy bed, so I retreated to the loungeroom and spent the night on the three-seater couch. I yawned and stretched my aching back and shoulders before quietly making my way to Fiona's bedroom. I gently knocked on the door. Fiona whispered, "Come in." We presumed the sergeant was asleep in the master bedroom and didn't want to wake him.

We grabbed our gear and crept down the entrance hall. As Fiona opened the front door, I placed a note and a pack of old playing cards on the dining table, thanking the sergeant for his hospitality. The sergeant had mentioned that he was a keen gin rummy player. I had won the novelty pack in a poker game a few years back. Each card displayed a picture of a naked woman in an erotic pose. They had been sitting at the bottom of my bag as I couldn't imagine showing them to Fiona. It's not as if I thought she'd be offended. I just didn't want to give her ammunition to take the piss out of me: *'Do you think the boobs on the ace of spades are natural?', 'Do you prefer a big ass like the king of clubs or a smaller ass like the queen of hearts?'*

The sergeant was a man of his word, our petrol tank was full, and we had an additional 100 litres of fuel stored in five 20-litre jerry cans in the Beast's boot. Within moments we were back on the road, heading north to Broome. If all goes to plan, which it rarely does (Bloody Murphy), the 610-kilometre journey should take about seven hours. Out of habit, I looked for a piece of wood to touch.

To make up for lost time, we decided to drive in shifts, with Fiona resting while I took the wheel for the first leg of the journey. We planned to make a quick stop off in Broome to fuel up, get some tucker, and then get straight back on the road. Fiona would drive the second leg to Kununurra while I caught up on some shut-eye.

The first leg was blissfully uneventful. I tapped my finger on the wheel and bobbed my head to David Bowie's lyrics while scanning ahead for human scavengers. Fiona's shottie lay at her feet, with her head resting against the side door panel as she snored for most of the trip.

During World War Two, Japanese Zero Fighter planes attacked Broome on four occasions, conducting strafing runs in the town centre. Almost ninety years later, they were incredibly fortunate to be spared the devastation of a missile attack during World War Three. Still, like most towns, their economy and livelihoods were utterly devastated. Before the War, tourists would flock to Broome to ride camels over the vast sweeping beaches under the cloudless blue sky and visit the pearl farms to learn about their 150-year-old industry. The ancient red rock cliffs jutting above the pure white sand and turquoise water of the Indian Ocean were among the many postcard images used to convince tourists to visit and spend their holiday dollars.

One of my more pleasurable duties at McGlennon and Graff Legal was meeting VIPs at the Broome International Airport and chauffeuring them to Matso's Brewery to wine and dine them. Memories of sitting outside with a view of the ocean while I sipped on a Mango beer and munched on tuna tempura in the hot, humid climate seemed like a lifetime ago. But, like many others, I took the simple pleasures for granted.

We arrived in Broome just after lunch. I'm not exactly sure what I expected, but I certainly didn't envisage a ghost town. The buildings on the main street were either boarded up or dilapidated shells of their former glory. Except for a couple of wild dogs roaming the streets, the town was completely deserted. I didn't even bother stopping as we passed the town's two petrol stations. Their smashed windows and missing bowsers indicated they had been ransacked long ago. I parked the car out the front of the old outdoor cinema, pressed stop on the tape deck and wound down the window to listen for any human activity. All I could hear was the wind, a dog yelping in the far distance, and Fiona snoring like a drunken sailor.

I decided to take a quick trip down memory lane and drive to Matso's. I parked the Beast on Carnarvon Street opposite the brewery and sat on the bonnet while I gazed at my former drinking hole. There are times when I feel a sense of gloom, like last year when I looked upon the Perth CBD for the first time since it had been nuked. It's irrational to compare a derelict brewery with the destruction of a capital city. Nonetheless, I was heartbroken as I inspected Matso's smashed windows and crumbling walls. I thought of my dream of owning a brewery and wondered if the liquor tanks, pumps, boilers, and chillers could be salvaged. My daydream was disturbed when Fiona yawned like a bear that had just woken from six months of hibernation.

"What's wrong?" she asked as she rubbed the sleep from her eyes.

"Nothing, I was just taking a trip down memory lane," I explained wistfully.

My eyes were drawn to an old Aboriginal man ambling towards us on the opposite side of the street. He was carrying a fishing rod and wearing a dirty singlet, ripped stubby shorts and a pair of thongs held together by gaffer tape. Around his waist, he wore a thin leather belt with a fishing knife sheathed near his right hip. I slid off the bonnet and stepped towards him with my hand raised in greeting.

"Hey mate, my name's Archie. How ya going?"

He stopped and looked warily in our direction as his hand slowly drifted to the handle of his knife. He ignored my question and continued his journey with one eye focused on me.

Fiona jumped out of the car. "Excuse me, Sir, do you know where we can get some fuel?"

The old fella stopped dead in his tracks and scrutinised us. "Are you monarch?" he asked as he ran his fingers through his thick grey beard.

Fiona turned to me and shrugged her shoulders with a quizzical expression. Over the years, my best mate Clarry has taught me a few Noongar words, which wouldn't help me in the slightest if this bloke were from Broome, as this is home to the Yawuru people. Fortunately, slang words like 'monarch' are used across nations. Pronounced like 'arch' as in 'archway', the term is a derivative of the 'English Monarchy' to describe the white men that arrived on their shores in 1788 and enforced the King's Laws. In the modern-day, the Aboriginal people use 'Monarch' to refer to police officers.

"Nah, we're not coppers. But we are bounty hunters."

I considered omitting our occupation, as hunters are not highly regarded in the Aboriginal community. Still, something about this bloke's cautious demeanour made me think that he'd read me like a book if I tried to put one past him.

"You need fuel. I know where to get plenty of fuel. You take me to my camp, and I'll show you."

"What do you want in return?" I asked.

"Take me to my camp, and I'll show you," he repeated.

"How many of your mob are at the camp?"

"My daughter and grandchild. I could use your help in shooting some vermin."

"What type of vermin?"

"Dangerous ones," he replied cryptically.

I felt like I was playing twenty questions with the cagey old fella, but I figured we didn't have any other options. Even though he'd be lucky to weigh more than fifty kilograms dripping wet, I was still concerned that he might knife us in the back on the way to his camp, so I asked him to sit alongside Fiona in the back seat. His rod protruded precariously out the window. I had no reason to distrust him, but as Sal preached – 'Don't trust anyone!'

On the way to his camp, he finally introduced himself. "I'm Johani Haji-noor. Your name's Archie?"

"Yep, Archie O'Connor."

"Why you have a wadjela name? Where you come from?" he asked me in a curious tone as he pointed at my dark brown skin.

He was asking me why I had a white fella's name, which I didn't take offence to. Due to my Irish name, I was often asked about my family origins. This was before the War when everyone was fixated on their identity. People have more significant concerns now, like where they'll get their next meal and what someone's willing to do to take it from them. Johani was just gathering information so he could decide whether to trust us. I gave him the same explanation I give anyone who asks.

"My Grandfather was a white man, my grandmother was a black woman, and my mum was Asian. So I'm what my grandad's generation would call a mongrel."

Johani nodded thoughtfully and squeezed my bicep. "That's good. Mongrels are strong."

I wasn't sure what to make of his comment, but I let it pass.

We drove northeast on Broome Road for about fifteen minutes until Johani directed me to turn right onto a red dirt track. As I entered the track, I read the old bullet-riddled sign, 'Malcolm Douglas Crocodile Park.' I had a sudden epiphany; my old man took me to this park when I was a kid. I remember being amazed and terrified when I witnessed a giant croc use its tail to rise from the water with incredible power and speed and chomp on a chook attached to the end of a long pole held high in the air by a park employee.

After that experience, I became obsessed with the dangerous reptiles, discovering with interest that they're closely related to prehistoric dinosaurs. Every so often, I would hear about a croc attack in a river, mangrove swamp or billabong. I recall reading about a fifty-nine-year-old NT fisherman who was almost killed when a croc jumped into his dinghy and chomped his shoulder. The rugged fisherman survived by ramming his elbow into its throat. Closer to home, a fifteen-year-old runaway not much older than me at the time was killed by a croc in a mangrove swamp 200 kilometres north of Broome. However, the typical victim was some dumbass tourist that ignored the warning signs and was lured in for a quick skinny dip by the inviting-looking water holes. Jack Lawrence had some wise words in his Peter Pan lyrics, Never Smile at a Crocodile – *'Don't be taken in by his welcome grin. He's imagining how well you'd fit within his skin.'*

We drove down the dirt track to a large bitumen carpark. Johani asked me to park in front of the tourist shop so we could go inside and speak to his daughter before he took us to the fuel. Call me overly cautious, but I parked at the other end of the carpark and decided to have a look around before we entered the abandoned building.

Just after we exited the Beast, Johani gestured to Fiona, "You bring your shotgun," he ordered.

"Why do I need my shottie, Johani?" Fiona asked.

"This place has dangerous spirits. Linygurra lives here." He gazed at me with a furrowed brow, "You know, Brother."

No, I didn't know. I did, however, note that Johani mentioned this 'Linygurra' in a reverent tone.

"Bring the shotgun, Fiona. It's good to have some insurance."

Johani quickened his pace before I could ask about this Linygurra fellow. We marched past empty animal cages that were engulfed by native bush. A thick wire fence enclosed a ten-square-metre artificial billabong. A thick layer of algae made the waters murky and uninviting. Fiona leaned over the waist-high fence and gazed into the water.

"Stay frosty, Fiona," I warned.

"A bit hard in this sweltering heat," she joshed.

A giant life-like crocodile head constructed out of fibreglass was erected as an ingenious entry to the tourist shop. As a kid, I remember looking up at the five-metre-high structure and gazing in wonder at its teeth.

I again attempted to question Johani as we approached the entry, "Who do we need to speak to? Who is Linygurra?" He just shrugged his shoulders in reply and pointed to the shop with its massive crocodile head entry.

My 'spidey-sense' was tingling. I pressed my lips and whistled as I unclipped my holster and drew my trusty revolver. Fiona instantly placed the butt of her pump-action against her shoulder and pressed the safety button to fire. We followed Johani through the warped timber door frame. The shop was a mess, with glass from smashed counters, furniture, and merchandise scattered all over the floor. A damp uninviting smell filled my nostrils. A man's booming laughter could be heard emanating from the rear of the premises. Johani drew his fishing knife and slipped out of his thongs.

"Johani, what's going on?" I whispered with urgency.

"You are good people," he stated as he suddenly quickened his pace.

I increased my stride to keep up with the small man while Fiona was forced to jog to stay by my side. Johani led the way as he marched through the doorway of a rear room, with Fiona and me following closely behind. I swiftly scanned the room for threats and conducted a split-second risk assessment. A slim, middle-aged man with shaggy blonde hair was sitting on a couch beside an Aboriginal girl who had her wrists tied. A glass coffee table with an uninviting plate of raw meat and fish was positioned in front of the couch. I turned to see a battered Aboriginal woman moaning in pain as she lay on her side against the far wall.

The blonde man rose from the couch, "What the fuck, old man?" he complained.

With his knife raised high above his head, Johani sprinted forward and jumped over the coffee table like an Olympic hurdler. His target reached for a pistol behind a cushion, but his reaction was too slow to stop the agile man hurtling towards him. The fishing knife with the long thin blade penetrated the side of the stranger's neck just under his jaw. With gritted teeth, Johani stabbed him repeatedly with savage ferocity. Blood splattered over his chest, the couch, and the plates of food. He only stopped his attack when he looked down at the young girl screaming in terror with blood dripping down her face. It's bizarre what thoughts come to mind during life-and-death situations, but she reminded me of the character Carrie in the gym scene of the horror movie of the same name.

A bald giant of a man with a massive bull neck entered the room through an emergency exit door that was left ajar. His eyes went as wide as saucers. He dropped two bottles of hooch he was holding and reached behind his back. Sal preached – 'Boy, no matter what, always watch their hands.' I instinctively fired three rounds into his chest. Hitting such a large target at a distance of five metres was like shooting fish in a barrel. I had time to admire my tight grouping as the big man grabbed his chest with his sausage fingers and fell face down, smashing the glass coffee table with his Neanderthal-sized forehead. I swiftly removed a SIG Sauer 9mm pistol from his waistband.

After Johani assisted the sobbing woman to the couch, he cut the rope securing the young girl's wrists and ankles. Then, he spoke to them with a soothing tone in an Aboriginal language.

I didn't want to break up the family reunion, but I was concerned there were more scumbags in the park. So, to gain his full attention, I gripped the old man's shoulders and looked him in the eyes. "Johani, are there any more men in the park?"

He lowered his eyes to the floor as he shook his head. I asked Fiona to grab the first aid kit from the Beast. While Fiona cleaned and bandaged the woman's cuts, Johani explained that he was taking his daughter and granddaughter to Kununurra for a funeral. On the tenth day of their journey, they decided to stop at Broome to rest for the night. They were sleeping in the tourist shop when the two men came across them. They threatened to kill his daughter and granddaughter if he didn't bring them food and alcohol. This explained why Johani was going fishing when we first met. Johani bent down to pick up the blonde man's legs and gestured for me to assist. Following the old man's instructions, I lifted the dead man under his armpits and carried him out the fire door exit to the fenced-off billabong.

"Lift over the fence," Johani instructed.

When the carcass hit the red dirt, his arm started to twitch. He then attempted to lift his head. Jeezus, he was still bloody alive! I jumped back from the fence when an enormous croc launched from the water and grabbed the man's head and upper chest in its monstrous jaws. His bloodcurdling scream was deafening. He dragged the screaming man into the water and barrel rolled over and over, drowning his prey so he could enjoy the rotting meat over the coming days.

Johani was standing casually with his arms resting on the fence as if nothing unusual had occurred. I doubt he had moved an inch during the attack. He gestured to the croc and giggled, "Good to be friends with Linygurra."

Suddenly lost for words, I gulped and nodded in reply.

Johani had cleverly used us to settle his payback. Before I helped him dump the fat man into an adjacent billabong, I checked his vitals to ensure he had indeed left for the underworld. I noticed two eyes hovering at the surface of the murky water, the only evidence that a croc the length of the Beast was considering its prey. I stepped away from the fence and diverted my attention to Johani, having no desire to watch the gruesome outcome.

"So, is there any fuel, or was this just a ruse?"

Johani giggled, "I don't lie. I just don't tell you the full story."

He led me to a tin shed that had three 20-gallon drums of fuel sitting against the rear wall. Two of the drums were almost full. It was more than enough to get us to Kununurra. WA is Australia's largest state, with a land area of 2.5 million square kilometres. South Africa and Pakistan could fit within the WA border, with land still to spare. The journey to Kununurra should take about eleven hours to travel the 1000 kilometres east, which on the map was within a bee's dick from the NT border.

I had just refuelled the Beast's tank and topped up the four jerry cans when Fiona approached me in the carpark holding two bottles of beer.

"Where did you find those?" I asked happily.

"Don't get too excited, Boss. They're warm," she warned as she handed me a bottle. "Do you reckon we can get to Kununurra without having to help anyone else? I feel like we're reviving the bloody Swiss Army," she protested.

I laughed, "If that's the case, we're not off to a good start. I've offered to give Johani and his family a ride to Kununurra. We can't let them walk."

I didn't have the heart to mention that she should be referring to the Salvation Army, not the Swiss Army. Without an education system, the Internet, and functional libraries, it is to be expected that youngsters who grew up post-war misconstrue 'old world' cultural references. I wondered what her generation would be named: Generation Y for 'Why did we fight another world war?' was already taken, maybe Generation W for 'WTF did you do that for?'

Fiona sighed, "Well, I guess it's the right thing to do. The young girl's sweet, but her mum's a bitch. I know she's been through a rough trot, but she's been asking me a heap of nosey questions. It's like she doubts our intentions. And we'll have to watch Johani. He's a cunning old fox."

# Chapter Twenty-Two

*Saturday, March 8, 2042 – Clarry*

The whirring sound of the large pedestal fan was drowned out in the confines of the laboratory by AC/DC's tune, *You Shook Me All Night Long*, blaring from the old but powerful Marantz speakers. The lab was built at the back of my 4000 square-metre property, alongside the stables, mechanical workshop, greenhouse, and expansive gym. My savings, combined with the gold Archie and Fiona gifted me, provided me with the funds to build my lab. The local builders placed two dongas side by side, and carpenters erected purpose-built benches and cupboards to operate and store my equipment. I have fitted the lab with all the necessities to conduct my research - test tubes, flasks, beakers, two microscopes, a Geiger counter, Bunsen burners, a centrifuge, a fridge, and various bits and pieces. In pride of place in the centre of the second annex sat my most valuable tools – an Apple computer and a DNA sequencer.

It's been almost twelve months since we drove into Perth in our hazmat suits to rescue young Raj. I remember feeling like a kid in a candy store upon entering the hotel's former business centre. Patterson had converted the centre into a laboratory, which he had fitted with all the bells and whistles. Before then, I hadn't used a computer for more than eight years.

We confirmed our worst suspicions; Patterson had used the lab to conduct unethical and cruel experiments on innocent civilians. After we rescued Raj, I took it upon myself to visit local hospitals and research centres to locate equipment that had been shielded from the EMPs to build my own laboratory. The lab is my pride and joy that I toil in tirelessly.

Before the War, I was a scientist working at the CSIRO's Health and Biosecurity unit. So when Archie presented me with Patterson's research papers, in which he claimed to have maintained the length of his subjects' telomeres, I'll admit that I was blindly optimistic. Some would say I became somewhat obsessed. I wanted to believe that Patterson had discovered the Holy Grail, the ability to cure diseases such as cancer while greatly extending the lifespan of Homo sapiens. Of course, there were side effects, such as turning his subjects' blood green and the requirement to use copious amounts of human growth hormone to keep them alive. Still, these were minor problems to be solved, considering this was an opportunity to reclaim our contaminated world. The human life span in Australia had reduced from eighty-nine years in 2030 to sixty-one years as of 2037, the last year of data collection before the Australian Bureau of Statistics was shut down. We were virtually living in the Dark Ages, with no education system, a sporadic power supply, skyrocketing levels of ultra-violent crimes, a near non-existent national health system and vaccine program, and worst of all, the cessation of scientific research and advancement.

My spirit was crushed when I performed an autopsy on one of Patterson's subjects and inspected his cancer-ridden organs. The outcome of Patterson's research was a poisoned chalice. His cure for immortality was short-lived, as his experimental drug only managed to maintain the length of one's telomeres for between three to twelve weeks, depending on the dose and size of the subject. This led to the requirement of progressively increasing doses and the inevitable escalation in the severity of concomitant side effects, ultimately resulting in catastrophic physiological consequences.

Nevertheless, despite all the challenges, there is always hope, and I will never give up. Antibiotics were a miracle discovery, with penicillin alone estimated to have saved 200 million lives. The discovery of antibiotics was convoluted, with the story beginning with the ancient Egyptians, who were known to apply mouldy bread to infected wounds. However, it was in 1928 when a Scottish microbiologist named Alexander Fleming fortuitously made the breakthrough. The scientist, known to keep an untidy desk, left inoculated staphylococci in culture plates on his lab bench when he went on holiday. Upon his return to the lab, he noticed that one of the plates was contaminated with a fungus. To his amazement, colonies of staphylococci surrounding the fungus had been destroyed. He identified the mould as being from the genus Penicillium. It may be hubris of me, but I have taken it upon myself to continue Patterson's research to develop a drug that will protect our species from radiation exposure and return our civilisation to the modern age of recent history. And even beyond!

I returned the glass slides I had been examining under the microscope to their containers and walked to annex A, where I removed my lab coat before slipping outside. The fresh southerly breeze blowing from the southern seas of the Great Australian Bight provided a cool respite from the confines of my lab. It was late afternoon; time to freshen up before meeting Pia for a bite to eat at her favourite restaurant.

My family, friends and gossiping members of the community regard me as a bit of a ladies' man. It's accurate that I enjoy the company of women. Who doesn't enjoy friendly conversation, a glass or two of a South West Shiraz and some dancing? It improves my mood and gives me the impetus to begin another day. But it is none of anyone's business who I spend my time with. And besides, a gentleman never tells.

I examined myself in the mirror as I shaved the whiskers from my cheeks and chin. Pia was meeting me at the Lucky Charm Chinese restaurant on Dempster Street. After dinner, we planned to watch a sixty-one-year-old movie called 'Alien'. An entrepreneurial council member salvaged an ancient projector and a cache of films. I enjoy a good sci-fi flick, and I heard from a reliable source, Geoff from the pub, that this Alien movie is one hell of a scary picture. I was committed to ensuring Pia felt safe by wrapping my arms around her to protect her from prowling aliens.

I dried my face with a towel and inspected my performance with the razor. My reflection in the bathroom mirror displayed cheeks that were as smooth as a baby's bum. My wide nose and intelligent eyes were inherited from my grandfather. I'm a proud Whadjuk man from the Noongar nation. My people called this land home long before the white man arrived on these shores. Aboriginal people have sung, danced, and told stories of the Dreaming for over sixty thousand years. It's not as widely known as it should be in this country, but when Captain James Cook first sailed into Botany Bay in 1770, there were 300 Aboriginal languages from over 500 different nations on this Island of nations, which is now known as Australia.

On that day in 1770, several Dharawal men observed HMS Endeavour approach them from the horizon. The Endeavour's expansive 2,777 square metres of sail resembled a low-lying cloud coming into shore. When the English landing party approached the men, the first of many misunderstandings took place. They reported that the *natives* warned them off with threats of harm. However, from the perspective of the Dharawal men, they believed the spirits of the dead had returned to their country, so they raised their spears and yelled "warra wai" to protect their nation from ghosts.

I slipped on my pants and favourite navy-blue shirt before selecting my lucky black leather belt and holster. Before the War, the only time I would carry a firearm was when I was hunting with my cousins. The way things are now, I wouldn't dream of leaving the house without my Browning nine-millimetre pistol. Archie, my best mate, would often preach, 'Be prepared.'

As I moseyed over to my green machine, a 1971 Volkswagen Beetle, Xena and Zeus came barrelling towards the car, hoping to catch a ride. They wanted to go to the beach and had no interest in hearing my excuse about romantic intentions. Zeus is an enormous rottweiler that I found two years ago in an abandoned drug lab. He was malnourished and abused, which gave him just cause to be mad as hell. However, we became great mates after I presented him with a juicy leg of lamb. Xena is a sleek Doberman who belongs to Archie. He adopted her after killing her owner in a violent altercation. Her owner was one of Patterson's green-blooded goons - homicidal supermen, whom I hope never to cross paths with again.

After I escorted the dogs to the backyard and secured the side gate, I promised them I would take them to the beach first thing in the morning. I waved them goodbye as I reversed the Beetle down the long winding driveway.

The Lucky Charm serves a western fusion of Chinese food that most Australians with Asian heritage would not touch with a barge pole. I tended to avoid fatty food for fear of raising my already high cholesterol, but Pia had requested this restaurant, and I'm not one to disappoint a lady, so the Lucky Charm it was.

The Chinese waitress greeted me at the front counter and escorted me to my table. She was an inch or two under five feet and wore a traditional blue cheongsam that matched the colour of her sneakers. After I was seated, the waitress politely asked, "What can I get ya?" in a thick ocker accent that wouldn't sound out of place in an outback pub. The Chinese have immigrated to Australia since the gold rush in the 1850s. As a result, most residents with Chinese features were as Aussie as any sixth-generation white fella.

As I checked my watch for the third or fourth time, the waitress brought another jug of water and a bowl of prawn crackers to the table. She gave me a look of pity and then hurried away to seat a couple that had just arrived. I missed my mobile phone and the ability to text a date and ask, *'Where are you? Do you want me to order? Is anything wrong? Have you stood me up?'*

I felt a firm grip on my shoulder and looked up to see Captain Ross standing above me. "Fancy seeing you here, lad," he said with a mischievous grin. The Captain had the physical characteristics and personality to be a shoo-in to play the role of Moby-Dick's Ahab in a town play. He's a gentleman in his early seventies with a prominent nose and a long white beard. The old salt was the Captain of the fishing vessel, Mother Teresa, and when I wasn't conducting experiments in the lab, I was his chief mate. It is hard to imagine that I was a successful and well-known scientist, having appeared on TV, the radio and even on the cover of Science Illustrated. While I appreciated the opportunity to make a living from fishing, science remained my greatest passion.

"I'm supposed to be meeting someone for dinner, but I guess something came up," I explained.

The Captain frowned, "Considering the name of this place, that's some tough luck, matey." He then pointed to a table at the other side of the restaurant. "Come and join the misses and me. We'd love to have dinner with you."

I was about to refuse when the Captain's wife, Elizabeth, started waving and gesturing for me to come over. A few years back, they celebrated their fiftieth wedding anniversary. During the party, he joked that it was their first day off from fishing and running the shop since they returned from their honeymoon. If there was any couple that personified the physics definition of a *couple*, it was these two; *when two equal and parallel forces act opposite to each other, then together they create a couple.* The Captain treated Elizabeth like his queen but drove her crazy in his quest for adventure. She, in turn, made every effort to keep him grounded and out of harm's way.

As I sat at their table, the Captain expressed a mischievous smile, "Loverboy here has been stood-up."

Elizabeth placed her hand over mine and said in a soothing tone, "Well, she doesn't know what she's missing out on."

Captain Ross raised an eyebrow, "I hope you're not speaking from experience, Love."

The Captain laughed raucously when he noticed Elizabeth's cheeks blush bright red like an English rose.

I couldn't resist joining in on the frivolity and turned to Elizabeth, "Let's leave this old fella with his prawn crackers and go for a walk on the jetty," I teased. Elizabeth's large breasts bounced as she giggled, and the Captain folded his arms and expressed mock offence.

We chowed down on the heavily battered sweet 'n' sour pork and salt 'n' pepper squid and washed it down with a couple of lagers and a glass of red. I could almost feel my arteries clogging with plaque. I would consider it ironic for a scientist whose expertise is diabetes to die from myocardial infarction whilst feasting on battered pork and beer. I chuckled at the thought.

"You going to let us in on the joke, son?" the Captain asked with a wink.

"I was just thinking about the mayor falling off the jetty last weekend," I lied, not wanting to discuss my more morbid thoughts.

The Captain and Elizabeth smiled. "Typical landlubbers. But we shouldn't make fun. The mayor is a good-hearted bloke doing his best for the community," the Captain pointed out with sincerity.

"Have you heard from Fiona and Archie?" Elizabeth asked.

Fiona stayed with the couple during Archie's recovery from his injuries and opiate addiction. They became close friends when Fiona worked as a deckhand on the Captain's fishing boat during the day and assisted Elizabeth in the fish 'n' chip shop at night.

I placed my hand over my mouth to hide the squid I was chewing. "Not since I received that postcard I showed you two months back."

Even though the Captain was adamant that he would pay for the meal, I told a white lie about needing to go to the bathroom and slipped out the back after settling the bill. During the drive home, I reflected on how my shenanigans would irk him and smiled all the way to the driveway.

The dogs were whining in the backyard, *'Play with us. Take us for a walk. Please! Please! Please!'* I collected the mail from the postbox and read the back of the envelope as I strolled into the loungeroom - *'From Archie O'Connor'*. With avid anticipation, I plonked down on the three-seater couch and ripped open the envelope. Feelings of delight and dread occupied my thoughts as I read that Archie and Fiona had a lead on Patterson's whereabouts and were journeying to the top end to investigate its veracity.

# Chapter Twenty-Three

*Sunday, March 9, 2042 – Archie*

Thankfully the first part of the trip to Kununurra was non-eventful. I fell asleep in the front passenger seat to the sound of Johani's daughter, Alicia, telling Fiona about her days as the headmistress of the Karratha Primary School.

Fiona woke me seven hours later to swap seats. Alicia was a chatterbox. She only stopped talking to take a breath or ask me inquisitive questions about my private life - 'Are you married? Do you have any children? Are your parents still alive? Have you travelled outside of WA since the end of the War?' The silver lining to her motor mouth was she kept me awake as I drove east on the desolate highway through the desert plains.

We arrived in Kununurra at 3:15 a.m. The town was located in the Kimberley region at the top end of WA, only forty-five kilometres west of the NT border. The Ord River Dam provided the residents with plentiful access to water all year round, which enabled the community to develop into an agriculture hub, growing melons, mangoes, sugar cane, and rice. Before the War, about 5000 souls lived in the area during the wet season, and then farm workers and tourists would flood the town during the dry season, resulting in the population doubling. Unfortunately, I had no intel on how the town had fared post-War, and our passengers were of no use, having not left their home in recent times. So I wasn't sure what we would find - a ghost town? A gang-ridden cesspit? A thriving community?

Driving down the National Highway past the regional airport, I noticed several derelict light aircraft scattered along the side of the runway. I imagine they provided a fantastic play area for mischievous kids. It was sobering to contemplate that today's children have never seen a plane in the air. And, of course, pessimists would argue they never will.

I gazed at the moonlit river flowing underneath as we passed over a bridge. When I returned my attention to the road, my frame of mind switched from one of calm composure to dread. In the distance, I could see two large caravans blocking the road, each hitched to four-wheel drives. *No, not again, I fretted.*

"Heads up, Fiona," I said anxiously as I nudged her shoulder to wake her.

"Johani, do you know how to use a shotgun?" I asked.

The man nodded in reply, setting the weapon on his lap in preparation. Fiona shook her head and wiped the sleep from her eyes before drawing her Glock. Grasping my revolver, I rested my wrist on the steering wheel while I considered the barricade before us and contemplated our next move - *I could do a uey and head out of town, but where would we go? We don't have enough fuel to travel anywhere else that's populated.*

I stopped the Beast about 250 metres from the caravans. I held my binos to my eyes and scanned for threats. Flood lights mounted on the caravans suddenly lit up the entire highway. After recovering from temporary blindness, I squinted to observe a middle-aged Aboriginal bloke and two white fellas standing near the caravans holding assault rifles.

Johani leaned forward from the passenger seat and asked to use the binoculars.

I passed him the binos, and two heartbeats later, he proclaimed, "I know that boy. He's my nephew."

"Which one?" Alicia asked. "You have about a hundred of them."

Before I could stop him, Johani exited the Beast and jogged down the road shouting at the men, "Hey boy, it's your uncle."

The Aboriginal bloke ran down the road towards Johani with a rifle in his grasp. Fiona grabbed her rifle and stepped out of the vehicle. "No, don't," I instructed.

The younger man grabbed Johani in a bear hug and spun him around in circles. Then, after returning Johani to terra firma, he laughed cheerfully as he waved us over.

After hearing his uncle's story of how they escaped the crocodile park, Johani's nephew offered to escort us to Kununurra's visitor centre. He explained that it was law for all non-residents to apply for a visa to enter the town. He must have read my mind, as he put my concerns at ease by explaining he would personally vouch for us as friends of his family. He shook my hand, "You saved my blood. You are my blood," he declared.

We tailed Johani in his light brown Datsun 180B to the visitor centre. We were gobsmacked by the town's appearance. It was an oasis in the desert. The street lights were working, the roads and public buildings were clean and well maintained, each home had mowed lawns or bush gardens, and vehicles lined the streets. We almost had to pinch ourselves. I never thought I would ever see a town like it again.

True to his word, Johani's nephew paved the way for us to receive visas to visit the town. He introduced us to the town administrator on duty, a thin, stern-looking woman who handed me a four-page application that took thirty minutes to complete. When she stamped the form and presented us with the seven-day visas, I stated, "We'll be leaving in two days."

The officious administration replied, "A seven-day visa is the minimum I can issue. If you want to stay longer, you must return and apply for an extension."

It had been a long time since I was required to deal with a bureaucrat. I bit my tongue rather than reiterate our intentions.

She peered at our holsters, "You can wear your handguns overtly, but it's illegal to conceal firearms or any other weapon. And you cannot brandish long arms within the town limits."

I forced a smile and thanked her before glancing at my watch: 4 a.m. We wished Johani and his family good luck before parting ways to find a hotel to book for the night. We felt dispirited after being told there were no vacancies at the first two hotels we visited.

Hopefully, the third time's the charm, I thought as we pulled into the Kununurra Hotel carpark. I was relieved when the weary-looking receptionist told us she had two rooms available. Unfortunately, we were getting low on funds, and the room rate was daylight robbery, so we settled for a room with two single beds. As we trudged towards our room, Fiona raised her eyebrows and pointed out the clean and inviting-looking pool.

"What's with this place? It's like the War never happened. Why haven't we visited here before?" she asked.

"I don't want to be a pessimist, but I'd prefer to investigate the town in the daylight before I make any judgements. It all seems a little bit too good to be true," I replied uneasily.

Fiona was cleaning her Glock as I settled into bed. Before I hit the sack, we agreed to stay in town for a day to resupply and recharge our batteries. We needed to fill our jerry cans and water bottles to travel the 830 klicks to Darwin, the capital city of the NT and Patterson's last known whereabouts. But before we left, I was curious to have a quick squiz around town. We could return one day, and it was always helpful to know the lay of the land. With that thought, I switched off the light and fell into a deep sleep.

# Chapter Twenty-Four

*Sunday, March 9, 2042 – Fiona*

Archie was still fast asleep as I slipped out to explore the hotel. The sun was directly above, and it felt like the day was heading north of 35-degrees. The heat didn't bother me as much as the high humidity. The best way to describe this weather is *oppressive*. I had only walked fifty metres, and my t-shirt was already sticking to my skin like glue. Archie mentioned the top-end has a tropical climate, and we were nearing the end of the wet season.

The hotel pool was calling to me like a siren's song. A couple of giggling kids threw an inflatable ball back and forth while their mother sat on a deck chair reading a book. Memories of a childhood holiday in Thailand hit me like a sledgehammer to the chest; dad playing with me in the resort pool, mum taking me to a cooking class, and buying me toys and clothes at the markets. I pushed the memories to the back of my mind and slid into the deep end. The cool water felt glorious as I let myself sink down and hover above the tiled bottom. This is the life I dreamed of. All I have to do is forget the past and focus on the present. Easier said than done.

When I returned to the hotel room, I found Archie sorting through his pack and making a list of supplies we were running low on. One word to describe Archie is fastidious. A normal human being would be itching to dive into the pool and enjoy the hotel's luxuries. But not Archie. When the man was in operation mode, he had only one train of thought, *complete the mission!*

I felt a cool caress against my skin that I hadn't experienced for a long time. "Fuck me! Is that air-conditioning?"

"Now I know why this place is so expensive," Archie quipped.

"Wait until you take a dip in the pool. Do we have to leave?" I joked.

"We do if we don't want to be poor and destitute. Anyway, forget about that. Let's go for a drive and get something to eat before we purchase fuel and supplies."

I gave him a nod and went to the bathroom to shower and change. "Bloody glorious! The shower has hot water with a ton of pressure. I'm in heaven," I bellowed.

"Nah, if we were in heaven, I'd have a beer in my hand, and the footy would be playing on the telly," came the shout from the bedroom.

~

After we stopped at a petrol station to fuel up, we drove past tennis courts, where residents were playing singles and doubles matches. It was hard for me to comprehend how people could play tennis in this heat. Then, I noted a sign that read, 'Welcome to the Ord River Sports Club – Bowls – Indoor Cricket – Pool Tables.' Playing tennis, bowls, indoor cricket, or any form of competitive sport sounded ludicrous. I pondered, how do these people have the time or desire to play games? I was experiencing a bit of a culture shock.

"It's like we've gone back in time," Archie remarked.

"I hardly lived in that time."

On the way to the town centre, we were surprised to see numerous vehicles parked around the edge of a football oval. There were too many cars to count. It was obvious that some type of event was in progress. I morbidly pondered whether they were hanging someone. Archie managed to find a spot to park down a side street. We strolled towards a raucous sound that brought back memories from long ago, a blast from the past. It was the sound of a carnival. People actually having fun. I was transported back to when I was a ten-year-old running around the Perth Royal Show.

As we walked onto the grass field, my senses were overloaded.

Hundreds of people congregated and busily moved between food stalls, carnival rides and side shows. Rock music was blaring from speakers while carnies shouted and plied their trade. Kids and adults of all ages were eating fairy floss, toffee apples and popcorn as they laughed and held hands. A clown bustled past me on one side, and kids were being led on ponies on the other. The kids on a tea cup merry-go-round were screaming in delight as they spun with dizzying speed.

"Now, young lady, stay close and avoid the haunted house. And if you're a really good girl, I'll buy you a show bag," Archie laughed.

I was about to retort with one of my typical smart-ass comments when a beer and food hall caught my eye. Men and women of all ages, shapes, and sizes sat at timber benches, drinking pints of beer and devouring a variety of fried and grilled meat. The aroma of cooked steak filled my nostrils, making my mouth water.

Archie must have observed my craving. "Come on, let's get something to eat," he said with a smile.

"You don't have to ask me twice, Boss," I replied.

Oh my god, I thought. Archie may be human, after all. He actually appears to be enjoying himself.

I devoured a T-bone steak, mash, and a side of fried crickets, while Archie wolfed down a plate of pork ribs and chips. We drank more than a few pints of lager and enjoyed the venue's atmosphere. We chatted with a couple sitting at an adjacent table, who were more than willing to brag about their town. The town was doing better than just surviving. They were thriving. They boasted a full-strength police force supported by a local militia, ambulance service, medical centre, and an elected government. When asked why we were visiting their town, we explained we were just passing through on our way to Darwin, where we were hoping to locate our sister. I had learned the hard way to trust no one.

We left the hall feeling sated and tipsy. The sun had disappeared over the horizon, and a rainbow of lights illuminated the carnival rides and sideshow alley. I instantly recognised two men I hadn't seen for more than a year standing beside a towering bright red circus tent. I might have thought my boozing was making me see double if I didn't know any better. Excitedly, I grabbed Archie by his forearm and pulled him toward the four-foot-tall identical twins. Wearing matching navy blue dapper suits, they stood under a sign that read, 'Come and Witness the Marvellous and Exotic Carnival.' One of the twins wore a purple tie, while the other wore a red cravat, their way to help people tell them apart.

I pointed first to Jesse with his purple tie and then to James with his red cravat, "Look, Archie, it's Jesse and James," I stated for Archie's benefit. Archie could cite numerous regulations and legislation off the cuff and list all thirty-four parts of a Glock pistol, but he was absolutely hopeless at remembering people's names.

The twins looked up with beaming smiles. "Ah, the beautiful Miss Fiona and her handsome sidekick, Master Archie," Jesse proclaimed as he prodded his brother with his elbow.

"Fancy seeing you two here. Have you got the whole crew with you?" I asked.

"Yes, ma'am, and a few extras. All but Blane and Evelyn will be performing in...." James glanced at his watch. "Just under five minutes."

"Blane should be here to assist, but his fire show isn't being exhibited until the midnight show. Evelyn has her tent on the western side of the oval," explained Jesse.

I was relieved to hear Blane was missing in action, as he's a real asshole that I'd rather avoid. The first time we met, he just about scorched my eyebrows when he sprayed fuel on a campfire I had just started.

The twins turned to one other and simultaneously announced, "You're welcome to see the show. No charge for friends."

We thanked them before stepping through the flaps and entering the packed tent. The performers stood on a raised dais and exhibited their weird and wonderful bodies and skills while bohemian music blasted through enormous speakers. A stagehand in the corner of the tent operated a smoke machine to create a fog that drifted around the performers' feet.

Members of the audience 'oohed and aahed' and applauded, while others pointed, gaped, and stared at the extraordinary entertainers. On the left side of the dais, a pencil-thin man who stood at least eight feet tall danced with a tiny woman the size of a three-year-old child while a contortionist bent his back and joints like rubber. On the other side of the tent, a lady flexed her bulging, rippling muscles, making men in the audience feel either inadequate, mesmerised or turned on. Beside her was a man wearing a G-string exposing elaborate inked art tattooed over the entirety of his body. In the centre of the stage sat the fattest man I have ever seen. You could hide a child within his folds of belly fat. He chortled with glee while he slapped his enormous gut and man boobs.

When we first encountered 'The Marvellous Carnival', I was surprised to witness Archie hooking up with Evelyn, the carnival's beautiful fortune teller. Archie was still so distraught over the loss of his wife, and throughout our travels, he usually didn't spare a second glance at attractive women. But, on reflection, I shouldn't have been shocked. Evelyn was a gorgeous lady who could have been a model in the old world, with her long, lithe legs, knock-out hourglass figure, and luscious black hair that fell to her waist. She also came across as someone who always got what she wanted; to be honest, the tryst with Archie was more of a seduction on her part.

I stood on my tiptoes and spoke loudly into Archie's ear, "Why don't you go and catch up with Evelyn?"

He gave me a sideways glance and then pointedly ignored me, but I persisted. "Don't be rude. She'll be pissed off if she finds out you were here and didn't say hi."

He sighed and peered at his watch before replying, "Ok, I'll meet you at the front of the tent at 10 p.m. on the dot. Agreed?"

"Whatever you say, cowboy. Don't do anything I wouldn't do," I teased.

Not long after Archie left the tent, Jesse closed the show by announcing into a bright red megaphone, "Thank you, ladies and gentlemen, for your attendance. We hope to see you again soon. If you can spare a coin or two, please drop it in Magilla's hat. Good night everyone."

A monkey dressed in blue denim overalls sitting in a saddle strapped to a black Labrador was weaving through the crowd. He was holding out a red felt bowler hat and grinning at the punters as they flipped him a silver coin. Noticing a small child with an ice cream cone drop a coin in his hat, I realised it had been over a decade since I had the pleasure of eating my favourite childhood dessert.

I approached the twins, still standing on the stage and asked, "Where can I buy ice cream?"

"Turn left after you leave the tent, and you'll see a stall next to the bumper cars that sells a myriad of flavours. Tell 'em JJ sent you, and you might get an extra scoop," Jesse replied with a smile.

As I zigzagged my way through the crowd, I noticed a woman that looked mighty familiar. Then, after a moment, it suddenly dawned on me. *Shit!* Bloody Lesley Maka, the fucking psycho bitch that murdered her three kids.

I retrieved a folded paper from the back pocket of my jeans and quickly examined the mug shot. Yep, it was Maka, without a doubt. Thinking back, I remembered a barmaid at Maka's local saying she'd run away with a carnie. I could have kicked myself. I should have joined the dots and considered the possibility of her being here. But there wasn't time to be self-critical. I needed to quickly devise a plan. The smart thing to do would be to wait for Archie to return, but I'd been looking for this witch for months, and I couldn't risk losing her. So I decided to follow her until I had a clear shot with no kids around. I didn't consider Archie's rules relevant at this time, place, and circumstance. *I mean, come on, she murdered her own kids. If she doesn't deserve a bullet, then who does?*

After I exited the tent, I felt someone tap my waistline. I looked down to see Jill, the little person from the show skipping alongside me. "Do you want to grab a drink, Fiona? I know a great bar that's as cheap as chips. Why are you walking so fast?" she asked breathlessly.

"I've actually got something important to do. Maybe later."

Jill wouldn't be dissuaded. "I've got nothing better to do. So what are you up to?"

I maintained a five-metre distance as Maka strolled down the sideshow alley without a care in the world. I ignored the carnies as they stood behind their sideshow booths and used their best lines to convince me to throw a hoop at a peg, fish for a prize, place a ball in a clown's mouth, or throw darts at a balloon. Little did they know that I was already planning on winning a prize at my favourite game – pistol shooting.

I was so focused on stalking Maka that I had forgotten entirely about Jill. "Where are we going?" Jill chirped.

I was too distracted to be polite. "Ah, look, you know what I do for a living, don't you?" I asked her while my eyes were locked on the back of Maka's head.

"Yes, sweetie, but you don't want to advertise your vocation around here," she warned.

"Well, there's a lady I need to have some harsh words with, so it's best that you return to the tent."

Maka made a sharp turn and walked behind the alley toward a shabby-looking caravan. I couldn't have asked for a better kill zone. There was no one around, and we were hidden from the crowd. I double-checked to make sure Jill had heeded my advice before drawing my Glock and quickening my pace. My heart pounded as I closed the gap and raised my pistol, placing my finger on the trigger.

As I pointed the muzzle at the back of Maka's skull, I felt a sudden restriction around my neck. The sensation was a familiar one. After rolling with Archie for almost a year, I instantly knew I was in deep shit. Someone had me in a rear-naked choke, tightly squeezing the arteries running down the side of my neck. Before I could react and lower my base and force my weight forward, my attacker pulled me backwards, so my heels dragged across the grass. In desperation, I jerked the trigger before dropping my pistol and gripping the arm wrapped around my neck. The gunshot was barely audible as my vision blurred. The dark tunnel enveloped me as I journeyed into oblivion. My last thoughts were honest - *'I'm a fucking idiot! Archie will never know ........'*

# Chapter Twenty-Five

*Sunday, March 9, 2042 – Archie*

I followed the twin's directions and found Evelyn's tent across the way from the bumper cars. The gold glitter sign at the front of the tent read 'Oprah the Oracle.' I had a sudden feeling of uncertainty as I stepped inside her tent.

I heard a bell ring above my head. I found Evelyn, her back turned, searching through a silver jewellery box. "Take a seat, honey. I'll just be two secs. I'm just looking for my old cards as I'm not feeling the magic with the new set."

I followed her command and sat on a cushioned chair, waiting patiently with my lips sealed. She was wearing a long figure-hugging purple dress with a loose gold belt. As I gazed at her hips, memories from our last liaison flooded my thoughts.

As if she could read my mind, she turned to face me and expressed a knowing smile that reached her eyes. "Archie O'Connor," she uttered in a husky tone.

I watched the sway of her hips as she walked past my shoulder, touching the back of my neck with her long, red-lacquered fingernails. She hung a 'Be Back Soon' sign outside her tent and tied the tent flaps closed.

"I missed you, stranger, and it wasn't just for the polite conversation," she purred as she straddled my lap and kissed me firmly.

She reached down to my waist and unclipped my belt, dropping my holstered revolver beneath the chair. Evelyn had a way of disarming me like no other person alive.

# Chapter Twenty-Six

*Sunday, March 9, 2042, from 10:15 p.m. – Fiona*

After waking up in a groggy haze, I thanked my lucky stars I was still alive, because I knew God had nothing to do with it. As my eyes adjusted to my new surroundings, I attempted to break free from the bonds that secured my wrists behind my back. The first thing I looked for was my firearm and knife. Both were missing. I was lying on a concrete floor in a dimly lit shed. A single light bulb was hanging from the tin roof, illuminating a variety of tools scattered on a workbench, some of which could be used to cut my binds. My main hurdle was the rope binding my ankles. I had a classic chicken and egg problem. I needed the tools to stand, but I couldn't stand without the tools. It was infuriating, but I couldn't let the red mist cloud my judgment. My life depended on staying calm and thinking of a solution. I scanned the shed and spotted a rusted old lawnmower sitting in the far corner. I scurried over the pavement like a crab walking sideways along the shoreline. After two deep breaths, I slid my fingers under the front axle of the mower and dug my heels into the concrete. Perspiration dripped from my hairline as I succeeded in flipping the machine onto its side. I shuffled my backside towards the underside of the mower and had just started to rub the ropes binding my wrists against the blades when the shed door suddenly swung open.

I froze and peered up to see a broad-shouldered man grinning at me with a set of perfect pearly whites. It was difficult to make out his facial features in the low light, as his skin was so dark that it was almost purple. But, disturbingly, I could see intelligence sparkling in his piercing eyes, like a cat considering its prey. The realisation that I wasn't dealing with a dumb thug, but a calculating predator, sent a cold shiver down my spine.

"Well, well, you are a resourceful young lady, aren't you?"

I didn't waste any time. I screamed as loud as I could muster, "Heeelp meeee. I need HEEELP!"

The asshole laughed as he folded his arms across his chest. "Screech like a whiney little bitch as much as you want. Nobody's gonna hear you out here."

"What the fuck do you want with me?" I yelled.

"You killed one of my girls. She wasn't a big earner, but she was still one of mine. And that pisses me right off!" he yelled, leaning forward, spittle spraying my face.

"You mean Maka? Are you telling me you're her fucking pimp? She murdered her three kids," I retorted in desperation.

"I don't give a flying fuck if she personally nuked Perth. You destroyed my property, and you're gonna make it up to me. Now you're obviously useless to me as one of my girls. You'll do a runner the first chance you get. But with some luck, Salkov will pay good money for you. You've got no tits, but you have great teeth, a nice bone structure, and a firm ass. If you're into boy's bums, that is. And trust me, many are." The asshole chuckled at his own wit.

It would have been a waste of energy to grovel or plead for him to let me go. So, for now, my fate was sealed. But I planned on escaping at the first opportunity I got, and if there was an opportunity to kill the fucker in the process, that's a bonus I'd jump at.

He bent down, threw me over his shoulder with ease, and carried me as if I was a ten-kilo bag of salt. I craned my neck and scanned my surroundings, but I could only see scrub. He then lowered me into the boot of a large sedan with greater care than I had anticipated. After he disappeared, I scanned the boot for anything I could use to break free, but sadly, the boot was as clean as a whistle. The asshole returned a minute later with a Camelbak hydration pack, which he placed near my shoulder with the blue drinking tube facing me.

"There's three litres in the pack. You need to make it last over the next six hours or so. Don't die on me," he sneered.

The asshole slammed the boot shut, leaving me in total darkness. I heard the motor start and felt the car accelerate. I slowed my breathing and focused on two thoughts – Escape and Retribution.

# Chapter Twenty-Seven

*Sunday, March 9, 2042, from 10:30 p.m. – Archie*

I had been waiting at the carnival tent, speaking to the twins for at least half an hour. It wasn't like Fiona to be late. She was a little tipsy earlier, but she's not one to get drunk and reckless. Rather the opposite. She's a control freak! So as I walked up and down the sideshow alley, I wondered, *where the hell is she?*

After walking around the grounds for an hour trying to locate her, I returned to the carnival tent, hoping to find that she had returned. Instead, I found the diminutive woman from the show fervently conversing with the twins, who each had an identical grave expression.

"What's going on? Is something wrong?" I worriedly asked.

"Jill just told us that Fiona was taken by one of our employees," explained James.

I locked eyes with Jill. "Take me to her now," I demanded.

"He grabbed her, and then I heard a gunshot. He dragged her away. There was nothing I could do," she cried.

I took a deep breath and composed myself; losing my cool now would only waste time and hinder my mission. "Who took Fiona?" I asked with as much composure as I could muster.

"Jeremy," she answered.

"Jeremy Olaoluwa is employed as the manager of our female entertainment," Jesse explained sheepishly.

"He's your pimp?" I asked angrily.

"Our clients have a wide range of desires. Some want to see a freak show, while others want to get their rocks off. We're a business. We supply a service based on the demand," Jesse explained defensively.

"Just take me to where she was grabbed," I insisted.

Jill led us to a rusted caravan parked behind the sideshow alley. I held my breath with dread when I saw a woman lying face down on the grass and then felt great relief when I noted her clothing and size. I grasped the woman by her shoulders and rolled her onto her back. Even in the dim light, it was clear to see she had been shot in the forehead.

Jill placed her hands over her mouth. "Poor Lesley," she cried.

The woman looked familiar. "Lesley Maka!" I exclaimed.

Fiona had an absolute hard-on for this bounty. She must have followed Maka here and was taken by surprise after she shot her.

I turned on my torch. "Jill, point me to where Jeremy took Fiona."

Jill pointed toward a gap in the caravan between a tree and a green wheelie bin. There weren't any drag marks, so I surmised he must have carried her.

"What's in that direction?" I asked.

"The carnies carpark," the twins replied in unison.

Jill and the twins followed me to the edge of the oval, where at least fifty vehicles of various makes and models were parked. I was disappointed to find the immediate area devoid of any witnesses.

"What does Jeremy drive?" I asked the three concerned faces.

"He drives a light blue Ford Falcon XY GT with black pinstripes. I know the car well because I've offered to buy it. It's a nice ride," Jesse explained.

After searching up and down the parking lot, my worst fears were confirmed. He'd already left the carnival. I prayed that Fiona was still alive.

Thinking back, I recalled an informant in Geraldton telling us that Maka had moved up to Darwin with a carnie. Even though every fibre of my being was urging me to jump into the Beast and race full speed to Darwin, I tempered my impulse and interviewed each of the carnies to learn anything that could help me locate Fiona.

A carnival troupe is similar to a large family in that they cannot help but pry into one another's affairs and gossip about what they discover. I quickly learned that Jeremy had spent his childhood in

Darwin. His Nigerian parents were refugees who immigrated to Australia in the early noughties and had worked day and night to establish themselves in their new country. They had built a fast-food empire selling Nigerian dishes that were both cheap and healthy. Jeremy had wanted for nothing – private schooling, a luxury car, and a generous allowance. Unconcerned by his parents' anguish, he took his circumstances for granted and hung out with the wrong crowd, dabbling in crime: stealing cars, snorting coke, and breaking into homes. He was destined to receive attention from the law. He was before a magistrate a week after his eighteenth birthday, charged with dealing in methamphetamine and trafficking girls for prostitution. He had been working as the carnival's pimp, a step down from his previous venture as the owner of a popular brothel on the outskirts of Darwin. It was rumoured he left the city when he couldn't pay his gambling debts. Supposedly, the people he owed were not ones to forgive and forget.

Before leaving for Darwin, I used my instant camera to take a photo of Lesley Maka's corpse and asked Jill and the twins to corroborate her death by signing my notebook. When Jill questioned my motives and accused me of wasting time, I explained that Fiona would be the first to jump down my throat if I failed to claim the reward.

The twins approached the Beast as I turned the ignition. "Jeremy has stolen the safe from our caravan. We've lost ten ounces of gold. Our entire savings. We'll give you a thirty percent finder's fee if you return it to us," declared James.

I swiftly accepted their deal before taking off toward Darwin. As I drove the Beast down the empty highway, I couldn't prevent dark thoughts from creeping into my mind. *Why did I leave her alone? She was drunk, for God's sake! I just wanted to get my rocks off! If she's dead, I'm never going to forgive myself. What am I going to do if I can't find her? I'm a bloody failure!*

# Chapter Twenty-Eight

*Monday, March 10, 2042 – Fiona*

It was impossible to gauge how long I'd been trapped inside the boot. The stifling heat and darkness made me feel like I was being transported in a mobile coffin. I had resisted drinking from the Camelbak as I was concerned the asshole had spiked the water. It's common for pimps to get their girls hooked on drugs to make them loyal and obedient, which no amount of drugs would succeed in doing in my case, but if I had any hope of escaping, I needed to keep my wits about me.

"Are you still alive in there?" I heard the asshole yell from inside the vehicle.

*Fuck you!* I thought, refusing to answer.

The vehicle swerved erratically to the left before violently stopping, causing my back to slam into the steel interior. Immediately after the asshole opened the boot, I was blinded by a torchlight.

"What the fuck?" I yelled.

He moved the beam to the Camelbak and shook its contents back and forth. "We're only halfway there. If you don't drink, you'll die. Your choice," he sneered before slamming the boot shut.

At least another hour passed before my muscles spasmed, my head throbbed, and I felt like vomiting. It didn't take a visit to the GP to diagnose that I was experiencing severe dehydration and heat exhaustion. What a fine medical practitioner I am. I'm also a wonderful patient. For a minute or so, I giggled at the thought. "You're going mad. Get a grip, girl. You're not dead yet," I whispered to myself.

Eventually, my desperate thirst won out. I pressed my lips over the tube and sucked a mouthful of water and, God knows what else. I counted to 400, and when I didn't feel any side effects, I took another sip and started counting. When I struck 400, I greedily sucked from the tube until the Camelbak bladder was empty.

Thankfully my symptoms were lessening, and my head started to clear. Next, I needed to think of an escape plan. I was sure of one specific detail; they would have to kill me before I let anyone take advantage of me again. After failing to think of a way to escape the boot, I tried my best to relax. This wasn't easy in the circumstance, but I intended to gather my strength to attempt a Hail Mary run for it as soon as my feet hit the ground. And if that failed, I planned on fighting to the death.

I had never felt such fatigue and yet couldn't fall asleep. The frustration and hopelessness of the situation overwhelmed me, and finally, it was all too much. The best I could do was muffle my sobs so the asshole wouldn't receive satisfaction from hearing my despair.

~

A wave of emotions washed over me as the boot popped open. At first, I was relieved to breathe fresh air, and then a surge of adrenaline gave me the energy to consider avenues of escape. I willed myself not to flinch as the asshole held the point of a flick knife below my right eye.

"Try to run, and I'll carve your pretty little face like a Halloween pumpkin," the asshole warned before cutting the rope securing my ankles.

As the asshole lifted me from the boot, I could hear multiple gunshots firing in the distance – *pop, pop, pop*. When my feet struck the dirt, I was shocked to feel sharp pains in my quads and calves. I found myself suddenly immobile with cramps. Before I could recover, he dragged me towards the rear of a large white brick building. We were surrounded by dense bush; spinifex grass and acacia shrubs carpeted the ground under the tall furniture, eighty-metre-high eucalypt trees. With my hands tied behind my back and my legs cramping, I rated my odds of breaking free from the asshole and escaping into the bush as one in ten thousand.

The asshole banged his fist against the rear door three times and hollered, "I'm here to see your boss and pay what I owe."

As he waited for a response, I noticed his knuckles were smooth, and his fingernails were clean and finely manicured. His hands were soft and feminine in comparison to my calloused knuckles and chipped dirty nails. The asshole was about to bang his fist once more when the door suddenly opened.

A pimply teenager gestured with a pistol for the asshole to follow him inside. Without warning, the asshole grabbed my arm and pulled me down a poorly lit corridor to a crib room. I had to step around a two-seater grey leather couch blocking the entry. A square dining table occupied the centre of the room, and a battered fridge stood in the far corner.

The asshole violently shoved me into the leather couch. 'Fuck you," I hissed. I scanned the room for weapons and noticed a bread knife lying near a loaf of bread on the kitchen bench. The blunt blade would neither cut my binds nor slice the asshole's throat. However, I could brain him with the sandwich maker. On the opposite wall hung a dartboard with a couple of darts sticking into the bullseye. Again, the darts may not cut my binds, but I could use them to stab him.

I watched pimples tear a piece of bread from the loaf and take a bite before turning towards the asshole and mumbling, "The boss will be wiv ya soon," before sauntering from the room like it was situation normal.

Heavy metal music was playing from a stereo system deep within the building. The music was so muffled that I couldn't recognise the song or the band.

"So, what the fuck are you going to do with me?" I spat.

The asshole grasped the back of my neck and leaned so close that our noses were almost touching. "Shut your fucking hole, bitch," he yelled. I could practically taste his putrid breath as his spittle sprayed my face.

I was about to take a bite out of the asshole's nose when a muscular

Asian bloke resting a shotgun over his shoulder entered the room, followed by a nondescript white guy dressed in a brown suede jacket. I noted my potential escape route was blocked by a heavy-set bald man leaning against the door frame with an assault rifle in his grasp. Interestingly, the asshole instantly altered his posture and body language. With a beaming smile, he removed his hands from his pockets and placed them by his side, narrowed his wide stance, and slightly dipped his head. At that moment, I sensed that Mr Average was more than he appeared.

"Thank you for taking the time to meet with me, Sir," grovelled the asshole.

Mr Average glanced in my direction before turning his focus to the asshole, "Tell me why I shouldn't cut your throat where you stand?" he said calmly. He spoke with a thick European accent that I couldn't pin down to any specific country.

"Sir, I have your money, and I also brought you this girl," he pleaded while pointing at me.

As the asshole reached into his jacket pocket, the Asian guard sprung forth like a cobra and shoved the muzzle of his pump-action shottie under his jaw.

"Slowly remove your hand from your pocket," the guard hissed while pressing the muzzle higher.

I couldn't help but smirk at his sudden change of fortune. He literally looked like he was about to shit himself. The guard reached into the asshole's pocket, retrieved a leather satchel, and then passed it to Mr Average, who weighed it in his palm before peering inside.

"I haven't weighed it, but I'm positive it's about ten ounces, Sir. That's everything I owe you," whined the asshole.

Mr Average stepped forward and bitch slapped him across his cheek.

Yelling, '*Suck shit!*' was on the tip of my tongue.

Mr Average pointed his finger at the asshole's face like a headmaster telling off a naughty pupil. "I'll tell you what you owe me. Has your monkey brain ever heard of a concept called interest?" he asked.

The asshole placed his hand on his cheek and looked at his feet.

"But I also brought you the girl, Sir," he mumbled.

Like a hundred men before him, Mr Average looked me up and down, undressing me with his eyes.

He sighed and rubbed his chin. "She'll do, I guess. I may be able to use her tonight. Your debt is paid, but I want to speak to you about other business matters, so you'll wait here until I'm ready to continue our conversation."

Mr Average approached the bald-headed guard at the door and whispered in his ear before leaving with the Asian enforcer.

# Chapter Twenty-Nine

*Monday, March 10, 2042 – Archie*

Even though I had a fierce desire to speed to Darwin, I refrained from putting the pedal to the metal. I was mindful of treating the old girl with respect to avoid a hissy fit and a blown gasket. I did my utmost during the journey to keep self-recriminations from invading my thoughts. Instead, I focused on formulating a plan to find Fiona – what information I needed, where I would go, who I would see, and what action I would take once I found her. Possible situations and various contingencies were at the forefront of my mind. Unfortunately, the thought of the killing spree I would initiate if anyone harmed a hair on her head made it difficult to remain rational. Guilt will do that to you.

The last time I visited Darwin, the capital city of the NT, was just over nine years ago, right after the end of the War. Whether it was a strategic decision by the enemy or just plain luck, Darwin was just one of two Australian capital cities to be spared being nuked. In the process of destroying each other, the world's most powerful countries also destroyed civilisation as we knew it. There wasn't a formal surrender or declaration. We didn't receive a discharge from the defence force. Instead, when the enemy finally left our shores, we abandoned our posts to return home and attempt to locate our family and friends.

It took me almost eight hours to drive 800 kilometres to the bustling city. Before the War, Darwin had a population of 300,000 souls. I had since heard the population had doubled, with those that crave a city existence flocking to the top end like seagulls to a discarded bucket of chips.

Plan 'A' involved visiting the seedy liquor establishments until I found an informant who could tell me the whereabouts of Jeremy Olaoluwa. Over three hours, I visited Monsoons, Throb, Opium, Nirvana, and the Squires Bar. Each time I entered a club, it didn't take long before an arms merchant, prostitute, or drug dealer propositioned me. When I attempted to purchase information, I was either thrown out by the club's bouncer, whose customer service consisted of trying to rip my head from my neck, or I was politely advised to buy a bottle of hooch and mind my own business by those who wished to retain my patronage. Unfortunately, Plan 'A' had failed miserably to discover even a whiff of a lead.

As I entered the Slow Greyhound, my resolve had not weakened, but my confidence was taking a hit. It was time to try a different tact. I approached the bar and purchased a pint of lager. The barman wore a pink mid-drift top with a red tie and brandished a gold chain that linked his diamond-studded nose ring to a belly button ring. It was hard to fathom why people wore neckties that could be used by an adversary to choke them. My legal colleagues who wore expensive Salvatore Ferragamo silk ties would look sideways at my cheap clip-on. I kept my opinions to myself, conscious of my father's influence. A man who saw shadows amongst shadows and was always ready for a fight.

The barman leaned over the well-used bar. "Would you like anything else, cutie? I get off in an hour. Maybe I could help *you* get off," he said salaciously, followed by a wink.

"I appreciate the offer, and I'm truly flattered, but I'm actually looking for a different kind of action. Where would a high-stakes gambling man go for a good night out, especially if he requires house credit?"

"Well, I can't say I'm not disappointed," he said with a long sigh. "I'd point you to the Casino, but they won't give you credit. Mmmm, let me think." He placed a fingertip to his lips. "You won't get a poker game at the High Horse unless you have a considerable buy-in. You could get credit at the fights, but I'd hate to see a pretty face like yours messed up. If you lose and can't pay, you'd better run. And run real fast."

"Cheers, I'll keep that in mind. Where do they hold the fights?"

"Micket Creek, right next door to the Darwin Pistol Club. It's just twenty kilometres out of town, not far from the cemetery. It's a convenient place to dump patrons that don't pay their debts. If you know what I mean," he warned.

"Thanks, I know where it is," I said appreciatively.

"No worries, honey, and don't say I didn't warn you. If you change your mind or need a bit of TLC afterwards, come back and visit me. I work the night shift seven days a week."

~

Long before the War, I attended the Darwin Pistol Club to compete in club tournaments while serving with the Army Reserves. It was supposed to be just a bit of fun, but when I approached the firing line with my .38 revolver to compete in the practical matches, I would put my game face on and give it my *best shot*. The course required you to move quickly to designated areas and engage multiple cardboard and steel plate targets at distances ranging from five to twenty-five metres. It was a high-speed, high-energy, and quick-thinking discipline. I even managed to win the cup on one occasion. When one of my mates asked me how I managed to beat the club champion, I repeated my old pistol instructor's saying, '*slow is smooth, smooth is fast,*' even though the truth was more akin to the phrase, '*every dog has his day.*'

I cautiously drove the Beast down a bumpy, pot-holed gravel road that led to a large carpark, where thirty or so vehicles and two ancient school buses were parked. At least seventy-five horses were tied to a row of hitching posts on the far side of the carpark. I walked past the horses thinking of how much I missed my old mate, Roger, before entering a cream brick building that, from the outside, looked like an 'old world' leisure centre. An obese bowling ball of a man handed me an entry ticket after I placed two silver coins in his meaty palm.

Heavy metal music was thumping as giant fans spun from the ceiling in a futile attempt to cool the packed venue of 500 punters, most of whom were sweaty men aged between eighteen and forty. The pungent smell of body odour, tobacco, mull, and spilt alcohol was all too familiar in my line work. An eight-square-metre octagon cage took centre stage, with a bar selling beer and spirits positioned to the right of the entry and an area designated for the bookies to the left. Aluminium stands of at least twenty rows stood on the far side of the venue, allowing the audience to peer down at the centre of the cage. Plastic rows of high school seats with numbers written on the backrests were positioned around the cage. I inspected my ticket, 'R30 S452', and found my seat in one of the rear rows. A skinny bloke with dreadlocks wearing an AC/DC shirt and a skull nose stud was sitting in seat 453 with a plastic cup of beer in each hand. I sat down beside him and gestured a greeting with a nod of my head.

"Hey, I'm Shaky. Here, have a beer," he offered in a Welsh accent. His hand shook as he passed me a full plastic cup of beer, spilling some of the contents on my jeans. "Shit, sorry mate, I have Parkinson's. That's why they call me Shaky Shaun," he explained before laughing at his own expense.

I wasn't sure how to respond to his cheerful self-deprecation. "No problem, mate. Thanks for the beer." I shook the man's hand as I said, "Archie's my name. Are you a fight fan, Shaky?"

"Yeah, sort of. I'm here to support my younger brother, who's fighting on tonight's card. He's a fucking good boxer, and I'm not just saying that because he's my bro. He was a golden gloves amateur that could have gone all the way as a pro," he said proudly.

I skulled the watered-down middy of beer. "What's your brother's name? I might place a bet on him."

Shakey stuck his chest out and replied, "Joshua Blevins. He's competing in the second fight of the night against a talented young Aboriginal boxer with lightning-fast hands. It'll be a tough fight, but Josh should have the edge on him with power and experience."

I nodded. "Thanks for the tip, mate. What are you drinking?"

"They only sell this awful shit they brew on-site," he replied, holding up his half-empty cup.

I got up and weaved through the boisterous crowd to the betting area, where five bookies stood behind frayed velvet barrier ropes taking money and issuing betting slips to a throng of punters eager to win big. Two armed guards stood at the corner stanchions, diligently protecting the gold and silver.

A bookie's assistant handed me a flyer listing the eight fighters and their pathway to the final of the mixed martial arts (MMA) tournament. The fighters' odds of winning their first fight and the entire competition were listed on a blackboard behind the podium. Before the start of the first fight, punters could lay a wager on who they favoured winning the entire tournament. Then, during the comp, they could place bets on each fight as long as it was placed before the bell was rung.

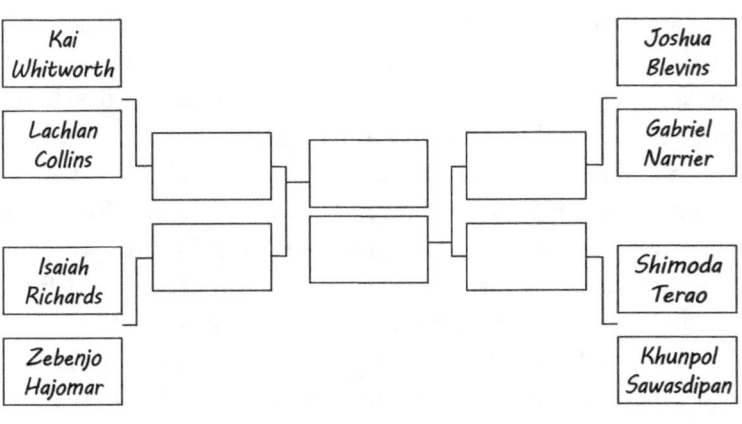

| Fighter | Weight | Height | Age | Style | Wins/Loses |
|---------|--------|--------|-----|-------|------------|
| 1) Kai Whitworth | 79kg | 5ft 11 | 25 | Brazilian Jiu-Jitsu | W: 28 L: 1 |
| 2) Lachlan Collins | 139kg | 6ft 5 | 34 | Street-Fighter | W: 18 L: 0 |
| 3) Joshua Blevins | 84kg | 5ft 10 | 31 | Boxer | W: 23 L: 2 |

| | | | | | | |
|---|---|---|---|---|---|---|
| 4) Gabriel Narrier | 83kg | 5ft 8 | 20 | Boxer | W: 63<br>L: 5 |
| 5) Isaiah Richards | 98kg | 6ft 6 | 33 | MMA | W: 4<br>L: 1 |
| 6) Zebenjo Hajomar | 102kg | 6ft 4 | 37 | MMA | W: 12<br>L: 0 |
| 7) Shimoda Terao | 62kg | 5ft 6 | 29 | Karate | W: 19<br>L: 11 |
| 8) Khunpol Sawasdipan | 74kg | 5ft 7 | 39 | Muay Thai | W: 136<br>L: 31<br>D: 4 |

Beneath the odds of each fighter winning, the competition format and rules were listed in chalk. The tournament's victor would need to win three fights, requiring the competitor to either knock or choke his opponent unconscious or make them submit. To submit, the opponent could tap their hand on the ground or their challenger, typically due to an unnatural limb extension or chokehold. They also had the option of verbally capitulating - 'I give up.' Each fight consisted of one round with no time limit. The fight could last three seconds or two hours, although most were done and dusted within ten minutes. There were only three rules: no eye-gouging, biting, and fish-hooks. A fish-hook involves inserting a finger into the mouth or nostril of their opponent and pulling, often tearing their orifice.

I feigned interest in gambling while I scanned the crowd for Jeremy Olaoluwa. I'm not much of a gambling man, but to keep up my charade, I placed a couple of silver coins on Shaky's brother, Joshua Blevins, to win his fight. As yet unable to locate a man fitting Olaoluwa's description, I sauntered to the bar to join the line and buy a couple of drinks. It was common for punters to attend several events a night, so I was prepared to be patient in the hope he would make an appearance. Normally I would enjoy a good 'fight night' such as this, but my concern for Fiona was foremost in my thoughts to the exclusion of all else.

After purchasing two beers, I kept an eye out for Jeremy as I moseyed back to my seat. Shaky gave me the thumbs up and smiled his appreciation when I handed him a beer.

Shaky noticed the fight card in my lap. "Can I have a squiz?" he asked. His hand shook as he took the card from my grasp.

It cost a small fortune to purchase medications for conditions such as Parkinson's, and it was a death sentence if you were diagnosed with a disease like stage 3 melanoma. But, unfortunately, this wasn't the only worry. After the collapse of the national juvenile vaccination program, we were nervously waiting for diseases and viruses from the past to rear their ugly heads. Vaccines that most people, including myself, took for granted. Parents feared for their children born after the War, with mumps, polio, rotavirus, meningococcal, rubella, and whooping cough being the primary concerns. The most severe effects of these diseases included paralysis, deformities, deafness, brain injury, blindness, kidney failure, and of course, death. The mere thought of a pandemic in this day and age sent a chill down my spine.

My fatalistic reverie was interrupted when the ceiling lights were switched off. Most punters were seated or in the process of finding their seats, with some latecomers placing last-minute bets or purchasing drinks.

The music stopped, and powerful lights illuminated the centre of the cage. An announcer dressed in a schmick, light grey suit held a microphone to his mouth and boomed, "Welcome, ladies and gentlemen, to the Killer of the Cage."

'Killer of the Cage' sounded ominous indeed. As a spectator, I have attended numerous fights, and in my late twenties, I competed in local MMA tournaments. Before society crumbled, it was almost unheard of for an MMA competitor to die in the cage. Unfortunately, it was now a regular occurrence. And there are sicko punters who love to see pain and death; gutless men that wouldn't dream of competing in the cage but get a kick out of watching fighters beating the crap out of each other.

After I lost Janet, my family, and my career, I had no plan or purpose, so I foolishly popped pills to dull the mental pain and picked up a job as a tent fighter. We travelled throughout the rural areas, entertaining the locals by providing their young bucks with an opportunity to fight the talent. It didn't take long for me to realise it was a mug's game. I was in constant pain for low pay, so I chucked it in and started working as a bounty hunter.

"Am I missing the obvious? Why do they call it Killer of the Cage?" I asked Shaky.

Shaky's brows furrowed in concern. "Mate, these events were always rough, but now they're insane. The promoters hired some new talent that enjoys killing. Josh wouldn't be fighting for this mob if it weren't for my meds," he said ruefully.

"Before we commence tonight's event, I would like to introduce and thank our benefactor, MR SALKOV DENISOVICH," the announcer proclaimed.

A spotlight beamed into the stands on the far side of the venue, illuminating a roped-off area at the centre. Four armed guards stood between the punters and the VIP they were protecting. Salkov was an unremarkable middle-aged man of average height and average build with grey wavy hair. I wouldn't bat an eyelid if he were introduced to me as the town's mayor or bank manager. However, his apparel was the one prominent aspect that set him apart from the average family man. He wore a luxurious red silk gown that flowed to his knees with a gold pendant the size of a fist hanging from his neck.

I almost jumped out of my chair when I noticed the man sitting alongside Salkov. Doctor Noel Patterson, the man I had been chasing for nearly twelve months! Suddenly so close yet so far from my grasp. I retrieved a picture of Patterson from the inside pocket of my leather jacket. It was hard to believe he was the same man depicted in the instant photo taken only two years ago. The experimental drugs that he designed and self-administered had altered his appearance, transforming him from a slim handsome gentleman with a full head of hair to a muscular pockmarked bald man that you wouldn't want to meet in a dark alley. Even though my priority was to find Fiona,

I was not one to look a gift horse in the mouth. Apprehending this psychopathic scumbag was now a very close second on my 'to-do' list.

"Mr Denisovich will graciously award the winner of the competition five ounces of gold. And in a sign of gratitude for the victor's bravery and fortitude, he's also very generously awarding a bonus prize. Bring out the trophy," hollered the announcer.

# Chapter Thirty

*Monday, March 10, 2042 – Fiona*

I had the displeasure of witnessing the asshole pigging out on anything he could find for the past half hour - biscuits, fried chicken, ham, and cheese. Then, having cleaned out their fridge, he started demolishing the loaf of bread left on the counter. I was about to tell him to stop munching like a cow near my ear when a heavily made-up woman in her early forties entered the room. She wore 'come fuck me boots', a plaid pattern tweed mini-skirt, and a midriff top that proudly displayed her muffin-top. My mum would have described her as mutton dressed as lamb. She swiftly looked me up and down before leaving the room without saying a word.

A minute later, Ms Mutton re-entered the room and threw a plastic bag of clothing at me before addressing the asshole, "Cut her loose. She needs to be ready in five."

The asshole roughly grabbed my arm and turned me sideways before cutting the rope binding my arms behind my back. I rubbed my red, sore wrists and rotated my shoulders to get the blood flowing.

Ms Mutton pointed to the bag. 'Put that on," she demanded.

I opened the plastic bag and dumped a matching metallic gold G-string and bra, along with a pair of transparent stripper heels, onto the couch.

I stood up from the couch and held the scant items in front of her face. "You can get fucked! I'm not wearing this," I sneered.

She placed her hands on her hips. "Listen carefully, you little bitch. I'll be back in five, so be ready, or the guys here will strip you and dress you."

I gave her the finger as she left the room to return to whatever snake hole she slithered out from.

It felt like a lifetime ago, but before meeting Archie, I worked as a skimpy barmaid, parading topless while serving drinks to patrons. Even though I hated the job, I still did it every night for two years. So, I pondered, why am I thinking about fighting to the death for the sake of pride instead of just slipping into the slut-wear and waiting for the perfect time to make my move? Finally, I decided, fuck my ego: making each one of these fuckers pay was now my primary objective.

# Chapter Thirty-One

*Monday, March 10, 2042 – Archie*

I had just left my seat to have another look for Jeremy when the announcer mentioned something about the victor being awarded a 'bonus prize'. I assumed it was a gimmick to motivate the fighters and excite the crowd.

A moment later, a spotlight illuminated a goon escorting a scantily dressed woman down the stands. The crowd whistled, jeered and yelled crude and abusive comments - *'Suck my cock,' 'She left her tits backstage,' 'Show us your pussy,' and 'I'll be your daddy.'*

The goon led the poor girl by a chain connected to a neck iron into the centre of the cage. As I weaved through the crowd towards the bookies, I turned around to see the unfortunate girl standing shoulders back and head high beside the announcer, a fierce look of defiance on her face rather than the defeated expression one might expect from a girl in her situation.

I felt a mixture of emotions - relief, joy, and pity. I had found her. Thank God!

As she was paraded around the perimeter of the cage, the announcer explained that Fiona would be awarded to the tournament's victor. I thought about trying to show my face to let her know I was there, but it would have drawn too much attention. And I had no idea how she would react. It was far too risky!

After a couple of laps, I watched the goon lead Fiona back to her seat, with Salkov seated between Fiona and Patterson. Rescuing her without getting us both killed was my number one priority. I decided that the smart plan was to wait until the end of the tournament, follow her after she was "awarded" to the victor and execute the rescue at the first opportunity thereafter - a piece of cake!

The announcer proceeded to introduce the first two fighters. I was so focused on Fiona that I didn't notice the fighters enter the cage.

"In the blue corner, you have a Brazilian jiu-jitsu fighter, standing 181 centimetres tall, weighing 79 kilograms, with a fight record of twenty-five wins and one loss." The announcer paused for dramatic effect before screaming, "Kai the BOA CON-STRICTOOOR WHITWOOOORTH."

Whitworth raised his fists to the crowd and flexed his six-pack before stamping his foot on the canvas mat toward his opponent. Shit! I looked over at his opponent. He was a Hulk - a nickname I gave Patterson's freak-shows, men that he dosed with a concoction of steroids, methamphetamine, radiation, and his experimental wonder drug.

"In the red corner, you have a street fighter, standing 195 centimetres tall, weighing 139 kilograms, with a fight record of 18 wins and no losses." The announcer screamed, "Lachlan the HAMMERRRR COLLIIIINNNSSS," extending the syllables as the crowd roared.

I hoped for Whitworth's sake that he was a world-class black belt because he was in for a world of hurt if he wasn't. I had tangled with Patterson's hulks in the past. They had incredible pain tolerance and extraordinary strength. I noted that the referee failed to bring both fighters to the centre of the cage to reiterate the rules and provide them with an opportunity to touch gloves. Instead, he yelled, "FIGHT!" I noticed the gamblers at the pit hurriedly make their final bets before the bell rang - Ding, Ding.

The Hulk rushed forward and swung wildly at Whitworth, who instinctively ducked under the haymaker and dove forward for a double-leg take-down, attempting to pull the enormous man's legs out from underneath him and toss him on his back. It was a clever strategy, but the Hulk was wise to the shot and sprawled his hips and legs backwards, leaning his chest on Whitworth's back. The Brazilian Jiu-Jitsu (BJJ) fighter knelt on his shins like a turtle under the 140-kilogram ball of muscle. The Hulk instantly stood and struck Whitworth with a closed fist to the back of his head and neck with several bone-crushing hammer blows. Whitworth instinctively rolled to his back in an attempt to play guard and protect himself.

Even though the grappler looked barely conscious, the referee made no effort to stop the fight. A part of me didn't want to watch, but I couldn't take my eyes off the carnage. The Hulk grabbed Whitworth's ankle, threw it to one side, and then stomped his size-14 foot down on his face and neck repeatedly. Finally, the referee stepped in and stopped the fight, but it was far too late for Whitworth.

While the Hulk played to the crowd, two guards dragged Whitworth's corpse from the cage by his outstretched arms. When the monster raised his fists and roared like a juiced-up grizzly bear, the crowd emphatically responded by rising from their seats and cheering. I love to fight, but I was grateful that I wasn't locked in the cage with the freak of nature.

# Chapter Thirty-Two

*Monday, March 10, 2042 – Fiona*

I decided to stick to the plan and wait for the ideal time to attempt my escape. Getting bludgeoned to death for refusing to wear slut-wear was not a smart move. Within ten minutes of making the decision, I already regretted it. The guard secured a steel ring around my neck and pulled me by a chain into a stadium full of jeering men, where I was humiliated and shamed on a grand scale.

After the guards shoved me into a seat beside Mr Average, I pulled myself together and reminded myself of who I was - a bounty hunter who managed to kill and scrape my way out of worse situations than this one. With new resolve, I scanned my surroundings. I was sitting in a roped-off section, looking down on a fight cage surrounded by hundreds of men full of bloodlust. Four armed goons were standing outside the barrier ropes, protecting Mr Average and a bloke to his left. Mr Average had put on an elaborate red gown with a gold eagle pendant the size of a tennis ball hanging from his neck. He was fixated on the action in the centre of the cage. I craned my head to get a look at his companion. I couldn't fucking believe it. I was eye-balling psycho fucking Patterson. Mutherfucker! He was glaring in my direction. I pondered whether he recognised me or I was just being paranoid. After all, it had been almost a year since he escaped, and he wouldn't have given me much more than a momentary glance at the time.

A suit in the centre of the cage was announcing some bullshit when a guard grabbed my chain and pulled me down the steps toward the cage. A blazing spotlight almost blinded me as the operator concentrated the beam in my direction. Then, while shielding my eyes, the announcer pointed to me. "Please welcome our trophy for the night......MISS KITTTTTY!"

I wondered, who the fuck was Miss Kitty? Is that supposed to be me? My senses were overloaded. I was struggling to fully comprehend the situation. Fucking assholes in the crowd were yelling nasty shit. I would have given my right leg for an assault rifle and a thousand rounds.

The guard pushed me through the cage doors. I stood in the centre, looking through the wire at the hundreds of sickos shouting and glaring in my direction. As if that weren't degrading enough, I was then paraded around the boundary like a poodle at a dog show.

Once the spotlight was mercifully switched off, I was shoved and pulled back to my seat. The announcer introduced two fighters. I focused on the fighters to help take my mind off the situation. I had been training under Archie's tutelage for over a year, working hard to improve my stand-up and ground game.

Whitworth looked fit, and with a ring name like the boa constrictor, I was interested to see how good his chokeholds were. After the announcer introduced Whitworth's opponent, I looked over at Patterson, who was smiling like a smug kid given a chocolate cake at his birthday party. No wonder he was happy; poor Whitworth was fighting one of his chemically enhanced goons.

I watched the fight with dismay as Whitworth struggled to even grab the goon, let alone attempt a 'boa constrictor' choke. Instead, the gorilla hammer-fisted and stomped him into the canvas until he was done and dusted. Having fought Patterson's goons with knives and firearms, I doubted his opponents would have any chance of beating him. I looked at my feet for a glass bottle or anything I could use as a weapon. I decided that when the ugly fuck won the comp, I would rather die fighting than be handed over as some trophy.

One of Mr Average's guards stepped over the rope and leaned over me to whisper something in his boss' ear. He reacted angrily, shouted for the guard to 'sort it' and gestured toward the crowd.

Moments later, the suit spoke into the microphone, "Ladies and gentlemen, I have been advised that one of the fighters, Gabriel Narrier, has been removed from the card due to injury."

The crowd started to boo loudly and throw their betting slips into the cage. This did not deter the suit. "All of your bets will be reimbursed. We want to call on anyone in the audience who would like to replace Mr Narrier and fight for five ounces of gold and our hot young trophy sitting in the stands to raise your hand and come forth to the betting pit."

After witnessing the enormous freak smash his opponent into mush, who would be dumb and desperate enough to raise their hand and die a painful death in front of a jeering crowd?

Mr Average turned to me. "Do you think someone in the audience will volunteer to be your hero?" He gestured to Patterson, "My good friend Noel mentioned that he looks forward to owning you after his fighter wins the tournament."

They laughed after I gave them both the middle finger. For a split second, I mistakenly believed the crowd was laughing at me until I saw the spotlight focus its beam on a grey-haired old man raising his hand and walking to the betting pit. Great, I thought, I have a senior citizen who desires to win my hand.

Another two men from the audience walked toward the betting pit, but I wasn't sure if they were seeking their reimbursement or were crazy enough to fight in the cage. The spotlight danced over the crowd, landing on a bloke raising his hand on the far side of the venue. At least he looked relatively young, tall, and fit. As he stepped through the crowd, I recognised him and felt a tear rolling down my cheek. The silly bugger was about to risk his life for me. I quickly wiped away the tear and crossed my fingers and toes.

# Chapter Thirty-Three

*Monday, March 10, 2042 – Archie*

I didn't hesitate to raise my hand when they announced the opportunity to replace Narrier. However slim my chance of winning, this was an opportunity to rescue Fiona. And I wouldn't be able to live with myself if I didn't give it my best shot.

Before approaching the betting pit, I looked over at Shaky. "Sorry, mate. I'll try to do right by your brother," I said solemnly.

Shaky momentarily looked shocked before quickly recovering and raising his chin. "Don't apologise. It's your funeral, mate." As he spoke, I noticed the shaking in his hands had intensified.

There were five men lined up in front of the bookie's table. As I joined the end of the line, an older gentleman cleared his throat, "My job is to select Narrier's replacement. Take off your shirts so I can get a good look at you."

The bloke in front of me, who must have been at least seventy years old, struggled to lift his jumper over his head. Just by having a quick gander up the line, my stiffest competition was the bloke at the very front. From what I could see of him in the dim light, he was about five-foot-eight, with a thick muscular back and broad shoulders. As soon as I slipped off my shirt, the man making the decision approached.

"Okay, bloke, can you fight?" he asked as he gazed into my eyes like he was evaluating my very soul.

"I was a tent fighter for about twelve months and won my fair share of fights. I've also fought in the cage."

"What's your record?"

"I'm not sure. In total, I've had about seventy fights and lost three or four of them," I replied unconvincingly. I had no idea how many times I had fought, as most of my fights were in WA towns against local men. They were tough blokes, but they weren't professional fighters.

He sighed deeply before stating, "I'll take your word for it, sport. It doesn't really matter, anyway. Whoever I pick is meat for the lions." He looked me up and down and then asked me to turn around. "Far out, you've got a lot of scars. Do you have any injuries?"

"Nope, I'm as fit as a fiddle," I declared as I stuck out my chest.

He chuckled, "You won't be for long." He picked his nose like he was mining for gold before asking, "What's your style?"

"Kung fu," I lied.

The selector laughed and turned to the bookies. "This is the one. He's full of shit, but he'll be entertaining. Put his style down as kung fu." He picked up a notepad and pen, "What's your name, and how old are ya?"

"Bolo Yeung, thirty-six," I managed to reply with a straight face. By his reaction, he obviously wasn't aware of Bolo's performances as an enforcer and executioner in Bruce Lee's movie, Enter the Dragon.

He scribbled my name on the pad before asking me to take off my boots and jeans and step onto a scale. "Eighty-four kilograms," he called out to the bookies. Next, he gestured for me to stand against the wall and used a tape measure to ascertain my height, "Six-foot-two." He then rummaged through a cardboard box behind the bookie's podium and handed me a groin cup, a pair of black shorts, and four-ounce fingerless gloves, which I quickly slipped on.

I was about to ask the old fella if he could tape my hands when he told me to follow him to the cage. The announcer introduced my opponent as I stepped into the cage. I heard my pseudonym being announced over the speakers and wondered if any Bruce Lee fans were in the building. I peered up into the stands at Fiona, which solidified my resolve to win the comp.

My opponent was shadowboxing on the far side of the cage, throwing combinations and bobbing and weaving with fluidity.

Shaky wasn't exaggerating about his brother's skill. Joshua looked and moved like a physical specimen. I predicted the fight wouldn't be easy.

I started formulating my tournament strategy as soon as I stood in line to be selected. I didn't want to fall into the trap of thinking too far ahead, as Joshua was a talented pugilist who demanded respect. Still, if I beat him, my next opponent would be a Thai boxer or a karate fighter, whose kicking prowess could present a painful challenge. So I planned to unveil my grappling skills when I needed them. Keep it in my back pocket, so to speak. Then, hopefully, I could catch one of these masters of the kicking arts off guard. My strategy to deal with Shaky's brother was the exact opposite. Distance would be my ally.

The referee approached me as I leaned against the cage wire and stretched my hips. "The only rules are no eye-gouging, no biting, and no fish-hooks. Everything else is legal. Do you understand?"

"Completely. Just don't wait for one of us to die before you decide to referee the fight," I warned, pointing at his chest. He gave me a puzzled look before returning to the centre of the cage.

Upon the referee yelling, "FIGHT," I heard the ding ding of the bell. I put my fists up and stepped towards my opponent. Joshua was quick for a light heavyweight. He skipped to the centre of the cage and settled into an orthodox boxer's stance, with his left side leading the dance. He immediately threw a double jab, missing my nose by a whisker with the second punch.

Joshua vented his frustration when I circled and danced out of his reach. Then, to the crowd's approval, he gestured with his hands for me to plant my feet and fight him. "Not in this lifetime, buddy," I whispered to myself.

As Joshua stepped towards me to throw another jab, I reacted by teep kicking him to his lower stomach with my front foot, forcing him back a step. He caught me off guard when he instantly recovered, launching an explosive cross-hook combination smashing into my left eye and right ear. Even though I was familiar with the sensation of losing my equilibrium after being struck behind the ear in previous altercations, I was still unable to alter the inevitable outcome. I was a slave to my perception. The canvas moved like the deck of a boat in a huge swell, causing me to fall awkwardly onto my backside against the side of the cage.

Surprisingly, Joshua yelled at me to stand rather than follow me to the ground and continue his onslaught with some 'ground and pound'. The crowd cheered at the prospect of witnessing further carnage. My vision was blurred. I was still dazed as I grasped the chain link fence to pull myself up from the bloodied canvas. Just as I had risen to my feet, like any good fighter, Joshua pounced, taking advantage of my defenceless posture by punching me to my liver, followed by a hook to my cheek. By pure instinct, I managed to duck the next punch, which gave me a fraction of a second to skip backwards to the far side of the cage. I felt blood dripping from my cheek as the crowd told me what they thought of my tactical retreat - 'BOOOOOOOO! BOOOOOOOO! BOOOOOOOO!'

From my perspective, the fight was not going well. Before he knocked my block off, I needed to start connecting with some offence and earn his respect or forget about my cloak-and-dagger tactic and revert to what I do best, grappling. My head began to clear as he stalked towards me with an abundance of confidence written all over his face. In his mind, he had already won the fight. He just needed to finish me off. It suddenly struck me that disrupting his footwork was the key to winning this fight.

Joshua effortlessly slipped my jab as I expected, so I immediately followed up with an inner thigh kick, striking him with my left shin just above his knee. Before he could counter, I stepped to the side and whipped my rear leg down in a kicking motion similar to an axe striking the base of a tree. My shin was the axe head, and his calf was the trunk. Joshua's grimace betrayed his valiant attempt to mask the effect of the devastating kick. His leg buckled as he closed the gap, but he somehow managed to stay upright and counter with a straight right, corkscrewing his knuckles toward my face. However, his clenched fist fell short of his intended target because of my well-timed teep kick to his lower stomach, followed by another calf kick.

He lumbered forward to counter but lacked the power, grace, and speed he displayed at the start of the fight. As the fight progressed, I kicked his thighs, calves, and stomach at every opportunity while evading his punches with ease.

Joshua's bruised and swollen thighs and calves were so beat up that he struggled to stand upright. So when I hammered my shin to the outside of his lead calf for the final time, I couldn't help but feel pity when he crumbled to the canvas in agony.

I glanced at the referee and shouted, "Do your job, mate, or my next kick will be aimed at your ribs."

The referee gulped nervously and waved off the fight. The crowd erupted with boisterous cheers when my hand was raised in the middle of the cage. I felt contempt for the fickle, bloodthirsty audience who booed me earlier in the fight but now applauded my success. Shaky's brother was stretchered from the cage as I returned to the betting pit to await the outcome of the next fight.

While I took small sips of water to rehydrate, I watched the next fight between Richards and Hajomar. They were both highly-skilled mixed martial artists who fought in an engaging back-and-forth contest. They battered and bruised each other with kicks, punches, and throws for just over twenty minutes, with Hajomar finally forcing his opponent to tap when he caught him in a beautiful guillotine choke. Hajomar looked physically spent as he exited the cage and limped past me, collapsing in a heap behind the bookie's table. In a gesture of sportsmanship, I leaned down to hand him my flask, which he rudely snatched from my grasp. He spat blood at my feet before guzzling the water. Lovely to meet you too, I thought to myself.

I scanned the fight card as the announcer introduced Sawasdipan and Terao. They were fighting on my side of the draw, meaning one of them would be my next opponent. The fighters entered the cage to a standing ovation. I watched the fight closely, looking for holes in their technique and formulating strategies that would lead me to victory. With artistic ferocity, the Thai fighter obliterated his Japanese opponent with solid knees, kicks, and elbows, ending the fight in under three minutes.

Hajomar was still seated behind the bookie's table, looking angry and dejected. As the fight official spoke into his ear, he vehemently shook his head. The official sighed before announcing that Hajomar could not continue due to injury. I wondered if the prospect of fighting the Hulk had anything to do with his decision. I wouldn't blame him if that was the case.

With the Hulk automatically progressing due to Hajomar forfeiting, I was told to enter the cage sooner than expected. The Hulk voiced his displeasure at Hajomar's decision by yelling "Coward" and spitting in his face. He then strutted up to me, stopping within an inch of my face and tracing his thumb from one side of his throat to the next. I gazed up at the monstrous man, locking eyes with him until a bookie attempted to separate us. I wasn't deluded into thinking the bookie was concerned for my welfare; instead, he didn't want to return the punters' coin due to a no-contest. When I held my ground, the Hulk shoved me with both hands towards the seated spectators, hurling me into a biker's lap. "Settle down, mate. You haven't even bought me dinner," the biker jested. Before I made my way to the cage, I glared at the Hulk, who yelled insults and threats.

I shook off my encounter with the Hulk and thought about my next fight. There was no doubt Sawasdipan would be a formidable opponent, but I was quietly confident my strategy would give me a distinct advantage.

Sawasdipan was performing the Wai khru ram muay, translated in English as 'war dance saluting the teacher.' The Thai fighter paid gratitude and respect to his instructor, parents, and ancestors by circling the cage counterclockwise and praying at each corner. Wearing his headband called a Mong Kon, he knelt on the canvas in the centre of the cage and bowed three times before starting to dance. He knelt on one knee, circling his arms as he bounced his kneeling lower leg before rising to his feet and rolling his fists in front of his chest as he brought his knee forward and then rotated it to the outside. It was a beautiful dance that the punters 'in the know' would carefully watch before laying their bets because it displayed the fighter's skill, flexibility, and coordination. I wondered if Sawasdipan was dancing to a Thai orchestra playing in his head.

Then, finally, the bell rang, and the Thai stepped towards me with both fists raised and a determined look. Even though Sawasdipan was more than four inches shorter and ten kilograms lighter than me, chances are he would thrash me in a stand-up fight. I took a deep breath and steeled myself, silently praying that my strategy was sound or this would end badly for me and Fiona.

# Chapter Thirty-Four

*Monday, March 10, 2042 – Fiona*

I was almost sick with nerves as I watched Archie get repeatedly punched and then almost knocked out by a hard-hitting boxer. "Take him down," I screamed. I was about to yell some more advice when I noticed Mr Average and Patterson glare in my direction. So I clamped down on my teeth and continued to send Archie instructions mentally like some believer in telepathy. 'When he throws his one-two, level change and take him down to the mats with a double leg. Control him until he tires, and then submit with one of your three favourite moves – triangle choke, rear-naked choke, or heel-hook.' Instead of heeding my advice and grappling, Archie continued dancing around the cage, keeping his distance and kicking the boxer's stomach and legs until he could no longer stand and went down. TKO! I couldn't contain my emotions any longer and cheered with the crowd.

The next two fights passed in a blur. I was either worrying about Archie's next fight, looking for a way to escape, or fantasising about killing the asshole and Patterson. I returned my attention to the middle of the cage when the Muay Thai fighter started to dance. I was mesmerised by how he rolled his arms, loosened his hips in a circular motion and pretended to shoot an arrow with an imaginary bow.

The bell rang, and I watched with anticipation as the Thai fighter and his Japanese opponent met in the centre of the cage. With his cows rather than calves and thick tree trunk thighs, the Thai's savage kicks and elbows overwhelmed and tore through his karate opponent like a katana through butter. The fight ended within minutes. If Archie planned to trade kicks and punches with this dude the way he did against the boxer, then we were both fucked!

Not long after demolishing the Japanese fighter, I was surprised to see the Thai re-enter the ring, with Archie following closely behind. I overheard the punters discussing the matchup. They predicted an exciting and brutal kickboxing contest – I fucking hope not!

While the Thai danced, Archie warmed up by shadowboxing near the edge of the cage. The striations and veins running along his lean muscles were exposed as he worked up a sweat, whipping punch and kick combinations through the air. The zig-zagging scars over his chest and back from knife and gunshot wounds told a story of violence and survival that the punters would not ignore. They crowded the bookies, frantically laying bets before the bell rang. I wouldn't be surprised if they underestimated Archie after his last performance.

# Chapter Thirty-Five

*Monday, March 10, 2042 – Archie*

My old mentor, Sal, would often preach, KISS – 'Keep it Simple Stupid.' With that in mind, along with Sun Tzu's philosophy of 'know the enemy and know yourself', I formulated my strategy for defeating Sawasdipan. Thai fighters typically start slow, easing into the fight and gauging their opponent's skill before engaging with full ferocity. I wasn't planning on allowing him to set the pace and use his art of eight limbs – two fists, two elbows, two shins and two knees – to overwhelm me with his skill and power. I was already battered and bruised from the previous fight and knew that if I had any chance of beating the Hulk, I needed to finish this fight quickly and unscathed. So I planned to make the Thai think I was going to fight toe-to-toe, then when he countered my strikes, take him down and submit him. *The plan sounded straightforward but executing it was another matter entirely!*

The fight started with the Thai throwing jabs, low kicks and feints to gauge the distance and test my reactions. As expected, he was easing into the fight, so I overreacted to his feints and allowed him to touch me a few times, encouraging him to move forward while I waited for my opening. Then, as soon as the Thai stepped within range, I focused all my speed and power on my favourite combination - a right cross to his face, a left hook to his jaw, and a right kick to his ribs. He blocked my fists with his forearms, checked my kick with his shin, and then smiled as he instantly countered my attack by launching a rear leg kick aimed at my thigh. In anticipation of the kick, I bent my knees and lowered my level to enter for a single leg take-down, grabbing his kicking leg and sweeping his standing leg. I hung onto his kicking leg, and as soon as his back hit the canvas, I dropped my ass to the mat, hooking his heel with the crook of my forearm before leaning back and rotating inwardly with violent torque. The tearing of his knee ligaments sounded like fabric ripping apart. I felt a little guilty as the brave Thai reached for his knee and writhed on the canvas, gritting his teeth in agony. I sighed with relief as I looked up into the stands and saw Fiona cheering.

# Chapter Thirty-Six

*Monday, March 10, 2042 – Fiona*

I am a highly competitive person who strives to win at all costs, so when I spar and roll with Archie, I aim to beat him up and submit him. After thirteen years of training, Archie received his Black belt in BJJ from an instructor whose lineage can be traced back to the family that developed the art. I often wondered how much effort he uses when we grapple. Does he hold back on using his strength and skill? My question was answered when he took the Thai fighter down to the canvas within moments of the bell and latched under his heel before savagely twisting to destroy his knee. It finally dawned on me just how good he really is. On reflection, getting to the top of Everest would be an easier mountain to climb than tapping Archie. The injured Thai fighter had to be carried from the cage on a stretcher. He was putting on a brave face for a bloke with a totally fucked up knee. His misfortune certainly didn't stop me from cheering. After all, *my life* was on the line.

During the ten-minute intermission, there was a hive of activity at the betting pit, with punters swarming around the bookies, swapping gold and silver coins for betting tickets. Archie must have been waiting at the far side of the venue as I couldn't see him. I picked up a fight card lying by my feet to study his final opponent's stats. I'd be a fool to think Archie's next fight would be a walk in the park. From where I sat, his chance of winning was as good as a coin flip. Patterson's goon was fresh, having fought for less than a minute in his only fight for the night, and he outweighed Archie by more than fifty kilos. He also had an opportunity to witness Archie's fighting style, including his strengths and weaknesses.

While a techno-rap song from the early thirties boomed through speakers hanging from the ceiling, the monstrous goon ran into the cage and lifted his fists to the crowd, who responded by either cheering or booing. An Australian audience without a home-grown hero to support tends to cheer the underdog. And I'm guessing the spectators considered Archie the massive underdog.

The crowd erupted with cheers as AC/DC's song 'Jailbreak' blasted through the speakers. Archie told me over one of our many campfires that the band was one of his favourites. At nine years of age, he was mesmerised by the rock gods when his grandfather took him to an outdoor concert in Perth. Feeling the vibration in the seats from the thundering drums, the electrifying guitar tearing through the stadium, and the lead singer screaming at the top of his lungs turned the young Archie into a fan. He couldn't have picked a better song to get the crowd on his side, as most people in the venue could relate to the lyrics.

The referee repeated the rules, or lack thereof, and asked the fighters if they wanted to touch gloves. Archie glared at the giant as his opponent stepped within an inch of his face and yelled, "You're dead, cunt!" The crowd cheered. I crossed my fingers and toes and screamed for Archie to 'kick his ass'. Unfortunately, Archie's response was not picked up by the microphone, but whatever he said infuriated the giant because he shoved the referee aside and threw a looping right hook. Archie bobbed and weaved under the massive fist as the bell rang.

Archie circled out of reach, dancing to the other side of the cage. He lost the crowd's support each time he evaded the goon's strikes - BOOOOOOO! He repeatedly made the goon miss. His fists swung at Archie's head but struck nothing but thin air, with Archie ducking, slipping, and parrying the punches. The crowd continued to voice their dislike of Archie's evasive strategy - BOOOOOOO! But it was working. The goon was gulping oxygen while Archie smirked and goaded him on to try harder. He yelled one-liners at the giant, "Come on, put some effort in!" "You're as weak as piss!"

and "Are you going to punch me or what?"

The goon lumbered forward while Archie started to stick and move, throwing a jab and then stepping back and off to the side. He peppered him continuously, cutting his cheeks and lips, breaking his nose, and swelling his left eye. The crowd pointed and gasped in amazement as they witnessed the freak's green blood flow from his wounds. From where I sat in the stands, Archie was like an artist, creating his masterpiece with every blow. But instead of using paint, he used the goon's green blood as it sprayed and dripped over the canvas. As Archie's confidence grew, so did his combinations - hooks, uppercuts, and kicks combined with his jab to batter his opponent.

The frustration and humiliation must have been too much for the goon, as he gave up trying to strike Archie and ran forward, reaching for his waist to tackle him to the ground. Archie sprawled on top of the giant and transitioned to his enormous back, gluing himself to his back like a koala bear hanging onto its mother. He hooked his legs around the goon's hips and wrapped his arms around his shoulders like a seatbelt. The monster had no idea how to defend the position and roared angrily in desperation. His roaring was silenced when Archie slid the ridge of his right hand under his chin, circling his neck with his arm and grabbing his own bicep, squeezing the arteries on both sides of his massive neck, preventing his green blood from carrying oxygen to his brain. It was a magnificent rear-naked choke. In my excitement, I forgot about the neck chain and attempted to rise to my feet and cheer, only to be shoved back down in my seat by one of Mr Average's fuckhead guards.

# Chapter Thirty-Seven

*Monday, March 10, 2042 – Archie*

Even though I knew I had a sound strategy, the fight went much better than I had planned. The Hulk barely managed to graze me as I easily evaded his lumbering punches. Confident that his cardio would be his biggest weakness, my plan was simple - make him so angry that he chases me around the cage and throws strikes with all his might. His freakish muscles were an impediment under high-intensity exertion. His heart had to work much harder than the average person's to pump oxygen around his massive frame, causing a higher heart rate and a lack of breath.

He fell into my trap from the word go. I responded to his banal challenge, "You're dead, cunt," by asking him, "Where did you attend your elocution lessons?" After a split-second of confusion, he shoved the referee aside and started throwing down. Much to the crowd's displeasure, I ran like a scared child. However, the tables swiftly turned when he began to fatigue. I threw my jab to gauge my distance and soften him up before launching some of my favourite combos. He was exhausted, humiliated, and a bloody mess when he attempted a desperate take-down. The rest is history. I don't care how strong or enhanced he is, he still needs blood to flow to his brain.

I rose to my feet, and the referee raised my hand as the Hulk lay unconscious, face down by the side of the cage. There was a mixture of shock, anger, and elation in the crowd, with spectators either throwing their betting slips on the ground in disgust, wallowing in silence, or raising their slips in the air and cheering with glee. The announcer brought forth my five ounces of gold, and I pointed to Fiona, gesturing for the Russian to bring her down to the centre of the cage.

From my periphery, I saw a sudden flash of movement. I jumped back as the edge of a blade narrowly missed my stomach. Gripped with fear, I had a sudden flashback of when I was sliced open with a machete blade. The Hulk had regained consciousness and was stalking me with a bowie knife in his grasp, passing it from one hand to the other. The voice in my head, my former mentor Sal, calmly instructed me: '*Don't turn your back and run. He'll stick you like a pig. Focus on his knife-hand. Stay in the middle of the cage. Look for an opportunity to grab his hand. And fight like fuck.*'

When you're unarmed, the best thing to do in a knife fight is to put as many obstacles as possible between you and the attacker. And then run for your life. But, standing in the cage, the only option I had was to wait for him to close the distance.

Just as the Hulk was within slashing range, a short, muscular bloke sprinted into the cage and grabbed the Hulk from behind, wrapping his arms around his waist and lifting him into the air before arching his back and throwing him rearward in an impressive, suplex wrestling move. As the Hulk's head hit the ground, I heard a distinct cracking noise, similar to a cricket bat snapping in two. His neck was positioned at a grossly unnatural angle as he lay motionless on the canvas.

My saviour was grinning from ear to ear. "Do you call that a fucking fight? It wouldn't have taken me more than sixty seconds to win that bout."

"Um. Gizzarelli," I said in amazement. "What are you doing...?"

Before I could finish my question, automatic gunfire erupted throughout the venue. For a split second, the audience went silent. Then, in a mad rush, the crowd pushed and fell over each other to exit the building. A boom of a shotgun and the crack of rifles' firing echoed as men and women stampeded towards the exits in panic, bumping and trampling the spectators unable to maintain their footing.

I pointed to the stands where Fiona was being held, "Can you give me a hand, mate?"

"What the fuck do you think I've been doing?"

Before I could respond, Gizzarelli sprinted past the cowering announcer, shouldering his way through the panicked crowd like a rugby player running towards the try line. As I followed in his wake, I peered up to see Fiona being manhandled down the stands by two guards. Unfortunately, I lost sight of her just after Gizzarelli started a fight with a guard who was blocking his path. I bumped and pushed through the stampede until I was nose to nose with a large Māori guard who sported an imposing full-face moko tattoo. For reasons I could only guess, he graciously stepped aside and let me pass. When I reached a corridor at the rear of the building, I heard three sharp blasts of a whistle. I knew immediately what the signal was communicating: *The poo has hit the fan, and I need urgent assistance.*

# Chapter Thirty-Eight

*Monday, March 10, 2042 – Fiona*

Seeing a guard pass the goon a knife, I jumped out of my seat to run down the stands and help Archie. However, in my desperation to go to Archie's aid, I forgot about the guard behind me, who ferociously yanked on the chain secured to my neck, hurling me backwards like a yo-yo. The fucker then grabbed me in a headlock and forced me down the stands and into the crib room. Once inside, he threw me onto the couch next to Mr Average, who was red in the cheeks and breathing heavily, sucking in oxygen like he had just competed in a two-hundred-metre sprint. As soon as he saw the guard, he started screaming in European, "Blyat Pizdets Yobanaya suka!" The guard apologised to his boss and quickly retreated from the room, standing rigid outside the door.

The asshole was sitting at the dining table, sheepishly gazing up every which way other than the couch, where his boss was venting his fury. After taking a deep breath to calm himself, Mr Average stood over me and grinned with such evil intent that he made my stomach clench. In that instant, I knew that some bad shit was about to happen.

"Hold this bliad down, Jeremy. All this excitement has made me horny," Mr Average instructed the asshole with an evil grin.

Taking the whistle from my pocket, I blew three sharp blasts, hoping against all hope that Archie would hear me. When Jeremy stepped towards me, I jumped from the couch, intending to lift my knee into Mr Average's groin, but instead I was grabbed from behind and felt my tormentor's knuckles smash into my nose. Before I could recover from the onslaught, I was thrown to the ground, landing hard on my back. The asshole knelt above my head and held me down by gripping my wrists.

"Fuck her good Boss, and then it's my turn," the asshole sneered.

"No problem, you can have my sloppy seconds," he laughed.

Watching Mr Average leering at me as he undid the clasp of his belt, I gritted my teeth and squirmed and twisted my hips with all my strength. When the asshole lost his grip on my right wrist, I seized the opportunity and bit through his pants into his inner thigh, gnawing at the muscle with as much savagery as I could muster. The familiar metallic taste of blood, along with his shrill scream, gave me a moment of satisfaction.

Sadly, the satisfaction was short-lived. The intensity of the pain I felt when the asshole's fist slammed down onto my busted nose made me vomit and then cough violently as last night's dinner retreated back down my throat. My screaming in pain and anguish, snot, puke, and blood running down my chest did nothing to deter Mr Average as he spread my legs apart. I had almost lost all hope as I thrashed and kicked out in horror.

Through my tears, I saw Mr Average grinning as he lowered himself toward me to begin the next phase of my torture. Then, with his face hovering over mine, the evil intensity of his gaze turned to shock and then bulged in panic when a bronzed muscular forearm wrapped around his neck. Mr Average squealed as Archie violently threw him across the room. He dropped to the ground against the brick wall and raised his arms in a futile attempt to protect himself from the onslaught of punches, knees, and kicks reigning down with ferocity.

I averted my eyes from Mr Average's beating as my focus was on one thing and one thing only, REVENGE! I grabbed two darts from the board and held them in my fist like wicked knuckle dusters. The asshole was cowering against the wall as Gizzarelli towered above him, grinning like a Cheshire cat about to play with his food. I was too numb and disconnected to even question Gizzarelli's presence.

"This asshole's mine!" I said through clenched teeth.

Gizzarelli took two steps back. "I wouldn't have it any other way, young lady. Don't be afraid to make a mess. I'm not one to judge."

I didn't think. I just raged. I stabbed the asshole's neck and face with pure hatred, puncturing his skin over and over again. I only stopped when I felt Archie's hand on my shoulder. Before I walked away, I considered my handiwork. The asshole had more holes in him than a soggy red pincushion.

When I turned to face Archie, I glanced at Mr Average lying on the ground behind him and laughed mirthlessly. He looked like he had been in a horrific car accident. Then suddenly, an overwhelming sense of relief washed over me. I stepped forward and grabbed Archie in a bear hug, sobbing uncontrollably against his chest.

After ten or so seconds, I broke his embrace. "You're a cunt, Archie," I exclaimed, wiping my tears and runny nose with the back of my bloodied hand. When his expression shifted from concern to confusion, I couldn't help but giggle like a crazy woman. "Before last night, I can't even remember the last time I've cried, and now you've made me cry twice in the space of two hours," I explained.

I heard someone grumble by the door. "I don't want to break up this heart-warming family reunion, but I'm gonna get a move on," declared Gizzarelli.

Archie marched across the room to shake his hand. With his arms crossed, Gizzarelli ignored his outstretched hand. "We're not mates, O'Connor. You two did me a solid, and now we're even. Nothing more, nothing less."

Archie rubbed the back of his neck. "Yeah, well, thanks anyway," he mumbled.

When Gizzarelli turned to face me, I was surprised to see him give me a warm smile. "You stabbed anyone yet with the knife I left you?"

"Nah, but give me time," I replied, half-joking.

"Here. I took these off the bloke you turned into a dart board," he said as he handed me my Glock pistol and the matching knife he gifted me.

Archie grabbed the back of Gizzarelli's shoulder as he turned to leave the room. "This better be good, O'Connor. I've got places to be and people to see."

"You were standing in line to volunteer to fight, weren't you?" Archie asked inquisitively.

"Yep, and as usual, you spoiled what would've been a fun night," he replied with a sneer before marching to the exit.

"Hang on," I said before reaching down and ripping the gold eagle pendant from Mr Average's corpse.

I marched over to Gizzarelli and placed the eagle in his hand. He held my gaze and flashed me a toothy grin before leaving the room to engage in whatever chaos he had planned.

# Chapter Thirty-Nine

*Monday, March 10, 2042 – Archie*

There were only two bodies in the room, so I chose the shorter one. I removed the Russian's pants and unbuttoned his bloodied shirt. Fiona was whippet-thin, so I found a flick knife in the pimp's pants and cut some new holes in his belt.

"This will have to do until we get back to the hotel," I said as I handed her the belt and clothes.

"Beggars can't be choosers," she replied in a daze.

After she slipped the pants on and secured the belt around her waist, I manipulated the cheap padlock with the tip of the knife, releasing her from the neck iron before throwing the horrible apparatus to the side of the room.

While Fiona was putting on the Russian's shirt and shoes, I searched the dead pimp and found what I was looking for. "Hallelujah!" He had hidden the twin's ten ounces of gold in a waist belt.

I picked up a pump-action shotgun that was lying beside a lifeless guard. His was the second neck that Gizzarelli had snapped this evening, and I was quietly thankful the grumpy bastard was on our side this time.

"I'm sure you're aware that Patterson was in the stands. We need to ascertain if he's still here. Are you up for it?" I asked.

Fiona completely ignored my question. Instead, she released the mag from her Glock and inspected the number of remaining rounds before reloading the pistol. She then picked up the flick knife I'd left on the table and started playing with it, repeatedly opening and closing the blade in a trance-like state.

Fiona had been through hell - she'd been kidnapped, chained, paraded around a stadium, and attacked by psychopaths. Understandably, she wasn't acting like her usual self, but I needed her to watch my back.

I placed my hand on her shoulder. "Fiona, are you ready to search for Patterson?"

"Of course, why wouldn't I be?" she replied with a stone-cold expression.

We cleared the corridor and entered the main stadium. The venue was empty and silent except for a couple of bookies packing their belongings. I didn't expect Patterson to be waiting in the stands for us, but we had to ensure he hadn't been trampled to death or gravely injured during the spectators' panicked exodus. We walked to the betting pit, where I slipped on my jeans, shirt, and boots. Thankfully my revolver and carry pack were still where I had left them. As I had hoped, the crowd was in such a mad rush to evacuate that no one thought to stop and pilfer my belongings.

Walking from the venue, I noticed that all but two men had vacated the carpark. Recognising Shaky and his brother Joshua sitting under the foliage of a large gum tree, we headed over to them. Joshua's thighs and calves were bruised and swollen from being pulverised by my shins.

"What are you still doing here?" I asked Shaky.

Shaky shook his head. "The bloody bus left us here, and thanks to you, he can't walk," he exclaimed, gesturing to his brother.

"Settle down, Shaun, we were in a fight, and the best man won. And look at his cheek. At least I scored on him. By the way, you're not so good at walking either," jested Joshua.

"You hit like a jackhammer Joshua. You were, without a doubt, my toughest fight tonight. Fiona, can you give us a hand lifting him? We're giving them a ride home."

"Why not? I wouldn't expect any less from the Swiss Army Major," she replied.

I noticed Shaky and Joshua's confused looks. Mental note, find the right time to correct Fiona on her Salvation army metaphor. Joshua placed his arms over our shoulders, and we supported most of his weight as we shuffled towards the Beast.

The brothers lived in a dilapidated fibro house hidden by tall palm trees on the outskirts of town. I parked near the front door, and we helped Joshua to the living room, plonking him down on a rickety couch.

"Do you want to stay for a couple of beers?" asked Joshua.

"No thanks, mate. It's been a long night, and I'm looking forward to hitting the hay."

Even though I could really use a beer, I declined because Fiona looked dead on her feet, and we still needed to find a place to stay for the night.

Shaky walked us to the front door and thanked us for the lift. I said goodbye and was about to turn to leave when I felt a pang of guilt. I reached into my pocket and placed the five ounces of gold I won from the tournament into his palm. "Buy your meds, Shaky, and get some ice for your brother." Shaky was speechless as he gazed at the gold. "Oh, by the way, what's the nicest hotel in Darwin?"

Shaky's reverie ended when I clicked my fingers in front of his eyes. "Yeah, sorry mate, the Hilton is where the rich people go. And thank you, this means so much," he replied while feeling the weight of the gold in his palm.

While driving to the Hilton, I told Fiona, "I gave him the gold because he needs meds for his Parkinson's, and his brother won't be able to work for at least a week. Besides, I recovered the gold the pimp stole from the twins, and our cut is three ounces."

"Fine, whatever. I don't give a shit, Archie. I just want to go to bed," she said tersely.

In a misguided attempt to cheer her up, I placed the instant photo of Lesley Maka's corpse on her lap. She glanced at it before staring out the passenger window in silence.

# Chapter Forty

*Tuesday, March 11, 2042 – Archie*

I spared no expense by booking interconnecting rooms at the Hilton. The rooms were luxurious; they had electricity, hot water, clean linen, air-conditioning, and an ice machine in the hallway. I almost jumped with joy when I found two bottles of beer in the fridge. After a quick shower, I lay in bed and stared at the ceiling while sipping a local brew. Fiona had been in the shower for at least an hour, and I was undecided whether to check if she was okay or call it a night and go to bed. I took the coward's way out and chose the latter. As I was losing consciousness, I felt Fiona climb into my bed. I was far too exhausted to contemplate her motives or state of mind.

I woke eight hours later with a big toe pressing into my cheek. While I dressed and checked my pack for supplies, Fiona remained curled up under the covers.

When she started to rouse and open her eyes, I asked, "I'm going to run down to the foreshore and do a light workout before fetching some brekky. Do you want to join me?"

"Nah, I'm good," she replied while gazing off into the distance.

It was unlike Fiona to refuse an invitation to work out. She was usually dragging me to the track. I couldn't recall a time when she hadn't taken the opportunity to work up a sweat. And I still had no idea why she had slept in my bed. *Very weird!*

"Okay, I'll see you when I get back."

Even though I was bruised and sore from head to toe, I've found it helps my recovery to get the body moving and the blood pumping. I ran at a moderate pace along a track that followed the foreshore;

the deep blue ocean and tropical vegetation provided the idyllic backdrop. If it weren't for the prevalence of the Box and Irukandji jellyfish at this time of year, I would have gone for a swim. The Box jellyfish is as deadly as they come, with up to sixty tentacles with thousands of stinging cells that can inject venom into a person's skin through millions of harpoons. Within twenty minutes of contact, your heart rate increases, you feel severe pain in the back, stomach, and chest muscles, followed by vomiting, and in rare cases, fluid builds up in the lungs, causing respiratory failure.

At about the four-kilometre mark, I felt my hammies and quads loosen, so I picked up the pace and sprinted to the Cenotaph War Memorial. The plaques at the base of the 120-year-old statue commemorated those Australian soldiers who either died in service of their country or were killed in action during World War Two, Korea, Malaya, Borneo, and Vietnam. I pondered whether memorials would be erected for soldiers who lost their lives during World War Three.

Upon returning to the hotel, I purchased two black coffees and an egg and bacon roll for myself and an egg and cricket roll for Fiona, who, as it turns out, was still curled up in bed. Before placing her brekky on the bedside table, I double-checked that I was giving her the cricket roll. That's not a mistake I wanted to make. The very thought of eating creepy crawlies made me want to vomit. I mean, yuck!

I gently nudged the bed until Fiona opened her bleary eyes and gazed up at me, looking slightly confused. "I've bought you brekky. After I chow down, I'm going to drop by the bondsman's office and collect the reward for Maka. I then plan to visit the pubs to see if I can gather any intel about Patterson. Someone around here has to know where he's staying."

Fiona replied by ducking her head under the covers and mumbling something indecipherable.

After I finished brekky and had a quick shower, I reviewed my notes. I had more questions than answers - What was Patterson doing with Salkov? Does he live in the city? Is he still experimenting on people? I decided to check if he had set up shop in one of the local hospitals. Now that I had my work cut out for me to locate Patterson, I regretted not taking the opportunity to interrogate Salkov. But when I found him on top of Fiona, I saw red mist, and before I could regain control of my senses, it was too little, too late.

I moved to stand back at the bottom of Fiona's bed. "I'm heading out, mate. You sure you don't want to come?"

Fiona rolled onto her side, turning her back towards me and wrapping herself tighter into her covers. She yawned before replying, "I'm too tired."

"Okay, no problem. Rest up," I replied before quietly leaving the room, ensuring the door was securely locked behind me.

It was going to be a long day as there were over twenty-five pubs in Darwin. While I drove from one pub to the next, I pondered the situation with Fiona. She obviously needs time to recover, but that doesn't change the situation. I need her head in the game to help me apprehend Patterson. Not only do innocent people deserve payback, but his capture is worth a life-changing sixty ounces of gold.

My modus operandi (MO) didn't take a genius to conceive. There are only so many ways to find someone without the luxury of the Internet. I would order a beer at the bar, strike up a conversation with the bartender, and casually mention that I was trying to find my long-lost mate from the War – 'His name is Patterson. He's a bald, muscular white bloke in his mid-forties that's a bit shorter than me. Oh yeah, he likes to hang around big blokes that lift weights.' I would carefully judge the bartender's body language for deception, but so far, they each responded with a frown and a shake of their head with just the right amount of eye contact.

I parked the Beast and sauntered to the front door of an Irish pub named 'Shennanigans'. I speculated whether the sign writer deliberately misspelled the name for comic relief or genuinely couldn't spell the word. This was my tenth pub for the day, and I was starting to get a bit tipsy. Of course, I was only drinking a midi of beer at each venue, but that's still nine midis over two hours.

I stood at the jarrah bar with a beer and continued my MO

with a pretty young bartender, who must have read the script, as she answered with a frown and a shake of her head. She obviously misread my disappointment as she informed me of a 5 p.m. happy hour at a local gay bar. I casually inspected the pub's occupants and mused over her comment about the gay bar. I wasn't going to ask her to elaborate, and besides, how would that conversation begin – 'Why did you mention the gay bar?' 'Excuse me, do you think I'm gay? Not that there's anything wrong with that.' That's a conversation that would be far too awkward for an introvert like me.

I noticed a big man sitting alone at a table, recognising him as someone I hadn't seen in more than fifteen years. I'll be damned, I thought - Uncle Chris - one of my old man's army buddies whom he served with in the Iraq War. As a kid, I would run to the fridge to fetch them bottles of beer while they sat under the backyard pergola and reminisced about good times and bad. Dad never talked to me about the War, so I would hide around the corner and listen to their yarns during their drinking sessions. They would take the piss out of one another and recall the jokes they played on their Special Air Service Regiment (SASR) mates. A vast majority of their stories were centred on childish pranks, which I found hilarious at the time – 'Spooning Vegemite into a mate's socks,' 'Accessing a mate's email and mentioning the prospect of marriage to their girlfriend,' 'Hiding rubber snakes in their kit' and so on. I really wanted to hear those war stories. Every so often, they would recount a story about engaging the enemy, performing heroic acts, and partaking in actions my grandfather called 'dastardly deeds'.

Now in his mid-seventies, even with the extra pudge around his gut and neck, Uncle Chris was still someone I wouldn't want to face in a barroom brawl. At six-foot-five and weighing about 120 kilograms, Chris Roberts was a formidable warrior who had probably forgotten more about warfare than most soldiers learned. I bought a jug of beer and sauntered to his table with two glasses.

Uncle Chris nonchalantly placed his right hand under the table as I plonked down on the chair across from him. Then, his eyes narrowed, "Do I know you, son? Because I tend to be suspicious of strangers bearing gifts," he warned as he nodded towards the jug.

I couldn't help but grin as I kept my palms on the table in clear view of the old boy, so he didn't get any rash ideas and shoot me. "Relax, Uncle Chris," I replied with a wink.

In a flash, his expression switched from puzzlement to happiness. "Get fucked! You've got to be bloody kidding me! Little Archie! The boy has become a man," he professed before laughing. The big man raised from his seat and hobbled around the table to give me an almighty bear hug.

After he released me and returned to his seat, I poured him a beer and asked, "What's with your limp?"

He waved his hand. "Ah, it's nothing. I hurt my hip when I was surprised by a feral pig protecting her litter. She was just being a good mum, but it didn't stop me from turning her into bacon burgers and sausages," he jested.

"It's great to see you, Uncle Chris. I have a hundred questions, but how are you keeping?" I asked.

"I'm going as well as can be, I guess. I've got a job as a guide in Kakadu, teaching people how to hunt and survive." He drained his beer and poured himself another glass. "You know how it is. People weren't prepared for the new world. Most of them can't even shoot, let alone butcher an animal."

"Yep, it's fair to say a lot has changed. And that's an understatement," I laughed dryly. "But I'm glad to hear that you're doing well," I said with sincerity.

The Kakadu National Park was a protected World Heritage Site located 170 kilometres southeast of Darwin. The battalion I served with trained in and around the park in preparation for the War. At almost 20,000 square kilometres, the area the size of Wales has been the home of Aboriginal people for at least 65,000 years. However, with the demise of the United Nations, UNESCO-protected sites are a concept of the past, with most residents hunting and occupying land based on the premise of 'first in, best dressed'.

His expression changed to one of sadness as he gazed down at his glass. "Look, I'm sorry about your mum and dad, Archie. They were like family to me. I would have walked through the gates of hell if your old man were by my side," he stated solemnly.

"I miss them greatly," I replied, lowering my eyes while trying to keep my voice from breaking. Seeing Uncle Chris brought back a flood of memories I wasn't prepared for. I quickly changed the subject before the dam wall burst; letting my tears flow would be just as uncomfortable for him as it would be for me.

"What do you hunt?" I asked quickly.

"Mostly buffalo and pig. Sometimes we'll target crocs, horses, and roos. There are *other* animals out there, too, that you need to watch out for."

I wondered what he meant by other animals, but I didn't want to look stupid in front of the senior man. Old habits die hard.

"Your old man kept me updated about your deployment during the War. It sounded like you had some wins?" he asked.

"You know how it is. I kept my head down and did what I was told." I provided a vague response because, like my dad, I had no desire to discuss the War.

He raised an eyebrow and leaned forward. "I heard different, but let's not dwell on the past. So, what are you doing with yourself? What brings you to Darwin?" he asked.

"I've been working as a bounty hunter. I'm actually up here chasing a bloke by the name of Noel Patterson. Haven't heard of him, have you?"

"Nah, but there's a lot of people around these parts. It's a bloody population explosion. With plenty of game and lots of water, it's an attractive place to settle, especially if you want to get lost and escape your past."

Running into Chris may actually turn out to be a blessing in disguise. Chris was a sniper with the SASR, a special forces unit of the Australian Army that operated in small teams to conduct long-range covert reconnaissance missions in enemy-controlled territory. After the end of the Iraq War, he was tasked with training soldiers at Campbell Barracks before they deployed to Afghanistan. I lived in Perth's western suburbs, a stone's throw away from the barracks where Dad and Chris trained. I could hear the *pop, pop, pop* sound that you could have been excused for thinking were fireworks being set off in the distance but were actually the report of gunfire during military exercises.

"Can I ask a favour?"

"For you, boy, anything. Just name it," he replied.

"I don't want you to feel obliged to help me out, but I have a business partner that's been through a rough time and needs something to take her mind off recent events. She's a great shot but has never had any formal training in sniping, especially in camouflage, stalking, infiltration, surveillance, and target acquisition. Of course, I'll pay you to train her."

Chris looked disgusted. "I'm not taking payment from you, boy." I was about to protest, but he held his trigger finger in front of my face to silence my argument. "Taking your gold would be enough to make your old man turn over in his grave!"

Chris stroked his chin and sculled the rest of his beer. "Do you drink whisky?" After I nodded in reply, he shouted at the young lady behind the bar, "Two glasses of Willing, two fingers, please, darling."

When the two glasses arrived, we clinked our glasses before taking a swig. "This is some good whisky," I remarked appreciatively.

"They distil it locally," he added. "Now, how long do I have to train this lass?"

"I was thinking ten days. I have some investigation work I need to do, and if that doesn't work out, I'll be chasing some local bounties."

"Just don't capture any of my clients," he requested half-jokingly. He downed his whisky. "I'm leaving to go on a hunt to supply some of the local stores and restaurants. And I've got a mate I owe a favour to. I'll kill two birds with one stone and train her during the trip. Bring her here tomorrow at 0700 hours."

"Thanks, Uncle Chris. I really appreciate this."

"No problem, boy. Now tell me some of your wild bounty hunter stories," he said before asking the barmaid to bring the bottle to the table.

# Chapter Forty-One

*Wednesday, March 12, 2042 – Fiona*

Hearing the door open, I peeked out from under the doona to see Archie tiptoe into the hotel room. Remaining still, I watched him pick up his pack and quietly carry it to the interconnecting room like a ninja on a mission. He wreaked of alcohol. I wondered what he had got up to.

While Archie was out all night, the only time I got out of bed was to go to the toilet or refill my cup with water. My head was throbbing after a rough night's sleep. Every two hours, I woke in a cold sweat, with my heart racing and the memory of a terrifying nightmare.

After I completed my apprenticeship with Archie, I felt like a new woman. I was no longer the abused girl treated like a pretty little rug brought out when the guests arrived, just to be tread on and then placed back in the cupboard after they left. Over the last 15 months, I had transformed into a badass bounty hunter in control of my destiny. At times I even felt invincible. I had taken down killers, protected a water train from a marauding gang, freed a town of enslaved citizens, and rescued a kid held in a contaminated city by a Nazi and his monstrous goons. Now in just twenty-four hours, the Asshole and Mr Average had stolen what I had fought so hard to earn - my dignity, self-worth, and sense of control.

I could hear Archie have a shower and move busily around the adjoining room. Then, annoyingly, he marched through the door with a purpose and flung open the curtains, permitting the sun to immerse the room with intense light.

"Wakey, wakey princess. I think you've had enough beauty sleep for now", he said with a wink. I know he was just trying to lighten the mood, but it still irritated the shit out of me. "The bad news is that I had no luck finding a lead on Patterson, but I haven't given up hope. I haven't even visited half the drinking holes yet, and I plan on dropping by the hospitals next. I also intend to speak to anyone with access to drugs. So pharmacies, dentists, vets, and dealers will be a good start." He ignored my exaggerated groan as I placed the doona over my head while he persistently continued to jibber jabber. "I have some good news, though. I met an old family friend whom my old man swore was one of the best sniper trainers in the country. A genuine hard-ass SASR vet named Chris Roberts. The great part is that he's agreed to train you to snipe out in the Kakadu. I know, awesome, right? But don't thank me yet, the training will be hard, but I'm sure you'll love it. You're going to learn from the very best."

*Is he fucking clueless?* I wondered. I can barely raise myself from the mattress, and he wants me to go bush with a special forces veteran to learn how to be a sniper.

"You've got two hours to get dressed, prep your weapons, and pack. I looked up to Uncle Chris as a kid and still do, so don't let me down. You're extremely fortunate, Fiona. This is a terrific opportunity to improve your skills, one that doesn't come along very often, if ever. I'm bloody excited for you."

I burrowed my face into the pillow and raged. Fuck! I've never heard him so chatty. Why doesn't *he* do the bloody training if *he's* so excited? So he thinks I'm fortunate? And I should be brimming with gratitude, I suppose; *OMG, thanks so much, Archie. Fuck you very, very much!*

After ten minutes of stewing in my thoughts, I allowed my anger at Archie's callousness to slowly subside. I had to remind myself that he had not only supported my new life but had treated me as an equal. The very least he deserved was my trust.

"I'll do my best not to let you down," I sighed.

After a quick shower, I examined myself in the bathroom mirror and decided I needed a fresh look for a fresh start. So I retrieved the scissors from the medical kit and cut off my blonde locks. As I inspected my new hairdo, I gazed at my reflection and whispered a pep talk – "You're a lean, mean, fucking killing machine. Don't ever fucking forget it. Don't let *cunts* like Mr Average and the Asshole take what you've earned."

When Archie reentered the room, I was perched on the bed cleaning my Blaser R93 Tactical 3 Sniper rifle. He stopped at the foot of the bed and looked down at me disapprovingly.

I subconsciously rubbed my dome. "What? It's bloody hot in the top end, and I wanted to try a new look," I snapped.

He placed his hands on his hips. "Good for you, but why are you cleaning your rifle on the bed?" he muttered, shaking his head.

I should've known that was what had irritated him. As if he'd give a shit about my hairstyle. "The sheets are rank. They need a clean anyway," I quipped to cover my annoyance at myself.

Archie left it at that but then placed my pack on the bed and combed through it with an expression of dissatisfaction.

"What do I need to bring?" I grunted.

"You'll only need enough water and food for two days. You'll be hunting, and there are plenty of watering holes. Oh, and you can borrow my handline in case you go fishing. We'll make a move in thirty minutes, so be ready."

I checked my pack, removed the items I didn't need and re-packed with additional ammo and water.

We met Chris at a pub 300 metres down the road. It was only 7 a.m., so I was surprised to see him sitting under the verandah, drinking a pint of beer. For an old man, he was a big and dangerous-looking dude with broad shoulders, sporting a buzz cut and a grey beard. A beautiful Bull Terrier lay on her side near his feet. She had a broad, muscular white chest and a short black body, and when she yawned, I noted her long powerful jaws.

Archie shook the man's hand and then turned to introduce me. Standing up from his seat without the typical groan of a man of his years, Chris shook my hand firmly. Then, before releasing his clasp, he looked me up and down, not in a sexual way like most men do, but as if he were appraising a racehorse or greyhound.

"The lad here told me you want to be a sniper," he grinned, displaying a gold upper incisor. There was something reptilian about his eyes - as if they were declaring – 'Be careful, I'm a killer.'

'Linygurra', Johani's name for crocodile, suddenly popped into my head.

There was an uncomfortable pause before I answered, "I appreciate the opportunity to learn from you, Sir."

"Don't call me Sir. I work for a living. Just call me Chris," he responded swiftly.

He glanced back at Archie before meeting my eyes, "Let's get a move on then. We have a five-hour drive. By the way, this is Penny. She's the love of my life," he said, giving the Bull Terrier a scratch behind her ears.

~

We had been travelling in silence down the Arnhem Highway for two hours in Chris' old light green Land Rover. I don't know much about four-wheelers, but it looked like a Lego block on wheels, with the spare tyre on the bonnet, a bull bar at the front, and an impressive roof rack with spotlights attached to the front and side rails. The noisy engine and rough ride didn't suit my style, but on the upside, there was plenty of room in the back for our gear – my rifle and pack, Chris' rifle and shotgun, three jungle-camouflaged duffle bags, and four steel ammo boxes that had '200 cartridges .338' stamped on the side. When I asked him how he came by so much .338 ammo, he double tapped the side of his nose with his trigger finger and told me that just after the War ended, he visited an army supply depot and *borrowed* some equipment and supplies.

Penny sat in the front seat, resting her muzzle on Chris' lap or sticking her head out the window with her tongue out. For most of the journey, I had been content staring at the dense woodlands and wildflowers as we dawdled down the highway at no more than seventy clicks per hour. Then, a sudden loud clap of thunder startled me so badly that I jumped out of my seat and almost struck my head on the roof. Penny whined and looked at Chris for reassurance. Dark clouds now covered the sun, transforming the highway and tall thin trees into a gloomy landscape. A few fat drops that struck the windscreen quickly turned into a deluge, with the rain bucketing down so hard and fast that I could barely see out of the windscreen. I had never seen rain like it. Chris had just flicked switches near the dash to turn on the wipers and the spotties when a small roo bounded onto the road in front of us without warning. Chris didn't even bat an eyelid as the 4WD's bullbar narrowly missed the dim-witted marsupial. I turned in time to see the outline of the fur ball hop into the thick foliage. *'Your lucky day,'* I thought to myself.

"That's a pity. We could have had wallaby stew and mash for dinner," Chris shouted over the downpour, which struck as a bemusing contrast to my thoughts.

The weather up here is strikingly different from the dry heat I'm used to in the Goldfields. When it rains where I'm from, it's usually cool weather, not so stinking hot. I felt like I was being steamed like a Chinese dumpling. Chris must have noticed me wipe the sweat from my brow and neck as he reached behind the seat and handed me a towel.

"They have six seasons up here. We're in the monsoon season, which the locals call Kudjewk. So there'll be plenty of heavy rain and thunderstorms, and it'll be as humid as hell, with averages of 35 degrees and 70 percent humidity. So be prepared to be uncomfortable little lady," he chirped.

"You know how you don't like to be called Sir because you work for a living? Well, I like to be called Fiona because I'm not a *fucking* little lady!"

Chris responded with a smirk and a mock salute.

# Chapter Forty-Two

*Wednesday, March 12, 2042– Archie*

After trying my luck with the bondswoman - she hadn't even heard rumours concerning Patterson's whereabouts, let alone any reliable intel - my plan for the rest of the day centred on hitting the pavement and visiting the remaining pubs on my list.

Strolling past an obese bouncer in a Hawaiian shirt, I entered a three-story, red-bricked venue named 'The Peach Pit'. If the peach had been left on a deli counter for three months, it would aptly describe the state of the rancid establishment. The appalling smell hit my nasal cavity like a baseball bat swung by Babe Ruth. Decades of old spilt beer and vomit will have that effect. The soles of my boots stuck to the dark purple carpet like velcro.

The DJ played eighties pop music that relied on synthesisers to drown out the dreadful vocals. Three floor-to-ceiling poles were being straddled by tired-looking naked women who, like a sixty-year-old boxer who comes out of retirement, should have just stayed home.

Moseying toward the bar, I noticed a bloke tip a pole dancer. She was upside down, gripping the pole for dear life with her hands and legs. Her huge breasts and stomach made her manoeuvre appear death-defying and actually rather impressive, all things considered. It took a second glance for me to recognise the tipper as the Englishman who shot Gizzarelli and tried to steal our bounty.

His name came to me as I approached his table. "Hello, Jon. Fancy meeting you here at this fine establishment," I shouted over the terrible music.

By the state of his red and blistered cheeks and nose, he had yet to invest in a wide-brimmed hat and a tub of sunscreen.

Obviously taken completely by surprise, Jon jerked around at the sound of my voice, looking like a stunned mullet. "Hello, um. Sorry, I've forgotten your name."

"Archie," I reminded him as I raised my hand to grab the waitress' attention. "Keep your elbows on the table, Jon. I don't want you and I to have any type of misunderstanding. We didn't exactly part on friendly terms last time we crossed paths, and it's left me a bit agitated, if you know what I mean."

"Yeah, no worries, Archie. What, um, what are you doing here? I mean, why are you in Darwin?" he asked nervously, keeping his arms completely still.

Before I could reply, a young waitress with tight denim shorts and a red lace bra approached our table with a wan smile. I ordered a scotch for myself and a beer for Jon, and as we were the only patrons in the bar, I asked her to turn the music down.

"Relax, Jon. I'm here looking for a bounty. But it's not me who you should be worried about. I caught up with Gizzarelli a couple of nights ago. He's in Darwin too," I warned.

I didn't owe Jon any favours by any stretch of the imagination, but even the thought of what Gizzarelli would do to him sent chills down my spine.

"Who's Gizzarelli?" he asked with a confused look.

This bloke is a daft bugger, I thought. "The fella you shot at Devils Creek," I explained.

"Ooooh, him, yeah, well, thanks for the heads-up," he nodded appreciatively.

"So, what are you doing in these parts? Have you given up bounty hunting?" I asked.

"Um, I'm in the process of applying for my license. I'm sort of looking for a fugitive," he said, rubbing the back of his neck.

The atmosphere instantly altered when the music was turned off and the ladies left the stage, with the venue appearing even more degenerate without the added distractions. When our drinks arrived, I tipped the waitress handsomely, asking her to share it with the dancers.

My eyes narrowed as I placed my elbows on the table and leaned forward. "Who are you looking for, Jon? You know you can't collect on the bounty without a license."

"I know someone that will take him in for me," he replied defensively.

"Who are you looking for, Jon?" I repeated.

He looked nervously around the bar as if people were listening to our conversation. "A bloke called Patterson. He's supposed to be a mean son of a bitch. I've got a whiff of him as well," he answered confidently.

The son of a bitch, I thought. Beaten to the punch by an amateur is a hard pill to swallow. But, on the other hand, he could be completely full of shit, I reminded myself.

"Maybe we can help each other out, mate. Go fifty-fifty on the reward. I've been chasing this bloke for a while, and like you said, he's a mean son of a bitch. But I'm only willing to deal if you've got some genuine intel."

I kept my fifty-ounce civil contract with Mr Singh to myself, figuring that fifty percent of the formal bounty is still far more than this douchebag deserves if we manage to bring Patterson in.

I watched Jon closely as he leaned back in his chair, now seemingly comforted by the knowledge that I wanted something from him. He placed his hand across the table. "Okay, deal. Fifty-fifty split," he said eagerly.

I smiled, "Hold your horses, mate. I need to know how good your intel is before we shake on a partnership."

Jon should avoid the poker tables, as you could read his emotions like a book. His expression of hurt and then frustration was almost comical.

"Yeah, right! Then you'll just take my lead and run with it. I wasn't born yesterday," he protested with flushed cheeks.

"Alright, mate, settle down. We'll do a deal," I said before reaching across to shake his hand. "Okay, now that that's settled, partner, lay your cards on the table and tell us what you've got."

Like a gasbag bursting to tell his mate a secret, he said excitedly, "An old prospector mate of mine from way back knows a bloke that....."

I quickly interrupted him, "Keep it down, mate," I hissed. "We don't want everyone in the bar to know our business."

"Oh right, sorry," he whispered. I gestured for him to continue. "My mate knows someone that said he worked for Patterson. He said they were playing pool, and this bloke started to talk crazy weird shit about experimenting on people and stuff like that."

I couldn't help but get my hopes up. "Where exactly are these experiments taking place?"

"He didn't say."

"Who didn't say?" I inquired in a frustrated tone.

"The bloke he was playing pool with," Jon explained.

I let out a long sigh and decided to take a step back and treat him like the total amateur that he was. "Okay, Jon. What's your mate's name and address?"

It was a promising sign when he retrieved a notepad from his pocket and opened it. Maybe I'd judged him a bit too harshly, I thought. "I'm not giving you my mate's details. But the bloke he was speaking to is known as Mickey Diamond. Patterson must be paying him a lot of coin, as he's bunking at the Vibe Hotel."

"Drink up, Jon. You and I are going for a little drive."

# Chapter Forty-Three

*Wednesday, March 12 to Thursday March 13, 2042*
*– Fiona*

After driving for about four hours, Chris turned onto a bush track, which gave me hope we were finally approaching our destination. Chris skillfully navigated either around, through or over the mud holes and large rocks. I hung on for dear life when he drove down steep descents, pressing my hands against the dash and the roof to prevent being thrown around the cab like a sneaker in a washing machine. The tree branches and bushes scraped against the windows and side panels of the vehicle, with ear-splitting screeches that reminded me of a horrible teacher I had in primary school who would scratch her fingernails on the blackboard to get the class's attention.

My bony ass was battered and bruised by the time we arrived at a man-made clearing roughly 20 metres across in diameter. Chris pulled up outside a small log cabin and asked me to help him unload the vehicle. The clearing was surrounded by dense bush, and when I looked to the sky, I could see an enormous, awe-inspiring rocky outcrop reaching towards the heavens. A fire pit was situated ten metres east of the cabin, and a wood pile was stacked against a cabin wall, protected from the rain by a slanting tin roof.

It was a simple one-room cabin with a bunk bed and cupboard on one side, a cook stove and kitchen bench on the other, and a small timber table in the centre.

After unpacking the equipment and supplies, Chris suggested we have lunch, and he opened three combat ration packs that he must have *borrowed* from the army depot. He kindly offered me a choice of braised beef and gravy or satay chicken. I was pleasantly surprised when I took my first bite of the chicken, as it didn't taste all that bad for a twelve-year-old can of mush. Penny sat at Chris' feet, scoffing down the beef like she hadn't eaten for a week. For dessert, I was treated to a bowl of peaches and chocolate. Penny tilted her head, licked her lips, and stared at me with her puppy dog eyes, clearly asking, 'where's mine?'

After we ate, like an actor after hearing the director shout 'Action!', Chris' personality suddenly changed from being easy-going and polite to behaving like an arrogant prick. He turned a steely gaze on me and menacingly cracked the knuckles on both hands before speaking. "Archie mentioned you've had a rough time. I'm not here to give you any sympathy. My role is to train you, nothing more and nothing less."

"Good, because I don't want your sympathy," I retorted, inwardly cringing at the sound of my whiny voice.

"The boy said you're a good shot. I'll be the judge of that. Grab your rifle and a box of ammo," he ordered.

I bit my bottom lip to prevent myself from firing another salvo. Great, I thought, I've got ten days with this prick.

I followed Chris outside, carrying the ammo box in both arms with my rifle over my shoulder. At least it had stopped raining. He stood at the edge of the clearing with his hands on his hips.

As I approached, he passed me a pair of binoculars. "Look one hundred metres down the clearing and you'll see a tree with a target. There's a target at every one hundred metres for one kay. This is our range."

Somehow he had carved a corridor through the bush, creating a narrow firing range. It must have been a hell of a job. At the centre of each trunk down the range, he had placed a white sheet of paper with a circular outline about the size of a basketball, with four inner rings and a dark red bullseye in the centre.

"Is your rifle zeroed?" he asked bluntly.

He must have noticed the confusion on my face as he asked,

"Have you ever shot at anything over 200 metres?"

"I've shot Roos at about 300 to 350 metres."

"In the chest or head?" he snapped.

After I pointed to my head, he gestured for me to pass him my rifle. He extended the bipods before kneeling on the dirt and lowering himself onto his belly, pointing the muzzle down range in a manner that suggested he had done so 10,000 times. He looked through the scope and then adjusted the focus dial on the left-hand side of the scope - the only dial I was familiar with. Next, he turned the top dial. "When zeroing your scope, ensure the '1' on the elevation dial is lined up to the elevation index line," he said gruffly. He then checked the dial on the right-hand side of the scope but didn't make any adjustments. "Then ensure '0' on the windage dial is lined up with the windage index line."

He placed the butt of the rifle snugly between his chest and shoulder and fired three rounds at the one-hundred-metre target. I peered through the binoculars and saw three holes in the bullseye. With smooth, robotic motions, he then swiftly changed the magazine and adjusted two dials before firing three rounds at the 1000-metre target. I couldn't help but whistle in appreciation when I looked through the binos and discovered that he'd once again hit the bullseye with every shot.

Chris reloaded the rifle before raising himself to his feet. "Put three rounds into each target, starting at one hundred metres," he ordered, passing me the rifle. "Cease firing *when* you miss the bullseye."

Feeling just a little anxious after seeing Chris nail every shot, I lay on my belly and gripped the rifle. I took a deep breath and prayed for the best before taking my first shot. I sighed with relief when I sighted the bullet hole in the dead centre of the target.

I bullseyed each target until I aimed at the 500-metre mark, where I missed the bullseye by a bee's dick on my second shot. I thought I was shooting pretty well until Chris sighed and commented, "We have a lot of work to do. C'mon, let's get training, and we'll see if we can fix some of those bad habits."

During the first day of training, Chris assessed my shooting style and then put me under the pump. He balanced a silver coin precariously on my scope as I lay prone and prepared to dry fire the weapon. I squeezed the trigger while holding my breath, and the coin fell to the ground. He had me dry firing for an hour, squeeze after squeeze until the pad of my index finger was red and sore. Frustratingly, the coin fell from the scope nine out of ten times I squeezed the trigger.

After watching me repeatedly fail, he tasked me with working on my breathing cycle and trigger squeeze, repeating the acronym BRAS over and over – Breathe naturally, inhaling and exhaling to the natural respiratory pause; Relax as many muscles as possible: Aim true; Squeeze the trigger, applying constant pressure straight to the rear without disturbing the lay of the rifle.

Easier said than done. But I was too proud to give up. Finally, after hours of practice, something just clicked. He placed the coin on the scope and asked me to try again. As I exhaled, I put my finger on the trigger and squeezed during my respiratory pause. The coin barely wavered while I squeezed the trigger. After achieving the same outcome for the next fifty squeezes, I was pretty chuffed.

By dusk, a painful blister bulged from my index finger. I washed the injured finger with soap and then pressed a hot towel against the fluid-filled bump, encouraging it to rupture. When I covered the wound with tree tea oil, my finger felt like it was on fire. Mindful that Chris would be watching, I gritted my teeth to stop myself from crying out in pain. From the corner of my eye, I caught the bastard grinning while I placed a dressing over my finger.

~

Chris advised me on the morning of day two that we were moving on to the next stage of the training, which I assumed was a good sign. I was surprised when he asked me if I liked mathematics. Not that I would confess it to Chris, but maths was my strongest subject at school. I could even calculate problems that troubled the nuns. Which, to my delight, they didn't like at all. To Chris, I just replied with an indifferent shrug.

"You've been shooting from feel without considering the bullet's trajectory and how gravity and drag will affect your accuracy. If you're targeting a bloke at 800 metres and aiming for his chest, the round will hit him in the ankles. The instant the bullet exits the muzzle, gravity will take effect and start to exert a downward force. You need to learn how to make elevation adjustments to compensate for gravity. Drag refers to the effect the atmosphere has on the speed of the bullet. The greater density of the air, the greater the drag. The drag is also affected by the temperature, humidity, wind, altitude, and efficiency of the bullet. Luckily for you, I learned to snipe *without* the fancy tech to gauge factors like distance to the target, elevation, windage and so on. Which means you get to learn old school."

We sat down at the small dining table on which Chris had placed paper and pen, and some laminated sheets that he explained were to assist in calculating the bullet's point of impact based on the target's distance coupled with wind strength, speed and direction. Due to time constraints, Chris was adamant that we focus mainly on those factors.

"When you look down your scope, do you know what the dots represent on the crosshair?" he asked.

"No. I just aim dead centre," I explained.

Chris shuffled through the paper and placed a picture of a crosshair in front of me. He pointed the tip of his pen to the dots on the crosshair. "Each of these dots is called a mil-dot or MRAD, which is short for milliradian. The space between each dot equals one mil. You can use the mil-dot as a range-finding tool to estimate the distance of a target, as long as you know the approximate size of the target." He drew a rough-looking rabbit in the crosshair. "You take the size of the target in metres, times it by 1000 and divide it by the size of the object in mils. For example, if you see a twenty-five-centimetre rabbit in your crosshair and it's taking up one mil in your scope, it's 250 metres away." Chris then wrote the calculation below the target.

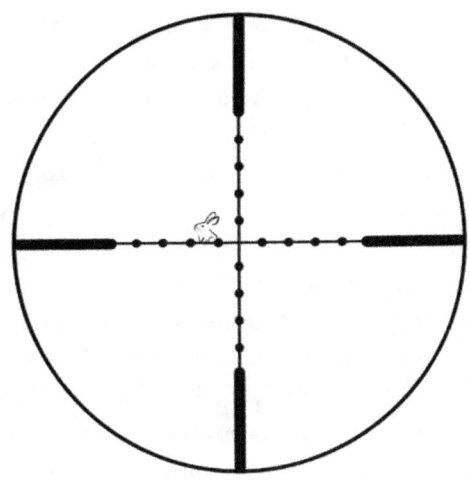

*0·25metres x 1000 / 1 mil = 250 metres to the rabbit*

"Alright, I want you to calculate the distance of a 183-centimetre man taking up three mils in your sight picture."

I jotted down the calculation.

*1·83 x 1000 / 3 = 610 metres*

I turned the page around so it faced Chris. He read the calculation, nodded, and then handed me one of the laminated sheets.

"Here are the tables that provide a distance estimation for both a standing and kneeling person," he advised.

*Why didn't you just give me the bloody tables instead of having me do the math? I thought.*

"But you should remember the calculation and write it in your notebook. You can't rely on paperwork in the bush."

*Oh, that's why. It makes sense, I suppose.*

"Alright, let's go outside, and I'll teach you how to determine the wind velocity."

We walked outside and stood in the middle of the clearing. I could smell the promise of more rain in the breeze.

"On the range, we can use flags, but in the field, just like an Aussie rules footballer who's about to kick for goal, you can use grass or leaves. Drop it at shoulder height, point directly to where it landed, and divide the angle between your body and arm by the constant for wind velocity, which is four. This will give you the approximate wind velocity in miles per hour. So if you point at the grass and the angle between you and your body is 40 degrees, then the wind velocity is 10 miles per hour. By the way, a mile is 1.6 kilometres, but the conversion tables are in miles per hour. Don't ask me why the yanks use miles in their tables for wind velocity when they use metres for distance. Okay, are you still with me?" I nodded, and he continued. "Now, the sights have windage and elevation adjustments in minutes of angle (MOA). An MOA is 1/60th of a degree. This equals approximately one inch or 2.54 centimetres for every one hundred metres. So, after you find the wind direction and wind velocity in miles per hour, you must convert it to MOA. The MOA conversion formula is (the distance to the target in metres, divided by 100) times the calculated wind velocity, divided by a constant related to the distance."

Chris showed me a table listing the constants. He then scribbled a calculation on a sheet of paper and said, "This is the formula for a target standing 600 hundred metres away with a wind velocity of ten miles per hour."

$$\frac{(600 / 100) \times 10}{14} = 4.28 \text{ MOA or } 4.5 \text{ MOA}$$

| 100 to 500 | "C" | = 15 |
| --- | --- | --- |
| 600 | "C" | = 14 |
| 700 to 800 | "C" | = 13 |
| 900 | "C" | = 12 |
| 1000 | "C" | = 11 |

For the rest of the day, Chris provided me with one math problem after another, only stopping for twenty minutes for a bite to eat. For each problem, he altered the size of the target, the mil size, and the wind velocity. Finally, he tasked me with calculating the distance to the target and the MOA. At sunset, my head was spinning, and I could feel a headache coming on. When Chris finally called it a day, I was none the wiser about whether he was satisfied with my performance. As my head hit the pillow and I closed my eyes, I pondered what tomorrow's activities would be. Even though my trigger finger was still raw, I prayed that we'd leave the confines of the "classroom" and go shooting.

# Chapter Forty-Four

*Wednesday, March 12, 2042 – Archie*

Jon and I strolled up to the reception counter at the Vibe, where a smartly dressed, severely thin gentleman with a prim and proper demeanour was patiently waiting to greet us.

"Welcome to the Vibe Hotel, gentleman. How may I be of service?" he asked politely.

I placed a silver coin on his side of the counter. "What room is Mickey Diamond staying in? I promise we won't make a mess."

With a thin-lipped smile, he placed the coin in his waistcoat pocket. "He's in room eighteen on the second floor. He hasn't been what I'd refer to as a splendid guest," he said before handing me a room key attached to a crocodile-shaped keyring.

We walked up the stairs to the second floor and stood outside room eighteen's closed door. I drew my revolver, and just as I was about to insert the room key into the lock, Jon drew his .45 Ruger pistol and lazily pointed the muzzle at my stomach. I shook my head and gestured for him to return the weapon to his holster. I cursed myself for not giving him instructions before walking up the stairs. I was so used to working with Fiona that I forgot about my new partner's capabilities or lack thereof. With him waving his muzzle around like a child with a magic wand, there was no way in hell I was prepared to clear a room with him. He'd probably end up shooting me in the back.

"You remain here while I clear the room," I whispered.

As soon as I unlocked the door, I swiftly entered the room and stepped to my left with my muzzle pointing forwards. Jon disobeyed my instructions and followed in my wake, foolishly walking straight into the middle of the room. Without warning, a muscular Pitbull Terrier leapt at him with savage ferocity, wrapping its powerful jaws around his ankle. I scanned for threats and saw a naked man with shoulder-length black hair running from the bathroom towards the king-sized bed. He reminded me of the bloke that played Tarzan in the movies. I stalked toward him with my muzzle pointed at his back. As he reached under his pillow, I shoved the muzzle behind his ear and barked, "Don't move. Now show me your hands real slow." Luckily for Tarzan, I maintained trigger discipline when the report of gunfire from behind made me flinch.

~

Mickey Diamond sat on the edge of the bed in his faux leopard skin undies with his wrists secured behind his back. Mickey was in his late twenties and looked like a man who could play in a glam rock revival band when he wasn't playing the lead as Tarzan.

Mickey's Pitbull was lying lifelessly on the carpet. Jon had put a bullet between the poor dog's eyes for doing its job. Jon was the one who deserved the bullet for not listening to my instructions. He was whining about the pain as he wrapped a hand towel around his ankle, placing pressure on the puncture wound.

I pulled a lounge chair to the edge of the bed and sat nice and close to Mickey. "Okay, Mickey. I have some simple questions for you. It's in your best interest to answer the questions honestly."

"Sure, man, whatever," he sputtered.

I took out my notebook and pen. "Where do you work?"

"At the Croc Hotel in Jabiru."

Jabiru is a small town of a thousand souls surrounded by the Kakadu National Park. Shaped like a saltwater crocodile, the Aboriginal-owned Mercure Hotel was a popular tourist destination for those who wanted to stay in luxury when they weren't partaking in adventure tours and cruises. I had never stayed at the hotel, but before the War, it was on my bucket list of things to do.

"Who do you work for, Mickey?"

"A prick called Patterson," he spat.

"What do you do for him?"

"I'm an electrician by trade, but I'm basically a glorified janitor," he moaned.

Without warning, Jon pointed his pistol at Mickey's forehead and pulled the trigger. Blood, bone, and brain tissue sprayed all over my face and neck. I instantly grasped his pistol on top of the slide and punched him hard with an overhand right to his jaw, knocking him onto his backside.

"What the hell did you do that for?" I boomed as I took the mag out of his pistol and ejected the round from the chamber.

While I glared at him in anger and frustration, he rubbed his jaw and remained sprawled on the carpet.

"What? We couldn't let him go. He'd warn Patterson, and then we'd lose the reward," he countered.

"After this job is finished, I never want to see you again. Do you understand?" He just stared at me dumbfounded. "Do you understand?" I yelled, stepping towards him.

Jon scooted backwards on his butt until he was backed up against the wall. "Yeah, sure thing, Archie. I, I, I got it," he stammered.

"Come on, let's get out of here before the cops rock up," I said bitterly.

"Hey, can I have my gun back?" he whined.

"You've got to be kidding me! Absolutely not! No guns for you during this Op. You've lost that privilege, buddy," I said with my ears still ringing from the gunshot.

# Chapter Forty-Five

*Tuesday, March 18, 2042 – Fiona*

Before I started training with Chris, I thought I was a pretty good shot by anyone's standards. Turns out I was wrong. But after firing hundreds of rounds under Chris' tutelage, my marksmanship has improved by leaps and bounds. My ability to consistently hit the bullseye from 1000 metres was evidence of my progress.

After sunset, we hunted buffalo and feral pigs for Chris' clients. I targeted a buffalo at four hundred metres during one of the hunts. I adjusted my elevation and windage dials and was about to take the shot when the cow was startled and ran off. Shortly thereafter, Chris pointed out a pig drinking from a water hole seven hundred metres away. As I squeezed the trigger, the wind picked up, and I missed the shot. I was pretty annoyed, but it made me think; It's all well and good to make your calculations and adjust your dials when you have the time, but what happens if the conditions suddenly change without warning, or the shit hits the fan, and you have to take the shot?

"What do I do in the field if I'm just about to take the shot and the wind changes or I need to engage a threat at a different distance?"

Chris smiled. "Ah, finally, you're asking an intelligent question. I was starting to wonder when you'd ask me that. It's called *holding off*. As I've said, if you aim at a target greater than the set range, the round will hit below the aiming point, and obviously, the opposite occurs at lesser ranges. So, for example, if your scope is dialled in at 400 metres and you have to engage a target at 500 metres, you would *hold off* by placing the first mil-dot five inches below the vertical line on the target's centre of seen mass, which gives you a 15-inch hold-off. Understand?" Once I had converted inches to centimetres in my head, I nodded in reply.

"Now, in terms of wind, it's a bit of an art. It takes a shit load of practice in windy conditions to adjust your point of aim on the fly. But the basic principle is if the wind moves from right to left, then *hold off* by adjusting your point of aim to the right, and vice versa if the wind moves from left to right. To be honest, you just have to get a feeling for it over time."

For the next two days, Chris had me shooting from various distances in changing wind conditions, often asking me to *hold off* and shoot on feel without altering the dials on my scope. I was getting pretty pleased with my efforts until Chris once again deflated my ego by declaring that hitting a stationary target was easy. The real challenge, he professed, is engaging a moving target.

Chris went on to teach me two methods to engage a moving target: ambush and tracking. He explained that the ambush method requires you to calculate the lead time by multiplying the target speed in metres per second by the time the bullet takes to reach the target. *For fuck's sake! More Math!* I thought to myself. However, I was relieved to find it was simpler than calculating the MOAs. He supplied me with another table listing an average man's walking speed in metres per second (MPS) and the method by which to calculate the lead time.

| Slow patrol | = | 0.3048 mps |
|---|---|---|
| Fast patrol | = | 0.6096 mps |
| Slow walk | = | 1.2192 mps |
| Fast walk | = | 1.8288 mps |

$$\underline{Time\ of\ Flight\ \times\ Target\ Speed}\ =\ LEAD$$

$$\frac{LEAD\ \times\ 1000}{Range\ to\ Target}\ =\ MIL\ LEAD$$

I reviewed the table and thought, what about the average walking speed of a woman? Maybe the person that wrote the tables didn't think a woman could be a threat. Perhaps they'd change their mind if they met *me*.

To start this phase of the training, I was tasked with concentrating on the mil scale (lead point) rather than the centre of the crosshair like I would for a stationary target. Chris warned that targets don't often walk back and forth at a constant pace, so I had to practice tracking them - moving my muzzle with their movement.

"In real life, you often need to combine ambush and tracking," he warned.

Tracking was hard as fuck! Chris placed a human-sized target on a trolley and used a twenty-metre rope to pull the target at different speeds while I utilised the ambush and tracking methods.

"Don't fuck up and shoot me!" he shouted.

I wasn't sure whether he was joking or not. But if I did shoot him, it certainly wouldn't be a mistake, I pondered mirthfully.

~

On the morning of day seven, I was eating breakfast in the cabin when I heard a knock at the door. I drew my Glock and darted to the side of the doorknob. Just as I was about to crack it open, I heard Chris speaking to another man in a friendly tone.

"Come on out the front, Fiona. I have someone I want you to meet," Chris shouted.

After holstering my firearm and letting the adrenaline settle, I sauntered outside and found Chris speaking to an elderly Aboriginal man. I couldn't help but wonder whether their gasbagging and laughing were at my expense – *'I'm training some hopeless sheila who thinks she can be a sniper, ha ha.'*

Chris gestured for me to come over. "Fiona, this is my mate Djiniyini. He's a well-respected Gunwinggu elder."

I held out my hand, and he squeezed it gently. "Good to meet you, Fiona. Welcome to my country," he said with an infectious smile and a sparkle in his eyes.

Djiniyini was a wiry man in his mid to late seventies wearing blue denim jeans, a black shirt, and a well-worn Akubra hat. He had a machete strapped to his waist and a .308 Winchester rifle hanging by its strap over his shoulder.

"Djiniyini's been kind enough to offer his assistance during the next phase of your training," Chris confirmed. Again, I felt a mixture of excitement and apprehension. "He's going to help me make you a silent killer. Get in undetected, set up your hide, take out the target, and then extricate yourself unseen like a ghost. Understood?" he asked.

"Sounds cool. I always wanted to be a ninja," I joked.

"Fucking ninjas can eat my 338." I heard Chris mumble as he walked back to the cabin.

~

We hiked through the scrub for about an hour with our packs on our backs and rifles in the carry position, with muzzles pointed to the ground. Chris took the lead with Penny by his side, and I followed behind Djiniyini. I needed to continually check my footing to ensure I didn't twist my ankle on a rock or fallen branch. And the last thing I wanted to do was upset a dozing snake. Djiniyini walked in, on, and around the scrub like he was taking a leisurely stroll in his backyard. He somehow managed to avoid leaving any indication of his passing in his wake.

I can run ten kilometres with a fifteen-kilo pack without much effort and consider myself to be pretty fit, but marching through this terrain was taxing my cardio and sapping my energy. When Chris finally announced we had arrived at our destination, I was breathing heavily and sweating like a bush pig. Djiniyini looked as cool as a cucumber. *I think that's how the saying goes.*

After I drained half my water bottle, Chris told me to unload my weapon before handing me four blank rounds to insert into my mag. Taking my live rounds, he shoved them into his pocket and then passed me a radio and earpiece. Djiniyini was still grinning like he knew a secret I was yet to learn. What the fuck have these two got cooked up for me? I wondered.

"Did you ever play hide and seek when you were a kid?" asked Chris with a wry smile.

"Excuse me?"

"No, wait, of course you didn't. Your generation was addicted to screens. You never played outside. Well, we'll make up for lost time and play a sniper version of the game. First, I'm going to turn my back for eight minutes to give you time to hide. Your task is to hide no more than 200 metres away and then get a bead on me. I'm going to hold a playing card under my chin. You need to remember what the card is so you can prove you had me sighted. You're then going to fire a blank, and Djiniyini and I will see if we can spot you. We'll keep repeating the exercise until you've fired all four blanks or we've spotted you. Got it?"

I nodded and folded my arms over my chest. "What do I get if I win?"

"Our admiration," replied Chris sarcastically.

Chris and Djiniyini sat on a boulder with their backs turned while Penny sniffed around the bush and marked her territory. "You have eight minutes, and then ready or not, here we come. GO!" Chris shouted.

I quickly scanned my surroundings and spotted a rocky outcrop about 120 metres away that was two metres high and covered with fauna. It was a flat surface with a perfect platform to lay prone and obtain a sight picture while being concealed by the thick bush. To misdirect them, I intentionally brushed past shrubs and kicked rocks to the east before slowly and carefully advancing to the west, where I set up my position.

About five minutes after Chris shouted 'Go,' I lay flat in what I thought was the perfect spot. Rocks and bushes concealed me, and I had a clear sight picture of Chris' back. Not long after settling into position, Chris turned around. I raised my rifle and lined him up through the scope to see the Queen of Hearts held under his chin.

I already knew what he would say when he placed the radio up to his mouth. "Take your shot," Chris commanded in my earpiece.

I fired the blank - CRACK. Immediately after the shot, I saw Chris and Djiniyini swing around to look my way through their binoculars. Chris then brought the radio back to his mouth, "You're lying in a prone position on a large rock to the west, hiding behind two smaller boulders and some *turkey* bush. Which is quite appropriate considering I found you so easily," he snickered.

"Fuck!" I hissed.

While I trudged back, I wondered how the hell they found me so easily.

I knelt and scratched Penny under her jaw as I asked, "How did you find me? I thought I had the perfect spot."

"The answer's in your question, Fiona. You chose an obvious location to set up a hide. I could also see the light reflecting from the lens on your scope. I'll tell you how to conceal your scope, but first, It's my turn to hide."

He shuffled the deck of cards in his hand before placing them in my palm. I sat on the same rock Chris had used as a perch and glanced at my watch. "Eight minutes starting now," I said.

I strained to hear the direction Chris was walking but gave up after his fifth step. I shuffled the cards until Chris whispered, "I'm ready," through my earpiece. I checked my watch and was surprised to discover that only three minutes had elapsed.

I'm highly competitive by nature, so I quickly scanned the bush with the binos, hoping to find him before he even had an opportunity to fire a blank. After having no luck spotting him, I placed the *five of hearts* under my chin. "Take your shot," I transmitted.

As soon as I heard the shot, I tried to pinpoint his location with the naked eye before peering through the binos to take a better look. I was almost positive the shot was discharged from the east, but I couldn't spot him anywhere, nor could I spot a decent place to set up a hide. Finally, I looked over at Djiniyini, who just shrugged his shoulders. I wasn't sure whether that meant, *'I can't see him'* or *'It's not my job to find him.'*

I repeated the activity three more times, and each time I asked

Djiniyini to search the areas where I thought Chris was hiding. I was beginning to feel irritated by my lack of success. Finally, Djiniyini put me out of my misery, cupping his hands around his mouth and shouting, "Penny, here girl," who responded by running over to him and obediently sitting at his feet in expectation. "Go find your dad. Go girl," he instructed. Penny wagged her tail in excitement and sprinted away at 12 o'clock. She eagerly barked and ran around a fallen tree about eighty metres away. I'll be damned! What appeared to be the earth rising from under the fallen trunk was actually Chris dressed in some type of camouflaged suit.

As he ambled back to us, I noted that he was wearing a jacket with a hood, a mesh face mask, and pants. The get-up had leaves, twigs, and bark attached, creating a three-dimensional chameleon-like disguise. I also noticed that the scope of his rifle now had a thin piece of black rubber fitted around the edge.

"This is what we call a ghillie suit," he informed me as he approached. "We'll teach you how to make yourself one. We'll also attach some rubber to your scope to prevent light from reflecting from your lens."

First, Chris made me do hours of math, and now he's tasked me with arts and crafts. So what's next? I wondered churlishly. It was Djiniyini who taught me how to make a ghillie suit that would help me disappear into the Northern Territory bush. We glued and lashed grass, leaves, twigs, and bark to a green hooded tracksuit. Chris converted a green t-shirt into a face mask which we also camouflaged with foliage.

Chris then taught me the six rules of movement. I should've figured the next subject would be Phys Ed. Rule One was – always assume you're being observed by the enemy; Two – always move slowly; Three – make every effort not to touch trees, bushes, and tall grass; Four – plan every movement in segments; Five – stop, look and listen before starting each segment, and Six – move during a disturbance (gunfire, vehicle movement, wind or anything that will distract the target's attention). He made me practice this by crawling over 300 metres through the bush, over rocks, branches, and scrub. I journeyed slowly over the terrain like some kind of stealthy sloth, praying that any snakes in my path would feel the vibrations and slither away. When I finally arrived at the hide that Chris had set as my destination, I sighed with relief and tried to forget about my elbows, knees and shins, which were grazed, bruised, raw and sore.

# Chapter Forty-Six

*Friday, March 21, 2042 – Archie*

The planning for this operation was a painstakingly slow process. I had no other option but to task Jon with gathering intelligence in the Jabiru townsite. I couldn't risk being seen by Patterson or one of his hulks. Each morning, I dropped Jon at the outskirts of town, so he could wander into local businesses under the guise of looking for work before winding up the day at the pub for a drink and a chin wag with the other patrons. On the fifth day of venturing into town, we finally caught a break when he met one of Patterson's guards at the pub and managed to talk his way into a job offer as a janitor at the Mercure Croc Hotel - Patterson's current place of abode and apparently the new location of his mad-science laboratory. The irony was not lost on me when Jon confessed he was replacing Mickey Diamond, the man he had executed. It still didn't make it right.

Sitting in the Hilton's café, sipping on a long black, I reviewed my operational plan to breach the Croc Hotel and apprehend Patterson. I would be the first to concede that it was more of a rough outline than a plan, as I was yet to have an opportunity to speak to Jon about the number of guards Patterson had on-site, their weaponry, layout, security protocols, and other relevant intel. I will learn more tomorrow morning after retrieving Jon from Jabiru. Then, hopefully, after twelve long months of searching for the bastard, Fiona and I will finally apprehend him and claim the reward.

I was about to order another coffee when I heard familiar voices emanating from the reception counter. An older gentleman with a commanding voice mentioned my name. Was that the Captain? It couldn't be! I turned to face the counter and was flabbergasted to see Captain Ross and my best mate Clarry Ugle questioning the fastidious receptionist. I marched to the counter and enthusiastically hugged them until the Captain grumbled about his back and Clarry complained of asphyxiation. After letting them escape my embrace, we sat at the café table I had made my office desk.

"What are you doing here?" I asked them both.

Clarry must have expected the Captain to answer as he glanced in his direction with an eyebrow raised. The Captain's an old salt in his late seventies, with skin like tanned leather and deep wrinkles around his eyes. He's been a close friend and somewhat of a mentor ever since I rescued his fifteen-year-old granddaughter from a sinister cult about six years back.

The Captain smiled. "After Clarry showed me your postcard, I convinced the missus to give me a leave pass so I could help you capture that bastard Patterson."

"And how exactly did you get Elizabeth to agree to that?" I asked suspiciously.

The Captain ignored my question and looked over his shoulder at the reception counter. "I'm going to sort out our rooms," he declared, groaning as he stood from his chair to hobble to reception.

I turned to Clarry and gave him a stern look. "When I sent you that postcard, I didn't expect you to travel up here, and I definitely didn't expect you to bring the Captain."

Clarry raised his palms. "I'm aware of that, Archie, but I've got some unfinished business with Patterson. And how could I pass up the opportunity to examine what he's been up to? He may be a bonified loon, but he's also a brilliant scientist. Who knows what breakthroughs he's made over the last year? Regarding the Captain, well, he didn't tell me the truth until we were halfway here. It turns out he left Elizabeth a note."

"He did what?" I asked incredulously.

"You know how he is, Archie. As he gets older, he becomes more and more stubborn. He doesn't listen to anyone, especially not me."

"Fair enough, mate. I'm not blaming you. It's just that Elizabeth will be seriously pissed at us." I sighed before continuing. "On a sinister note, I think Patterson has set up another Nazi research lab."

Fiona and I helped Clarry fund his lab so he could find a way to use Patterson's research for the good of the community. Even though Patterson's methods were pure evil, his research opened the door to possibilities that Clarry believed could fix many of the world's dilemmas. Clarry thinks science can fix everything. I didn't have the fortitude to play devil's advocate and argue that science was responsible for the nukes that destroyed half the planet and created those dilemmas.

The Captain returned to the table and gingerly lowered himself into his chair. "I've sorted the rooms. So, where's Fiona?" the Captain asked.

"It's a long story, but she'll be back tomorrow, and I'll let her fill you in. I'm glad you're here, as I think I know where Patterson is based, and I'll be able to confirm it in the morning. I was just telling Clarry that I've also received intel that he may have restarted his mad science experiments, again using innocent people as guinea pigs."

"Whatever you need, young man, we're here to help," affirmed the Captain.

I was grateful to have the two men I trusted the most in this world by my side.

# Chapter Forty-Seven

*Saturday, March 22, 2042 - Fiona*

For my final exercise, Chris tasked me with planning and executing a sniper operation. My mission was to eliminate an enemy staying at a holiday house twelve clicks northeast of Chris' cabin. He clarified that he would assess me on the knowledge and skills he had taught me over the previous ten days. As I reviewed a map of the area and planned my movements, Chris presented me with the enemy – a blue, torso-sized cardboard target.

Wearing my ghillie suit, I navigated to within two kilometres of the target and then slowly and deliberately walked until I was 150 metres from my hide. I scanned the surroundings before crawling to a fallen tree trunk surrounded by waist-high spinifex grass. Looking down my scope, I confirmed there was no movement around the property. I quickly determined the distance to the hut by the mil size of the front door and then calculated the MOA. I was 725 metres from the fibro home, and there was next to no wind. I then patiently waited.

It was bloody humid, and I had been looking through the scope for I don't know how long. It could have easily been over an hour or maybe two. I dearly wanted to check my watch, take a drink from my flask, wipe the sweat from my brow, take a piss, and scratch my ass. But I couldn't do any of these things as I needed to stay focused and ready to squeeze the trigger. I don't think I could ever live it down if I missed the shot.

At last, the door opened. I exhaled and then squeezed the trigger during my respiratory pause. I took the shot – crack. Unfortunately, the door then closed before I could verify the kill. Immediately, doubt started creeping into my mind. Did I succeed, or did I fail?

Static erupted through my earpiece. "Target is down," Chris transmitted in a monotone voice.

With every fibre in my body, I wanted to jump up, dance on the spot, and yell, 'FUCK YEAH!' But, instead, I suppressed the urge to celebrate with considerable difficulty, silently extricating myself from the hide and trekking back to Chris' cabin like a ghost.

Upon my return, Chris, Djiniyini, and his family sat around a fire pit, enjoying beers and buffalo burgers. They all clapped as I entered the camp. That's when I learned that Djiniyini and his nephews (Kumanjayi, Djon & Carbiene) had unsuccessfully searched for my hide as I lay ready to take my shot.

Djiniyini smiled, "We couldn't find you, little sister. You did real good."

When I noticed his nephews giving each other shit-eating grins, I figured Djiniyini was lying, and they had found me for sure. I was too tired to contemplate why they chose to keep their lips sealed.

Chris handed me a burger and the target. I had shot him straight through the middle of his upper chest. "You were competent," he affirmed. This was the only acknowledgement I received for my efforts during the entire training.

We ate and drank beer by the fire late into the night. I noticed Djiniyini's nephews had scars over their arms and necks, and Djon had lost an arm from the elbow down. When I asked the men about their injuries, they glanced at their uncle, who returned their silent request with a subtle shake of his head.

I was feeling tipsy after knocking back a six-pack. Chris sauntered to the cabin and returned with a bottle of 18-year-old whisky. After I downed two fingers, he poured me another, and when I tried to refuse, he bellowed that it was tradition to have a piss-up after a successful course and coerced me into sculling three shots. By 1 a.m., I started to feel sick and could feel the alcohol rising up from the back of my throat.

I was about to declare that I had had enough and was heading to bed when Djiniyini announced that he and his nephews had somewhere else to be. After I thanked Djiniyini for teaching me, he surprised me by handing me his machete. It had a beautiful, curved blade with a razor-sharp edge and a jarrah handle decorated with Aboriginal art. I was about to politely refuse when Chris piped up and said it's disrespectful to decline a gift from a warrior. I thanked Djiniyini for the machete before shuffling off to the cabin.

I collapsed into bed, too tired to remove my hunting clothes. A moment later, I felt a presence nearby and looked up to see Chris standing at the foot of my bed, grinning from ear to ear. "Good night, Fiona," he said cheerfully.

This was a day of firsts. I had never seen Chris so happy. And he actually wished me good night. I didn't think much of it other than the old man was as drunk as a skunk, which was something we had in common.

~

A thunderous bang jolted me from a drunken stupor. My brain was still clearing from a sleep-deprived fog as I jumped out of bed and furtively scanned the room.

Smoke, sparks, and gunfire filled the cabin. What the Fuck? Are we under attack? The brain fog was cleared instantly by a surge of adrenaline. When I reached for my Glock, I was comforted by the feeling of the cool polymer grip in my grasp.

"Grab your rifle, pistol, and ammo and meet me by the wood pile," I heard Chris bellow, feeling both relieved and petrified by the sound of his voice.

With the Glock in my grasp, I scanned the room for threats and couldn't mark anyone through the clearing smoke other than Chris standing at the cabin door in his ghillie suit with Penny barking at his side.

"What the FUCK are you waiting for? Hurry the fuck up, soldier!" Chris commanded as he left the cabin.

Chris wasn't acting like there was any imminent danger, so I calmed my nerves, quickly grabbed my rifle and newly acquired machete and went out to join him by the wood pile. Dawn was fast approaching as Chris ordered me to follow him into the bush. I had to jog to keep up with his quick march. Once we were in the bush, he passed me my ghillie suit and told me to put it on.

As I pulled the jumper over my head, he finally offered an explanation of sorts, "We have an enemy about nine klicks southeast from our current location. Our mission is to eliminate them.

"Wait, is this an exercise?" I asked, completely stunned.

"What do you think?" he asked tersely.

"Come on," he prompted before turning his back and continuing through the bush.

It was just light enough to see where I was stepping. Chris moved through the scrub like a cat stalking its prey while I rubbed the sleep out of my eyes and tried not to brush noisily past the shrubs and branches. Penny wagged her tail with excitement. I wish I had her enthusiasm for the situation.

About two hours in, Chris raised his hand, palm forwards at shoulder height, signalling for me to dip down into a crouch. I heard the distinct sound of gushing water and glanced around for the source. After a few moments, Chris motioned us onwards, signalling for stealth, and we crawled for a further 150 metres over the rocks and shrubs until we reached the edge of a clearing. The sound of gushing water had become a roar.

We lay on our bellies, hidden by vegetation, as we gazed into the clearing. Chris stroked Penny's neck as she rested her muzzle on the dirt. A magnificent waterfall cascaded over a three-hundred-metre cliff to plunge into a pool surrounded by a rocky gorge. It was the kind of striking view that 'old world' tourist companies would use in their advertising campaigns. Unfortunately, the idyllic scene turned hellish when I saw what was happening on the bank of the waterhole.

Three filthy men dressed in rags sat by a fire, busily tearing and chewing the meat from some bones. Behind them knelt a sobbing Aboriginal woman who was chained to a peg by a steel collar around her neck. Two large canvas tents were erected close by. I had seen some bad shit in my short life, but nothing could have prepared me for the grisly and distressing scene before me. The dismembered arms, legs, and torsos of men, women, and children were piled up by the side of a bonfire. Human heads were grotesquely stacked in a macabre pyramid at the waterhole's edge.

Chris nudged my arm to get my attention and gestured at my watch. "See those three cannibals sitting by the campfire. Take them out at 06:45 on the dot," he whispered.

Cannibals? Before I could ask him to clarify, he crawled off silently like a goanna on the hunt. I quickly peered at my watch: 6.32 a.m. "I guess this isn't an exercise," I whispered to myself. Archie's told me campfire tales about bands of cannibals roaming the top end of Australia, but I had waved them off as the type of horror stories your big brother tells you before bed to scare the bejesus out of you.

Peering through my scope, I quickly calculated my distance to the targets from the mil size of a cannibal standing by the fire cooking a human torso over the flames like a pig on a spit. I was only about 450 metres away from the sick bastards. I tried to ignore the ghastly scene by focusing on calculating the MOA and adjusting my scope's dials for elevation and windage.

I once again glanced at my watch: 06:44.45. Fixing my attention back on the targets through my scope, I focused on my breathing. Counting down, 15,000, 14,000, 13,000, I decided to take the bastards down right to left, 8,000, 7,000, 6,000, 5,000. I exhaled smoothly - crack – the first one didn't know what hit him. The second cannibal jumped to his feet as I pulled the bolt, but that's as far as he got - crack - he's down and will never rise again. The third one started to bolt after he saw his cannibal mates go down - tracking - crack - you're joining your buddies in hell.

When gunfire suddenly erupted from the side of the camp to my right, I instantly tracked toward the tents. Women and men were sprinting from the two tents in panic. Chris was out in the open, firing his pistol at the cannibals. I squeezed the trigger – crack - and took out a cannibal with a raised kitchen knife at the forefront of a group running at him from the side. Chris must have discarded his pistol as he swung to face the group, brandishing his machete, slashing at multiple cannibals now darting in and out with spears, knives, and machetes. Unfortunately, I was unable to obtain a clear sight picture as they moved to surround him. FUCK!

It was a split-second decision. I left my rifle on the ground, drew my Glock, and sprinted towards the action. Leaping over a series of rocks, the leaves on my ghillie suit rustled in the wind. When I was within twenty metres of the cannibals around Chris, I started firing my pistol – *pop, pop, pop, pop, pop, pop*. As three of them turned and rushed at me, I had no time to reload, so I drew Djiniyini's machete from the sheath and slashed at a cannibal's neck as he lunged at me with a knife. Like splitting the skin of a banana, his flesh opened, and blood spurted over me from the gaping wound.

With a somewhat panic-fuelled reverse stroke, I almost severed the head clean off the second cannibal's shoulders as he charged at me, yelling wildly with his machete raised. His filthy man-eating mate decided to run away, so I chased him down, cutting his hamstrings with a downward-angled slash. After he fell face down in the dirt, I hacked at his neck and spine until well after he had stopped jerking and twitching.

Whilst gulping down air, I turned to scan the scene. Penny was up on her hind legs ripping and tearing into a cannibal's groin with her powerful jaws as Chris ran his machete through the man-eater's wide-open mouth. Three aboriginal women in chains huddled together, sobbing by the bonfire. There were mutilated, hacked, and bullet-riddled bodies lying everywhere. The horrifying sight was like something from a 'slasher flick'. To top it off, I was suddenly aware of the sickly sweet smell of cooked human flesh and the distinct dirty aroma of burnt hair. Not registering any further threat, I collapsed to my knees in mental and physical exhaustion. The combination of a hangover, an adrenaline dump, and the ghastly spectacle surrounding me was too much to bear; I violently puked my guts up until nothing was left but bitter bile dripping down my bloodied chin.

As I staggered to the water hole to clean the blood and puke from my arms and face, I was overcome with fatigue. Reaching the edge, I dropped back to my knees and scooped water over my body, dazedly watching the red-stained fluid soak into the dirt around me.

Turning to the sound of a triumphant roar, I witnessed Chris holding his blood-soaked arms in the air while Penny ran around the camp, barking and wagging her tail in delight. *A mad bastard and his bitch.*

~

We escorted the three Aboriginal women to Djiniyini's camp. Chris spoke privately to the elder in his house while I treated the ladies' injuries, applying antiseptic and bandages to cuts and lacerations.

I was dressing my last patient's wounds when Chris and Djiniyini approached. "Djiniyini will take the women home tomorrow morning," Chris commented.

"They don't live here?" I asked.

"No, they live at a camp 30 klicks east from here."

Djiniyini pointed to the machete he gifted me, gesturing for me to hand it to him. He grinned as he ran his finger over the dried blood.

"It came in useful," I acknowledged. "Thanks again."

Chris and I said our goodbyes before hiking back to his camp in silence. In preparation for our return trip to Darwin, we cleaned the cabin and packed our gear into the back of the Land Rover. When I bent down to pick up my pack, I noticed a green canister near the foot of my bed. With everything that had occurred over the last seven hours, I almost forgot about the commotion that woke me this morning. I held the used M84 Flashbang Stun Grenade in my hand and whispered to myself, "You fucking wanker!"

Chris decided to have lunch before we journeyed to Darwin. He barbequed the thigh of a pig we bagged during our most recent hunt while I sat by the fire and cleaned my rifle. I had said hardly a word to him since the end of the operation, still majorly pissed off at being placed in such a chaotic and dangerous situation without any warning. Not to mention the state they got me into beforehand. *It was a seriously shitty thing to do.*

Chris leaned toward me with a pork bone in his grasp. "Here, have this. You must be hungry."

The smell of pork reminded me of the cooked human flesh at the camp, making me feel like dry retching. I pondered whether I would ever be able to eat pork again. "Not right now," I replied disgustedly.

By his confused expression, I figured he had no idea what I was feeling. He either didn't smell the cooked flesh at the camp, or it didn't bother him in the slightest. Probably the latter. Finally, after half an hour of awkward silence, he attempted to start up a conversation as he chewed meat off a bone. With a mouth half-full, he joked, "With all those cannibals we slaughtered, the crocs will have a banquet tonight."

I ignored him and focused on cleaning the mud from the bottom of my boots with my knife.

"You giving me the silent treatment? What's got you so upset?" he asked with a puzzled look.

I couldn't help but bite at the hook he was dangling. "Oh, I don't fucking know, maybe because you got me pissed, threw a fucking flashbang on the floor after I'd slept for barely three hours, and then took me on a crazy operation without any planning," I snapped angrily.

"Surely you didn't think the blue target was your test, did you? Being a soldier is about being resilient and dependable. You need to be ready and able whenever and wherever the unexpected bites you in the ass and the shit hits the fan."

"But I'm not a soldier, Chris. I'm a bloody bounty hunter. I wanted to learn to shoot, not hack people with machetes," I exclaimed.

"Don't you fucking get it, Fiona? Everyone has to be a soldier if they want to survive in this new world," he argued. "Anyway, you enjoyed it. I saw your blood lust when you killed those savages. People like you and me are born to kill. And thank god for us. Those sick fucks have been preying on Djiniyini's people for months. "

Penny was lying at his feet, gnawing on what I hoped was an

animal bone. Chris had cleaned her up, removing the blood stains from her white muzzle and broad chest. I called her over, and she responded by trotting over to sit at my feet. She turned her head to look at me as if to say – 'come on, pat me.' I complied with her request by massaging her back with my fingers.

"Anyway, you enjoyed it. I saw your blood lust when you killed those savages. People like you and me are born to kill."

I reflected on what Chris had said. "Archie has warned me about enjoying the kill. He says it's a slippery slope that can affect your soul."

Chris waved off the suggestion. "That's bullshit. What would he know? I love the boy, but I've known him since he was a young tacker. I remember watching him spar with his old man. He'd whine whenever his dad gave him a little love tap."

"How old was he when he was given these so-called love taps?" I asked sceptically.

"I don't know, older than 8, younger than 12. It was a bloody long time ago. Anyway, what's that got to do with the price of eggs?" When I didn't respond, he continued on his rant. "Now his dad and grandad were real men. Tough fucking bastards. His grandad skull fucked the gooks, and his daddy skinned the rag heads. So what did the boy do during his War? Rescue some fucking nurses on a boat. Big, bloody deal," he scoffed.

"Don't talk about Archie like that," I warned.

He ignored my comment. "You're different, though. Yeah, you're a bloody sheila, but you have that look. The look that says, bring it on! I saw your eyes when you hacked those cannibals. Your eyes told me that you loved bathing in that beautiful violence. You're like me. It gives you a real boner!" After reflecting on his faux pas, he looked at his feet in embarrassment, "Ah, well, you know what I mean."

Fuck! It suddenly hit me like a ton of bricks. Archie was worried that I was turning into someone like Chris. But I didn't want to be anything like Chris. I didn't want to enjoy killing, or as Chris put it, *Bathe in beautiful violence.* It all made me feel sick. What have I become?

# Chapter Forty-Eight

*Friday, March 21, 2042 – Saturday, March 22, 2042 - Archie*

For the past week, I felt like I had been twiddling my thumbs, so it was a pleasant change to have a busy morning. The Captain and Clarry joined me in picking up Jon, who was waiting at a truck stop two clicks south of Jabiru.

During the return trip to Darwin, I asked Jon to fill us in on everything that had occurred over the last four days, from beginning to end. I was mindful not to interrupt his story, knowing that we would only get one chance to hear his initial version of events before our questions influenced his reporting of events. When questioned, witnesses will often subconsciously or deliberately tell the interviewer what they think they want to hear, especially when the storyteller has a history of embellishment. Only after Jon had exhausted his memory would I ask him questions to clarify specific details.

Even though Clarry's mind was as sharp as a steel trap, he still took notes as Jon rattled off what he had seen and heard. He told the story like he was holding court in his London local and spoke non-stop for most of the three-hour journey. Given his lack of experience as a bounty hunter, I was impressed by his attention to detail. I guess a good memory is a survival mechanism for a prospector. They search for gold in the middle of nowhere and rely on their memory to recall features in the desolate landscape to find their way back to camp.

I felt like whooping with joy when Jon confirmed that Patterson was living and operating out of the Croc Hotel. My elation turned sombre when he further explained that he used the hotel's guest rooms to perform ghastly human experiments. His henchman lured drifters to the hotel with the promise of food and shelter. He would then keep them captive and test his pharmaceuticals on them until they either died or were transformed into one of his muscle-bound goons. Speaking of his Hulks, twelve of his monsters were guarding the hotel armed with pistols and shotguns. Jon also mentioned that nine non-combatants worked as cooks, cleaners, lab assistants, and handymen.

Clarry asked a poignant question that had been preying on my mind, "How does the town let him get away with it?"

"He pays them a generous bribe," Jon explained.

"Hear no evil, see no evil, speak no evil," the Captain rumbled in disgust.

I figured that Patterson must have access to a considerable stash of coin. I always suspected that he had raided the Perth Mint, which was abandoned when the nukes struck the CBD. However, I kept that information to myself as I didn't want Jon to get any wild ideas. After all, it was Einstein who said, "Three great forces rule the world: stupidity, fear and greed."

Upon our return to the Hilton, my day got even better when I found Fiona and Chris waiting for us in the lobby. I noticed that she looked leaner, which I didn't think was possible. I introduced Chris to the three men before we all moseyed over to the bar and ordered pints of lager. We clinked glasses and said cheers as we moved over to a table. I gestured for Fiona and Chris to sit across from me so I could catch up on all the details about the sniper training and fill them in on what I had learned about Patterson.

"So, how did it go?" I asked them both.

Strangely, it was as if Fiona didn't register my question. Instead, she turned to Clarry and started up a conversation.

"She was competent by the time we were done," was all I got out of Chris.

"Well, that's great, I guess. Thanks again, Uncle Chris. I owe you one. On another note, I've got another job for you if you're interested. It involves breaching a hotel and capturing a fugitive. But it's not going to be easy. He has twelve armed killers guarding the place. I'm paying two ounces of gold. Are you up for it? No pressure if you're not keen."

Chris straightened, and his moustache bristled sternly, "I'm up for anything, you cheeky little bastard. But like I told you before, I'm not taking your money. When I walk through the pearly gates, I don't want your old man waiting for me with a pair of fingerless gloves and a desire to rumble."

"You seriously think you're going upstairs?" Fiona scoffed before returning to her conversation with Clarry.

I now wondered whether the training went as well as I had assumed. Or was there something else going on? Chris just smiled and gave me a wink before sipping his beer.

I decided to swiftly change the subject. After all, I had bigger fish to fry. "Can you recommend any men that could assist us with this op?"

"Yeah, lad. I know four tough and reliable Gunwinggu warriors that have assisted me in the past. I'm sure they'd be up for it. It'd be fair to pay their leader, Djiniyini, two ounces and his three nephews one ounce each."

"Are you talking about asking Djiniyini and his nephews to assist with the Op?" Fiona cut in, to which Chris replied with a nod. "They're good people," Fiona stated with confidence.

"Perfect, that would give us an operational force of ten," I said.

After shooting the breeze with everyone over a couple of beers, I decided to head up to my room to type the operational order. I told them I would present the briefing tomorrow after lunch and wished them all good night.

~

I had just finished typing my op order on a well-used Brother Deluxe 240 typewriter that the hotel attendant was good enough to lend me when I heard a knock at the door and a familiar voice asking if they could enter.

Fiona plonked on the edge of the bed, holding a half-empty bottle of scotch by its neck. She looked a little worse for wear and smelt like she had more than her fair share to drink.

"You got some glasses?" she asked.

I found two glasses in the minibar and held them as she poured us four fingers, which was an unusually generous portion for Fiona.

"Sooo, what's up? Do you want to go through the op plan?" I asked.

"Please don't leave me, Archie," she blurted.

"What are you talking about? Did something happen during the training?" I asked with concern.

"No, I mean yes, but that's not the issue." She burped before continuing, slurring a little, "You said you'd leave me if I didn't respect your code, and I'm worried that I'm beginning to enjoy the pointy end of the ops, but I don't want us to split."

"Fiona, what going on? Fill me in, please."

"I know I've got issues and put on this act of being a badass. But I think you're just as fucked up. You may not want to die, but I don't think you care whether you live."

I was feeling more than a little confused by this turn of topic. Sometimes I feel like we speak a different language. I had absolutely no idea what she was referring to.

"What do you mean I don't care whether I live?"

"Archie, you put yourself at unnecessary risk at every opportunity. I mean, who volunteers to board a pirate vessel unarmed? You did the same thing when you walked into Norseman on the recon."

She had a valid point, but I felt that I had assessed the risk in both scenarios, and the reward was worth it. But I was still determining if she'd agree with my perspective in her current state.

"Okay, I tend to put myself in harm's way. I'll give you that. And there was a time after I lost Janet when I didn't care whether I lived or died. But that was then, and this is now. I have things to live for. I have Clarry, the Captain, Roger, and Xena. And I have you, Fiona. Believe me, I'm planning on sticking around. If for no other reason than to save your ass from the crazy shit you get yourself into," I added half-jokingly to take the edge off.

"I didn't enjoy shooting the bloke in the caravan. I was just overcome with an urge to get payback for Vanessa and her father. It was the same feeling when I killed the cannibals. Yeah, I admit I felt satisfaction from the killings, but I swear I didn't enjoy it. I've felt weak and helpless for most of my life, and I know what it's like to be vulnerable. I hated it and don't ever want to feel like that again. And I can't stand by as innocent people are victimised just because someone is bigger, stronger, and meaner. Do you get it, Archie? Was there ever a time that you felt that way?"

"Yeah, Fiona, I get it. When I was ten or eleven, my dad beat the crap out of me. One day I cried for two hours straight. That night I promised myself that I'd never show weakness like that again. But I guess that's why I also struggle with unnecessary cruelty." I was just about to take a swig of whisky when it suddenly hit me, "Wait, did you say, cannibals?"

"Yeah, long story. I'll fill you in another time if that's okay? But, I will say this. Chris is really fucked up in the head."

"Yep, he has PTSD, just like my old man. That doesn't change the fact that he's a good bloke and one of the best trainers and toughest bastards you'll ever meet. Ask yourself this, did he improve your skills?"

"You have no fucking idea, Archie. He's taught me to be a motherfucking killing machine with a rifle. But the training sort of made me think about where my life is heading. It's just that he....ah, don't worry about it. I shouldn't have even brought it up. And as I said, it's for another time."

I wondered what Chris had put her through. The training obviously made her confront some demons, and it would be better for her to talk about it, but I decided she was probably right. Now was not the right time.

"Are we good, Archie?" she asked in earnest.

I rose from my seat, "Come here," I said, moving in to give her a brotherly hug. Then, after I released her, I held her eye and said, "Everything will work out. And as long as you want me around, I'll be here."

~

I flicked the hotel receptionist with the flawless customer service a silver coin after he agreed to let me use the convention room to present the operational order. Fiona and the eight men were talking amongst themselves with notebooks and pens ready as I prepared my documents at the front of the room. I had typed nine copies of the 'execution phases' to ensure each team member understood their role. I sighed inwardly when I glanced at my horrible drawing of the Mercure Crocodile Hotel on the whiteboard. Don't quit your day job, I thought to myself.

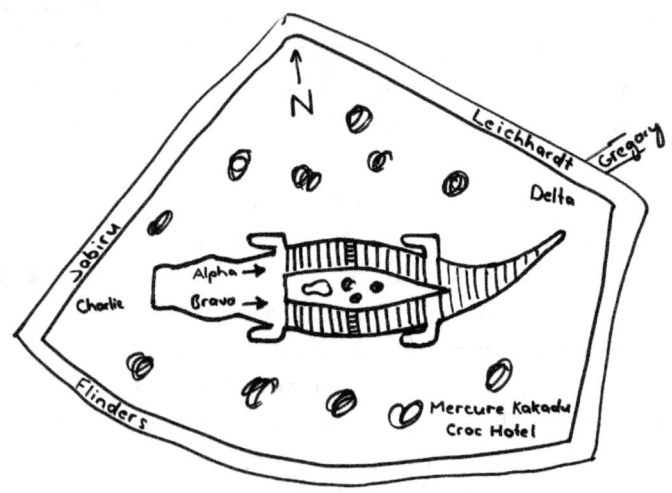

I signalled for the group's attention. "Alright, listen up. First things first, before I present the order, I want to thank you all for participating in this operation. Patterson is a sick criminal who must be detained for the greater good. And, of course, the reward." There was a release of tension in the room when they all laughed. "I'll give you all a copy of the execution phases after the briefing, but please take notes. I'll answer questions after I've finished reading the order. The situation is......"

After I read the situation, I glanced around the room to gauge the team's mood - the nephews were on the edge of their seats, looking eager, while the Captain and Chris were leaning back with their arms folded, looking calm and measured. Clarry was in his own world, staring off into the distance, Jon was fidgeting nervously, and Djiniyini was as happy as can be, grinning like a Cheshire cat.

I continued, "Our mission is to breach the Mercure Kakadu Croc Hotel in Jabiru and capture Noel Patterson on Sunday, March 25, 2042. I repeat, our mission is to breach the Mercure Kakadu Croc Hotel in Jabiru and capture Noel Patterson on Sunday, March 25, 2042."

#### **\*\*\*\* OPERATION VENGEANCE \*\*\***

**SITUATION:** NOEL PATTERSON WAS TRIED AND CONVICTED IN ABSENTIA FOR MULTIPLE MURDERS. PATTERSON IS NOW A WANTED FUGITIVE WITH A 'DEAD OR ALIVE' BOUNTY ON HIS HEAD. RELIABLE INTELLIGENCE HAS BEEN RECEIVED THAT PATTERSON IS BASING HIS CURRENT OPERATION AT THE MERCURE KAKADU CROC HOTEL, LOCATED ON FLINDERS STREET IN JABIRU. HE IS CONDUCTING ILLEGAL AND IMMORAL EXPERIMENTS IN VARIOUS GUEST ROOMS. INTEL SUGGESTS HE HAS AT LEAST TWELVE ARMED MEN GUARDING THE HOTEL, AND A FURTHER NINE NON-COMBATANTS WHO WORK AS COOKS, CLEANERS, LAB ASSISTANTS, AND HANDYMEN. THE GUARDS ARE ARMED WITH PISTOLS AND SHOTGUNS. ALL INGRESS AND EGRESS DOORS HAVE BEEN BARRICADED TO PREVENT CAPTIVES FROM ESCAPING. TWO ARMED GUARDS ARE POSITIONED AT THE FRONT ENTRANCE OF THE HOTEL. GUARDS ARE NOT KNOWN TO PATROL THE EXTERNAL GROUNDS OF THE HOTEL, BUT THIS CANNOT BE TAKEN FOR GRANTED.

**MISSION:** TO BREACH THE MERCURE KAKADU CROC HOTEL IN JABIRU AND CAPTURE NOEL PATTERSON ON SUNDAY, MARCH 25, 2042.

#### **EXECUTION:**

PHASE 1: AT 0100HRS, ALPHA, BRAVO, AND CHARLIE TEAMS WILL DEPART THE HILTON CARPARK AND TRAVEL IN THE CHARGER (VICTOR 1: DRIVEN BY ARCHIE) AND LAND ROVER (VICTOR 2: DRIVEN BY CHRIS) TO THE JABIRU BASKETBALL COURT ON LAKESIDE DRIVE.

PHASE 2: UPON ARRIVAL AT THE JABIRU BASKETBALL COURT (APPROX. 0400HRS), ALPHA, BRAVO, AND CHARLIE TEAM WILL PREPARE FOR THE ASSAULT (WEAPONS AND RADIO CHECK).

ALPHA TEAM: ARCHIE, FIONA & CLARRY

BRAVO TEAM: CHRIS, CARBIENE & JON

CHARLIE TEAM: DJINIYINI & KUMANJAYI

DELTA TEAM: THE CAPTAIN & DJON


PHASE 3:

VICTOR 1 WILL DRIVE DELTA TEAM TO THE CORNER OF GREGORY
PLACE AND LEICHHARDT STREET (THE CROC'S TAIL), WHEREBY THEY
WILL ESTABLISH COVER AND ELIMINATE ANY HOSTILE COMBATANTS
AND WAIT FOR RADIO COMMS IF BACK-UP IS REQUIRED.

VICTOR 2 WILL DRIVE CHARLIE TEAM TO THE CORNER OF FLINDERS
STREET AND JABIRU DRIVE (NEAR THE CROC'S HEAD), WHEREBY
THEY WILL ESTABLISH COVER AND ELIMINATE ANY HOSTILE
COMBATANTS AND WAIT FOR RADIO COMMS IF BACK-UP IS REQUIRED.

PHASE 4: ALPHA AND BRAVO TEAM WILL BREACH THE FRONT OF
THE PREMISES (CROC'S HEAD) AND CLEAR THE RECEPTION AREA
AND CONVENTION ROOM.

ALPHA TEAM WILL CLEAR THE NORTHERN SIDE OF THE CROC (LEFT
SIDE FACING THE HEAD), EVERY ROOM TO THE TAIL (55 ROOMS).

BRAVO TEAM WILL CLEAR THE SOUTHERN SIDE OF THE CROC
(RIGHT SIDE FACING THE HEAD), EVERY ROOM TO THE TAIL
(55 ROOMS).

CHARLIE TEAM'S MAIN PRIORITY IS TO SECURE THE HOTEL
PERIMETER NEAR THE CROC'S HEAD TO PREVENT COMBATANTS FROM
ENTERING OR ESCAPING THE OUTER CORDON, WITH THE PRIMARY
FOCUS BEING PATTERSON.

DELTA TEAM'S MAIN PRIORITY IS TO SECURE THE HOTEL
PERIMETER NEAR THE CROC'S TAIL TO PREVENT COMBATANTS FROM
ENTERING OR ESCAPING THE OUTER CORDON, WITH THE PRIMARY
FOCUS BEING PATTERSON.

CAPTURE AND SECURE PATTERSON (IMMEDIATELY ADVISE ALL
INVOLVED IF HE HAS BEEN CAPTURED).

PHASE 5: FIONA TO PROVIDE FIRST AID CARE AND TRANSPORT
PATTERSON'S VICTIMS TO THE JABIRU HEALTH CAMPUS.

PHASE 6: VICTOR 1 (ARCHIE AND CLARRY) TO TRANSPORT
PATTERSON TO DARWIN POLICE STATION.


**ADMINISTRATION & LOGISTICS:**

A TWO-WAY RADIO WILL BE ISSUED TO EACH MEMBER OF THE TEAM.

EACH TEAM IS TO CARRY DOOR BREACHING TOOLS IN THE VEHICLE AS
A CONTINGENCY (JIMMY BAR, RAM, HINGE PULLER, BOLT CUTTER).

EACH MEMBER IS TO BE ARMED WITH A SIDEARM AND LONG-ARM.

EACH PERSON IS TO CARRY SUFFICIENT AMMUNITION SUPPLIED BY
CHRIS (12-GAUGE SLUGS AND AAA, .223 CALIBRE, .45 CALIBRE,
& 9MM ROUNDS).

VEHICLES:

VICTOR ONE: ARCHIE, FIONA, CLARRY, THE CAPTAIN & DJON

VICTOR TWO: CHRIS, CARBIENE, JON, DJINIYINI & KUMANJAYI


**COMMAND & SIGNALS:**

CHANNEL 4

\*\*\*\*

After the briefing, the only question came from Jon, who questioned why he wasn't selected to escort Patterson to the Darwin Police Station. In a tone designed to curtail any debate, I advised him that he would be needed to care for and transport innocent parties and deal with detained guards.

Jon crossed his arms, stuck his chin in the air and just as he opened his mouth to argue the point, I raised my voice, "Thank you for your attendance, and I will see you all tomorrow morning in the Hilton carpark at 0100hrs."

Before returning to my room, I quickly chatted with Chris, once again, with my cap in hand. He kindly agreed to obtain the logistics we required to execute the operation – radios, ammo, vehicle, and maps. The man was a life saver.

# Chapter Forty-Nine

*Sunday, March 23, 2042 from 1 a.m. – Fiona*

Archie asked me to help him carry the ten coffees he made to the Hilton carpark, where the eight others were waiting by the Beast and Chris' Land Rover. I noticed that each man had a sidearm holstered to their belt and was carrying a long arm. Clarry held his F92 Austeyr assault rifle that Archie gave him last year, while Chris carried an F88 Austeyr rifle from his ADF stash. Jon, the Captain, and Djiniyini were armed with .223 bolt action rifles, and his three nephews were packing shotguns. Chris supplied the men with all the ammunition they could carry. Hopefully, they wouldn't need it, I thought to myself.

The Beast was fully loaded with bums on seats as we followed Chris' Land Rover down the Arnhem Highway towards Jabiru. The three-hour journey felt like a quiet drive through the countryside. I have not been calmer before an operation. I wondered whether the past two weeks of sniper training had desensitised me to pre-op nerves or if I was falling into the trap of overconfidence? Probably both, I figured.

Both vehicles approached the Jabiru Basketball Court carpark from the town's eastern side to avoid the Croc Hotel's entrance and Patterson's guards. As planned, we stopped at the carpark, conducted a weapons inspection to ensure our firearms had one up the spout and performed a radio check to confirm all members were on channel four and could receive and transmit comms.

After we dropped the Captain and Djon near the croc's tail, we sped off straight to the croc's head. Bravo team were exiting the Land

Rover as we pulled up alongside.

With my rifle strapped to my back, I swiftly drew my Glock from its holster. Alpha and Bravo teams advanced towards the hotel entrance with their firearms raised. Finally, I could feel my body prepping for the action: my heart started to race, and the adrenaline surged through my bloodstream. Ready or not, here we go.

Archie issued instructions just before we reached the mouth of the croc. "Fiona and I are clearing the left, Jon and Clarry go straight up the middle, Chris and Carbiene, you're on the right. Understood?" There were 'rogers' all around.

Fortunately, the two complacent muscle-bound goons guarding the entrance were caught completely unawares. Both men were standing on either side of the closed glass doors having a chinwag as we dashed quietly to within metres of the entry. Clarry, Chris, Jon and Carbiene unloaded on the two men - 12-gauge slugs and 5.56 mm rounds shattered the glass and ripped the two monstrous men to shreds.

Archie and I moved to our left, with his long legs stepping over one of the corpses, whereas I had to skirt around the body while I scanned for threats. We walked past the empty reception desk and cleared the lobby before entering a hallway with Aboriginal art hanging from the walls.

A diorama of a stuffed crocodile chasing a salmon caught my attention for a split second before a blur of rapid movement to my left shifted my focus. I turned to see Archie in a firefight with a goon who managed to get off a round from his shotgun. As I put two rounds into the goon's skull, the blast rattled my eardrums. I was relieved to discover that Archie was still standing, but the damage to the wall behind him revealed it was a close thing. With a quick nod to each other, we continued our advance into the croc's head. I could hear automatic gunfire and shotgun booms to my right, but I maintained my focus on my area of responsibility, trusting that Bravo team was engaging the threat.

Just after we entered a large dining room, Clarry let rip with his assault rifle in the direction of a goon who was shooting wildly at us from behind a marble bar with his pump-action shotgun. I felt a familiar stinging sensation in my right thigh and calf as Clarry strafed the bar, blasting wine glasses, bottles of spirits, and the attacking goon's face. After Clarry had eliminated the threat, he provided cover while Archie quickly bandaged the wound to my leg. I then limped behind them down the croc's body toward the hallway that provided access to the guest rooms. I knew my injury wasn't that bad, but the pain was still intense. I could feel the lead balls tear through my muscles every time I took a step. Fuck it - no choice but to bite down and finish the job.

Clarry and Archie cleared room by room while I watched their backs in the hallway. Archie either yelled 'clear' if he found the room empty or 'patient' if he found a victim of Patterson's sicko experiments. Whenever a victim was found, the door was left open as a sign to return after we cleared the hotel. Archie told us during the briefing that the only way to maximise the chances of finding Patterson was to methodically clear and search each of the 110 rooms, all the way down to the croc's tail.

We had only cleared half of the rooms when I noticed a door open about thirty metres down the hallway. A bald, muscular man who I instantly recognised as Patterson bolted from the room and sprinted towards the tail of the hotel.

"Patterson," I screamed.

"Stay with Fiona," Archie yelled as he took off after him.

He knew I was wounded and couldn't run, but he didn't want Clarry to leave me alone.

"Fuck that! Go after him, Clarry," I pleaded.

In response, Clarry just shook his head. He refused to disobey Archie's wishes. I hobbled down the hallway with Clarry by my side. When I attempted to jog, I screamed in pain and frustration before Clarry put his left arm around me to take some of my weight, making sure to leave our weapons hands free.

# Chapter Fifty

*Sunday, March 23, 2042 from 4 a.m. – Archie*

As we approached the hotel to commence the op, my usual jitters were present, but there wasn't time to reconsider the plan. After Clarry and Chris took down the two hulks guarding the entrance, Fiona and I quickly cleared the reception area before advancing through the lobby. A Hulk stepped out from behind a six-foot-high rock centrepiece shaped like a spear point and fired his shotgun over our heads as I fired six rounds into his chest. I ducked down and yelled, "reload" as Fiona finished him off with her Glock.

I could hear what I assumed was Chris firing his assault rifle in short bursts on the southern side of the hotel. Then, as Clarry cut down a Hulk using a bar as cover, I heard Fiona cry out in pain. We stopped so I could assess the wound in her lower leg and apply a bandage. She had been shot with buckshot, which was becoming a bit of a habit of hers. It would hurt like a bitch, but she would survive.

Clarry and I cleared each hotel room as Fiona watched our six and secured the hallway. In the fifth room we cleared, I found a pregnant middle-aged woman chained to a bed with a drip inserted into her arm. She was incoherently mumbling - obviously drugged out of her mind. It was difficult not to be overcome with sympathy for Patterson's victims and become enraged by his depravity, but I had to keep a cool head and stay on task. We found another four victims, but unfortunately, they were not long for this world due to stomach and head wounds – more evidence of Patterson's horrific experiments.

We had just cleared a room when Fiona screamed, "Patterson." The scientist ran east down the tail.

Stay with Fiona," I shouted to Clarry and gave chase.

For a big man, Patterson was surprisingly fast, but I was starting to close the distance. When he shouldered a door to his left, I followed him out of the croc's rear foot. We were running east through the hotel grounds - jumping over fences, garden beds, ponds, and along grass paths like we were performing in an amateur steeplechase event.

As I ran, I spoke breathlessly into the radio, "Alpha team to Delta team."

"Roger, Archie," the Captain responded over the radio.

My legs were pumping. "On foot...chasing Patterson.... toward you," I transmitted between gulps of air.

I brought the radio back to my mouth and was about to order the Captain to seek cover when I saw Patterson raise his right arm and alter his gait. I heard the shot a heartbeat before I dove forward, grasping Patterson around his waist and tackling him to the ground. We both rolled, but I was quick to scramble and dive on top of him. I instantly grabbed his wrist and wreathed a pistol from his grasp. My knuckles popped as I rammed my fist into his jaw.

I looked up to see the Captain lying on his side, just five or so metres from where I knelt. I was shocked to see blood pouring from the side of his head. My right hand shook as I stood above Patterson and pointed my muzzle at his chest.

"I give up. Take me in. Do your job," Patterson demanded arrogantly.

"You've just murdered a mate of mine, you piece of shit!" I spat in rage.

Patterson just shrugged his shoulders in contempt. "He was in my way."

I thought of my duty to tell Elizabeth that her beloved husband of forty years was gone. She had every right to blame me. If anyone deserved to die, it was Patterson. But not in this way. The families of his victims deserved to see him dance the jig at the end of a rope. They deserved closure as much as I did.

I was shocked to hear the Captain moan, and I looked over to see his hand shake before lying dead still. I made a fatal error. I took my eyes off him. '*For fuck's sake, boy, watch his bloody hands*,' Sal screamed inside my head.

Patterson smirked as he raised himself to a sitting position. It was too late! I saw the glint of a silver pistol in his right hand.

# Chapter Fifty-One

*Sunday, March 23, 2042 from 4:25 a.m. – Fiona*

I heard Archie over the radio as I hobbled with Clarry's help from the hotel. My right thigh was in agony, and my calf was cramping.

"Alpha team to Delta team," Archie transmitted.

"Roger, Archie," acknowledged the Captain.

I stopped and peered through the scope of my rifle as I heard Archie gasp over the radio, "On foot chasing Patterson toward you."

Several alarming events appeared to occur simultaneously. I saw the Captain fall to the ground - I heard a single shot - and I saw Archie tackle Patterson.

Archie was standing over Patterson within a heartbeat, pointing his revolver at him. "Take the shot, Archie," I whispered to myself.

They were about 150 metres away. After completing Chris' training, it felt like spitting distance.

"What did you just say?" Clarry asked.

Through my scope, I could see Patterson reaching behind his back. Fuck this, I thought. I squeezed the trigger. *Crack!*

The .338 round impacted Patterson's right eye socket at 940 metres per second, causing his skull to crack like an egg, but instead of yolk, green blood erupted from the bullet hole as he fell lifelessly to the grass.

Good riddance, you evil fuck! I figured he was now screaming while the Devil roasted his testicles above an open fire and shoved a pitchfork up his ass.

I couldn't help but boast. "Not a bad shot," I said with a wry smile.

I felt Clarry's hand on my shoulder as it finally hit me - the Captain had been shot.

I hobbled towards the Captain as Clarry sprinted past me.

# Chapter Fifty-Two

*Sunday, March 23, 2042 from 4:26 a.m. – Archie*

Raising my revolver, I experienced tunnel vision. My entire focus was directed at the muzzle of Patterson's revolver as it swung towards me. I was about to die. And there was nothing I could do to prevent it. And then I heard a shot - *crack!* For a nanosecond, I thought he had shot me. I had just one thought - Janet. As I registered the large hole where Patterson's eye used to be, I felt an odd mixture of relief and disappointment that I wouldn't be joining my wife just yet.

It was finally over. I turned to see Fiona hobbling over to us with her rifle in hand. I walked over to the Captain and fell to my knees alongside Clarry, overcome with grief.

~

I carried Patterson's head to the dining room, where all the surviving members of Alpha and Bravo team congregated. I was saddened to discover that Carbiene, one of Djiniyini's nephews, had been killed while clearing the hotel. A Hulk hiding behind vegetation near the empty pool had fired a 12-gauge slug into his chest at close range. Chris responded by mowing the guard down with his assault rifle, but it was too late to save the young man.

Alpha and Bravo teams had dispatched a total of eight Hulks. If Jon's intel on the number of guards was accurate, four of the guards had decamped during the breach. The non-combatant workers took their belongings and left the hotel in peace. Only the cook remonstrated about his loss of employment. Chris told him to skedaddle before he placed his size fourteen boot up his ass.

Of the twelve men and women we found in the guest rooms, only the pregnant lady, a teenage boy, and an old gentleman had survived. True to form, Patterson hadn't cared whether his guinea pigs lived or died. We buried the unfortunate victims on the hotel grounds as Jon and Fiona transported the survivors to the Jabiru Health Clinic.

As Clarry searched the hotel for Patterson's notes, patient charts, and lab equipment, I searched for something entirely different. It took me almost two hours to find what I was looking for. In a storeroom, under several chemical containers, Patterson had stashed a green ammo container full of minted gold bars. I counted seven one-kilogram gold bars and an assortment of 100-ounce, 10-ounce and 1-ounce bars, more than one million dollars of gold in pre-War old money. Normally a thing of beauty, the gold lacked its usual lustre under the current circumstances. I shed tears for the Captain as I loaded the stash into my pack.

When I finally returned to the dining room of the Croc hotel, the others were all patiently waiting. I apologised for my tardiness and explained that it was time to dish out what was owed. I gave Djiniyini and his two nephews double what they were promised and gave them an additional three ounces for the loss of Carbiene. They attempted to refuse the extra payment, but I insisted they take the gold. Djiniyini finally appeared happy with the arrangement after Chris explained that I was an honourable man impressed by their bravery and skill.

I asked Fiona and the men to wait in the carpark while I spoke with Jon. Jon looked concerned as he placed his hand on the grip of his holstered pistol.

"Don't even think about it, Jon," Fiona stated firmly from the doorway.

Jon turned around to see Fiona aiming her rifle at him.

"Let's just all settle down," I said while gesturing for Fiona to lower her weapon. "Listen carefully, Jon, because I'm only going to say this once, and I'm not here for a debate. I'm giving you all ten ounces of gold for this bounty." Jon was smiling until I told him the bad news. "But you killed a man in cold blood. Mickey didn't deserve to die. I'll ensure the authorities know what you did."

Jon's bottom lip dropped. "What the fuck? You're going to dob me in?" he sneered.

"Tell him about your code, Archie," Fiona said.

"Now, if I were you, I'd take those ten ounces, cross the border into Queensland, and never come back. Because by sundown, you'll likely have a bounty on your head and that gold you'll be carrying will make you an extra tempting target, if you know what I mean."

I slowly reached into my pocket and handed Jon the ten ounces. During our conversation, Fiona had ignored my request and kept her muzzle pointed at Jon's head.

Jon's cheeks were red, and it wasn't his sunburn. "Well, fuck you very much, Archie," he exclaimed.

"You best be moving on, Jon, because my trigger finger is starting to itch," Fiona warned.

# Chapter Fifty-Three

*Monday, March 24, 2042 –*
*Thursday March 27, 2042 - Fiona*

Over the last couple of years, I've come to accept that Archie almost always makes the right decisions at the right time, and that's why I didn't get stuck into him for handing Jon the ten ounces of gold. As soon as we left Darwin in the Beast, Archie looked at me in his rear vision mirror and told me to look in his pack, which was sitting beside me in the back seat.

"Fuck me! How much is this? Where did you get it?" I exclaimed.

"We're rich," he laughed.

"What are you two on about?" asked Clarry, who was riding shotgun.

I handed Clarry a one-kilo gold bar. "Oh, sweet baby Jesus," he whispered.

"And there's another six of them," I giggled.

"I had a suspicion that Patterson had raided the Perth Mint. Turns out I was right. We now have a lot to think about," Archie said with a grin.

~

We packed the Captain's body and Patterson's head in ice in the Beast's boot to keep the former presentable for Elizabeth and the latter recognisable for the coppers. I knew it was irrational, but placing that lovely man next to the evil bastard didn't feel right, so I stuck Patterson's head in an old Esky cooler.

Clarry suggested we honour the Captain by stopping off at his favourite fishing spots on the way down the west coast from Broome to Geraldton. Unfortunately, we didn't manage to catch fish at every stop, but we did share a beer and shed a tear as we remembered our boss, mentor, and friend.

Once we arrived in Geraldton, Archie and Clarry spent the morning picking up supplies and visiting Roger and Jasper at Bushy's stables. Archie paid a hefty sum to transport the horses to Esperance by float, but funds were no longer a concern.

I carried the Esky into the Geraldton Police Station. Nicky Allen, the volunteer officer who had assisted us during the debacle of an arrest warrant earlier in the month, was standing behind the station counter. He was dressed in uniform with a badge reading 'Police Cadet' pinned to his chest.

I placed the cooler on the counter and shook Nicky's hand, "Congratulations, Nicky. Your mum and dad must be very proud."

"Thanks, Fiona. Yep, they sure are. They held a street party for me and everything," he beamed.

Before I could warn him, Nicky opened the cooler lid and asked, "What have we got here?" Then, as quick as a fox, he jumped back from the counter.

"What is, I mean, who is that?" he sputtered, face pale.

"That was Noel Patterson," I clarified as I placed the wanted poster on the counter. Nicky examined the mug shot before reopening the cooler and having a quick peek. "Nicky, I need you to complete the handover documentation, so I can prove to the bondsman that I've honoured the contract."

"Sure, sorry." Nicky marched to the sergeant's office. "Sarge, where do I find the bounty handover documentation?"

Nicky returned to the counter twenty minutes later with the completed document in his grasp. "Sorry it took so long. It's the first time I've completed one of these," he explained.

I left Nicky at the counter, ogling Patterson's head like it was about to bite him, and strolled next door to the bondsman's office to submit the handover document to Brad Hill.

Brad whistled with appreciation. "Wow, ten ounces. I've never issued a reward worth so much." Brad opened the safe, counted the gold into a leather satchel, and placed it in my hand. "Don't spend it all at once," he teased. If only he knew about the gold Archie found at the Croc Hotel, he'd regard the reward as a pittance.

~

We arrived at Elizabeth's home in Esperance on the morning of the fourth day of our journey. I held Elizabeth in my arms as Clarry and Archie waited to offer their condolences. She explained that Helen, her adopted daughter, was staying the night at her friend's house for a birthday celebration. She didn't want to spoil Helen's night, so I stayed with her until she returned the following day. Helen had matured into a confident young lady in the six months since I'd last seen her, which gave me solace that Elizabeth would have someone close by her side while she grieved.

It was no surprise that more than half of the town attended the Captain's funeral. He was a beloved man in the community who helped those in need and supported the militia. Archie and Clarry spoke eloquently at his funeral, telling touching and humorous stories about a man who had been a beloved father figure to them both.

I was pleased to hear that Helen had decided to take over as skipper of The Mother Theresa and help Elizabeth manage the fish 'n' chips shop. It was hard to imagine the confident and competent young lady being scared and resentful just twelve months ago. She was fortunate to be rescued from a gang in Norseman by Archie and then adopted by the Captain and Elizabeth, who gave her the one thing she needed to heal: love. And now she's paying that love back in spades.

~

Archie and I were tearing down the road to the Singh's farm to collect our private fifty-ounce reward on the Patterson contract.

316

I wanted to explore what was next for us as a team, but I didn't know how to broach the subject, so in my new way of expressing my feelings, I just came out and told him what was on my mind.

"So Boss, what's next now we have all this loot? But before you answer, I want to make it clear that I'm keen on staying a team."

"I've been giving that a lot of thought. But first, I want to make sure you're all good with my proposal before I consider the finer details."

"Shoot," I replied, my interest piqued.

"As you know, my dream was to retire from bounty hunting and run my own brewery in Darwin. But after our trip, I changed my mind. I want to build one from scratch here in Esperance. You could split your time between helping Helen and me with the business if you wish."

"Archie, I...." I started to speak, but he cut me off.

"And I know what you're thinking, it's boring, and there's no action. But we could train the militia and ensure the region is safe from the gangs. We could even clear the border from the scum bags regularly crossing over and...."

It was my turn to cut in because I was about to burst with excitement. "Archie, I absolutely love the idea. I'm all in!"

Archie looked both happy and relieved as he drove the Beast to the main gate of the Singh property. The guards approached the vehicle while pointing shotguns in our direction.

After the guards recognised us, we were escorted past the Singh's red-brick mansion to a gazebo in the centre of a manicured garden. We had a picturesque view of the Singh's sprawling farm that spanned as far as the eye could see. An old tractor sat in the paddock, surrounded by tall wheatgrass blowing gently in the breeze. Sheep lay huddled under a gum tree to escape the day's heat. I could see myself back on a farm in later life, living and working off the land.

Archie placed the Esky at his feet and stretched his arms wide before slumping in his seat. He swiftly corrected his posture when he saw Mr Singh shuffling towards us. The elderly gentleman gestured a greeting before lowering himself into a cushioned ornate chair. A maid dutifully placed three glasses of lemonade on the table.

"When I was advised you had arrived, Mr O'Connor, I was hoping that you had brought Mr Patterson," admonished Mr Singh in a posh English accent.

"We did, Sir," Archie replied with a blank expression.

"Well, where is here? Is he in your car? The boot? My guards will collect him."

Archie picked up the Esky and plonked it on the table. "He's in there. He killed a close friend and was about to take me out when Fiona shot him."

Mr Singh opened the cooler and glared at Patterson's face before crudely spitting on it. He handed the guards the head and asked them to collect fifty ounces of gold.

"I would have preferred to get my hands on him, but a deal is a deal. Thank you for helping me achieve the vengeance necessary to retain my honour."

I nearly spat the lemonade from my mouth. I wanted to give the old fool a piece of my mind. His honour? I don't give a rat's fuck about his honour. The monster kidnapped his grandchild and committed mass murder. However, the ill-feeling quickly dissipated when I saw a grinning eleven-year-old boy run across the grass with a crossbow in his grasp. Raj was delighted when we agreed to spend the afternoon with him sipping lemonade and shooting targets with his crossbow. It was magic.

As the sun set over the paddock, we were ready to return to Clarry's with the gold in our packs. I inserted a mixed-tape into the deck and bopped my head to AC/DC as we roared down the highway towards our next adventure.

# DEFINITION OF TERMS

*Area of Responsibility:* When operators are tactically entering a room, the area is divided into pie like sections or sectors. The room can be cleared faster. If there are two operators in the room, they each have 50% of the room.

*Billabong:* An isolated pond left behind after a river changes course.

*Bliad':* A Russian word for slut or whore

*Bounty:* Payment or reward (especially from a government) for acts such as catching criminals or enlisting in the military

*Brazilian Jiu-jitsu:* A martial art and combat sport based on ground fighting and submission holds.

*Crib:* A meal break

*Donga:* A donga a transportable building with single rooms, often used on remote work sites. They can be made out of traditional building materials or even from converted shipping containers.

*Door breaching:* The use of equipment (ram, jimmy bar, hinge puller, bolt cutter) to gain entry to a locked and/or barricaded door.

*EMP:* A short burst of electromagnetic energy. A pulse's origin may be a natural occurrence or human-made and can occur as a radiated, electric, or magnetic field or a conducted electric current, depending on the source.

*Friendly Fire:* An incident involving the killing or wounding of friendly forces while engaging with what is thought to be an enemy force.

*Furphy:* Australian slang for an erroneous or improbable story that is claimed to be factual.

*Gallows:* A scaffold or gibbet used for execution by hanging.

*Geiger Counter:* A type of survey meter that estimates the radiation dose deposited in an individual or object

*Little Tacker:* Aussie slang for young child

*Longarms:* Longarm include rifles, shotguns and machine guns

*MILs, or milliradians:* Are a unit of measurement dividing radians in a circle. A radian is equal to 57.3 degrees, with 6.2832 ($\pi$ x 2) radians in a circle.

*Militia:* An army of non-professional soldiers, citizens of a state, who may perform military service during a time of need.

*MO:* A modus operandi is someone's habits of working, particularly in the context of business or criminal investigations

*MOA:* A Minute of Angle is an angular measurement. A MOA is 1/60th of a degree.

*Muay Thai:* A martial art and combat sport that uses stand-up striking along with various clinching techniques.

*NMG:* A gang from South Australia that has been wreaking havoc in Western Australia

*Operational Debrief:* A review of an operation in order to affirm and reinforce what worked well, and what requires improvement in order to refine and enhance future processes.

*Operational Order:* The order converts the Operational Plan into action and gives the team essential information and direction needed to carry out the operation. It is broken into five elements-: Situation, Mission, Execution, Administration and Command and Control

*Operational Plan:* An operational plan sets out the objectives, strategies, tactics and tasks that a team needs to perform in order to achieve a mission

*Oxycodone:* An opioid medication used for treatment of moderate to severe pain. It is highly addictive and is commonly used recreationally by people who have an opioid use disorder.

*Projy:* Short for projectile - the bullet

*Recce:* Slang for reconnaissance. Exploration of an area by military forces to obtain information about enemy forces, terrain, and other activities.

*Round:* Bullet

*Sarama:* Sarama is the typical melody that is played before (during the Wai Khru) and during the Muay Thai match. Instruments include the Pi Java, Klong Kaaks, the Ching instrument and the Kong Mong.

*Shottie:* Shotgun

*Six:* It refers to the 6 position on the face of a clock. If you were standing in the centre of a clock face, facing the 12 position, the 6 position would be immediately behind you.

*Specky:* A spectacular mark in Australian rules football that typically involves a player jumping up on the back of another player and catching the football.

*Teep Kick:* Also known as the push kick or simply as the teep, is a straight kicking technique in Muay Thai.

*Towie:* Tow truck driver

*UNESCO:* The United Nations Educational, Scientific and Cultural Organization is a specialised agency of the United Nations aimed at promoting world peace and security through international cooperation in education, the arts, the sciences, and culture.

# ACKNOWLEDGEMENTS

This book would not have been possible without the assistance of Corporal Mark Davies (ret). Mark served with the Australian Special Air Services Regiment from 1988 to 2012. Thank you for your assistance in training Fiona to be a sniper. I want to be clear, any mistakes made in this novel are mine and mine alone. Thank you to those that provided me encouragement and feedback throughout the journey - Lynne, Graham, Barney, Pete, Oscar, Damon, Paddy, and Jon. A special thanks to Ming and Knut for your editing and plot advice and Steve for the amazing cover work and design.

# FURTHER NOTES & REFERENCES

Most of the locations mentioned in the novel are accurate, and yes, the Mercure Kakadu Croc Hotel in Jabiru is shaped like a crocodile. It is a beautiful place to go for a holiday, and I promise you, Noel Patterson will not be a guest.

Mark Davies was invaluable in assisting me in planning Fiona's sniper training. Her training was not an attempt to replicate special forces training. I have also referenced the FM 23-10 United States Army Sniper Training Manual (1994), which was also helpful, given that Fiona was being taught 'old school' without using a laser rangefinder. The Blaser rifle is used in the Australian Army when writing this novel. However, the Blaser R96 Tactical Sniper rifle does not exist. I have adjusted the weapon's model numbers to consider the manufacturer's future improvements and developments.

At the time of writing this novel, the Royal Australian Navy operates a fleet of fourteen Armidale Class Patrol Boats. When protecting Australian borders, Patrol Boat crews are typically employed on a range of duties involving tracking, intercepting, stopping, and boarding other vessels, and sometimes arresting their crews and seizing cargo. Australia's current Armidale Class and Cape Class Patrol Boats are planned to be replaced with a single class of Offshore Patrol Vessel (OPV), under Project SEA 1180 Phase 1, to be built in Australia by German shipbuilder, Lürssen's subsidiary. The lead vessel, HMAS Arafura, is planned to enter service in 2022. I have used creative license when I suggested the Armidale Boats would be gifted to Indonesia and the Philippines under the agreement that they'd assist Australia in patrolling for people and drug smugglers. However, the Australian Government is known to gift boats to Australia's northern neighbours. For example, in 2017, the Australian Government provided nineteen new patrol boats to Pacific Island nations to combat increasing rates of transnational crime in the region.

The novel includes fictional Aboriginal characters from Western Australia and the Northern Territory. The First People of Australia's culture, customs, and beliefs are rich and complex, with over 300 languages from over 500 different clan groups or 'nations' around the continent. I encourage you to peruse The National Unity web page, which provides an informative map of Aboriginal countries http:// nationalunitygovernment.org/pdf/aboriginal-australia-map.pdf

## Songs Mentioned in the book (in order of appearance)

Sinclair, Marion (1932). *Kookaburra* (also known by its first line: "*Kookaburra sits in the old gum tree*") [Song].

Young, Angus. Young, Malcolm & Johnson, Brian (1980). *You Shook Me All Night Long* [song]. AC/DC. Atlantic, September 10. LP

Young, Angus. Young, Malcolm & Scott, Bon (1976). *Jailbreak* [song]. AC/DC. Albert Productions, June 14. LP

"Never Smile at a Crocodile" is a comic song with music by Frank Churchill and lyrics by Jack Lawrence. The music, without the lyrics, was first heard in the Walt Disney Animation Studios film Peter Pan.

## Map of Australia

Map is courtesy of Bruce Jones Design and FreeUSandWorldMaps.com

## Notebook and Journal Image

Images Purchase and licenses from Vector Stock Images

## Sniper Manual

FM 23-10 United States Army Sniper Training Manual (17 Aug, 1994) (Approved for public release; distribution is unlimited)

# ABOUT THE AUTHOR

James Thomson grew up in Western Australia's South West and Eastern Goldfields. He served in the WA Police Force, attaining the rank of Sergeant. He has completed two Master's Degrees and is the Director of a Registered Training Organisation focused on Emergency Management. James has also performed as a University Lecturer, Management Consultant and Training Manager. He has practised martial arts for over thirty years, earning two black belts, one of which is in Brazilian Jiu-Jitsu under the Jean Jacques Machado BJJ Perth Academy. He resides with his wife and son in Perth, WA.

# The Blood Journey

# Gallows Gold Series

# Book 3

*Written by James Scott Thomson*

*Excerpt from The Blood Journey – Book Three of the Gallows Gold Series*

Fiona ran from the room towards the front of the house. I glanced at Clarry before we jogged down the corridor after her. My back was pinched in pain when we eventually caught up with her. She was unlocking a gun cabinet in the study. "Taro, Yang, and Smithy, get tooled up. We're going to visit the Harrisons. They've taken Elly," she yelled. The men shouldered past me as they ran into the room. Fiona wasted no time handing out rifles, shotguns, and ammo to the three men with sidearms strapped to their waists.

Fiona ignored me when I asked her what was going on. I had to grab her by her shoulders to gain her attention, "Who are the Harrisons, and why do you think they've taken Elly?"

"Because we're feuding," she screamed with wild eyes. "So help me, God, I don't have fucking time for your questions, Archie. Are you gonna help me or not?"

I raised my palms in a sign of peace. Before I could answer, she turned on her heels and hurried out the front door. Clarry followed Fiona and attempted to reason with her while I hobbled to the back of the house where I had parked my midnight black Valiant Charger, which I had nicknamed the Beast years ago. I jumped in and quickly turned the ignition to hear my baby's recently reconditioned V8 5.6-litre engine awaken with a throaty rumble. Wasting no time, I sped around to the front driveway to find Clarry in a cloud of dust with his hands on his hips, watching two utes accelerating down the main road.

I put the pedal to the metal as Clarry was still in the process of closing the driver's side door. "So I'm guessing you didn't get any rhyme or reason out of Fiona?"

"Nope. I'm worried, Archie. She hasn't been this impetuous for years."

I caught up with the rear ute a couple of kilometres down the road. Fiona must have been leading the convoy as I saw two male heads through the Toyota's rear cab window. Out of habit, I touched the grip of my Smith and Wesson .38 calibre revolver and the pommel of my FS-Fighting knife. I looked over my left shoulder and glimpsed the 12-gauge shottie resting on the back leather seats. Clarry had a Browning nine-millimetre pistol holstered to his belt. He also had his F92 Austeyr assault rifle secured in the boot. After I left the Australian Defence Force (ADF) in 2033, I worked as a bounty hunter. I was involved in numerous engagements during my career, from being shot at by wanted criminals to battling heavily armed gangs. But for the past eight years, I haven't been in a gunfight or any type of fight for that matter. Fortunately, I haven't needed to. In 2049, the Western Australian (WA) state government finally got its act together and implemented armed patrols across the South Australian (SA) and Northern Territory (NT) borders. I still trained with the local militia once a month, but at fifty years old, I would be the first to admit that I'm rustier than an iron drum barbeque discarded in the outback.

The twenty-kilometre trip flew by with Clarry and I stewing in our thoughts. Both utes took a sharp turn down a gravel road and sped toward a neglected fibro farmhouse. The property was a mess, with battered machinery and beaten-up cars scattered around the front yard and nearby fields. Fiona and her workers parked directly in front of the house, suggesting Fiona was not considering a tactical entry.

"What's our play here?" Clarry asked.

I reached for the Remington model 870 pump-action shotgun. "I've got no idea what's happening here, so I'll just have to play it by ear. You grab the Austeyr and hang back unless the shit hits the fan."

Fiona and her three workers were already stepping onto the front porch as we exited the Beast. "Bloody hell, Fiona, would you just give me a second," I yelled as I shuffled over to her, my bad knee throbbing with every step. My heart thumped hard and fast against my chest when I heard the first shot ring out. I took a deep breath and swiftly scanned my surroundings as I disengaged the shotgun's safety and stepped onto the porch.

Fiona gestured for Taro to go to the back of the house before stepping through the front door with her two remaining men. Multiple shots rang out as I approached the house - *pop, pop, pop, boom, boom*. "Stay out here and protect our six," I yelled to Clarry before crossing the threshold. I couldn't help but curse when I almost tripped over Smithy, one of Fiona's workers, who was lying on his back at the entrance with gaping holes in his cheek and chest.